THE COLOR OF BETRAYAL

This book is a work of fiction. Any references to historical events, real people, or real places are used fictitiously. Other names, characters, places, and events are products of the author's imagination, and any resemblance to actual events or places or persons, living or dead, is entirely coincidental.

For information about this title, contact the author:
Hollie Smurthwaite
hollie@holliesmurthwaite.com
https://holliesmurthwaite.com

ISBN: 978-1-7371189-5-4

Cover Design by Sarah Hansen, Okay Creations
Interior Design by Olivier Darbonville
Edited by Joyce Lamb

Printed in the USA
First Edition

Also by Hollie Smurthwaite:
The Color of Trauma

THE COLOR *of* BETRAYAL

HOLLIE SMURTHWAITE

To my Aunt Karen, who I think will get the biggest kick out of being in a book dedication and Aunt Susan, who always makes everyone their favorite foods.

Also Uncle Jim, who would give me a bastard-calf look if I left him out. And the rest.

I truly have the best extended family ever!

CONTENT WARNING

Explicit sex scenes

References to alcoholism and recovery

Violence

Gaslighting

Profanity and not just a little

CHAPTER ONE

Jolene

AFTER ONLY THREE WEEKS OF DATING, JOLENE and Colton had fallen into a routine: dinner (both) and drinks (him), binge-watching various flavors of *CSI* at his downtown Boston condo (him), and a few hours of surreptitiously delving into Colton's memories (her). Jolene's practice run as a spy in the field was going well.

The late August night was cool enough for Colton to crack open the sliding glass door to the balcony to let the night air clear his lingering cigarette smoke. Jolene kicked off the stiletto heels and inwardly sighed. After some complex maneuvering, she managed to tuck her aching toes under her too-bright skirt.

The next part of the evening promised to be worth the discomfort of a thong up her ass crack to avoid panty lines.

Without asking Jolene what she would like, Colton switched on the obscenely large TV and pulled up Hulu, lounging like a czar on his pristine white couch, which was a stupid color for anyone but particularly ludicrous for a smoker who drank too much and worked with dangerous people.

In another life, he would have been regal with golden hair, long limbs, straight nose, and a boyish, charming smile. But this wasn't another life.

As a midlevel lackey in the Red Flames criminal organization, he was not proper boyfriend material, even if he made enough cash to buy a downtown place on a high floor and have it professionally, if foolishly, decorated all in white.

Jolene wiggled her toes into the plush cushion and ignored the stale-smoke smell mixed with Colton's spicy cologne. Any moment, Colton would slip into a *CSI* coma, and she would slip into his memories.

"This looks like a good one," she said. What she always said, because why mess with what worked?

"Yeah," Colton agreed, as he always did. He lit a cigarette and "politely" blew the smoke toward the balcony doors, tapping the ash into an antique crystal ashtray on the glass coffee table already holding three butts.

The first week, she'd been terrified he'd somehow feel her inside his mind, though she'd never had that happen before or heard of anyone sensing the process. Not that Jolene still had contacts in the memory-surgeon community, small as it was, but that sort of revelation would put memory surgery back in the 24/7 news cycle, like when they'd first been legitimized. Semi-legitimized.

This first assignment was nothing more than an exploration of what she could do on a real mission. Since Colton was a gangster and she had no close backup, fear nibbled, but confidence had outpaced her worry.

Jolene rested her head on his shoulder, slipped her arm through his, and slid her hand down his button-down shirt to rest on his hand. As soon as skin-to-skin contact was made, she mentally reached out to him. Colton's mind rose up inside her own. To boost her concentration, Jolene closed her eyes.

Within the blackness, bubbles sharpened. The different shapes and colors bobbed and slid around one another. In her mind's eye, she moved into the middle, staring at them as if in an aquarium. The memories never touched her, but she could reach out and sink into any of them. If she did, she experienced the memory in its entirety, exactly as Colton had lived through the event at the time. If she wanted, she could remove memories, but that was a level of violation she resisted unless absolutely necessary. Besides, if she took something, she had to keep it, and she didn't want to keep anything of Colton's.

Jolene already had an entire dossier in her head of all things Colton. She'd cataloged his fears: multilegged insects like millipedes terrified him, as did his brother when his eyes went icy, and his jaw shifted to the right.

Shame occupied its own section: bed-wetting for a month when he was twelve. The time he'd slapped his girlfriend after she'd gotten pregnant and decided she didn't want it. Red Flames passing him over for job after job.

Still, inside, people were infinite, and she had more to learn. She avoided the pink bubbles, as they were filled with his worst memories, and her reactions to living them were difficult to hide. Reds gave her the best intel so far. Angers, suspicions, smackdowns.

Truthfully, she should have wrapped up the mission a week ago since she wasn't finding anything new. But playing spy and the unfettered access to Colton's recollections had been too enlightening to quit quite yet. Her skills had grown, and she didn't feel guilty about messing in his brain because of his criminal history. She was three weeks into her two- to three-week mission, so she needed to skip out soon.

Jolene decided to make a game to test her memory-reading skills. She had recently learned how to peek and not immediately experience a memory. It allowed her to see more since she didn't need any emotional recovery time, and she processed what she encountered more quickly.

Tonight, she wanted to test how many memories she could scan during commercial breaks, since Colton was too cheap to pay for the commercial-free version of Hulu. She'd hop through his memories like jumping into puddles.

Colton laughed at a dead body on the screen.

Commercial.

A mahogany memory: *his brother, Walther, stood over him, watching over his shoulder as Colton did algebra homework. Whenever Colton squirmed in his chair, Walther flicked his ear. It didn't hurt much, but Colton's face burned every time, and his muscles shook with the stress of not moving to avoid Walther's attention. "Knock it off," he grumbled, earning another sting. Colton tensed—*

A buttercup-colored memory: *"Mama, Mama, Mama," Colton said, running around his mama as she walked in the park. If he ran fast enough, he would fly, his head already lightening. He stumbled and giggled, his mama laughing. Something shiny glinted in the sun. What was it? His mama scooped him into her arms before he grabbed it. She smelled of flowers and oranges.*

CSI resumed, and Jolene steadied her breathing. Her head throbbed from the memory dumps. Too many memories too quickly hurt. She should let the recollections unfold in their own time and save the gulping down for emergencies.

Colton stubbed out his cigarette and pulled her closer. Too close. "You should stay the night tonight," he said in a husky voice, which might have been sexy if he hadn't reeked of nicotine, and if she hadn't known some of the things he'd done.

She cocked her head and looked up at him from beneath her lashes. "That's too tempting for me." Jolene clasped her hands together, losing access to his memories, but she didn't need them for this. "I'm sorry. You could be with anyone. I don't get why you stay with me."

Early forays into his memories to assess how she was doing revealed Colton found her denial of sex with him frustrating but also alluring. Although he pushed for more physical contact on every date, he liked her no-sex commitment, as it was somehow proof of purity.

She'd told him she wasn't a virgin, but he hadn't believed her. To Colton, a twenty-eight-year-old virgin (though she was actually thirty-four) was more believable than a sexually active woman rebuffing his advances. He lived in a world of saints and whores and nothing in between. He assumed she was holding out for marriage.

"Julie, baby," he crooned, sliding his hand up and down her arm. "Let me make you feel good."

His idea of making her feel good undoubtedly involved his dick—and she wanted no part of that. Even remotely sexual contact wasn't fun.

Jolene dipped her chin to give herself a moment. She thought about how she had no family left alive, how she'd lost her only friend when the Agency had faked her death. She remembered her grandmother's face the last time Jolene had seen her before she died. *Nobody* loved her.

As soon as tears welled on her eyelashes, she shoved the memories down deep into the cellar of her mind and looked up at Colton. "I just can't, baby."

As she hoped, the prospect of her weeping had him backpedaling. "No. No. It's fine—don't cry, baby. I love you just as you are."

"You're too sweet to me, Cole." Jolene put a hand on his cheek, and his memories opened again. She peered inside another, the closest one—Colton taking care of business in the shower, thinking about her. The fantasy of turning the good girl into a slut ran hot and fast.

Pass.

He wrapped both arms around her and kissed the top of her head. It wasn't real, and she didn't want *him*. She swallowed down a splash of bile. Time to bugger out. Past time.

Her headache thrummed incessantly, but she decided to push it since this would be her last night to explore her talent, and she needed to ensure she'd gotten everything possible. This time, she took Colton's hand but pretended to watch TV.

His memories blossomed again. "Hey, did I tell you I'm going to be getting some more responsibility at work?" she asked.

The bubbles shifted as he thought about his own job, but she didn't make her move, looking for a shade of violet for pride or blood-red for brutality.

Colton grunted. "What does that mean?"

She couldn't read his tone, so she kept going, half concentrating on her story and half on his memory spheres. "They might make me manager." The Agency had set her up with a perfume-counter job at Saks Fifth Avenue at the Pru.

"Why you gonna want that?"

"I guess I don't, but it's nice to be appreciated, and I could use the extra money."

"You saying I ain't looking after you?"

"What? No. I want to take care of you too, baby."

Colton's face pinked, and his bottom lip jutted in a pouty sneer. "I don't need some skirt taking care of me."

Skirt? Had he time-traveled to the fifties? A frisson of danger speared through her.

Jolene inhaled and placed a tentative, reverent hand on his chest. "You would take care of *me*?"

Colton's gaze scraped over her for a few seconds. She kept her chin tilted down and her hand steady over his beating heart. Eventually, his shoulders relaxed, his grip on her other hand no longer menacing.

The corners of his eyes crinkled. "Of course I will, Julie baby. You're it for me."

His phone rang. For a moment, she thought he might ignore it, his eyes flipping to a nebulous longing that made her skin tight.

"Yeah?" Colton's voice was wistful as he answered the call. "Who? . . . Why?" Colton frowned. "Okay, you can send her up."

He hung up and gave Jolene an uncomfortable grin. "My brother's girlfriend is downstairs."

"What's she doing here?" Jolene wondered if she should use the woman's arrival as an excuse to bail for the night—and forever.

"Apparently, she wants to talk about Walther's birthday."

In person at ten at night? "Kind of strange."

Colton nodded and rolled his eyes in a way that included his entire head. "Right? She's a piece of work. You'll see what I mean."

Jolene didn't want to see what he meant; she wanted to leave. He opened the door before the girlfriend knocked. "Hey, Saffron," he said.

Of *course* his brother dated a woman named Saffron. Walther was a slicker, smarter, more dangerous version of Colton. Stadler had determined

Walther was too tough a target for Jolene's first mission. She'd seen enough of Colton's memories of Walther to agree with her handler.

When she spotted the woman in the doorway, though, she realized Stadler had decided Walther was not too much to handle for someone else on his team.

"You two know each other?" Colton asked when he saw Jolene's expression.

"Uh, no," Jolene said. "She's—you're just so pretty."

Sara wore a silver top with thin ties around the neck and back that molded the fabric to her round breasts, a black microskirt, and silver, sparkly heels towering at least five inches, bringing Sara to over six feet tall. She looked stunning with her natural blond hair falling artfully over one deep-blue eye, stopping just below her shoulders.

Jolene wasn't breathtaking like Sara, her own attractiveness more niche. She was fit, noticeably muscular in the ass and shoulders—too muscular for some—and she would have liked C-cup breasts to balance out her lower half, instead of her B-cups, but overall, she was pleasing enough, the kind of attractive that made men think they weren't shallow for dating her.

Sara showed no hint of recognition. "Aw, Colton, she's so sweet. You didn't say you had your girlfriend over. Hope I didn't interrupt anything." She waggled her brows like a teenager.

Jolene's face flamed, though she wasn't sure why.

"Don't tease. Julie, Saffron. Saffron, Julie." He beamed at the introduction.

"Hey, Saffron, nice to meet you," Jolene said, voice strained. Sara had trained her in what she'd called "feminine wiles," which essentially amounted to letting him talk and acting interested. It had worked. Still, Jolene didn't want Sara grading her on this assignment.

Sara walked over to the sofa and shook Jolene's hand, and it wasn't until their hands no longer touched that Jolene realized she hadn't gotten anything from Sara's mind, though she was in a memory-receptive mode.

It was as if Sara had no memories at all. Maybe Jolene's tricked-out affinity worked only with people comfortable with her.

Jolene didn't linger on the concept of Sara not trusting her.

Although they'd both been part of Stadler's team for over four years, he'd kept Jolene separate from the rest of the team—*compartmentalizing*, he'd called it. She'd thought Stadler finally believed in her, since he'd given her this shot. But he didn't, or he wouldn't have sent in Sara to babysit.

Okay, yeah, she *had* been playing with her gift, but he didn't know that.

"Whatcha got to drink around here?" Sara asked as she surveyed the room like a sailor searching for land. When she spotted the alcohol cart, recently tucked into an alcove so Jolene didn't have to see it, Sara strutted to it with an exaggerated sway to her hips. "Julie, can I get you something?" Sara knew Jolene was in recovery but had to pretend she didn't.

"No, thanks."

"Jules doesn't drink," Colton said with a note of pride in his voice, as if her alcoholic genes made her superior to a person who could imbibe without ruining everything.

"Too bad," Sara purred.

Fuck you, Sara, Jolene sent out psychically, wishing telepathy were real. "I'm fine."

"I'll say. Colton didn't mention how adorable you are." Sara looked her up and down and pursed her lips as if in invitation. "I've found blonds really do have more fun. What about you?"

Jolene's blond hair was longer and warmer than Sara's, a butter-blond that came from a bottle. It was not providing an entertaining time at the moment.

Sara sashayed to the couch where Colton had rejoined Jolene, sitting with his thigh touching hers. Sara handed Colton his glass. "A toast." She held up her amber beverage, likely whiskey. "To true love."

Colton echoed her, smiling at Jolene, who smiled back. Sara and Colton clinked glasses and drank.

As always, Colton finished his drink in a few swallows. His alcohol consumption hit professional levels, but he wasn't a sloppy drunk and didn't seem to *need* alcohol. Bastard.

Sara sat in the stiff, pearl armchair adjacent to the couch and crossed her long legs. "You guys can hold hands."

Stadler had sent Sara to facilitate Jolene's job. Total. Bullshit. Jolene didn't need assistance.

Colton took her hand and smiled at her again in a too-real way. She reciprocated, her stomach riding the teacups until nausea rolled through. His memories popped into view, but not as clear as earlier, probably because Sara made him nervous, which closed him up some.

"How's work?" Sara asked, glancing at her thin, gold watch.

Sara was breaking the first rule she'd taught Jolene: act how they expect, and nobody will question your cover. She'd been right. And this was definitely not how she should be behaving. Head-on inquiries raised suspicions, and nobody dating someone in the business asked about it. They were only there to look pretty.

"Fine." Colton's tone was clipped.

"Colton doesn't like to talk about his job," Jolene said with some bite in her own voice.

"That's the problem, isn't it?" Sara said with an eye roll.

Jolene accidentally squeezed Colton's hand as the rest of her body froze. Was Sara losing it in the middle of Jolene's first assignment?

"Work's boring," Colton said and tilted his chin up so he appeared to look down on Sara.

"No need to talk about it, if it makes you uncomfortable," Jolene said as she glared at Sara.

All the while, Colton's memory bubbles shifted. A raspberry-colored one glowed a little. Jolene shifted her attention to the edges, saw a dark bar and experienced a wave of Colton's anxious anticipation. She dipped inside. *The drop should have happened five minutes ago, and Colton scowled. He'd asked for the Stefano organization contact's name and description but had gotten nothing. Now, he was eyeing every passing asshole like he was prowling for a date. Like he was some kind of loser.*

A drop? She hadn't found that one yet.

"The way Walther tells it, Colton just plays a small role in the organization, nothing important, so what he has to say ain't worth hearing anyway," Sara said, as she sneaked another look at her watch.

Jolene plunged deep into the memory, absorbing it fast, making her headache throb from the pressure, but she needed to focus to save the situation. "I don't like your tone," she said to Sara, letting all her frustration color her words as the memory blossomed inside her.

* * *

An older man, Hispanic, wearing a fedora and no facial expression, caught Colton's attention. Colton chin-nodded, and the man narrowed his eyes, his gaze falling to the briefcase in Colton's hand.

Colton wondered again what was in it. Money? Drugs? Harry had told him it was papers, but Colton didn't believe that. Paperwork could have been sent by FedEx or a delivery person; they didn't require a back-alley meeting.

* * *

"YOU BEING MY BROTHER'S PIECE OF ASS DON'T GIVE YOU NO RIGHT TO insult me in my own home." Colton's face and neck pinked. The canned lighting made his blond hair glow.

* * *

The exchange was silent and cloak-and-dagger enough that Colton started feeling part of something cool and dangerous. It took the edge off his irritation. The man handed him a black business card with a fancy S *on it and nothing else—no name or phone number or email address.*

Colton shifted the briefcase to the man while tucking the card into his pants pocket. The entire interaction took less than five seconds. His brother had insisted Colton was nothing more than a messenger or low-level lackey, but he'd done a drop that ran smooth as baby shit. Walther never got cool tasks like that one.

* * *

THE MEMORY CARRIED INTO ANOTHER, BUT BEFORE JOLENE COULD GRAB it, Colton pulled his hand away and everything blanked. He stood and took a step toward Sara. "I said, get out."

"It's for the best," Jolene added. "You're obviously intoxicated, and we don't need to be around that." She decided that before she left for the night, she'd take his memory of Sara's visit, just in case the drunk excuse didn't quell his suspicions.

"We don't like drunks around here." Colton sneered and towered over Sara.

Sara smirked. "Take a seat, Colton."

Colton hauled Sara to her feet. Jolene jumped up but debated if she should step back and let Sara handle it on her own or team up with her.

Sara pushed Colton's chest with two fingers, and he flopped onto the couch, his eyes glazed. "That's what I thought," she said with a giggle.

"What did you do to him?" Jolene asked as Colton's pupils took over most of his irises.

"Nothing serious. A little GHB is all."

Jolene gaped at Sara. "Why the fuck would you do that?"

She shrugged. "To help you."

"I don't need assistance!" Jolene looked back at Colton in time to realize he'd stood, but before she could react, he struck the crystal ashtray from the coffee table into the side of Sara's head.

Sara crumpled to the ground, barely missing the armchair, blood trickling down her temple, spattering the white carpeting. Cigarette butts dropped to the floor like shell casings.

Colton seized Jolene's throat, gripping so hard she couldn't breathe. Stadler had trained her in hand-to-hand combat, even getting out of chokeholds, but he'd never actually choked her, and her brain stopped dead. She scratched Colton's hands, trying to pry them from her neck, but it didn't work.

Jolene kicked his shins with her bare feet as spots danced behind eyes threatening to pop free, as his memories grew brighter and brighter. Out of instinct, she brushed against a beet-red bubble of memory.

* * *

"Walther! Wait for me!" Colton tripped over a root hidden beneath a layer of leaves. His backpack kept snagging tree branches, and he wished he'd left it at school. He was graduating in the spring and had no interest in college, so why bother with homework?

"Go home, Colton. Now," his brother called back.

Well, he wasn't going home. He'd be eighteen in less than a month and had no intention of letting Walther order him around anymore.

It took Colton half an hour to find the party, and relief overshadowed his triumph. The sun was setting, and Colton didn't want to be alone in the woods. He hadn't moved into the firelight yet, so nobody had noticed him—certainly not Walther, who had his hand up the skirt of Colton's girlfriend, Angela. His angel. Walther had his tongue so far down Angie's throat he probably tasted pizza. Colton knew, because they'd had lunch together.

For an hour, Colton sat where he'd collapsed onto the ground, watching his brother and his girlfriend cheat on him.

* * *

Jolene pushed the memory with her will, directing it . . . up? It felt like up. Her intention to overrun Colton's mind with his own memory in the hopes it would give her a moment to break free or at least catch one more breath.

He gasped, and his hold loosened. Jolene finally remembered one of the chokehold-release moves. She interlaced her fingers into a giant fist, then punched straight up. It worked better than intended, because her double fist connected with the underside of his chin. Luck did the rest as he stumbled backward and tripped over Sara. Colton hit the floor with a boom. Jolene scooped up the bloody ashtray from where Colton had dropped it and stood over him, ready to brain him if he moved.

He groaned and stilled. His chest rose and fell, so Jolene knew she hadn't killed him. Thank Christ. She'd never have washed away that stain on her soul, even if she'd done it in self-defense.

Jolene poured the remains of Sara's whiskey over Sara's face. Thankfully, the woman gasped and sat up, one hand moving to the wound on her temple.

Sara looked from Colton's prone body to Jolene. "You?"

Jolene closed her eyes briefly in relief. "No, it was the Dumbass Fairy who stopped by looking for you." She sounded as if she'd smoked a carton of cigarettes. Jolene rubbed at her sore neck and gulped in air. "What the hell were you thinking?" Sara's field skills were legendary.

Sara blinked up at her, sitting cross-legged on the floor, giving Jolene a show with her microskirt. "He should have been more out of it. I waited ten minutes." It had been five. Sara looked around the apartment as if coming out of a blackout, blood trickling down her long neck. "That totally should have worked."

Jolene jogged to the kitchen, though she had yet to catch her breath, and grabbed a white hand towel. She avoided Colton's unconscious body as she returned to Sara. "Let's get the hell out of here before he comes to."

Sara pressed the towel to her wound and gasped. "That hurts." She moved her feet as if preparing to stand. "Oh shit. This is bad."

"It's fine." It wasn't fine. "He probably won't remember the fight, not with the GHB in his system."

"What if he does?" Sara stood like a newborn colt, her legs threatening to buckle. "I'm not worried about him, but Walther . . . He's not someone to fuck with. If he thought we—"

Sara picked up her sequined silver clutch and pulled out a small plastic bag of powder. Her hands shook, and she sniffled. "We have to be sure he can't tell Walther anything."

"Whoa!" Jolene put a hand over Sara's as she tore it open. "What is that?"

"It might not kill him."

Not the answer Jolene had wanted or expected. Her heart and stomach switched places, acid burning up her throat, blood throbbing in her middle. "No." Jolene bent over, coughing, trying to control her lungs. She couldn't let Sara do something they couldn't undo. "No, we don't need to do that. I'll just—I can take all the memories from tonight. He won't remember, and we can tell whatever story we like."

"The assignment is still wrecked, but yeah." Sara bobbled and dropped the bag, unleashing a puff of powder.

Both women stepped back, though only a tiny amount broke free. Sara scooped up the small baggie and dumped it into her clutch. "I almost—" Sara took a few, cleansing breaths. "Wipe his memory, and let's go."

Jolene squatted next to Colton and put her hand on his face. Memories popped to life.

Colton's cell rang. Sara's phone pinged.

"Shit!" Sara scrambled to her feet. "Walther's here. He wasn't supposed to come for another half hour. If he comes upstairs, we're dead." Sara clutched her purse to her chest with one arm, pressing the bloody towel back to her cut. "Hurry! We can't be here when Walther gets here."

Jolene shuffled through Colton's memories, finding the threads of that evening and pulling everything from tonight. Every memory she took she had to hold inside herself. Colton's affection for her festered under her skin, and his fury stung as sweat trickled down her back.

"Come on," Sara hissed.

"I got it," Jolene said, casting one last look at all of Colton's bubbles.

One bright snippet took over her mind, lingering.

* * *

How did I get so lucky?

Colton pulled his hand from Julie's and stroked her soft cheek. Kissing made her forget herself, and his chest sizzled with pride. His kiss set her on fire. He kissed the top of her head and tucked her close to his body. Julie was the one. He'd finally found her, and before Walther had met someone special. Saffron? She was a gold-digging slut that wouldn't last more than a month. Julie was going to be his for the rest of his life.

* * *

JOLENE DIDN'T WANT TO SEE COLTON SO VULNERABLE AND REFUSED TO hold those tender feelings of his inside her. She pushed the memory back. It wasn't as if that recollection would come back to bite them in the ass.

"We have to *go.*" Sara stood at the door, practically dancing in place.

Jolene grabbed her purse and shoes and took one last look at Colton, her throat aching both internally and externally. Fuck.

"We better take the stairs," Sara said as she ran down the hallway in stilettos so tall Jolene wouldn't have been able to stand in them. Sara kept the dishtowel against her head, preventing a blood trail.

The elevator chimed as they shot into the stairwell. They didn't bother to check if it was Walther who got off or not.

CHAPTER TWO

Jolene

JOLENE SLID INTO THE BOOTH OPPOSITE SARA AT some dirty, twenty-four-hour diner with cracked, red seats and harsh, yellowish lighting that made everyone look like a user. They both panted, though they'd just spent ten minutes in an Uber and should have caught their breath by then.

"What the fuck, Sara?" Jolene finally said, now that she could unleash in relative privacy.

Sara's hands shook as she covered her face. Mascara raccooned her eyes. "He should have been out of it."

Jolene wanted to kick her under the table. "Why didn't you wait? No—why didn't you reach out to me beforehand? I would have told you I had everything under control."

"Why didn't you check in?"

Because she hadn't wanted Stadler to pull her. Jolene said nothing, letting her bitch face talk for her.

Sara grunted. "Stadler got impatient and Walther got controlling and—and . . ." Sara shook her head, then *thunked* her forehead onto the sticky tabletop. "Ew." She finally straightened and looked at Jolene. "Look, I thought it might be fun."

Jolene gawked at her, the moment stretching and stretching. Was Sara insane? Fun. *Fun?* Their eyes connected in an epic glare-off.

The absurdity hit her low and deep. They both burst into laughter.

"I would *not* call that a festive time." Jolene wiped her eyes.

Sara shook her head again and recoiled as she checked to see if her temple had stopped bleeding. Her platinum hair was streaked with red, and she looked exactly like she'd gotten brained. A smear of crusted blood remained on her collarbone, and she reeked like a distillery from the whiskey Jolene had poured over her face. Luckily, the diner had a fuck-all feel to it, and the server didn't appear to notice Sara's injury or Jolene's bruised neck.

"What can I get you?" The waitress looked thirty but sounded eighty.

"Fries," Jolene said. It was something this sort of place might do right, and it was a decent comfort food.

"Coffee for me," Sara said. "Black as my soul."

The server snort-laughed and said, "You got it, hon."

Once the server stepped away, Sara perched her elbows on the table, fingers interlaced as if in prayer. "You're positive he won't remember we were there?"

If Jolene said she wasn't sure, the Agency might send someone to kill Colton. Part of the reason their branch of the DEA was off the books was so they could do questionable shit like that. Still, she'd never imagined they actually *assassinated* people.

"I got it all." Even if she hadn't, the alcohol and GHB would cloud anything he did remember. He'd doubt everything. "We're safe."

"Okay. Awesome."

The coffee came, the scent half coffee, half ash, and they sat in silence as Sara took careful sip after careful sip. Jolene's neck ached as if she had whiplash, and she brushed her throat along the pain fault line. That bastard.

Jolene pulled out her phone.

"Who're you calling?" Sara said, her voice too high and brittle.

Jolene understood Sara's distress. She dreaded talking to Stadler too.

"I'm sending Colton a breakup text. It'll explain the blood on the carpeting and my disappearance."

"Oh." She nodded and ran a hand through her hair on the uninjured side of her head. "Smart thinking." Sara cocked her head to the side. "What are you going to say?"

Jolene swallowed hard. Her throat ached as if she'd been gargling glass. She spoke as she texted, "*I can't believe you would attack me like that. I thought we had something.*" Colton didn't know shit about love. Of course, neither did she. "*I've gone to the emergency room. Then I'm leaving town. Don't try to contact me. I'm tossing the phone after this message. I never thought you would hurt me, but I was wrong*. Send."

Sara exhaled in a long stream. "Perfect. He'll believe it, you think?"

Jolene pulled out the SIM card and dropped it into her purse. "Yeah. He'll have a big gap in memory and assume he drank too much." Her fries arrived, as overcooked as Sara's coffee. "We'll have to tell Stadler eventually."

Sara wiped her eyes with an elegant finger. Her nails were a deep red and didn't have a single chip. She trembled.

"This can't be the first time things have gone pear-shaped," Jolene said, suddenly finding herself comforting Sara instead of laying into her. She wondered if she cared too much about Sara or cared too little about herself. "Just own up to your actions."

"Easy for you to say; you're irreplaceable. Me . . ." Sara swallowed down the last of her coffee and signaled to the server for more. Her shoulders slumped as if she'd been slugged in the gut. "Not my first fuckup, I'm afraid. Apparently, I have impulse control issues. Stadler's been awfully cranky lately with all the pressure from the director. I might be out permanently."

Jolene didn't think Sara's mistake was firing worthy. Her errors needed addressing, but Sara was a chameleon. Jolene had seen video clips of Sara on various assignments. She was brilliant. And Jolene couldn't have pulled off her ruse with Colton without Sara's coaching beforehand.

"You're too talented for them to let go. What would you do?" Jolene tried to envision Sara behind a cosmetics counter trying to sell makeup or outside a dressing room asking if the fit was right.

"This is all I want to do," Sara said, her voice thick. "This job makes me use every part of myself, you know? I get to be a different person every time, and you can't let your attention wander for a moment. If you do . . . Well, you saw what happens." She covered her face and groaned. "What was I thinking?"

The server filled Sara's coffee cup. "You girls need anything else?"

They both shook their heads.

"I didn't need your help," Jolene said.

"Probably not, but I thought it would be fun to double-team him."

Jolene snorted at the innuendo. "He would have loved that. But seriously, Sara, I can't read minds. Seems like Spying 101 to let your partner in on the plan."

"I know. Part of it is my love of improvisation. I never feel more alive than when I'm in the zone. But mostly, I needed to up the timeline and trying to signal something would be far worse than counting on you playing along."

Jolene wanted to ask her to clarify, but Sara kept talking.

"You did great, by the way." She gave Jolene a tight, rapid handclap. "Perfect girlfriend responses."

"Thanks." Jolene had to admit that Sara's prodding had dredged up something. "I did catch something new."

"No shit?" Sara bounced forward, the plastic seating erupting in a fart-like noise they both ignored. "Tell me, tell me."

"As we already knew, he's not so high in the Red Flames organization, but he wanted to move up, so he stuck his nose in a few places he shouldn't, and I did manage to catch a memory of a drop." Jolene huffed a laugh. "Colton was sure it was the most important job he'd ever done."

"How long ago?"

"A month. Just before we met."

"That might save us." Sara wiggled in her seat and stirred cream and sugar into her second cup of coffee.

Jolene had never known anyone to take their coffee more than one way, unless forced. Another example of how flexible Sara was. Jolene smiled. "I think you're underestimating your value."

"I'm a woman in a man's game," Sara said with a sigh. "Seven years I've been with Stadler's team. I like it, I do, but Walther . . ." She pressed her wrist against her chest and winced. "He's one scary psycho and absolute shit in bed. Seriously, I think he thinks I liked all that slapping and biting."

"He *bit* you?"

Sara gingerly worked down her silver top to show purple and red indentations on the inner side of her left breast. Teeth marks.

"Holy shit," Jolene wheezed. It hurt just to look at the injury.

AC/DC started up, "Back in Black" in midsong, then immediately cut out.

"Did you tell Stadler?" Jolene asked.

"I'm okay." Sara's eyes grew glossy, and she managed only a weak smile. "Just glad this is over. Walther's the kind of guy to 'accidentally' kill a girlfriend."

Jolene's stomach rolled over and splatted beneath her skin. No wonder Sara had attempted to push up the timeline so recklessly. "What if I take the blame for screwing up?"

Sara's eyes widened. "You don't have to do that."

Jolene scratched her eyebrow with her thumb. "My pride can take the hit." She hoped it was true. Disappointing Stadler would hurt more than her bruised neck. Maybe the sight of her bruises would soften his response. Even as she thought it, she knew he'd tell her she deserved them and worse for letting a drugged mark almost take both her and Sara out.

Since Sara had opened up to her, Jolene allowed herself to voice her fear. "I can't go back to how it was before."

Sara nodded. "Not so exciting?"

"Boring days of nothing to do interspersed with midnight calls to some seedy hotel to pull blackmail material out of some low-life douche. I give

Stadler everything, he writes the report, and back I go. If I complain, he threatens to send me back to the lab for their bullshit tests. 'What color am I thinking of?' 'What did my wife say to me on my wedding night?' They're either poking me with needles or making me into some sort of one-woman game show. It's such a waste, and I feel like I'm not doing enough to shut down these drug cartels."

"I get it. I'd go crazy stuffed away by myself," Sara replied. "We'll find a way to take what you've learned and make it valuable." She bit her lip. "If we don't, we're both screwed."

CHAPTER THREE

Jolene

JOLENE WOKE WITH THE SURETY SHE WASN'T alone. Light filtered through the white sheet over the window. It was barely morning. Sara had gone somewhere else for the night, so only Jolene stayed in the safe house.

Slipping out of bed soundlessly, clothed in her sleep shorts and tank top, Jolene unplugged the lamp, the only weaponlike object in the sparsely furnished room. She pulled off the lampshade and rolled the cord around her wrist. The base had heft.

Downstairs, the wood floor creaked. She'd left her phone charging in the kitchen, so she'd have to handle this herself. She should wait for whoever was in the house to come to her so she'd have the advantage of surprise, but her nerves insisted she act now.

Keeping tight to the wall, Jolene stalked barefoot along hardwood, lamp raised over her shoulder. At the end of the hall, she peeked down the stairs.

Gavin Stadler stood in the center of the living room, which was empty of everything but a ratty blue sofa, watching her.

"Oh, fuck me," she said, lowering the lamp. "Why didn't you ring the doorbell?"

Stadler assessed her in a way that stopped short of a glower but made her just as uncomfortable. He wasn't traditionally handsome, with acne-scarred cheeks and a mustache that tried more than succeeded, but he had quick hands and a quicker mind. And beefy arms, like oh-my-God-is-he-going-to-pop-out-of-those-sleeves muscles. Above-average height. Nice teeth. Bad attitude—which should have been in the deficit column, but Jolene appreciated his grumpy, misanthropic personality. She detested men who hated women but liked the man who hated everyone.

He wasn't so likable at the moment, however. "Heard you had a long night."

As Jolene tromped down the stairs, making extra noise to compensate for her earlier stealth. Stadler's eyes focused on her neck. She'd forgotten. She wasn't sure how, though, because her throat ached as if she'd swallowed a handful of thumbtacks.

"What's your plan with the lamp?" Stadler asked.

She shrugged. "I thought I'd entertain you with my Statue of Liberty impression."

No laugh. He walked into the tiny kitchen without making a sound. The creak earlier had been intentional.

"Sit," he said, gesturing to the pine bistro table and two white metal chairs. On top sat a cardboard Starbucks carrier holding two drinks.

Jolene dumped the lamp base on the floor, unwrapped the cord from her wrist with painstaking care, and tumbled into the seat, her back to the wall. The tea and coffee were a sort of joke between them. When either wanted to apologize, they brought Starbucks. A chai tea for her and a black coffee for him. Why would he need to say sorry?

Stadler set two ibuprofen tablets before her with deliberate care, like an accusation. He didn't seem concerned at all, as if their personal past meant nothing. Which was as it should be, but still . . .

Jolene swallowed the painkillers dry in some lame attempt to look tough. Once they were three-quarters down her gullet, they stuck, so she sipped the tea casually. She'd thought she'd hit maximum pain in her throat. Nope. The lump finally moved, but a phantom pill remained.

"So, what happened?" he asked, pulling his coffee out of the carrier and taking a sip. His eyes fixed again on her neck.

Jolene rolled her eyes. "Jesus, Stadler, sit down already."

He didn't smile, but his rigid posture loosened as he slipped into the seat across from her. "Happy?"

She let the cup of tea warm her hands but didn't drink again. "Did you not see this?" she asked, pointing to her neck.

"Caught my attention. Now spill."

Jolene knew he wanted details on what happened, but she wanted to delay the inevitable. "We trained for a chokehold, but I blanked when he grabbed me." She spun her cup in a circle, the light, scraping sound a distraction from the tension. "What's the point of practicing if everything's going to fall out of my mind when I need it?"

He leaned back in the chair, as close to a slouch as he got. "You didn't drill enough for muscle memory. If you had, you wouldn't have needed conscious thought."

"Really?"

"We discussed this in training."

She remembered but kept pushing. "I wasn't expecting him to grab me like that. Colton never showed any violent tendencies."

"Anyone can become vicious, Jolene. Better to assume everyone can turn on you."

She sipped her tea. He gulped his coffee.

His eyes hit her hard enough to bruise. "Somehow, I'm going to have to find a way to write this clusterfuck up on an IR-109 in a way that won't get the entire team fired. The worse the fuckup, the sooner I have to submit. The bosses are not as forgiving or as patient as me. People have been terminated for less."

Jolene disappeared for a moment, all sensation gone, time stopping as her brain filled with a white mist. Not literally, of course, but inside her, the world ended. The job was all she had and the only avenue available to her to make a difference in curbing the drug trade.

"I was working on Colton," she said, her voice surprisingly normal, "when Sara showed up. She slipped some GHB into his drink, and he'd already had quite a few." He'd had three, which wasn't much for Colton, but she figured the more incapacitated he sounded, the less incompetent she and Sara appeared. "We waited a good fifteen minutes, and I started asking him leading questions."

Stadler nodded at her pause but didn't ask anything. It was a clever tactic to encourage her to overexplain.

"He was wobbly on his feet and slurring some. We thought he was ready." Jolene swallowed the sour distaste of taking the blame, but she needed to keep the band together. "I got through two questions, and then . . ." This part was mostly truth. "He was suddenly lucid, though still stumbly. He figured out I was pumping him for information, and he attacked us. He clocked Sara in the head and then choked me. I've never seen him so angry."

Stadler interlaced his fingers except for his pointers, which he extended and tapped against his lips for a few seconds. "You're always careful about phrasing, even with secured targets. What made you sloppy this time?"

Shame slicked over her. Jolene savored the spice of the chai as she chewed the inside of her lip. She didn't want to lie, but maybe it was too late.

"I was sort of distracted by Sara."

"It's Sara's fault?"

Yes! Ninety-five percent. "No. I didn't say that. It's not Sara's responsibility to keep me attentive." They needed to move on to another topic. "Who cares? What's done is done. Let's talk about how we can fix it. I think—"

Stadler knocked his knuckles on the table. "Sorry, Jolene. I thought you were ready."

"I *am* ready." Goddamn it. She couldn't backtrack and couldn't think of a way to convince him she wasn't incompetent. "Don't you want to hear what I've learned?"

His eyebrows arched.

She took a steadying breath. "The Flames are working on an expansion, something big." This wasn't more than what they'd already suspected.

"Colton was involved in one drop. He was smart enough not to open the briefcase, but it wasn't heavy enough to be a large sum of money, and Colton didn't work with the people supplying product, so it wasn't drugs. Paperwork of some kind."

Jolene's lazy perusal of Colton's mind hadn't just honed her craft but had sharpened her understanding of how his brain worked. Odd snatches of various, random memories clicked together like a puzzle, and a picture formed.

"Colton noticed a Hildy Walker was spending a lot of time at their offices. Hildy is a realtor specializing in residential properties. He overheard her once bragging about her deep connections in New York, Boston, Tampa, and Chicago and they dropped the name Stefano." Jolene thought back to the black business card from the drop with only the *S* as an identifier. "If you track her sales, or sales associated with her realty firm, you might be able to figure out their plans, but it's probably got something to do with that Stefano guy. It's either buying or selling real estate. It's a solid lead."

"You got all that in the midst of a fight?"

She snorted. "Of course not. What do you think I've been doing for the last three weeks?"

Stadler didn't smile, but the corner of one side of his mouth quivered. "How?"

"How does it work, or how did I manage it?" Jolene didn't like questions about memory surgeons. However, she'd answer anything he asked if it made Stadler look on her and Sara less harshly.

"*You*. Other people don't matter, only our team."

She smiled, pleased to be considered part of the group. "It's about connection. They open, and I open, and I see bubbles of memory—other people see strings or hear musical notes, though I think most memory surgeons are primarily visual."

Stadler nodded as if he'd heard that before.

"Anyway, over time, Colton opened more and more to me, and it became easier to access his memories. It gave me more opportunities because I needed less focus."

"How'd you leave things?"

She closed her eyes, Colton's hurt and anger abrading her heart and mind. "He won't remember anything from last night."

"Better a blank memory than death." Stadler smirked, and Jolene thought he might have been a bit proud of her.

"What was that powder Sara had, anyway? Would it have killed him? Has she had to do that before?" Jolene tried not to ask too many questions. Part of the advantage of working for the hidden side of the government was they had real flexibility to do what was right without the morass of red tape. The disadvantage was that without accountability, they might turn into something worse than what they fought.

"Fentanyl. And it could have killed him, depending on the dose. Sara's never taken out anyone. I gave it to her because Walther's got a history of violent behavior toward women. She needed something in case she had to escape." He pulled back his elbows to stretch his chest. "It's also cut into the main drug the Red Flames are selling right now."

"I'm glad she didn't use it on Colton. He's an immature asshole but doesn't deserve death."

"And the extra paperwork when someone dies is a pain in the ass." He eyeballed her neck as if he wouldn't have minded the work this time. Stadler stood, his attention somewhere else. "Pack up. We're moving out today. Go back to the apartment in Virginia."

"What?" There was nothing in Richmond but walls and boredom. The in-between. "Aren't we going to follow the trail?"

"The team, yes. You, no." His impassive face made her lungs ache. She was done. "A little more training and—"

"It's been over four-and-a-half years. I'm sick of sitting on my ass all by myself with nothing to do until a call at three a.m. to pluck a secret knock pattern from some passed-out junkie." She stood. This was why he'd brought her tea. "I've got less than six months left in my contract and nothing to show for it. Give me something."

"You have helped. All those memory reads gave us information nobody else could have gotten. We've shut down gangs with what you've found."

She groaned, which hurt her throat. "It doesn't feel like it. I'm completely removed from everything. It's not enough, Stadler."

He held out his massive arms, accentuated by the too-tight black T-shirt. He stood close enough for her to catch the woodsy scent of his cologne, deceptively comforting. "I gave you a chance."

"You promised I would be part of the team."

"If you succeeded."

"I did succeed. I got you the information you wanted, didn't I?" The odds she would win this sort of logic argument with Stadler were slim, but she didn't stop trying. "Why did you give me all that physical training and coach me on people's thought patterns if you were only going to bring me in on cases where none of that was needed? Or do you just get off on wasting people's time?"

Stadler's chest froze for a moment before returning to the regular rise and fall. For Stadler, it was as if he'd dropped his mouth open. He hated wasting time, and she'd picked the wrong stick with which to poke him.

"You think you're owed a place on my team because you're a memory surgeon?"

Sara thought so, but she had been speaking from her own assumptions and not anything Stadler had said. Jolene kept her posture loose, her face cool. She would not cry. She would not beg.

"I'm not asking for special treatment. All I want is to be treated like a human being and not some tool you pull out of your ass whenever the mood strikes you. I want to use my brain and not just my gift." Her face flamed hot enough that he had to notice. "But you know what? Fuck you."

He arched one eyebrow. She told her thudding heart he didn't scare her.

They stared at each other. Jolene refused to blink, even as her eyes roasted.

Stadler huffed a laugh and shook his head. "I'll make you a deal. You can join the team on the next assignment. You finish whatever task we've got for you in the allotted time—this time without the fuckup—and you'll become a permanent part of the group."

Jolene grinned. "And if I fail?" She wouldn't fail.

"You go back to before." He held up his hands to her imminent protest. "But I'll give you the reports on how the information you uncover is used. You'll see what a difference you make." He finally flashed her a smile. "And I'll cycle you in when I think you're set. A softer transition." Stadler stuffed his hands in his pockets. "The next stage is going to be a big deal. You've just confirmed we're heading in the right direction. Stefano isn't just a person, but a drug syndicate. We're going to move from the small-time Red Flames to the big-time Stefano organization. You ready for it?"

This was her chance to make the last four years count, to make her entire life count, to grab everything she wanted: purpose, friends, and atonement for all her previous mistakes. Right here and now, she would establish her family legacy, her jewel in the family sword hilt.

"I am."

CHAPTER FOUR

Walther

"SHE'S ONE OF THOSE WITCHES," COLTON SAID, pacing around the island in Walther's newly renovated kitchen and snagging chunks of carne asada as he passed by the steaming plate. "I'm telling you, that snotty girlfriend of yours stole my memories."

Saffron had sent Walther a breakup text the same night Julie cut Colton loose. She'd told a different tale. "Cole, if you don't remember, ain't it more likely you got blackout drunk than Saffron put some kinda spell on you and lifted your memories?" Colton never took responsibility for his actions, and Saffron's story of Colton pitching a fit over some imagined slight and smacking Julie hard enough to break her nose was far more likely.

"I don't drink around Julie," Colton replied, his tone mulish.

Walther stopped stirring his homemade salsa and raised one eyebrow at his brother.

Colton scuffed his shoe against the base of the island. "Whatever."

He moved to snatch another piece of meat. Walther slapped his hand. "That's for dinner, which is in five fucking minutes. This is a perfect example of your lack of impulse control."

"I don't drink past a buzz," Colton amended, ignoring the assessment of his character, like always. He pursed his lips, looking more like a teenager than a man in his late twenties, but then, Colton had never grown up. At the time their dad kicked it, Colton had been too young for the back of their father's hand, so Colton's relationship with their father had been positive, based on fantasy. Between Walther and their mother, they had raised Colton, and neither of them had been equipped to deal with a petulant child, so they'd always given in to his tantrums and moods. He was regretting that now.

"Uh-huh," Walther said, not believing Colton. The aroma of spiced meat, raw onions, and blanched tomatoes made his nose happy, and he decided they needed to change topics, or Colton would ruin the meal.

"Her dad was an alcoholic and a mean drunk," Colton said. "That's why she don't drink. So, there ain't no way I got so sauced I can't remember dinner."

Walther pulled out a plate and poked Colton in the stomach with it.

Colton piled too much carne asada onto the dish and not much else, only a sprinkle of cheddar and onion. "And what about that white powder I found all over my carpeting? Where did that come from?"

"You need more vegetables than that. Take some of them peppers at least."

"I don't touch none of that shit," Colton said, ignoring his brother again. "I never done the hard stuff."

Walther worked to ensure the hard stuff never came across his brother's path. But Colton wasn't stupid. If he wanted to find drugs, he could find them. "But you said you don't know what you did."

They took their plates outside to the glass patio table where Walther liked to enjoy the cooler hours and admire the fancy landscaping of his quarter-acre yard.

"Okay, then why was your girlfriend asking me about business? It's the only thing I remember from the whole fucking night. She said you was telling her I was some nothing in the organization. Did you say that?"

Cicadas chirped and whirred. A light breeze cooled Walther's sweaty neck.

"Of course not," Walther said, lying on instinct and without pause. He had told Saffron that one night. Why would she say something like that to his brother? Then again, if Colton had hit Julie, he could see Saff flinging that insult at him in retaliation. She had spark.

"Should I tell—?"

"No!" Walther pinched his nose. "Colton, if you tell the Flames anything, they're gonna think you blabbed and made up this ridiculous story to cover for yourself."

"I didn't say nothing!"

Walther chose not to point out Colton had just said he didn't remember the entire night, which meant he might have told anyone anything. "So why mention it?"

"They'll help me find Julie."

"To kill her."

Colton gasped. "She ain't done nothing. That bitch of yours fucked with her memory and made her think I hit her."

"You said there was blood on your carpeting."

Colton stood from the patio table. "Saffron did it! She's the one broke Julie's nose, then changed her memories so she'd think it was me. Once I explain—"

"Cole, sit down." Walther used his father's voice, the one that promised violence.

His brother sat, though his red face and lack of eye contact displayed his stubborn streak.

Walther leaned forward and waited for Colton to look at him. "There's no proof memory whatevers ain't nothing but con artists. They can't testify, and a shit-ton have been outed as fakes."

"But—"

"Even if they're real, there ain't that many around. You honestly think someone who can read fucking minds or whatever are gonna bother with us? No, they're gonna be hanging around day traders and stock market guys, cashing in on hot tips." Walther saw Colton was not yet convinced.

"Look, I know Saff pretty good, and no way she's one of them memory whatevers. All she knows how to do is look hot."

"But—"

Walther slapped his hands onto the table, the glass cool and smooth beneath his palms. He gentled his voice. "Do you trust me?"

Colton nodded once.

With a firm hand squeeze on Colton's arm, Walther spoke as if instructing him on how to diffuse a bomb. "You cannot mention any of this to the Flames. Not one word to any of them or anyone else. Understand?"

His brother nodded again.

"Because if they so much as suspect you've leaked information, they'll kill you, Cole."

Colton swallowed as if he finally did comprehend the seriousness of his situation. "Okay."

Walther shouldn't have indulged his brother, but it had become a habit. "Maybe she'll snap out of it and come back."

The smile Colton gave him reminded him of why he and his mother had spoiled him. He might have the disposition of a child, but he had the guilelessness of one too. Colton was easy to please and easy to love.

Walther would personally track down Julie and fix this mistake.

CHAPTER FIVE

Jolene

JOLENE GAVE UP HOLDING ON TO HER PARANOID edge after her second week in Chicago. Her near panic attack at being back in her hometown after the Agency had faked her death five years before had dissipated. There was only one person likely to recognize her with her now-blond hair and toned body. And Kiera, unless she'd changed radically, was practically homebound and living by Lake Michigan.

Without an assigned role yet, Jolene wandered around her Wicker Park neighborhood apartment being herself, whatever that meant. Mostly, she arranged her bookshelf full of thrift store finds, most of which she'd already read, and worked out compulsively to keep her anxiety at a tolerable level and to help her sleep better and longer.

Her grandmother had been one of those people who valued industriousness, and she'd tried to instill that virtue in Jolene.

She ate every meal out and shopped more than she should, paying cash. Deciding it wasn't a violation to hook up to people's memories, she let her fingers brush others', trying to connect to their experiences as quickly as possible.

As expected, the more interaction she had with someone, the more accessible the memories. She joked with waitresses, checkout clerks, and the entire staff of the Starbucks she frequented. In just a few short weeks, she could reach even strangers' memories. Adequate progress, but the next logical step was to peek into them. Then dive inside for the full experience. She hesitated, the violation a step too far. Regular people deserved their privacy. But she needed the practice. Jolene struggled with the choice. Did the end justify the means, or was that something assholes said to legitimize their unethical behavior?

* * *

Usually, at just before seven, Starbucks had few patrons, but a small line waited when Jolene stepped through to the coffee bar. Her favorite barista, Rick, was working the register, while Moll and a teenage-looking kid whose name Jolene couldn't remember worked the machines. She stared at the exposed-brick wall and sank into her mind, preparing to link to Rick when it was her turn.

"Where is the goddamned cinnamon?"

The surly voice snapped Jolene out of her meditation. It wasn't one of the reality-impaired homeless people who occasionally popped in, but a douche-canoe in a suit. "I need some fucking cinnamon, people."

The teenager came out from behind the counter with a huge Costco-sized container of cinnamon. Jolene would have to learn his name.

"Hurry it up, tardo. I've got places to be."

An old memory popped into her mind, as one always could with the right trigger. Before the Agency, Jolene used to perform memory surgeries, removing traumatic memories, her specialty torture and war crimes.

Tardo. One of her refugee clients from Syria, Haamid, had been only eight, fresh to the US and struggling with the cultural adjustment and not over his ordeal. The reek of exploded concrete and burned flesh was seared into his nasal passages, and he still waited for bombs to go off, for his mother to die like his father and brothers had. On top of that, he didn't speak English, and some of the kids assumed he was stupid. *Tardo.* After everything he'd been through, he felt as if that sort of teasing should have been nothing. But like wild animals, certain children sensed his weakness and tore into the soft spot without mercy. His mother admonished him to swallow his anger, to fit in at any cost. He'd burned with humiliation but had done nothing. Powerless. Always without power.

Jolene had raged as him and for him as she'd sucked away those memories, keeping them tucked inside herself, locked away until some arrogant asshole in a Starbucks freed them with just the right key.

"Hey," she snapped, her frustration with her own life merging with Haamid's incandescent fury. From her place near the back of the line, she was only a few feet from the dude. "He's a human being. Treat him with some respect."

People throughout the coffee shop were staring at her when she should have been keeping a low profile. All she needed was to show up in some viral video on TikTok, but she had this prick's attention now, along with the rest of Starbucks.

"And watch your fucking mouth."

The name on his cup was Skip, which was too perfect. Skip wasn't any older than forty with a face that was all forehead and too-wide teeth. He turned conniption red and took a step toward her, a tremor in his coffee hand. Was this guy seriously looking to throw down in the middle of a Starbucks on a Tuesday morning?

Someone grabbed the back of her long-sleeved T-shirt and yanked. She stumbled back one step before an arm banded around her middle and hauled her back into a hard, flat chest as Skip hurled his cup. The top shot off like an exploded grenade, landing where she'd just been standing. Coffee splashed up toward her legs, but whoever had pulled her back took another step, away from the liquid.

Skip stared at her, wide-eyed, mouth agape. Nobody moved. The kid with the cinnamon clutched it to his chest like a shield.

Jolene should have let the tantrum go but didn't. "You missed."

"Screw this," Skip said, spinning around.

She thought he was going to grab the sugar container and hurl it at her. Instead, he bolted for the door, fancy oxfords sliding, a hard, black briefcase slapping into his leg as he stumble-ran out.

The entire Starbucks remained frozen, the scent of coffee heavy, the only sounds the hiss of the steamer and some song from the eighties over the speakers. Everyone wore a did-that-really-just-happen expression. People stood from the padded benches, several moving to the windows to watch Skip's escape.

The moment felt more like a dream than reality.

Jolene turned to face the man who'd saved her from a likely burn and certain stain. Wide eyes flicked from her face to her arm, which, at some point, she'd flung in front of his body. She dropped the protective gesture, her face flaming with adrenaline and confusion.

He was handsome, caught midway between rugged and pretty. His chin and jaw were strong, but his cheekbones delicate, lips full and pouty. Oh God, had she just thought he had a pretty mouth?

Yes. Yes, she had.

She recognized him as a regular, often there around the same time she was. He also ordered tea, though he drank London Fog lattes instead of chai. That was why he was so memorable. Certainly not because of his broad shoulders or his shoulder-length, dark hair that looked as lush as a mink stole.

When he smiled, his teeth were white, with one canine that was twisted and shy, breaking his perfection into pieces that made him seem almost attainable. Part of his roughness, she remembered, were his forearm tattoos, which she couldn't see now through his Henley. Even when his forearms had been exposed, she'd been too self-conscious to look all that closely, but she remembered the black ink with a tribal flare, sharp with thorns in places. He had elegant hands with long fingers he raked through his hair, the movement exposing a black hair elastic around his right wrist.

As if someone had given a signal, people reanimated. They talked to each other in fast, clipped tones about what they'd all witnessed. A young woman with several facial piercings asked Jolene if she knew the guy. An older man said Skip was a regular but usually came in an hour earlier. Jolene doubted he would ever return.

"Jolie Jolene." Rick said the nickname he'd given her in a voice that carried, breaking her gapefest. "We'll be making you a chai latte. On the house."

"That's . . . nice. Thanks."

"Cass, my man, fine job." Rick stretched his fist over the glass partition, and the man who'd kept her from getting burned twisted his body to fist-bump the barista. Rick grinned. "Your London is coming right up too."

The teenage employee refilled the cinnamon, his face blotched red, his movements jerky. Poor kid. Jolene shuffled closer to her gorgeous savior, who studied her warily, as if unsure if he should tell her that her fly was unzipped. It wasn't. And she didn't have toilet paper on her shoe.

Maybe he hadn't appreciated her final taunt at Skip. Admittedly, not her finest moment. But her dredged-up anger still hadn't abated. *Tardo.* Such a hateful word. Jolene also squirmed internally at the feel of everyone studying her.

Side by side, she and Cass picked up their drinks. *My God, he smells amazing, too, like warm spice and leather with a hint of citrus.*

"Cass?" she asked, wanting to make sure she had his name right, that Rick hadn't given him a nickname too. She had to thank him for the save.

"Short for Cassidy," he said, as if she'd questioned his name rather than confirmed it. "My mom was a huge Shaun Cassidy fan."

"Why didn't she name you Shaun?"

He cringed. "That's my brother's name."

Jolene laughed. They walked together toward the door. "So, when she called you guys in for dinner, did she yell, 'Shaun Cassidy, get in here right now?'"

"Pretty much."

"And your dad didn't care?"

"He thought it was funny."

They reached the street, the sun a dagger to the eyes with a clear shot down North Avenue. "I don't think that naming kids is the time for humor," she said, wanting to stretch out the conversation for just a few more minutes. In the natural light, she noted his eyes, which she'd thought were brown, were actually an earthy green. Her own eyes were a middling shade of brown made prettier by her dyed-blond hair, but they weren't as striking as his. Not that this was a contest. "Thanks for the save back there, by the way."

"Hey," he said, resting a hand on hers, the one holding her tea. "You're shaking."

Jolene scrunched her eyes closed for a second, then opened them. She reached out for his memories in a trained reflex and found them less crowded than most people's. He watched her with an unnerving intensity. What had he said? "Oh." Her hands *were* trembling. "Just adrenaline. I'm fine."

"It's okay if you're not. He could have seriously burned you." Cass looked down Damen Avenue, toward the 'L' stop, possibly looking for Skip.

She wished she could tell him she was a memory reader so he would understand a little coffee throwing wouldn't cause a blip in terms of trauma. But many people were uncomfortable around her gift. He'd probably jerk away his hand, though she hadn't peered into his memories, not even the tiny bubbles.

"I bet he's pretty mortified at this point." Jolene imagined his mental horror, either for losing his cool or for missing her with his coffee assault. "He'll be thinking about those moments a lot longer than I will."

The man had lost control for a moment. She wanted to give him the benefit of the doubt she'd wanted from others back when she'd been a drunk. It didn't matter that he didn't deserve compassion or understanding. Or maybe that's what made it matter at all.

Cass moved his hand from hers and squeezed her shoulder. "You're a lot more forgiving than me."

She'd never thought of herself as magnanimous. Hell, she still hadn't forgiven her parents for dying, and that had been nearly thirty years ago. Jolene's feet buzzed with the need to move, her body desperate to shed the chemicals still swirling through her, spurning her to action even though the excitement was over.

"He caught me on a benevolent day."

Cass held his tea with both hands and inched closer to her. "You seem . . . unsteady. Should we sit down?"

"No." She shook her head for emphasis. "I actually need to move. I'm—I don't—" Jolene laughed at her own ridiculousness. "Walking is better for me. I think I'm just going to walk the park." Not that there were many paths in Wicker Park, a strange triangular configuration with only a baseball diamond, fountain, and a squat administrative building. "You want to come with me?"

"Okay."

They walked to the corner of the busy, three-way intersection of North, Damen, and Milwaukee and waited for the light. The curb was steep, as if the street had been lowered at one point, so Jolene took an extra-long step when the light changed. Cass mimicked her and kept flush to her side.

"I've seen you a few times but never said hi," he said as they made their way to the park.

"That would have been weird," she replied, thinking of how much she wouldn't have appreciated that friendly gesture. "You're just supposed to nod or something when you recognize people you don't actually know."

"Is that right? What would you have done if I'd said hello?" His playful tone warmed her where she had no business warming.

"I would have said 'hey', but I'd be judging you the whole time." They cut into the park and headed toward the fountain sitting in the center of the concrete patio. "I'd be wondering what the hell was wrong with you."

He chuckled and sighed dramatically. "So many things."

"Like what?" This was the first time in forever she could take the time to make friends with someone. The moment was normal and easy, and she'd forgotten what it was like to just be a regular person for two damn minutes.

When he smiled, she noticed his crooked tooth again. "I'm an artist, but I haven't been able to paint much lately. I've had some kind of creative blockage, and it's made me unsettled, like it might be permanent."

They walked past the baseball diamond on their left, houses on their right.

He nudged her with his elbow. "So, what's wrong with you?"

She should have anticipated he'd quid pro quo her on her faults. Although she couldn't tell him everything—and wouldn't if she could—she found herself wanting to tell him only true things. "I'm a recovering alcoholic, and I'm told I mention that too often. Apparently, some people think that after someone stays sober beyond a certain milestone, they're supposed to consider themselves cured, like it's cancer or something. You paint for a living?"

Cass nodded.

"What kind of stuff?" She hoped he didn't talk in art terms, like perspective or . . . Perspective was the only art term her brain conjured.

"Abstracts, mostly."

"Is that because you can't draw people?"

He laughed. "Harsh."

Oh shit, that *was* rude. "I don't know anything about art."

"I could do portraits if I wanted." He grinned, but an edge had crept into his voice. "But I don't have a spark to paint something a camera captures better."

Good point.

"I don't want to be confined to what I can see with my eye." He sighed. "But right now, I'm halfway through a painting, and I can't finish it. That's why I have to leave the house every day. Otherwise, I might cut off an ear in frustration."

"Van Gogh was considered a success only after he died, so I wouldn't go emulating that guy."

His hand bumped hers as they walked. They both mumbled apologies and shifted apart, though not far. A comfortable silence knit them together.

He smiled. "What do you do?"

She wished she had a cover job not meant to incite boredom. "Medical billing." After that landed, she pushed on. "Despite what anyone believes about the insurance industry, I like to think of myself as helping people. Not as exciting as being an artist."

"How did you get into the medical billing business?"

He was the first man on Earth to not want to talk about himself. Or she hadn't hit upon the right topic yet. But she didn't want to discuss her fake job when it was such a beautiful day. The drowsy energy between them made her want to hum. "I don't want to think about work."

"Okay. What do you do for fun?" Their hands brushed again. He didn't edge away from her this time or acknowledge the contact.

She swallowed the urge to apologize. Had she done it on purpose without realizing it? "Exercising. Running."

"Do you ever run on the 606?" he asked.

"All the time." The 606 was a short walk away. The lakefront had a longer running pathway and a better breeze but getting there required a bus ride. The lake path took her close to Navy Pier, close to where her friend Kiera lived—had lived—likely still lived. She wasn't supposed to contact anyone from her previous life, so being near Kiera's condo felt like holding her palm over a candle flame. She dared herself to come as near as possible, even if it burned her.

"Want to run together sometime?"

"Sure," she replied, because that's what people did, proposed vague plans to meet when they had no intention of doing so.

They both took sips from their drinks. He tapped his cup with an index finger. "What about tomorrow?"

CHAPTER SIX

Jolene

JOLENE SAT ON HER FUTON COUCH, HER KNEE bouncing, her thoughts pinging everywhere. Of course, the minute she'd gotten a date—well, social engagement—Stadler texted that the team was meeting tomorrow afternoon at her place to start the new mission.

With a huff, she dropped and did twenty push-ups. Not enough. Ten pull-ups and fifteen jump squats. Not enough.

Jolene jerked on her walking shoes. She wouldn't fail. She needed to be part of something, not just an awkward appendage.

She avoided the 606, not wanting thoughts of tomorrow's plans to distract from tomorrow's problems. Instead, she stayed on the quieter side streets. The dappled sunlight from all the trees and the somewhat muted sounds helped her focus. Leaves blazed in reds and glowed in yellows, the air crisp in a clear, cleansing way. A beautiful fall day.

Jolene might have suffered a touch of nerves, but she was ready for her new role.

A man walked his chocolate Lab puppy in her direction, and she was glad for the break in her thoughts. The fluffball pranced more than walked, occasionally twisting her head back to chew on the leash.

"So cute," she said with a wide grin. "Can I pet her?"

The man was about her age or a bit younger, with overly gelled hair. Trendy, he oozed confidence and the arrogant security of his place in the world. The ring finger on his left hand had an indentation from a recently removed ring. He vibed all wrong. "Sure. This is Trudy," he said, stopping. "She loves people."

"Hey, Trudy," Jolene said, squatting to better pet the squiggling puppy. "How old is she?" Trudy's back end almost blurred it moved so fast, and her fur was fluffy soft.

"Nine weeks."

Trudy nipped at Jolene's fingers, her puppy teeth sharp. "She's so adorable and sweet."

"So are you."

Jolene looked up at him. His flirting while obviously being married justified practice time. She stood and extended her hand. "Jolene."

He took it. "Ferris."

His memory bubbles were enormous and almost sheer. One of them throbbed, only half formed, looking like a lopsided *C*. She'd never seen anything like it.

"As in Bueller?" Since they were strangers, she couldn't hold on to his hand for more than a few seconds. If she wanted to read his memories, she had to act fast. A win would bolster her confidence. She needed that. And he was a cheating bastard. Probably. Jolene touched the odd bubble in his mind and sank inside.

* * *

Smoking hot. Her body glowed with sweat as he maneuvered her onto her hands and knees. Oh yeah. *Grab that blond hair and wrap it around his fist.* Yes, arch your back just like that, you little slut. *She moaned, and her cunt squeezed him as she begged him to pound her harder.*

* * *

HOLY. SHIT. THIS WASN'T A RECOLLECTION FROM THE PAST BUT A MEMORY he was building as they spoke. She was literally reading his mind as the fantasy he would revisit later formed.

Jolene fixed a pleasant expression on her face and kept hold of the man's hand a few more seconds, despite how much she detested having to live his imaginings about her. She grew wet with arousal from his own lust and then queasy in reaction to her reaction. Although she comprehended she couldn't stop feeling what he felt, it was still creepy.

"Yeah, as in Ferris Bueller." He smiled like a youthful Viagra ad and rubbed his thumb over the back of her hand.

* * *

"I want your dick in my mouth," Joanne begged, her tits swollen with nipples so hard they could cut glass. "I want to swallow your man milk."

He smirked and took hold of his cock.

* * *

JOANNE? THE FUCKER DIDN'T EVEN GET HER NAME RIGHT. SHE WAS TORN between wanting to shake free of this man's daydream of her and exploring this new aspect of her gift.

* * *

A flash of his wife, Michelle, making him an omelet for breakfast interrupted his awesome fantasy. He pushed her aside in his mind and concentrated on the heaving tits of the woman in his mind's eye.

* * *

"Do you live around here?" Ferris nudged Trudy, who'd lost interest in the adult conversation and started chewing on some grass. His fingers squeezed Jolene's.

"No." She should let go of his hand, but—

* * *

He was going to come. Her red lips slid up and down his pole as she slurped and sucked and made wet sounds that pushed him over the edge.

"I'm gonna come on your face."

"Please," she said, his manhood slicking out of her mouth with a pop as she reached down and frigged herself, coming as the first jet of his cum landed on her cheek. She opened her lips to catch the next stream.

* * *

"Thanks for letting me pet your puppy," she said, taking a step away, testing if she could keep the connection without the contact, but the moment they no longer touched, his thoughts disappeared.

Thank fuck. But still. Damn it.

"Want to grab a coffee sometime?" he asked, his smile almost guileless.

"Only if your wife joins us," she said, moving around Trudy, who was chomping on a short stick.

He made a few "eh" and "uh" noises but formed no actual words. Jolene didn't wait for his response. She wanted to go home and shower, shake the residual arousal.

After she turned the corner, she giggled. Man milk. What the hell? And what was up with the breast augmentation? She laughed out loud at the absurdity of men.

Jolene stepped on a fat, brown maple leaf, the crunch satisfying. A shudder shook her body, and she blew out a breath. The seriousness of what she'd done soaked into her vertebrae. She read minds, sort of, with only a touch.

CHAPTER SEVEN

Walther

WALTHER STARED AT HIS LITTLE BROTHER, inanimate and chalky on the metal table under unforgiving lighting. He tried not to see the bullet holes in Colton's forehead, glad the ones in his chest were covered. Double, double-tapped. Executed. No witnesses or DNA evidence.

Unbeknownst to Walther, his brother had been dead two weeks.

The police suspected a professional hit and had far too many questions about what Colton did for a living and who his closest associates were. Walther couldn't say—not because he didn't know, but because those colleagues weren't the sort of people you named.

The Red Flames didn't give two shits about Colton's death and wouldn't put the proper effort into finding who'd done it and making sure they died a slow, terrible death. That would fall to Walther. Colton was dead, and someone had to pay.

He had a place to start—with those bitches Saffron Struthers and Julie something. Colton's phone was missing, but Walther had the password—Pu$$yLover. He smiled and winced at the reminder. Colton had been so immature, indulged by everyone.

Walther squeezed his eyes shut and nodded to the morgue guy, who tugged the sheet to cover the face of his dead baby brother. The cold of the room seeped through his suit jacket and into his DNA. The sound of a pen scritching on the paperwork for Colton's permanent sleep made Walther's fingers twitch.

He should have kept a closer watch on Colton. When he'd bitched about that cunt trying to frame him, Walther should have taken that seriously.

Tonight, Walther would get shitfaced and buy a few rounds in honor of his brother. In the morning, he'd dive into Colton's life—his past life—and find those bitches.

CHAPTER EIGHT

Jolene

THE RHYTHM OF HER FEET ON THE SIDEWALK, THE shush of traffic, the smells of the city—car exhaust, coffee, doughnuts—the sights of people scurrying to work or daycares . . . The essence of her hometown washed over Jolene. Like a favorite coat, she wrapped the neighborhood around herself as she hurried to meet Cass.

She passed Starbucks on her way farther north. The place was both familiar and foreign at this odd time of day. A shiver zinged up her back.

Her steps faltered as she thought about how she'd fallen into a schedule. She glanced behind her, but no one paid her undue attention. The people across the street moved, no one lurking or watching.

Her scalp tingled and itched, making her want to dig her nails into her hair and scratch until she bled. Nobody followed her, but she'd broken the pattern, hadn't she?

Stop it!

Jolene hadn't experienced this level of paranoia in years. She tried to squash the thoughts, but they slipped and slid out of her grasp.

Why would someone as hot as Cass strike up a conversation with her?

Wait. She'd started talking first.

Had Skip been a plant meant to draw her out?

Anyone knowing she'd confront someone like that right then was unlikely. If she'd been in a different mood, she wouldn't have said anything. She wasn't a consistent person.

Her eyes scanned as her brain categorized. Nothing out of the ordinary.

She was so engrossed in her surroundings that by the time she spotted Cass, he'd seen her first.

It was 6:05 a.m.

"Was this too early?" he asked as she approached. He was probably one of those always on time guys. "You don't look happy to be here."

She smoothed her face. "It's not too early. I don't like being late. Sorry."

"It's fine. I enjoy people watching."

Jolene didn't enjoy her people watching at all. "Shall we?" She gestured to the curving cement entrance ramp.

* * *

THAT PART OF THE 606 HAD A HEDGE HIGH ON ONE SIDE, ONLY THE roofs of condos or apartment complexes visible. The other side had a fence laced with vines. It felt private, sheltered.

They took the trail at a walk for the first few minutes. Jolene thought about how much easier it was to hang out side by side instead of facing off. The weather tipped toward cool, which was perfect for a run, and she looked forward to shedding her jacket soon.

Cass wore all black, like her, the swirl of blue on his shoes the only spot of color. His hair, thick and long enough to be termed a pelt, was down. It would be stifling later. Then she noticed the elastic around his wrist.

"Hey, stranger," she said, finally calm enough for a proper hello.

His smile flashed as if he was happy to be with her. "Hey, yourself."

If the Skip drama had never taken place, they wouldn't have bonded as quickly as they had. With Jolene's reticence, they would have never gone beyond "hey, how are you?" She would have missed out on the strange combination of ease and tense attraction he pulled out of her.

Jolene thought about her paranoia reappearing and wondered if it was some sort of brain-chemical response to making a connection outside the safety of work. She'd spent so many years—not happy but content—with Stadler and the job, but it wasn't healthy long term to associate only with the team and those they targeted. Certainly, she deserved to have a life of her own too.

She couldn't hear the traffic on Damen. The asphalt path had been renovated from old railroad tracks and had an eighteen-inch ribbon of padded surface along each edge, a considerate gesture for runners, though not enough room for two people to run next to each other.

"I warmed up by walking here," she said. "Are you ready to go, or do you need more time?"

"All good. I usually work up to speed, and I do all my stretching on the back end."

"That's what she said," Jolene replied, her pattern of banter with Sara bleeding through to Cass. She hoped it wasn't too much.

Cass laughed.

Their strides synced, their proximity too close for the newness of their friendship, yet it felt right. Their situation reminded her of the start of a great book, that moment, only a paragraph in, when she understood she would love the story. It rarely happened, probably less so with people than books. But already, she wanted to hang out with Cass, suck up his casual confidence.

"I'm thinking we go out to breakfast afterward, maybe grab something from Beard Papa's," he said.

"I haven't been there yet."

His conspiratorial grin and the cosseted feel of the 606 soothed her paranoia from earlier. She reminded herself she was the shadow in the dark now, and shadows didn't have shadows of their own.

"I run three days a week," Cass said. "Used to run every other day, but I tried to power through shin splints and learned a lesson."

Jolene held back the urge to say, *me too*, at everything he said, like a preschooler making her first friend. "I've been lucky not to have pulled anything in a while. If I don't exercise in some way, I feel like I'll scratch my skin off. It's my therapy."

"It's helpful in so many ways, isn't it?"

Jolene wondered if he wanted to chant, *me too*, like she did.

Weight-bearing exercises worked just as well as running, but jogging made her feel free. She ducked behind him and encouraged him to the right edge. "Go ahead and take the padding, shin-splint guy."

He bit his lip and narrowed his eyes at her in a playful way. "Not very gentlemanly of me to take it."

Jolene exhaled and started a slow jog. "Your secret is safe with me."

"Thanks," he said, matching her pace. "Do you want to hear another secret?"

She did and didn't. Sharing secrets should be reciprocal. "Sure."

"I've been wanting to talk to you."

Her foot hit the ground at a shorter length, causing a hitch in her step, but she quickly recovered. "Why?" He was going to ruin their friendship now.

"The way you joke with Rick," he said, surprising her. "It made me want to get to know you, but I couldn't imagine approaching you in any way that wasn't creepy."

She swallowed down her relief. "Rick's a cool guy."

"He is . . . Well, other than his godawful taste in music."

"What kind of music does he like?"

"Country."

"Hm. I like Dolly Parton."

He scoffed. "Everyone likes Dolly Parton. She's a national treasure, and she'll probably single-handedly prevent the apocalypse."

"So, country music like Shania Twain?" Jolene didn't listen to country, so she had no one else to suggest.

"Like the kind of country about cheating women and gun racks on trucks. I mean . . ." He growled a little, the sound making her stomach stumble and fall in an inappropriate way. "It's fine to like that stuff.

I just . . . I don't want to listen to music that makes me want to clean my shotgun or seed my lawn."

"Country music makes you want to seed your lawn?" She laughed so hard she started coughing. "So it's, like, motivational?"

"*Anyway*," he said, chuckling. "I'm glad we finally met properly."

"Me too." She shoved down the giggles, though her smile wouldn't fade. "Let's quit dicking around."

When she was upset, she sprinted straightaway to drain the stress. But having Cass next to her gave her an energy she didn't want dissipated. So she found a moderate pace her body adjusted to in five minutes.

"How was the rest of your day yesterday?" Cass asked, his long hair swishing from side to side.

Attraction was pointless. "I've got a new work project I'm excited and nervous about. What about you? Did you finish that painting?"

He increased his speed. "I did. Thanks for that."

"What did I do?"

"You restored my faith in humanity by standing up to the Skips of the world."

She might have wanted to be the kind of person who restored people's faith, but that wasn't her. How could you restore something that didn't exist? People, for the most part, sucked.

They passed a woman pushing a double stroller and two women in white T-shirts and pants, their heads bent together, moving slowly enough to be considered strolling.

Cass finally broke the silence. "Does this pace work?"

Jolene smiled. "I could go a little faster."

He caught her grin and bit his lip. "Is that right?" He slid off his hair tie and pulled his hair into a ponytail before edging ahead of her. His side-eye gave her a playful challenge.

Jolene's stomach swooned, sending a ping of energy through her body. He was baiting her, and she liked it. She unzipped her thin jacket and tied it around her waist so she wouldn't have to fuss with it later. Once secured, she pushed in front of him.

They passed under a rusted bridge, and she lengthened her stride, which made her move faster. Jolene's entire person—mind, body, and soul—distilled into a tight line of clarity with each strike of her feet, every pump of her arms, her breath and heart working overtime.

"How . . . long . . . do you . . . run?" Cass chugged next to her, his face red and covered in sweat.

"We can . . ." Damn it, she wanted to talk in easy, full sentences, but she was reaching her max. "Stop . . . when you . . . want."

"That's . . . how . . . it is . . . then?"

"Yep."

She stayed inside herself as her mind expanded, her limbs loosened, and her lungs pumped oxygen everywhere. Cass said nothing, his presence next to her felt friendlier than it had a right to, and though she should have rejected such a comforting reaction, she chose to enjoy it.

They continued for another five minutes, passing walkers and joggers. Finally, Cass dropped back and slowed to a walk, his hands on his waist, his chest heaving. "Goddamn, you've got some stamina," he said on one long exhale.

That's what she said.

She shrugged. "Competitive by nature."

Her lungs and heart continued to thunder in her rib cage, squeezing from the back of her throat to the bottom of her stomach. She wiped her forehead with the back of her arm, but she was sweating too much to do more than slick it around. Her legs wobbled as they walked off the run. She refused to check her heartrate on her Fitbit.

"That was good." Cass grinned as he huffed.

That's what she said.

She gulped in a few extra breaths to keep her lungs happy. "Yeah."

Cass grunted and peeled his shirt over his head, his eyes fixed ahead, which was fortunate because she openly gawped.

Holy hell, he was hot. Like, supermodel-rock-star-billionaire-playboy incandescent. She tore her gaze away before he caught her ogling him. At least she was already panting before he'd unleashed his natural glory. His six-pack wasn't *Men's Fitness*-defined, but she could scrub some clothes clean over his muscles.

His tattoos looked to occupy only his arms and shoulders. The forearm tattoos looked tribal, with thorns and skulls woven inside, one with a missing eye and one with the eye overlaid with crosshairs. All black. Beautiful. They weren't sleeve tattoos, so the absence of ink between the designs became as interesting as the tattoos themselves.

His tentative smile made her . . . feel too much. She had responsibilities and no time for a relationship.

* * *

Back at Churchill Park, they headed toward the north side of the small lawn, away from the asphalt dog run. It was a small park with a bit of grass, a tiny baseball diamond, and the dog area. She'd acclimated to his shirtlessness, though she had to concentrate to keep looking at his face.

Cass walked to a spot closer to the dog run.

"Have you ever done partner stretching?" he asked as he tossed his shirt to the grass.

"Is that a euphemism for sex?"

He choked out a laugh. "No."

"Then, no."

"Are you up for trying?"

She really wished it was a euphemism for sex. "Okay."

The cool morning had warmed some, and her core temperature had yet to drop enough that she needed her jacket, so she pulled it free of her waist and dropped it next to Cass's shirt. She wore only running tights and a sports bra, so when he grabbed her shoulder, his hand touched bare flesh.

"You hold on to me at the same time, and we use each other for balance to stretch our quads."

His skin retained a slight sheen of sweat. She tried not to assign significance to their skin-to-skin contact. Luckily, standing stretches required concentration. Using her opposite hand, she grabbed her foot and pulled it to her ass, breathing into the quad stretch. Nobody in the park paid them any mind. When she glanced at Cass, he was studying her.

"Other side?" Had his voice gotten deeper?

They both turned in place and grasped each other again. She watched him for several seconds before deciding that might be creepy for him. Neither of them wobbled, but she still enjoyed the security of having something to hold on to.

"Are you going to do an Ironman one day?" she asked. He seemed the type.

"No, I don't swim."

"For real?" She wasn't a great swimmer, but she knew how.

Jolene hadn't connected to his memories. Not once. For weeks, she'd done nothing but hook into others' minds with every touch. Not today. She wouldn't, not even to practice. Shouldn't.

"What happens if there's some meteoric, cataclysmic event, and Lake Michigan swallows up the city? You'll drown." She was joking, of course. Mostly.

"I'll hide out at the top of my apartment building."

She'd done memory surgery on a survivor of the 2004 Indonesian tsunami. The sound, a roar like a jet in a thunderstorm, sometimes haunted her dreams, or the churning, pulling, grasping way the water had clung to him and slammed him into things. She wondered if he still dreamed about the noise even though she held those memories. Did they creep back into his subconsciousness as some generic unease, or had she completely taken the triggers?

"I'm going to teach you how to swim." Not that swimming had saved Ernesto—only luck. But everyone should learn how to swim.

"Really? Do you swim a lot?"

"Enough." Enough to prevent drowning.

They sat on the ground facing each other, legs spread, feet touching.

Jolene couldn't do the splits, but she had decent leg flexibility, matching Cass's longer legs, though she had to stretch to do it. Cass held his hands out in front of him, and she took them. His elegant fingers were cool, and his hands encompassed her own. His cuticles had small dots of paint: ecru, moss, and blood red. A thrill of energy that was all lust and none of her gift traveled up her arms into her chest, and she had to work to steady her breathing.

"Okay." Cass leaned back, pulling her forward, her groin muscles protesting but acquiescing. "Where and when should we go swimming?"

They balanced each other, their motions suspended by their counter movements. The stretch itself bordered on uncomfortable, but she enjoyed the connection with him. A mutual connection.

"Saturday?"

After a million minutes, he nodded, and she leaned back, way back, stretching him. Cass was one limber motherfucker. "Saturday's fine."

He was naked underneath his clothes. Everyone was naked underneath their clothes, but she'd never thought about it until that moment. His green eyes watched her as if fascinated.

"I'll find a place and open swim times," she said.

They exchanged phone numbers. Cassidy Stuart.

The next stretch was downright weird. She sat on the ground with her legs straight in front of her. Cass sat behind her, his feet planted against her lower back as he pulled her arms backward to stretch her chest. Although it felt good, she kept picturing him ripping her arms off.

"Relax into it," he said. Since he was behind her, she couldn't see what he was doing.

She didn't like anyone in her blind spots, not on the street or in her car, and definitely not while holding on to both her wrists. What if she needed to run? "Let's switch."

He grumbled a little about tightness but released his grip. When she tried to repeat what he'd done, it felt even weirder, like she was attempting to rip *his* arms off.

"You can pull harder," he said with a satisfied groan.

"Okay, but if your shoulder pops out of joint, you're taking yourself to the hospital."

"Will you come visit me?"

She huffed a laugh. "I'm pretty sure they don't admit people for dislocated shoulders."

"But what if they did? Would you visit?"

"Hell no. I'd ransack your apartment while you're out."

"Can you do some laundry while you're there?"

She laughed. She hadn't laughed so freely in a long time. Years?

They both struggled to their feet, and she was sure he tried as hard as she did to seem smooth. She'd pushed him as much as he'd pushed her. Jolene hadn't had a balanced relationship since she'd joined the Agency. Maybe ever.

"You okay?" Cass asked, his body angled as if avoiding facing her directly. It was as if he understood she'd gone someplace dark.

"Hell yeah. I'm all warmed up now. You ready to go for that run?"

He laughed.

* * *

In light of the amount of sweat they'd produced, Cass invited Jolene to his place for breakfast in lieu of a restaurant or even takeout. "I'm just a few blocks that way," he said, gesturing.

He lived in a modern three-flat on a tree-lined side street west of Damen. The stairs were narrow for a new building but clean. His apartment was neat and minimalist in a way that appeared cultivated, not like her general lack of shit. The books on the bookcase were arranged according to the color of their spines. A bonsai tree sat on the kitchen windowsill. The walls were all a cool blue, like fresh snow atop a glacier. He had an *L*-shaped couch in some microfiber fabric, a large television and not much else. No coffee table or end tables or lamps.

"Where are your paintings?" she asked, hoping that wasn't a rude question.

"My studio is in the master bedroom."

"Where do you sleep, then?"

"The guestroom."

"Damn, always a guest in your own place. That's got to sting."

He grinned. "It certainly makes it hard to find the motivation to clean. I mean, who cleans someone else's apartment?"

The space, however, had obviously been cleaned recently. She looked around and smirked. "You can be a guest at my place anytime."

"I'm going to remember you said that."

Her insides turned slippery, and a pleasant flipping sensation rolled through her belly. Their eye contact jolted her to attention as if it were a living thing.

"Are you going to show me your art?" Jolene asked.

She imagined art—real art, anyway—to be highly personal. Would she look at one of his paintings and confront his soul? More likely, she'd see swirls of paint, and she'd have to decide if she wanted to pretend to perceive more than that.

Cass bit his lip and tapped his fingers on his leg. "Maybe once I've completed a few more pieces?" It was more question than statement. "I'm just going to change real quick."

She watched him walk away, captured by the tight movement of his fine ass. Beyond the physical, he had an easy way about him she deeply envied. She was brittle. Jaded. Sour. Sharp.

What the hell was she doing here, starting . . . something . . . with this hot stranger? Friendship? More? She should be concentrating on the job, on the unique opportunity to do something bold and exciting, not attempting to carve out something mundane and comfortable. But Cass didn't seem to expect anything from her, which made her feel lighter, freer, as if she'd found a kindred spirit.

"Ready?" Cass asked as he walked barefoot into the room in a blue

T-shirt and paint-splattered jeans that were ratty at the hem. Holy mother of God, he was attractive. His long hair was loose and wild again, looking as if he hadn't combed it, only run his hands through.

From three feet away, she imagined the heat of his body, the presence of him as he propped himself over her, both of them naked. She turned away, her face blazing, and stared at the bookshelves.

Books. Review the books. He had quite a few fantasy titles she'd read, and many she hadn't. "A lot of space books here."

"Not into sci-fi?"

How could she explain how nonfiction science fiction was to her? She was a goddamned memory surgeon. The Agency insisted she keep that part of herself secret, even between jobs, let alone while on one. Nobody could know about her gift.

Something about Cass told her he wouldn't freak out if he knew. He'd ask thoughtful questions, weigh in on the ethics and struggles. It would have been an intense, real conversation.

But spies didn't draw attention to themselves. Maybe one day she'd tell him about her talent, regardless of her orders.

They stared at each other, and something pulled and twisted deep inside her lady parts. It grew the longer she held his eyes, like a dragon unfurling her wings, her throat warming up to spew fire everywhere. Only a foot separated them, and Jolene wasn't sure if she'd moved, or he had or both. Goose bumps popped up and down her arms. She'd never reacted to a man like that before, with such hunger and longing.

Cass's breath tickled her lips. "What do you want?"

She didn't say *you*, because yuck, but she did rise on her toes. He slanted his mouth over hers and kissed her. His lips were soft and lush, the kiss tentative, almost cautious. She dragged her teeth over that plump bottom lip of his. Cass growled, the sound trapped in his throat, a vibration that echoed inside her core. His arm wrapped around her and drew her snug to his body as he deepened the kiss.

Jolene floated for several seconds, her body weightless and filled with tingles and shivers. Just as she threaded her fingers through his deliciously soft hair, he took a step backward. A flush painted his throat and chest. "I'm sorry," he said with a pant. "I . . ."

All the sparkles throughout her body turned sharp and stung everywhere they touched.

"Look," he said, not looking at her. "This is going to sound lame, but I didn't mean to kiss you."

"Oh." Her insides began to turn inside out.

Cass huffed and tugged on the ends of his hair. "I just got out of a long-term relationship." He lowered his head, and his hair slid forward, obscuring his face. His hands opened and closed by his sides. "I'm not ready for another . . . and I don't do . . . I'm not comfortable . . . men are supposed to be all about sex, but . . ."

"Hey," she said, cutting off what was starting to look like a mini-meltdown, and she certainly recognized the signs. "You don't have to explain yourself to me or to anyone. If you're not comfortable with kissing, then we won't do it." She swallowed all the disappointment before it spread across her face. It's not as if a sexual relationship was a healthy idea for her anyway. "Do you want me to go?"

"What? No!" He stepped toward her, then back again. "Please stay. I didn't mean to"—he swung a hand back and forth—"do what I did."

"Set boundaries?" She snorted. "Wow. What an asshole."

He stared at her for a moment. "You're honestly not upset? Because I was sending signals."

"Oh, I'm going to be taking a painfully cold shower later, but no, I'd much rather you stop than regret it."

"I only meant for us to be friends."

Ouch. Friend-zoned after one kiss—granted, a hot, extended kiss—or had it been amazing only for her? "I'd like that." She poked her thumbnail underneath the nail of her index finger, though all her nails were clean, anything to avoid his face.

"Oh man, I *am* an asshole." Cass pinched the bridge of his nose, his face pink and pained.

"Want to hear a secret?" Jolene asked in a half whisper. "I'm an asshole myself."

He barked a laugh and gave her shoulder a playful push before moving to the kitchen to make them breakfast.

Jolene's smile fell once he'd passed her. This was why she didn't do relationships. Someone was always left behind. She wasn't going to let it be her.

CHAPTER NINE

Jolene

JOLENE HAD ATTENDED ONLY THREE TEAM meetings in the four-and-a-half years she'd worked for the Agency. Sometimes she thought Stadler kept her out of the group as a means of control or perhaps for protection. She longed to be in the midst of them, working toward a goal as partners, each playing a role.

The concept of not having to pretend felt like removing her bra at the end of a long day. She pushed thoughts of Cass to the side. *This* was the important part of her day.

"This is your chance," Stadler said as he and Jolene stood in her tiny dining room, both of the folding edges of the table flipped up so the table for two now sat six. The entire team consisted of five people: Stadler, Sara, Ryan, Jorge, and *her*.

Jolene asked Stadler once if he received orders from someone or ran things as he wanted. He'd grunted and muttered that everyone had a boss and mentioned a director. She couldn't picture the kind of person who'd order him around, and Stadler did seem to do as he liked.

While they waited for the others to arrive, Stadler filled her in on everyone's housing situation, and she pulled out dishes and silverware. The Agency leased a two-flat in Ukrainian Village, the neighborhood just south of Jolene's. Stadler was staying on the second floor, which would also serve as the safe house, while Sara stayed on the first floor. Ryan somehow managed to snag a loft studio in Lincoln Park, while Jorge was stuck in a garden apartment in Humboldt Park that apparently provided hot water for only ten minutes at a time.

Stadler held a stack of manila folders as she switched the forks from the left side of the plates to the right. Was that where they went? Ryan would know and might tease her if she got it wrong. She half hoped he would.

She studied the table. "Shouldn't they be here by—"

The buzzer squawked, making Jolene jump. She raced to the intercom. "Yes?"

"Hey, sweet thing," Sara crooned.

Jolene hit the entry button and opened the door. In seconds, Sara squealed and tackled her, the hug fierce, tight, and over almost as soon as it started. "I'm going to look around," she said, brushing past Jolene and perusing the open space.

"Hey, Jo," Jorge said with a broad grin and held out two plastic bags brimming with paper sacks that filled the room with the scent of Mexican food. He was in his twenties, scruffy in a curated way, thin enough to be all elbows and knees but with a surprising grace. His eyes were too close together, a beautiful golden brown a few shades lighter than his skin. "Tacos, burritos, chips, salsa, guacamole, and churros."

"Set those on the table," Jolene said, gesturing to the dining nook. "How's things?"

"Five by five." Jorge nodded to Stadler before dropping the bags onto the table. His computer bag was strapped behind him. He swung it around as if to unpack it, but Stadler shook his head once. Jorge frowned and stashed the bag in the corner. "Ryan?"

Stadler glanced at his watch, something that looked fancy but might be cheap. "Three minutes."

Ryan was a notorious stickler for time and never arrived a minute early or a minute late. Jolene walked to the window to see if he was standing outside, waiting for the minute hand on his watch to hit six p.m. Already, the sun was setting, the streets darkening. She didn't spot Ryan, but she cracked the window open for some air flow. The October afternoon was temperate, but this was Chicago. Soon, it would be too cold for an open window.

Sara was in Jolene's bedroom, opening dresser drawers.

"Seriously?" Jolene said, stalking into the room. "Have you no shame?"

She shrugged. "I'm curious."

"You're nosy."

Sara grinned. "That too." Her eyes flicked toward the other room, where Stadler and Jorge were standing together, neither talking. She lowered her voice, suddenly serious. "How've you been?"

Jolene understood her real question—how had Stadler taken their fuckup? "Fine." Jolene hadn't recovered from Stadler's disappointment, but it had brought her this new opportunity.

Sara perked back to herself. "I'm so stoked we're finally going for a big fish. We knock this bully off the block, and it shakes up the entire Midwest trade."

How did she already know that?

Sara bounced on her toes, then flounced over and plopped onto the couch, where Jorge had seated himself with his laptop on his knees, keys clacking in a frenzy. So much for obeying Stadler. As the tech guy, he was always on his computer. Sara's shoulder brushed his, and Jorge leaned into her for a few seconds.

The buzzer sounded again, and Ryan joined the group. He typically dressed in designer clothes tailored to fit him perfectly. Jolene supposed his underwear was made to his specifications. He was a little older than Jolene, dark-skinned with short, cropped black hair and a smooth-shaven face.

Ryan was the administrator of the group, the one who could find, buy, and arrange almost anything. If she could abscond with the superpower of one of the team members, she would choose Ryan's. He got his way through a mixture of attractiveness, charm, and that indefinable quality of the wealthy and powerful. People naturally wanted to give Ryan whatever he wanted.

"Tacos?" he asked as he stopped and kissed Jolene's cheek. He smelled like expensive cologne and money.

"Let's eat while they're hot," Sara said as she slammed the lid of Jorge's computer closed.

"Hey!" His glower lacked heat. He set the laptop on the coffee table before joining the others at the table.

They squeezed into the tight dining room, elbows close, more cozy than annoying. Jolene passed out food as Stadler passed out folders. She took a beef burrito and a mound of guacamole but no chips.

She opened her file along with everyone else, her food temporarily forgotten. The few times she'd worked with the team, Stadler had brought her in after this initial meeting, so she wasn't sure of the protocols. Butterflies zipped from one side of her stomach to the other, then did a few loop-de-loops.

It reminded her of how Cass made her feel. What would he think if he knew what she was doing at that exact moment? Would he be impressed by her actual work or horrified?

Nobody said anything as they turned through the pages, occasionally munching on their food, except for Sara, who poked at her chicken taco to painstakingly redistribute its contents.

Jolene's palms weren't dry, and her toes scrunched like a fist. No body part worked right. This was her opportunity to forge a worthwhile legacy. The alcoholic triumphing over the pushers. Finally, her nerves settled enough, and she unfolded her burrito to spoon guacamole inside before rolling it back into shape. Her first bite was too large, and a bit of sour cream oozed out of the side of her mouth. Only Sara noticed and smiled. Jolene shoved the excess into her mouth and continued chewing. It wasn't as warm as she would have liked, but the spice level was perfect, just enough to buzz but not burn.

Stadler swiped his lips with a napkin, his chimichanga destroyed. "I need a tracker on a couple of computers and cell phones. I want physical tracking and a look at whatever files are inside, particularly on Kenneth."

Jolene scrambled to read as much as possible, swiping away a dollop of sour cream that landed on the first profile. Stadler was talking about Diego Kenneth, top adviser to Stefano Sr. There were four different targets on this mission in addition to Stefano Sr. and his son, Stefano Jr. Most had only a few sheets of information that included their photo, name, address, physical statistics, role in the Stefano organization, and surveillance notes, such as places they frequented and their associates, schedules, and vices. Some of the targets' weak spots were also noted.

"Kind of sketchy," Sara said, crinkling her nose, not even looking at the file. "Where's the rest of it?" She played with the folder, swishing it back and forth on the table.

From the rampant grumbling, Jolene learned the notes were usually far more detailed with several pages and photos, sometimes audio clips, video footage, financial details, and browser histories. Everyone looked to Stadler.

Stadler didn't seem the least bit bothered by their scrutiny. He shrugged. "Sorry, spoiled children. This time, we're the *A* team, the *B* team, and probably the *C* team. Stefano Sr. is a paranoid motherfucker. That's how they've entrenched themselves in the market. We can't risk people noticing a tail or a break-in. All his higher-level people have tight home security. Even fuck buddies are screened and vetted. Their phones have extensive security, requiring both a fingerprint and a six-digit code that changes every two weeks to unlock."

Jolene bit the inside of her lip to keep from smiling, because Stadler wanted them to be somber and professional. But come on, how cool was it to be on a team that could break into a highly protected phone or laptop? This was some hardcore spy thriller shit. Her part would be simple—learn those codes. Well, once they figured out how to get her in a position to do it. Someone else would procure the fingerprints with careful surveillance and lifting tape.

"Four targets," Stadler said, his voice a graveled growl. "Twenty-year age spread and different levels in the organization. This isn't going to be easy. Ideas?"

Sara, Ryan, and Jorge all stared at one another. Sara shrugged. "I can take one of them, two if one is the kind to turn bored real fast."

Stadler returned his attention to Jolene, but she shook her head, not wanting to have to honey-pot ever again. One side of his mouth ticked up. "Don't get your panties in a bunch. Two new broads would only draw suspicion. And you're terrible at meetups."

Jolene bristled, though he wasn't wrong.

"Meet-cutes," Sara said, crunching into a plain tortilla chip.

He rolled his eyes, and Sara winked at Jolene.

"And she's not bad at them. It's just that I'm outstanding." Sara smirked at Jorge after that comment.

Jolene thought about what her grandmother would have said about her role in all this. She wouldn't have approved of the subterfuge, for certain, and she'd always bolstered the downtrodden rather than tearing down the monster. Would she have understood?

Sara tapped her lips with three fingers and made clicking noises. "Hm." She had a tendency to act out all her inner thoughts. "I was thinking." As if they hadn't all noticed. "I'll bet a lot of these guys work out and probably at the same gym. If we find out which one, Jolene and I could get in as personal trainers. We'd have direct access to their bodies and indirect access to their phones, right? In their lockers?"

Stadler nodded. "What do you think, Jolene, about setting you up as a personal trainer?"

"Sure," she said. She worked out enough to pull off that role. "As long as I don't have to teach yoga or Pilates."

Sara snorted. "You can get a lot done with a proper downward dog."

"Maybe *you* can," Jolene countered with a grin.

"Hell yeah, she can," Jorge said as he wiggled a cinnamon-and-sugar-dusted churro toward Sara's mouth.

Sara slipped her lips over the dessert in a suggestive manner.

"Focus," Stadler barked, popping all the camaraderie from the room. "Fuck around once we have all this figured out."

Jorge let go of the churro. Tension suffused the room, and everyone's postures stiffened, nobody looking at anyone else.

Stadler continued, "She needs a strength-training background, website, clothes. Jorge, work on figuring out which club. Ryan, get Jolene in there. Jolene, put in long hours. Be seen."

"What about me?" Sara asked, sounding more confused than irritated.

"You're in reserve," Stadler replied, ignoring Sara's frown. Or maybe not, because he added, "Good thinking on the gym."

"This will be fun for you, Jolene." Sara bumped her leg into Jolene's under the table. "I'm picturing badass, weightlifting-drill-sergeant bitch. Those rich pricks will pay out the nose to have you ordering them around all sweaty and whatnot."

Stadler stood. His focus lasered in on Jolene. "Come up with a backstory that explains the lack of social media presence, since we can't generate that fast enough. Anything else?"

"Can I pick your workout clothes?" Ryan asked.

"Sure. Just make sure everything is—"

"—black," Ryan finished for her. He grinned, and an atmosphere of family pierced her. He was a perfect older brother—slightly bossy and a little protective.

"Photoshop can help too," Jorge added with a waggle of his eyebrows. "I'm going to make her history centered in LA training a few B-list celebrities."

Jorge was how she pictured a younger brother—annoying, wheedling, but loyal and a bit reverential. He was the one in the group most impressed by her gift. Everyone had asked questions about memory surgery, but Jorge had done research beforehand, citing references and theories, always eager for a little more knowledge.

"Can I pick out the superstars?" Sara asked, rubbing her hands together.

Sara was the youngest, rebel sibling, the one always in trouble and the worst influence of the bunch. Her bravery and audacity stunned Jolene. Sara kicked ass or crashed and burned, rarely anything in between. She ran on guts and gumption.

"B-list or lower," Stadler said. "Anything else?"

Stadler was the father figure. As a strict authoritarian who showed he cared by acting like a prick, he was the backbone of the team.

A weight settled in Jolene's chest as a lump formed in the back of her throat. She was the fucked-up middle child. If she wanted to be a solid part of the family, she had to deliver.

Ryan suggested they approach each target in very different ways to keep from raising suspicions. Jorge wanted to orchestrate a global shutdown of the Stefano organization's tech to slip something in when everything got recovered, infecting SIM cards, or something like that. Sara ruminated on the possibility of orchestrating an orgy. Jolene was fairly certain Sara was joking.

Everyone suggested something except Jolene. She didn't want to extend herself and fail, but if she didn't have any ideas, then she wasn't contributing enough to the team. That would give Stadler a solid argument to keep her out of the group. She had to pitch something. Anything.

She studied the dossiers, looking for inspiration. And it actually came.

"What if we hit everyone at once?"

All movement in the room—twitches, taps, sighs—ceased.

"Explain." Stadler was as alert as someone fresh off a bump of coke.

She pulled out a sheet that showed schedules. "There's the birthday party for Stefano's niece two weeks from Saturday. All of our targets should be there, right?"

"Yeah," Sara said, licking her lips, probably to hide a smile. "Go on."

"That restaurant has private dining, of course, but it also has a bar. These guys, once their family obligations are done, might want a drink, right? With a bar right there? Is there a way to make it especially appealing? Create some event that would bring in a lot of women?"

Everyone nodded, catching her idea. Well, Stadler only stared at her, but that was as good as a nod.

"I'll show up with the personal-trainer cover," Jolene said, her head light, almost high on the adrenaline of finally being part of the discussion.

"If you can get me into the health club fast enough, I'll have a reason to interact with them because they'll recognize me from the gym."

"What makes you think you can read memories in a crowd? What's changed?" Stadler didn't look remotely convinced. "This isn't the time for you to dick around."

She pushed out a breath. "I want to try." She didn't tell him she'd been practicing because she didn't want him to try and take that over. Better to manage expectations. "I got quite a lot in Boston, and I'm ready to up my game. You going to let me or not?"

Stadler turned to Jorge. "I want that website up by tomorrow." His attention shifted to Ryan. "She's working at whatever health club the biggest players use by Monday. Five days isn't a lot of time, but you can pull it off."

Ryan, it seemed, was Daddy's favorite. He grinned. "I'll make it happen."

"What about me?" Sara asked, her posture straight, though her body shook from her wiggling foot.

Stadler smirked. "If we set you up as the venue's event manager—"

"Support staff?" Sara rolled her eyes. "Bo-ring. I want to go as Jolene's friend. We can be at the restaurant or bar together, which is far less suspicious than her trolling around alone."

"I'd like to participate too," Ryan said, dabbing his mouth with a napkin before folding it and tucking it under his fork.

"Okay, you can both be friends." Stadler stood and stretched his arms behind him.

The movement reminded Jolene of partner stretching with Cass. What was he doing right at that moment? Painting? Eating? Thinking about her?

Sara grinned at Jolene. "Let's celebrate something. Birthday? That could be—"

"Divorce," Jolene countered.

"Yes!" Sara rocked in her chair. "Definitely divorce. It's the perfect excuse for me to drink too much and hang on pretty much everyone."

Jolene ignored the visions of herself drunk at a bar, her weakness blown open for the team to witness. She sipped her water and reminded herself she wouldn't have to fake drunkenness. That would be Sara's job. Manageable.

Stadler nodded, but his posture remained rigid. If she failed, Jolene had no doubt Stadler would deliver a come-to-Jesus moment.

CHAPTER TEN

Jolene

THOUGHTS OF YESTERDAY'S MEETING WOULDN'T stop spinning. Preparation would calm her nerves. Sitting cross-legged in the divot of her futon couch, Jolene reminded herself she brought something unique to the group with her deep understanding of a variety of people, their different thought patterns, values, and coping mechanisms.

People assumed others were like them, but what broke one person barely fazed another. An unforgivable act to one person might mean nothing to someone else. Jolene was uniquely qualified for this task.

She grabbed a spiral notebook from her bookcase and flipped it open. Stared and stared. Worked on chewing off a persistent hangnail, telling herself to fetch the clippers but not doing it. She bit off half with a snap and a burn of pain but didn't get it all.

Jolene wrote *Triggers* at the top of the page and underlined it.

Pulled out her phone and tried to find an appropriate playlist. Watched video of a live performance of "Shame Shame" by the Foo Fighters. Made a cup of tea. Curled her hair, then put it into a sloppy bun.

Then she listed everything she imagined might cause a person to think about their own security code. She let the ideas flow without judgment:

memorization, losing a phone, someone else losing a phone, hacking a phone, hacking a computer, mnemonics for remembering, number patterns, favorite numbers, forgetting a password, someone else forgetting a password. Even when the list got downright weird—alien abduction, past-life regression, Scientology—she kept going.

When she faltered, she reminded herself to keep an open mind. Her free-range brain, however, drifted to thoughts of Cass. He was a distraction she didn't need. He wasn't available for sex, and she couldn't do a relationship. And yet . . .

They could watch movies together. She pictured curling up next to him on his couch, his arm slung across her shoulders. Yeah, right. Jolene amended the scene to them sitting upright in their respective corners, a bag of microwave popcorn between them like the Berlin Wall.

Their fingers touch as they simultaneously reach into the bag. As if choreographed, they both pull away and laugh. She kicks the popcorn off the couch and straddles his lap, licking butter and salt from his lips as she teases him for several seconds before kissing him properly. His hands grip her waist, pulling her against his erection.

Jolene's phone buzzed with a text message, breaking her free from her fantasy. *Strategy session tonight 7. What food*

Stadler was fastidious in everything except his texting protocols. He sent messages like a middle schooler.

I'm available at seven. Please bring Thai. Thanks.

She had less than three hours to figure out at least one approach that would work. Otherwise, he might yank away the opportunity. Stadler was a sink-or-swim mentor.

Swimming. Cass in a swimsuit. Plump lips. Heat. A tractor beam kind of attraction she wished worked in the opposite direction. She wanted Cass at home mooning over her when he was supposed to be working, and she wanted her own traitorous brain to prioritize the goddamned job.

Jolene set a timer on her phone for ten minutes. She allowed her mind to linger on Cass the entire time while she envisioned showering with him, entrenching the fantasy with sensory details like the sting of hot water contrasting with the bite of cold tile, the smell of his skin underneath the scent of her body wash, droplets of water trailing down his sharp cheekbones, sucked up by her mouth before reaching the angle of his jaw. She slipped her hand down her yoga pants, bringing herself to orgasm fast enough she still had time to get a tall glass of water before the alarm sounded.

Jolene walked a circuit around her living room. Pinned her brain in place. Thought. Made more notes. She pushed away the slice of pain over the idea she'd never done enough with her life. Her grandmother had worked tirelessly to help drug addicts. Jolene was working to cut off the source of drugs altogether or at least curb it. Failure wasn't inevitable. She thought about impressing Cass. No, astonishing Stadler.

Damn it, why couldn't she focus for more than a few minutes at a time? She hadn't gotten clean to just sloth her way through life. This was her time, her opportunity, so why was she so damned distracted? And the way Stadler had eyed her at the meeting hadn't screamed, *Hey, I think you're going to do awesome.* Jolene had something to prove. Now.

She dropped onto her palms and executed ten perfect push-ups.

Jolene paused at the top of the last push-up, planking, keeping herself still. Get the codes. Get close to Stefano's crew. Practice the finger-smithing with her gift. Move forward. Live up to her family legacy. She ignored the fleeting thought that most people didn't have to continually remind themselves what they wanted. Or, at least, they didn't have to convince themselves they wanted what they wanted.

* * *

STADLER STRODE THROUGH THE DOOR CARRYING THREE OVERSIZED, white, paper bags. His wet brown hair appeared almost black. He handed Jolene the food as he toed off his shoes and gingerly removed his rain-spattered duster.

"Are the others coming?" Jolene asked over her shoulder as she dropped the assortment on the dining room table.

"No. I'm hungry."

She shook her head, then jogged to the closet to grab a towel for Stadler. With just the two of them, nobody would witness her failure—not that she'd fail, because she had come up with several decent plans. She needed to chill out and treat this like any other assignment.

"Ever hear of this invention called the umbrella? It's really cool. It looks like a fat stick, but when you press a button—"

"Fuck you, Nova." His voice held no heat, and his eyes were relaxed.

"Are you . . . amused?" She squinted and pretended to study him as if he were baffling. "And calling me by my last name . . . Is that a sign of . . . respect?"

"You are no comedian," he said as he wiped the towel over his face, then scrubbed at his hair.

"So massive amounts of respect, then."

He huffed a laugh that was only ten percent condescending and tossed the towel back to her. "You do something respect-worthy lately?"

"Ow." She had done commendable work. At least for some of the day. "Keep that up, and I won't share my brilliant plans."

Stadler arched an eyebrow, the one with a thin scar through it. "Tell me while we eat."

It looked as if a bomb had detonated and spewed Thai food over the table. They piled a bit of everything onto their plates, sitting kitty-corner to each other. She should have opened the folded ends for more room. Jolene poured them both oversized glasses of ice water.

"Tell me," Stadler said around a bite of pad thai.

Jolene swallowed a gulp of water to cool her burning mouth after a significant helping of pad prik king. When that didn't help, she ate a bite of plain rice. Her throat tickled with the need to cough, but she managed to hold it back.

Stadler studied her, waiting.

"Okay." She shared only her best ideas.

Stadler didn't comment on any of them, but she could almost feel his mind whirring, cataloging her information. When she finished, he settled into his seat like a stingray into sand. "What about Stefano Sr. or Jr., the white whales of this mission?"

She hadn't given much thought to them. They weren't likely to stay and mingle, and no way would security let her within touching distance of either one. Was he asking to trip her up?

"I can introduce myself to Stefano Jr. with a handshake, say I recognize him from the club, pitch personal-training sessions." This suggestion sucked more than all others. "I can try to trip him into thinking of his passcode by mentioning a discount code for the training. It might work."

It would never work.

Stadler gave her zero feedback on her ideas, leaving whatever confidence she'd scrounged together melting like Frosty the Snowman in Miami for spring break. In a few minutes, there'd be nothing left but a corncob pipe.

"You need to do something you're not going to like," he said after he'd polished off his first plate of food. Stadler always ate two.

"What else is new?" she grumbled. The heat of the curry had cleared out her nose and burned out her taste buds. Her body felt oddly hollowed out.

"Your diet starts now." Stadler tapped his chopsticks on his empty plate. "The more cut we get you, the better."

Jolene paused with a pad thai peanut halfway to her mouth. She didn't mind extra workouts, but she hated dieting. "Oh man." Well, it was actionable. "For the record, you suck."

"At least you won't have to," Stadler retorted.

She snorted, and they both grinned before looking away. Her peanut fell from her chopsticks with a plink.

"You do your trainer homework?" Stadler asked.

Jolene nodded, glad they'd moved on to surer ground. She listed a shit-ton of exercises for training others. Her research included different ways to incorporate squat racks, ballet barres, kettlebells, elastic bands, and BOSU balls. Innovation would attract attention almost as much as her appearance, though the bulk of her repertoire would remain the classics: pull-ups, push-ups, squats, lunges, burpees, and jump squats. The list seemed shorter, though, with how fast she spewed it out.

Stadler took in that information the same way he had all evening. "Okay."

Her insides finally rioted, all churning storm clouds and flashes of lightning. "Is that all you're going to say? About any of it? Do I need to change tactics?" She squeezed both hands into fists under the table.

Stadler smiled at her, a genuine smile he didn't share often. "You don't need me to tell you you're doing a great job."

"Yeah, I do." She managed not to yell it. "What kind of management technique involves giving absolutely no feedback?"

"You care too much about what other people think." He burped into his fist. "You're pleased, so fuck me if I'm not."

She laughed, more relieved than anything else. If he hadn't been satisfied, of course he would have said so, outlining why point by point. She'd done enough. Contributed. Pulled her weight. Her body zinged in celebration.

He clapped his hands together and stood. "Now for some physical training."

Her energy dipped. "What about your seconds?"

"Gotta work up my appetite, and you need to burn some calories." He pushed the coffee table to the side with his foot.

She rose and circled her neck, overfull but resolved and ready. "I hate you."

He grinned. "No, you don't."

CHAPTER ELEVEN

Jolene

Cass and Jolene met at Eckhart Park Pool on Chicago Avenue during open-swim hours. The indoor space reeked of chlorine. Though it was an overcast day, the square glass panes of the outer wall let in enough light that the overhead lighting was off. Most of the panels were clear with a few red, green, and yellow squares set in randomly.

She wore a tankini, simple in the front with racer-back lacing. Black, of course. She didn't wear a swim cap, though she should because of her long hair, but she'd wrapped it in a tight bun on top of her head. The brown and tan tiles of the floor were ugly, but that was expected from the park district.

Except for a guy swimming laps, though the pool wasn't set up with lanes, Cass stood alone at the shallow end, delineated from the deep end by a banner of red and yellow flags hanging from the ceiling. His hair was unbound, and he wore maroon swim trunks. They came down about as far as boxer shorts, fitted without being too tight. His abs and chest were well-defined and proportional to the rest of him. No way he had that kind of body by accident.

His arm and shoulder tattoos turned him into living art. His torso reminded her of firefighters on calendars. So beautiful. She wanted to eat off him.

He looked her up and down, then focused on the thin strip of skin between her bikini tank and bottoms.

She stepped down the ladder into the water, fighting a blush. The pool was several degrees cooler than Jolene would have liked. "Fuck me, that's cold. Those park district people are cheap motherfuckers." She grimaced. "We're going somewhere else next time."

"We're doing this again?"

Oops. "You could drown at any time, so this is urgent." And once the Agency mission gained momentum, she wasn't sure how much time she'd have for him.

"Your dedication to my well-being is touching."

She wished there was touching—lots and lots of touching. She could use the release.

The man swimming laps splashed quite a bit but never slowed, keeping to the other side of the pool. Jolene winced her way into the water up to her chest, then ducked down to her chin. "Fuuuuck."

Cass huffed a laugh and dunked himself. "Teach me to swim before my balls shrink to the size of marbles."

It wasn't until that moment that Jolene thought about the actual teaching. The truth was, although she could swim, she was terrible at it. She was the last person who should instruct anyone.

"There's actually not much to it. Hold your hands like this." She held her fingers tightly together and slightly curved, like little bowls.

"You're starting with how to position my hands?"

"Hey, which one of us knows how to swim?"

He scraped his bottom lip with his teeth before mimicking her hands.

"Perfect." Maybe. "Now, when you're swimming, you have to tighten your abs like you're supporting yourself on top of the water." She bit the inside of her cheek. "And try to keep extra air in your lungs so it's easier to float."

"Okay." He sounded as if she were pitching a timeshare in a swamp.

"And then kick your feet." She blew out a breath. "That's about it."

He stared at her with an intensity that made her skin itch everywhere. "Let me get this straight. I hold my hands like little scoops, suck in my abs, and kick? That's all you've got?"

His breakdown was spot-on. She'd sounded like a complete fucking idiot. "Pretty much."

"Show me."

"Surely, you've seen people swimming before. I don't think a demo is necessary." The truth was, she loved pools but never really swam. Mostly, she bounced around in them, tried to walk as fast as possible, and kicked off the sides to see how far she could glide before she sank.

Cass frowned. "It doesn't seem like enough, how you've described it. What about breathing? When should I put my face in the water, and when do I turn my head to take a breath?"

"Oh, I keep my head out of the water." She didn't even stick her face in the shower, only splashed her face.

He looked as if he were losing the battle not to smile, because his lips twitched to one side and then the other. "This I have to see."

"I'm here to keep you from drowning, not to entertain you."

"You can't teach without demonstrating. Do it." He was kind of sexy when he bossed her around.

She decided to go for it. "Prepare to be amazed." She kicked off the side of the pool, deciding swimming the width was manageable. Her body jetted for a few feet with her propulsion, and then she kicked and windmilled her arms, her hands in a convenient paddle shape. The pool was wider than she'd anticipated. She moved about as fast as an eighty-year-old who'd just had a hip replacement, so she made little progress, but she refused to give up. At long last, she slapped her hand onto the other side. Panting, she turned around to grin in triumph at Cass, but her smile died a quick and vicious death at the sight of Cass's face, beet red from laughing.

"Oh my God." His voice filled the space. "That is the funniest thing I have ever seen."

Her own face, already hot from the exertion, went thermonuclear. "You need to get out more. Maybe I'm not the most graceful swimmer—"

He full-on cackled, and she decided continuing that sentence wouldn't make her feel any less stupid. Cass waved his hands. "I'm sorry. Just give me a minute."

The lap swimmer splashed past her.

Cass continued to laugh. She should have left him to drown. At least she wasn't cold any longer.

"You can do better?" Jolene lobbed back. She might have looked ridiculous, but she could swim.

"Okay, okay!" He held up both hands as if being robbed, then cupped them as she'd shown him. "Ready?"

"Quit stalling and do it already, before that guy comes back."

Cass nodded, took a breath, sank under the water, and kicked off the side of the pool. He glided underwater, his body extended like Superman flying, hair flowing like silk. Jolene watched him, his body ghostlike, moving faster than she would have thought possible. Then he moved only his arms, and his body rocketed forward. Jolene's mouth fell open. Cass propelled himself once more, right to her. He blew out air and gently broke the surface. "How'd I do?"

Water clung to his dark lashes and dripped from his chin. The ends of his hair trailed in the water.

"You . . . asshole." She struggled to form words. "You said you couldn't swim."

"No, you asked if I was planning to do an Ironman, and I said I *don't* swim. Not in lakes, anyway. I like pools."

The urge to tell him she felt the same way warred with her outrage at what a complete ass she'd just made of herself in front of an Olympic-level athlete. "Why did you agree to let me teach you, then?"

"You insisted, and it was a way to see you again."

Her belly purred, and she wanted to slap herself. He was not charming. "That wasn't real swimming anyway. It was all underwater." She was amping up her humiliation.

He grinned at her, tipped his head to the side, and freestyled the length of the pool, deftly avoiding the lap guy, tilting his face out of the water every few strokes, making it to the other end in a few breaths. When he returned to her, he arched his eyebrows at her.

She held up her arms. "I'm a genius teacher!"

* * *

"How did you learn to swim like that?" Jolene asked as they sat at a black plastic table on the sidewalk outside Black Dog Gelato. Well, Cass ate gelato, and Jolene kept him company while sipping a Solo cup of water.

"Army."

As soon as he said it, she saw the evidence in the way he moved, his fitness level, and his calm demeanor.

The sun had yet to make an appearance, but with no wind, the temperature was fine for outdoors. In Chicago, you had to capitalize on every pleasant day. Cass sat on a cheap plastic chair as Jolene settled back on the wooden bench seat across from him. "From soldier to artist?"

He shrugged with one shoulder. "Artist to soldier to artist. My dad was in the military. So was my brother. I joined the army for the GI Bill and served for eight years." His gelato had become very interesting, holding all his attention.

Jolene didn't want to force him to talk about what clearly disturbed him, no matter how curious she was. She couldn't picture him with buzzed hair and a massive gun. "Do you like it or hate it when people thank you for your service?"

He huffed a laugh and grinned at her. "You never say or do what I expect." He rubbed an eyebrow. "Sometimes it's satisfying to be appreciated, because you do make sacrifices when you serve, especially if you see combat, which I did. Other times, though, it seems like words people say because they think they're supposed to, like saying 'bless you' when someone sneezes."

She suspected nobody would ever comprehend the depth of his sacrifice. Even if she entered those memories, she knew she'd find only pieces. She wouldn't see how they all fit together to form the whole of his experiences. The way he carefully sheared gelato with that tiny, pink plastic spoon told her some trauma still clung to him.

Jolene rattled the ice in her cup but didn't drink. "There's no changing the past, but—"

He squeezed her hand. "I wouldn't want to."

"Good."

Something heavy remained between them.

"In case it makes a difference, there's something—" Cass looked at her, his expression the kind of blank that indicated he'd armored himself. "I was a sniper, Jolene."

He delivered the news as if he were telling her he'd drowned kittens for fun and profit.

She placed her hand on his forearm. "You seem concerned about my reaction. Does that bother some people?"

"I had a girlfriend who was very into soldiers. When she found out I was a sniper, she became obsessed with it. She was always asking me what it felt like to kill someone." He stirred his gelato as if it were heavy. "Truthfully, I never spent much time thinking about it. Sometimes the world is a better place without certain people in it. I covered my guys. I took out warlords, human traffickers—you know, bad dudes. I did my duty."

Of course he had. Jolene wanted to tell him she was a memory surgeon who'd seen inside enough people to recognize the upstanding ones, and he was exemplary. But telling him that would open herself to questions she couldn't answer honestly.

"Was this the long-term girlfriend you mentioned before?" she asked.

Cass stopped stirring and stabbed the spoon into the gelato. "No, this one was worse, in a way. I think she got off on the thought I'd kill for her if she were ever in trouble. The constant questions brought up a lot of shit I thought I'd moved past. And then I started to wonder if I shouldn't have let go of everything so easily."

Jolene trapped one of his feet between her own under the table and leaned forward, catching the scent of chlorine still clinging to them both. "You think you need to feel guilty in order to be a decent person?"

"No, but sometimes I wonder if good people feel guilty regardless of the situation."

"You're fine," she said, moving one foot on top of his, hoping the playfulness might disperse some of the tension. "Some people are more resilient than others. I don't think morality has anything to do with that."

"Sometimes people are scared of me after they find out what I did over there. That's why I usually only say I was in the army. I've been out six years, and it feels like a lifetime ago, but . . . it's like I can't escape."

"You shouldn't let other people define you; they'll always get it wrong." She wiggled her foot. "Unless they're a true friend. Sometimes they'll see you better than you see yourself, but most people are clueless. They judge everyone through the filter of their own experiences."

"Do you judge me?"

"Oh yeah. Definitely. I judge everyone. I just usually keep my opinion to myself, because I'm aware I might be full of shit. Except about you, of course."

"And what's your judgment?"

His eyes dipped to her lips, and her belly swirled like the belle of the ball. The energy between them threatened to overtake her common sense.

She shrugged. "You're all right."

"Thank you," he said, voice soft.

They stared at each other for too many seconds. Too intense. Too real. Especially when she hadn't shared about her gift, something that could bond them tighter with their shared experience of dealing with unkind assumptions.

Damn the consequences. "You know—"

A dark-haired toddler with huge brown eyes careened to their table and grasped the edge to steady himself, plump fingers coated in chocolate gelato. The spell between her and Cass broke, stopping her ill-advised confession.

"Whoa!" A woman with a half-escaped bun tackled the kid. "Sorry."

Cass grinned at the child and then the mother—well, the presumed mother. "No problem."

"Hi," the boy said.

"Hi," Cass replied, his smile widening.

"Hold still, Jeffrey," the mother said, down on one knee, pawing at his sticky fingers with a wet wipe while he squiggled around, making faces at Cass.

Cass narrowed his eyes at Jeffrey, and they both laughed.

The mom's phone rang, and when she looked at the caller ID, she swore under her breath. "We're late," she said to Jeffrey, scooping him up and practically tripping away, wet wipe still in hand, diaper bag open and precariously bouncing against her hip as the boy squirmed.

Cass watched them go. Did he want that? Did he dream of the stability of a family?

"I'm never having kids," Jolene blurted, a cocktail of mixed emotions fizzing around her heart.

Cass studied the departing mother and child for another second. "It's not always like that."

"I got my tubes tied at twenty."

He studied her and tapped a thumb on the tabletop. "Can I ask why?"

She paused long enough to not sound defensive. "I wasn't exactly a responsible drinker, and I don't want kids. Ever." It had taken three tries to find a doctor willing to perform a tubal ligation despite her young age.

"You could get that reversed later, though, if you want, right?"

Her laugh was dry. "No way. I've never regretted it. Not every woman wants to be a mother." The complete sacrifice of personal needs involved in becoming a mom made her want to vomit, even now, five years sober. "And being young doesn't mean you don't know what you want."

He nodded. "I get it. I assumed I'd have kids, but I can't see it now."

"Maybe *you'll* change *your* mind in the future." They weren't dating, just friends, so his stance on having children didn't mean anything. "You'd be a great dad."

"Doesn't make it something I want."

She suspected one day he'd find some nice woman who'd want to bear his young, and he'd forget all about this conversation and her.

Jolene stretched dramatically, keen to change the subject. "So, I taught you something—very well, too, I might add. What are you going to teach me?"

He cocked his head, the tension in him easing. "What do you want to learn?"

She played with the zipper of her jacket, giving that some thought. She didn't want to shoot a gun or paint anything, but she still wanted to spend time with him.

Cass laughed, the intensity between them glowing. "You are such a fidgety thing. Would you like to learn some meditation?"

"God, no." She held up both hands. "I already meditate, and I *hate* it. Fifteen minutes a day to focus myself, but it doesn't work. I've been doing it for a while, too." Ever since she'd screwed up in Boston. She'd thought it might clear her head.

He chuckled. "Do you sit still and close your eyes?"

"Yes," she said, her tone more defensive than she'd intended. "I set an alarm, too, so I don't punk out early."

He pointed at her. "That's your problem."

* * *

THEY WENT TO HER PLACE BECAUSE CASS WANTED TO SEE IT, AND JOLENE couldn't think of a reason not to let him. It wasn't as if she had spy stuff lying around. Her notebook and files were under her bookcase.

While Jolene hung their coats on the hooks on the wall and stowed her workout bag in her bedroom, Cass pulled the coffee table to the side of the sofa, giving them a square of cleared space. "This'll do."

The qigong movements were easier than she'd anticipated, the motions flowing, using a decent range of motion. Gentle. As light faded from the room, she breathed with Cass, following him as he transitioned seamlessly from one move to the next. The pressure to impress him, to be an exemplary student, kept her mind engaged.

"Breathe in." Cass let his arms rise, his hands cupping an imaginary ball over his head, cradling what he called universal energy.

She followed.

"Breathe out." His arms dropped, hands still holding the ball, bringing it down to his chest, continuing to push down until his palms turned flat to the floor and sent the flow into the ground.

He stopped and shrugged. "That's a start."

Jolene wiggled her hands a little, her body energized but not overflowing. Her mind wasn't a calm pool, but it no longer darted in forty-three opposing directions. She smiled. "That was *much* better than meditating."

He brushed a lock of hair from her face, his body close. "It was still meditating, just a different kind."

Jolene had always been restless, even as a child. Her teachers had complained about her wiggling in her seat or leaving it entirely. When drunk, she'd often pace and stumble around. Of course, the calm she felt now might simply be because of Cass's presence. His personality—centered, honest, funny, and considerate—made it easy to be around him.

"So, what happened that caused the breakup with your last girlfriend?" she asked.

Cass sighed. "She cheated on me." He moved to look out her window. Since she had an unimpressive view of the tops of a few trees and the building across the street, he was avoiding her. "A lot. She was a sex addict. At least she claimed that's why she'd done it. The sex between us was good, but I realized later that was all we'd had. Our relationship was a lie."

Jolene's toes scrunched in her shoes. She, too, was a liar. Her lungs squeezed for a moment as she prepared to tell him about her gift.

He turned, resting his butt on the window ledge. "What about you? How did your last relationship end?"

This was a chance to give him some truth without revealing any secrets. "Coworker. It didn't end badly or anything. It just . . . It couldn't go anywhere. And I think neither of us wanted to ruin our working situation. I'm actually pretty proud it didn't. Made me feel mature or something."

Of course, at no time during her two-month affair with Stadler had she felt anything as powerful as what she was experiencing with Cass. Thinking about it reminded her that she hadn't had sex in over three years.

Neither she nor Cass said anything for several seconds, the energy between them solidifying. For all their banter, something tender and real wound around them, cocooning them together. Cass felt it too. Or was she imagining that like she imagined people watching or following her?

He visibly swallowed, and her stomach flipped. She'd never wanted anyone like this, the sensation of ardent pining infusing every cell in her body until her pussy ached and her hands shook.

Cass looked away and pushed the back of his hand against his lips.

He wasn't ready. She had a job to do. Mostly, though, he was too perfect, and she was too flawed. He had fought for his country, and she'd fought with an elderly grandmother, scientists, and most of the world. She was making amends, but she hadn't come close to earning a man like Cass.

CHAPTER TWELVE

Jolene

The next morning, Jolene stepped out of her bedroom and gasped, rocked fully awake.

Stadler had manspread himself in the middle of her couch, his weight pulling the ends of the cushion up a few inches like a smirk. He wore jeans and a crimson T-shirt that stretched over his shoulders and biceps. "Where were you yesterday?" His voice was calm, but the sharp energy in the room warned her he wasn't as collected as he sounded.

"Swimming."

"Alone?"

Damn it. If she thought she would get away with it, she'd lie, but Stadler had an uncanny ability to detect lies, and he knew her too well. "I was teaching a friend how to swim."

"You barely swim yourself."

She shrugged. "Just because you suck at something doesn't mean you can't teach it."

"It means you shouldn't." He walked to her, his footfalls silent, his body language predatory. "You missed training."

"We didn't have anything scheduled." She shook out her hands, her mouth dry. *He's not threatening you*, she told herself.

"We did."

Jolene fetched her phone from the kitchen counter. Two mugs sat in the sink like a guilty secret. Shit. There was something in her calendar. "When was that set up?" She never forgot training. Had Cass muddled her brain that much?

"Ryan entered it into your itinerary yesterday morning."

Oh. She flung out her hands. "If you want me to know about stuff, you have to tell me, not just sneak it into my calendar like some fucked-up kind of test. I don't check my phone or calendar every two minutes."

"Start checking." He was only a few feet from her, looming in the pass-through.

Her irritation pushed common sense aside. "Why?" She crossed her arms and tucked her hands under her armpits. "I don't like power games, Stadler."

"You want on the team; you accept my authority like everyone else." He stared at her in a way that pierced through her.

"I'm not—"

"Jolene." His clipped tone shut her up like a punch to the larynx. "I let you do your thing because you made it work, and it was just the two of us then. Being part of a crew means no special treatment."

"I'll check my schedule every morning from now on."

He backed away from her. "Change so we can train."

She didn't want to, but training always bonded them by the end, so it would be for the best. As she dressed in yoga pants and a sports bra, she grumbled to herself about the importance of boundaries.

Special treatment. Because she was a memory surgeon or a woman? Or was it because of their past? She never brought that up.

"Shoes or no shoes?" she called out.

"Shoes."

He knew Jolene preferred shoes, so maybe he'd calmed down and wasn't in one of his prove-a-point moods. By the time she exited the bedroom, he'd pushed what little furniture she had to the sides of the room. The action reminded her of Cass's qigong instruction, except this time everything hugged the walls, opening up as much space as possible. That shouldn't have made her twitchy.

Stadler's face said nothing, his body nothing, his energy nothing.

She didn't like it. His blankness sent a creeping sensation up her spine to land at the base of her skull. Her instincts screamed unhelpful instructions, like *Run!* Jolene couldn't conjure the confidence to stride up to him to stand toe-to-toe like she wanted. Her eyes were probably Bambi-wide.

He opened and closed his hand to beckon her forward.

Jolene stepped to him, shoes squeaking on the hardwood. She tried to swallow and failed, which kind of hurt. "What first?"

He whipped out his hands and grabbed her, wrapping them around her neck. She should have expected it, since it was the attack they practiced most after the incident with Colton, but Stadler didn't restrain the pressure.

Her adrenaline spiked high enough to blank out her mind. Blindly, she scrabbled at his wrists, trying to pull them off her, then she raised her right arm and brought it down, elbow first, turning her body, breaking the hold. She should have followed up with a punch, but she backed away, needing a moment to gather her thoughts.

"Good," he said, not smiling but not scowling. "Almost there."

Jolene comprehended the need to go through the throat stuff after Colton had almost killed her, but the practice wasn't having the desensitization effect Stadler had promised. Every time he grabbed her, her body expected to die.

For the next half hour, they sparred and reset continuously. The mental concentration combined with the brutal physicality wore down her strength. She pretended to trip into Stadler—a trick he'd taught her. He'd warned her it wouldn't always work, but the move could change the dynamic of a fight. He reached out to steady her—not because her ruse succeeded, but because he wanted her to practice. Jolene rammed her knee into his groin, or would have, if he hadn't shifted so she nailed his thigh instead.

Even so, he grunted. She hadn't held back, and a knee to the thigh still hurt. Stadler bent over enough that she could lower her center of gravity and pull him over her shoulder. His back hit the hardwood floor, but he popped to his feet before she could take advantage. Goddamn, he was quick.

Fatigue swamped her, and she couldn't catch her breath. She hoped Stadler would end the lesson soon.

Suddenly, he grasped her behind the neck with both hands. She stumbled, this time unintentionally, and as she toppled forward, his knee came up, connecting with her ribs in an explosion of agony.

He tossed her to the ground, or let gravity do the work. She fell onto her side and rolled to her feet, though she couldn't straighten. Maybe he'd broken a few ribs, because the pain made her brain slow and her mind muddy. Stadler watched her, waiting for her to counter as expected. It was his biggest rule: Never stop fighting until she incapacitated her opponent enough to confidently get away.

If she didn't retaliate, he'd come for her again, and he wouldn't hold back. Already, he'd given her time to recover, something a real attacker wouldn't do.

"Use your environment," he barked.

Jolene grabbed a hardback off the bookshelf and hurled it at him, wincing as her ribs protested the action. Stadler twisted to dodge the book, which *thunked* into the door before sprawling open on the floor.

"Wasted movement and energy," Stadler said. "Pick another book. Smack me in the head, arc it into my balls, block a shot to your face, but don't throw it away."

"What the hell, Gavin?" she hissed, gripping the left side of her body.

"That's what happens when you don't fucking focus," he replied, showing no sign whatsoever of fatigue. "This isn't a game, Jolene. If Stefano's people suspect you're working for the government, they will kill you. Find out you're a memory surgeon? They'll peel strips of skin from your body until they get everything they want. *Then* they'll kill you."

"I know," she replied. She knew more about torture than Stadler could ever imagine, thanks to her former work with war refugees, and she had no desire to experience that firsthand again. But if she spent every second concentrating on the danger, she'd freeze in the field, and then she'd be left with nothing but mini projects like the ones from the last four-plus years. Alone. "Believe me, I'm taking this seriously."

"By hanging out in swimming pools?"

Her gut pinched in guilt and dread, and anxiety turned her insides to ice. "Jesus Christ, can't I have a few hours to myself? Mental health breaks? When have I ever taken time to do something just because I wanted to do it?"

"You bitched I never let you do enough. *Now* you want to explore your inner self and make friends? You don't want to do this, say so. I don't have time for self-sabotage."

"I'm not—" She stopped. As a recovering alcoholic, she didn't have the luxury of disregarding that sort of criticism. "I don't think that's what's going on." Jolene wasn't about to talk about how much she liked Cass, how he lightened the load she carried whenever they were together. It was as if she'd been living in a cramped box, and Cass's presence let her stretch to her full height, roll her neck and shoulders, and finally take a deep breath.

"What's happening, then?" Stadler crossed his arms.

All the energy inside her disappeared like a delusion in the light of day. "I just like him."

Stadler's chest rose and fell, his face stoic. "You're going to have to make a choice. Take today off. On Sunday, you tell me in or out, but nobody's half-assing this mission. Your health club job starts Monday, so—"

"I don't need time."

He stalked to her; his eyes so intense she thought he might attack her again. "This team is everything. Take today off. *Think.*" His eyes zipped up and down her body. His wood-spice cologne invaded her nose, another kind of assault. Slowly, he reached out and prodded her ribs in a few places. She winced but didn't cry out.

Stadler blew out a sigh. "Nothing broken, but ice that, yeah? Run the fight in your head, making better choices. See yourself winning. If your head isn't in the right place, you'll fail."

Jolene nodded once and waited until he'd left before she gingerly stroked her sore ribs, refusing to cry. She kept imagining how amazing it would feel to take a drink and forget everything.

Maybe she was doomed to fail no matter what she did.

CHAPTER THIRTEEN

Jolene

THE AA MEETING ROOM LOOKED LIKE A CORPORATE retreat with almost everyone wearing business casual, even on a Saturday. The square room was too big for the circle of a dozen folding chairs and one card table near the door that held a samovar for coffee and an assortment of cookies from the Jewel bakery.

Jolene wondered if she would have to trust-fall with her too-light head and aching ribs at some point. Or sign up for a Roth IRA.

Still, she liked this setup better than the bigger groups where you had to stand in front of everyone, sometimes behind a podium or on a platform. Thank God there were AA meetings several times a day across the city. She needed the comfort of the familiar. Although she'd never been to this particular meeting in Uptown, she knew what to expect.

A scruffy guy a few years younger than her ducked into the room wearing ratty jeans and a vintage Megadeth T-shirt under a denim jacket. The chair squeaked as he plopped next to her. She immediately felt a camaraderie with him, and if he asked to go for coffee afterward to talk about their blue-collarness, she decided she'd say yes. Anything to keep her mind off Cass, Stadler, and the job. And the decision she had to make.

In the hours since Stadler had left, her ribs hurt more, not less.

The woman in charge wore chunky jewelry the same shade as her red lipstick, probably called Poppy Passion or something similar. She started the meeting with the Serenity Prayer, which the dude next to her didn't say with the group. Jolene arched a brow at him, not in condemnation, but in question. He quirked one shoulder and smirked. She liked him.

Of the sixteen people there, Scruffy volunteered to share first. "I'm Billy, three years sober. My girlfriend is chapping my ass about drinking a toast at her sister's upcoming wedding. She's all, like, 'It's just one sip of champagne' and shit. I mean, what the fuck, right?"

Jolene expected the corporate crew to scowl at his language, but all they did was nod. The takeaway here: She was the asshole in this situation by preemptively judging others.

None of the attendees had an emergency or anything pressing to share, though an executive in his seventies told the same story twice. The way everyone patiently responded told her he did that often. Dementia, maybe. The urge to touch him and investigate his memories washed over her.

She could tumble into the old dude's life, and he'd never know. No one here would ever know. Stadler would say that meant it didn't matter. But down to her shriveled soul, she knew that it did. Stadler didn't make her a better person, but together they were creating a better world.

Her ribs ached despite her doubling up on the ibuprofen. She deserved the pain for losing focus, for letting her selfishness distract her when she'd finally gotten a shot at being integral to taking down a criminal organization.

Someone put a hand on her shoulder. People stared at her. "Sorry?" she asked.

"You aren't required to share; we just want to give you the opportunity," Poppy Passion said, though it had been Scruffy—Billy—who'd touched her. Luckily, Jolene hadn't taken off her jacket, so she had a few layers of clothing between their skin. She didn't want the temptation to glimpse at Billy's memories.

"I'm June." Might as well start using the personal-trainer name Ryan had chosen for her. Even in her safe space, she was a liar.

They greeted her.

"Five years sober." People smiled and nodded, but although it had been a respectable run, no alcoholic was ever done. She sighed. "I'm . . . not liking myself very much lately, not that I'm ever exactly enamored."

Polite laughter.

"I've got no decent options. My job . . . I've been asking to join this team for years, and I finally got in, and I thought it would make everything better, but somehow everything is worse. My boss isn't happy with my work, and he's questioning my commitment." She shrugged. "*I'm* questioning my commitment. And I met someone, but he just got out of a relationship, and it's bad timing all around, and what the hell am I doing? And I can't stop thinking about how getting wasted would solve everything. I'd get fired, so I wouldn't have to worry about the job situation, and the guy wouldn't find drunk me attractive." Bonus: she would get to eat real food again. "But I'm not going to do that." Maybe saying it out loud to the group would make it true—AA's particular kind of magic.

"Do you think you're afraid of success?" Brenda, a Black woman in an expensive pantsuit, asked afterward as they stood around the table of refreshments. The acrid scent of coffee warred with the cigarette stench clinging to most of the group.

Jolene shook her head. "I'm terrified of failure."

Billy stuck to her like a bodyguard. "When has alcohol made a fucking thing better? You need to remember how much worse it makes everything."

Brenda nodded. "Hold on to the person you want to be and fight for that. Maybe you need a new job, a new man, or both. Just because you're in recovery doesn't mean all that goes wrong is your fault. We have to take responsibility for our actions, but not those of others. Just remember—do the next right thing."

AA advice was rarely prescriptive, though rife with catchphrases for each person to apply as needed. *Do the next right thing* was a common refrain, a way to make decisions exactly like this one, when the answer didn't glow in the dark. "Thanks, you guys."

Stadler was an epic ass, but he wasn't wrong. Cass had been commandeering her heart, which needed to realign itself with her important work. She couldn't choose herself when there were so many lives more innocent than her own on the line.

CHAPTER FOURTEEN

Jolene

On Sunday, decision day, Jolene's belly wouldn't settle. It was human nature to want—right now—instead of waiting for the appropriate time. The selfish part of her suggested she might have both Cass and career in a sort of pay-as-you-go kind of karmic redress.

The next right thing.

She texted Cass and asked if she could stop by and bring lunch. He said yes and sent a string of nonsensical emojis that made her laugh.

Her heart keened, begging her to change her mind, hold onto their friendship, but she'd made her decision.

* * *

Jolene's meal consisted of a giant salad of veggies and chicken breast without dressing, dried fruit, nuts, cheese, or croutons. She hated the "shred" diet and the water pills, the deprivation, and the endless glasses of water. It had been only two days, but it felt like a month already.

For Cass, she'd brought a cheeseburger and fries. She could live without the fries, but the burger smelled charred, smoky, and absolutely delicious. Her life sucked.

The skin over her ribs had turned from red to bluish purple, and though she'd consumed a steady dose of ibuprofen, they still throbbed. At least they reminded her of what was at stake, and they helped support her resolve. She needed to earn her place on the team by giving one hundred percent.

As she waited for Cass to buzz her in, she considered her "higher purpose." She'd heard the phrase so many times in her early life. Her grandmother had worked tirelessly to help the community. That commitment made her happiest. Apparently, her mother and father had been the same. Service to others was in her blood; she just had to find the drive. This was a chance to have a bigger role in shutting down part of the drug trade. She wouldn't cock up this opportunity.

Cass buzzed her in without asking who was there. She could have been anyone—a burglar, serial killer, Jehovah's Witness. He'd left the door to his apartment open an inch. A woman would never have been so stupid.

"Hey, what if I was some kind of murderer?" she called out.

"I wish some criminal would try his luck with me," Cass replied, coming out of his bedroom, his hair wet from a shower.

Solid. Smiling. Sexy.

The shaking started in her hands, or maybe it was her belly, and quickly traveled everywhere. Why couldn't she have something for herself? Just a bit of happiness, small enough to fit in the palm of her hand. When she looked at Cass, her body experienced a sense of loss.

"What's wrong?" he asked.

Jolene used one hand to squeeze her neck muscles. "Tired."

He frowned. "Sorry to hear that. Have you been practicing those qigong moves I taught you?"

She nodded. "Much better than meditating."

Cass shook his head at her. "It *is* meditating." He tilted his chin at her bag of food. "What did you bring? It smells so good."

"Burger and fries." This was the last meal they'd share together.

He came over and scooped the sack from her hand. "What can I get you to drink?"

"Water." She should tell him now, get it out in the open, but maybe he wouldn't want her to stay then.

Cass pulled out plates, but as he reached for glasses, he looked at her and stopped. "Seriously, what's going on with you?"

It didn't mean anything that he always picked up on her emotions. Plenty of people would have noticed she hadn't come all the way into the kitchen, that she was standing in the door like an unwanted orphan.

"I'm fine." Heartbroken. *No.* That was an exaggeration. Histrionics. Tomorrow, she would start an important project, finally part of a team, like she'd wanted, and she couldn't be more excited. She. Was. Thrilled. Damn. It. "I'm starting a second job at Gold Coast Health Club tomorrow as a personal trainer."

"Congratulations! Gold Coast Health Club? Upscale. You'll have to tell me if you land any famous clients."

Like a drug lord's son? "I think famous people probably hire privately rather than rely on a club coach."

"Once they see you, they're going to want you to train them. What made you decide to get a job there?" He set up two TV trays so they could watch a movie while they ate, and she trailed him like a duckling from the living room back to the kitchen.

"I could use the money." The lie burned up her throat like bile. "And I've got too much free time lately. My brain doesn't do well in that scenario."

"Because of the recovery?" he asked, his tone gentle.

She nodded. "Yeah. Staying busy helps keep me out of trouble."

"The qigong can help with that too. I can teach you more later." He pulled out the food. When he saw her salad, he mock shuddered. "Since when do you eat girlie food?"

"Salads aren't girlie. I need to cut calories for some definition." She hated how that made her sound as if all she cared about was her appearance. "The more in shape the trainer, the more clients."

"Sounds like bullshit to me. It's obvious you're fit. I mean, nobody gets an ass like that by channel surfing."

Her ass *had* taken a lot of work to achieve. She extracted her nails from her palms. "It's necessary."

He stopped plating the food and gazed smack into her eyes. "Why?"

She shrugged. "People want a coach they consider aspirational. I need a six-pack and bitching about how much the dietary restrictions suck doesn't help." Not that she'd be able to expose her bruised midriff anytime soon.

"I know what you need."

She snorted.

"Not that." His smile made her want to return it. Goddamn it, this shouldn't be so hard. "You need one of my magic hugs."

"Magic, huh?"

"Yep." He held his arms open. "Come to the master."

She chuckled amidst the churning inside her.

His grin faded, and he sobered. "I really do give good hug, if you want one."

She did. A fitting goodbye, right?

Jolene wanted it too much to deny herself. She stepped forward and slipped her arms around his waist so her elbows protected her ribs.

Cass pulled her body against his with a gentle press. He smelled of soap and something chemical, like paint or turpentine. The cocoon of his arms warmed her. It wasn't sexual but comforting. One hand stroked up and down her back.

Her throat tightened. Prickles stabbed the backs of her eyes as her nose burned. Everything clamped down, crumbling from the inside.

She couldn't breathe.

His hand rubbed twice more up and down her spine and dislodged a sob. He didn't scrabble away or stiffen. "It's okay," he murmured into her ear, so present and caring.

Nobody had ever held her like this, making her feel cherished and safe, and of course she couldn't keep that. Even if the team embraced her wholeheartedly, invited her to every Thanksgiving dinner, remembered her birthday, let her help bring down a thousand drug dealers, it wouldn't feel as transcendent as Cass's hug. This might be the best she'd ever feel, and she wasn't enjoying it.

"Shhhh." His soft voice caressed her ear as he kept hold of her.

Her body shook, which should have mortified her into drawing away, but the humiliation only made her cry harder. Life wasn't any more unfair for her than for anyone else, but the bitterness of finding someone so valuable when she couldn't keep him made her want to curl into a ball and never move again.

Cass adjusted his hold and squeezed, the pressure pushing her arm against her bruised ribs. She hissed and jerked and cried all the harder. Stadler had hurt her, and yeah, it had probably been accidental, but still, he'd *hurt* her.

"What happened?" Cass pulled back, taking his warmth with him. Hands on her shoulders, he focused on her contusion as if he could see it through her clothes.

Jolene slapped the tears from her face and turned away so he wouldn't witness her ugly-crying. She held a hand protectively over her ribs.

"I was doing a little sparring, and I—" She wouldn't say those words so many other women said. And then she did. "It was an accident."

"Let me see." It wasn't a request.

"No."

"Who hurt you?" He shifted his weight between his feet and shoved his hands under his armpits as if afraid they might go rogue.

"Nobody. I just said it was an accident. Aren't you listening?"

His look called bullshit, and she couldn't hold his gaze. He sighed. "Here's the thing. When people hurt themselves unintentionally, they want to share with the world their stupidity or bad luck or whatever. I'm certainly not going to force you to show me, but the only reason I can think of for you not to is because you're ashamed. And why would you be embarrassed by an 'accident'?" His scorn as he said *accident* should have set his couch ablaze.

Fucking astute Cass. "Fine. You want to see it? It's ugly as fuck, but here you go." She yanked up her thin sweater and turned to showcase the discoloration. Finally, her brain gave her something helpful. "My shame is that I didn't counter the move. I've been remiss in my training."

Cass rested cool fingers on the edge of the bruise, his touch light. His jaw bulged as he gritted his teeth. "Motherfucker," he hissed.

"It looks worse than it is." She couldn't stop lying.

"This happened during sparring? Did your instructor kick his ass?" Cass looked as if he wanted to hunt down the culprit.

"The instructor was the one who did it." Part of her enjoyed calling out Stadler for his bad behavior.

"I hope you quit. What the fuck?"

She sighed. "I'm fine." His open-jawed glare had her hustling to continue. "I was distracted, so it's my fault."

"Look, Jolene, he's either got no control, and therefore you shouldn't learn from him, or he bruised you like that on purpose, which makes him a violent prick, and therefore you shouldn't learn from him. I had some fight training in the army. I'd be happy to show you some moves. I can assure you that proper instruction doesn't hurt like *that*."

Stadler was her lifeline to everything, so accepting the kinds of truth Cass mentioned didn't serve her. "I'll talk to him about it."

She wouldn't.

Cass pulled his hair back into a ponytail, then let it go, the long strands swishing forward and back. "Please don't. Just fire his ass and be done with it."

"Your burger's getting cold."

"I don't care about food right now."

She bit her lip until she realized what she was doing. "Look, you're just going to have to trust me." She rubbed her forehead. "I came here to tell you I'm about to get busy at work."

"You said you took a second job because you have too much free time."

She resisted the urge to roll her shoulders. "I can only do the billing for so many hours in a row, and I need other things to think about, but I'm about to be super busy with a new client, and I'm not going to be available to hang out for a while. Just wanted to let you know. I don't want you to feel ghosted or whatever."

He stared at her as if he didn't believe a word she'd spoken.

She grabbed her plated salad and left the kitchen, talking over her shoulder. "Maybe you wouldn't have noticed anyway, so I don't know why I'm making a big deal out of this. It's just . . ." She sensed him following her to the living room. "I haven't made a friend in a long time. But I've got responsibilities that have to take priority."

He set down his burger with a subdued *clunk*. "Let's eat."

* * *

THEY WATCHED THE NINETIES MOVIE *THE CRAFT* AND ATE IN RELATIVE quiet. Halfway through the movie, Jolene tucked her feet underneath her. Fifteen minutes later, Cass tugged one of her feet onto his lap and dug his fingers into the sole. She closed her eyes and enjoyed the pleasure of his ministrations.

"I didn't mean to push you earlier," he said. "I promise I won't bring it up again. Just, please, don't cut me off."

Her eyes popped open. Shit. He assumed she planned to disappear because she was abused and protecting her abuser. "It's not what you think."

"You say you haven't made a friend in a long time, but then you're willing to toss everything away? Couldn't we at least text? Or is it because I can't offer you more than friendship?" He rubbed the back of his neck. "We could try . . ."

Her belly flipped and sloshed as her chest tightened. "You should never give more than you're comfortable with, Cass. That stuff never works out." His eyes drilled into her. "Of course we'll still be friends, and texting isn't a problem." This was a simple compromise—not between her and Cass, but between her heart and her head. "But don't be offended if I don't respond right away."

His smile lit up his face, his crooked tooth on display. "I'm not that needy." He winked.

"Don't be a winker. Winkers are creepy."

He released her foot only to grab the other. "Winking is an art form, and I, as you know, am an artist."

As he wrung the muscles until they became liquid, she sighed. "You're not an artist but a witch."

On her way home, she suppressed her longing for Cass, comforted that at least he would still be connected to her via text. In a few weeks or months, the team would break the case, and somehow, she'd find a way to make work *and* Cass the next right thing.

She texted Stadler. *I'm in.*

CHAPTER FIFTEEN

Walther

JULIE AND SAFFRON WERE GHOSTS, AND WALTHER was no ghost hunter. Yet, he didn't give up. His brother, five weeks in the grave, couldn't rest—no, *Walther* couldn't rest until he'd avenged Colton.

Everyone he spoke to had a Colton story Walther had never heard before. He was discovering and losing his brother over and over again. It made his blood speed through his veins like oil in a racecar. Faster. He needed to move faster.

He stood outside a sad-looking bar in South Boston, ignoring the October cold snap and how the wind stung his face like Mother Nature slapping him for his failures. The building's bricks were crumbling in places, the windows wide, squat, and filthy. A few neon signs flashed, one half burned out. Why the hell had Colton hung out *here*?

Colton had wanted to better himself, move ahead, and yet, he'd associated with people who worked at a dive bar. Walther's brother never understood the value of networking and associating himself with people who were going places.

And now Walther was there, looking for someone to help *him* out. It was a waste of his time, but he was in the grip of something and couldn't turn away. So, he pushed inside, grunting at the cloud of cigarette smoke. He took a deep, pleasurable breath, questioning his decision to quit smoking. A whiskey and a cigarette sounded so good.

His heavy legs carried him to the bar on autopilot, his eyes gritty from lack of sleep. The bartender was a balding, overweight man with runny eyes. The tattoos on the pale skin of his forearms were blue and faded. He also looked bored as fuck. "Get ya?"

"Johnnie Walker Black, if you've got it."

The man grunted and poured him a Johnnie Walker Red. What the fuck was Walther doing there?

"Four bucks." The man's voice creaked and rasped as if he'd been choked recently.

Walther slipped a five from his wallet and laid it on the bar. "You know a man named Colton Bridges?" He sipped his whiskey, intending to stay all of two minutes to finish it, then find a classier joint where he could binge himself into a stupor.

The bartender cracked a smile to reveal surprisingly healthy teeth. "You must be Cole's brother. Look just like him, you do. How is ol' Coley? He marry that pretty thing yet? You tell him I'm pissed as crackers not to get an invite. I figure that's where he been, holed up with his hottie."

Walther stopped with the glass halfway to his lips. Married? His brain spun in place several times before the word came out of his mouth. "Married?"

The bartender shook his head. "Aw, fuck me. I done ruined the surprise, didn't I? I thought for sure he'd be hitched by now. He bought the ring in the summer, and that lad ain't one to think too hard about nothing."

Walther snorted at the assessment, his heart squeezing so tightly in his chest he thought he might pass out. "He was going to marry Julie?"

The bartender smacked his hand on his thigh twice. "Julie! That was her name!"

"You met her?"

"Once. Bit scrawny for my taste, but pretty enough."

The bartender wasn't getting it, and Walther had to grip the tacky bar top to keep from reaching over and punching him until his face was nothing but pulp. "She say anything about where she was from?"

"Why you wanna know?" The turn in the bartender's countenance was sharp and deadly.

Walther liked this version of the man far better. "Because Colton is dead, and she's gone." He kicked back the rest of his whiskey and nodded for another.

"Dead? How?" The shock on the bartender's face was genuine, and Walther softened a bit toward the old guy.

"Professional hit."

"Did they hurt Julie? Kidnap her?"

Walther wished. He imagined someone still torturing her. "I think she was part of the setup."

Emotions rushed across the bartender's face, his color draining white, then blossoming red. "That—she—he was gonna marry her. Said he'd knowed the moment he met her, and he was so happy about it. I thought he was an idiot, 'cause it ain't like he knew her good, but stranger things and all that." He shook his head and poured them both a glass of the Johnnie Walker. "He was so sure she was the one."

That cunt had a lot to atone for.

CHAPTER SIXTEEN

Jolene

For the next few weeks, Jolene enjoyed working as a personal trainer. She liked pushing people further than they would on their own, and she loved using all the equipment when she didn't have a client. The exercises she'd learned for the job were different enough to make her sore but in a good way. Her ribs ached but not as much as before.

Stefano Jr. and his men were often in the gym, mostly in the afternoons, but they ignored her. Jolene made a point of saying "hi" and greeting as many guests as possible so she would be noticed and remembered at Stefano's niece's birthday party.

Stadler hadn't shown up at her place again. Jolene hadn't seen Cass, though she continued to run on the 606. That didn't mean they had no contact. He texted her several times a day. She wondered if he was painting at all.

She still ached for him, but seeing him might decimate the equilibrium she'd achieved with her dedication to the team. To keep calm, Jolene practiced qigong twice a day and sometimes followed along with some of the YouTube routines while at work.

Unfortunately, as the night of the birthday party drew closer, the qigong worked less and less.

* * *

Jolene ignored the stuttered vibration of her cell phone. Cass had a habit of sending not just a text or two, but a barrage, a dissertation's worth of messages sent in bite-sized pieces. It was annoying and not at all endearing.

Tonight, they'd see if Jolene's plan to get close to the Stefanos and their people would work.

Her apartment buzzer sounded, and her stomach bottomed out. Oh no. Was Cass stopping by, and was that why her phone was blowing up?

She should have cut ties completely. What had she been thinking?

Jolene hit the intercom. "Yes?"

"Hey!" Sara.

The relief she'd expected didn't come, and she tapped her forehead with the pads of her fingers before hitting the button to open the lobby door.

"What the hell?" she hissed at herself.

Sara kicked the door. "Let me in!"

Jolene smiled and opened it to see a pile of clothes.

"I couldn't decide what to wear," Sara said and almost ran into Jolene as she stumbled into the apartment, her exotic and earthy perfume following in her wake. Jolene remembered the slightly smoky scent—Tom Ford Santal Blush—from her perfume counter days in Boston. Expensive.

Sara didn't stick to one fragrance or one genre of fashion. She and Ryan were the only members of the team who didn't travel light, their ruses requiring vast wardrobes—or so they claimed.

"So, you brought every item of clothing you own?"

"Hardly. We can get ready together. It'll be fun."

"How does sharing a bathroom turn into a chucklefest?"

Sara heaved her clothes onto the couch, put her hands on her hips, and studied Jolene. "Haven't you ever gotten dressed for a party or something with a girlfriend?"

"No." Quite frankly, the idea seemed like one of those fake rom-com things that wasn't actually enjoyable in real life, like having to share a bed with a stranger.

Sara rolled her eyes. "Well. This won't be as chucklesome sober, but you're going to laugh so hard you pee, so dress accordingly."

"Again, you are not making this sound fun." But Jolene grinned.

They were both right. Getting ready together was entertaining *and* annoying. Sara's eye for matching garments was obviously a gift. Sure, all Jolene's clothes were black, but Sara had a way of pairing things that projected an ensemble rather than a slapdash collection of clothing items.

She made Jolene switch outfits three times, barging in on her during the last costume change and spotting her bruise. It had faded considerably, but the lavender hue was unmistakable.

"Stadler?" Sara asked, her voice a rough whisper.

"Perils of training." Jolene tried to both snicker and shrug, not pulling off either. "Reminder of my need to focus."

Sara snorted. "What a prick. Tell him to keep his hands to himself."

"It was an accident."

"Huh." Sara tossed Jolene a sleeveless, stretchy top with strategic cutouts on the chest. "So, he said he was sorry, then?"

The current shirt fit Jolene especially well when paired with a push-up bra. "Stadler doesn't apologize."

"Right?" She tapped her French-tipped manicured fingernails on her hips. "Guess it explains why he gave me this to give you." She pulled a Starbucks gift card from her purse and held it out. "Twenty-five bucks' worth of bruising, apparently."

That amount paid for more than their usual tea and coffee. The gift card didn't make her feel better, but it didn't make her feel worse either.

Sara squeezed her shoulder. "I've got your back." Then she moved on, picking out more clothing. "We're locking in the top."

Jolene admired Sara's gift for letting go of negativity and anything awkward.

Sara selected a pair of black jeans and black shitkicker boots to complete Jolene's outfit. "I like it," Sara said when Jolene had changed. "Edgy and tough without trying too hard." She fished out dangly, diamond earrings from a small makeup bag filled with jewelry. "A bit of classy bling."

Jolene assumed her look was complete, but Sara insisted she lose the ponytail.

"You want your hair down. Men need to see how much there is to grab while they're fucking you." Sara smirked, then claimed the bathroom mirror, unrolling her makeup case like a surgeon fanning out scalpels. She applied black eyeliner, then expertly brushed a metallic dark gray shadow around her eyes. "Men want to be with the woman other men want. They want the shiny object. Of course, I'm going to be the shiniest." She winked and plugged in a curling wand.

Why was everyone suddenly winking all the time?

"But you'll sparkle, too, and that is only going to pull in more sausage. All we need to do is snag one man from the crew, and he'll do the bulk of the work by dragging the rest to us. Don't you worry." Sara grinned at her in the mirror. "Here. Try this red lipstick."

* * *

Jolene wished she could take a quick jog or execute a couple of burpees, but she was dressed up and made up, so that wasn't happening. Besides, the qigong moves would have been weird in front of Sara. So, she paced her apartment instead, boot heels clicking as she rehearsed inane conversations, trying to make herself sound natural.

"Are you talking to yourself?" Sara called as she shook her fresh curls into beachy waves. She wore a fire-engine-red catsuit that hid nothing—a literal beacon.

"I'm practicing being engaging. I don't think it's going to work. It was so much easier when I just had to sit and smile."

"You'll be great." Sara stared so intently, Jolene she felt as if she were naked. "What's really going on?"

"I think Stadler's testing me but not in a nice way."

Sara snorted and eyed Jolene's torso. The bruise, hidden from Sara's gaze, ached, and she had to resist the urge to clamp her arms down to protect the spot. Sara gave her a long look. "It doesn't matter, because you're talented."

Jolene studied her bookshelf. "What about Boston?"

Sara winced. "That was my fault. I shouldn't have been messing around with Colton." She put a hand on Jolene's arm. "I am sorry. I never thought Stadler would do something like that to *you.*" Her hand fell away, and she dropped her chin.

Had he done something similar to Sara?

Jolene needed to bring back the festive mood, or she'd fail before she started. "Is that because I'm Daddy's favorite?"

Sara tilted her head back and laughed. The motion exposed the long column of her throat. Jolene wasn't jealous, exactly, but she wondered what it would be like to be that beautiful.

"You *have* to call him Daddy in a meeting sometime. Please, please, please." Sara wiped a tear from her eye. "Please."

"I think I'm going to try to *not* poke the bear for a bit, thanks."

CHAPTER SEVENTEEN

Jolene

As they waited for their Lyft driver, a wave of irrational fear crashed into Jolene—at least she hoped it was irrational. She imagined taking a shot, feeling the bracing burn of alcohol down her throat, opening the beast precariously caged inside her.

I tell myself I'll quit at one, but I don't. The bar and restaurant torch to the ground, and I die wrapped around a bottle of Grey Goose.

The fantasy became so visceral, it felt inevitable. Jolene shuddered. "Make sure I don't drink."

Sara cocked an eyebrow and studied her. "I will."

When their ride arrived, Sara leaped into character. She slid across the back seat to make room for Jolene and announced to the driver, "I'm divorced today!"

The driver was a middle-aged man with more gray than black in his hair and a beard that looked far more trouble than it was worth. "Good for you." He had a surliness to him, which made Jolene suspect he was divorced and related more to the fabricated ex than to Sara.

"May the festivities begin," Jolene said, ignoring the bitter bastard's foul mood.

Sara whooped as if she'd had a few before they left. They swayed in the back as if dance music were playing. Sara grabbed Jolene's hand and held it up as if proclaiming her the winner. It was easy to fake happiness with Sara around.

* * *

THE BIRTHDAY PARTY FOR THE NIECE WAS HIDDEN IN A PRIVATE BACK room. Every so often, someone from the Stefano organization popped out to take a phone call or use the restroom. Jolene and Sara tracked their movements in the mirror behind the bar.

Ryan had somehow arranged a ladies' night with three-dollar well drinks for women from seven to midnight. Already, the place was full, but two men gave up their barstools for Sara and Jolene and offered to buy them their first beverages. Sara accepted a Jack and Diet Coke, and Jolene refused, ordering a pathetic, no-calorie club soda with lime. The bar was crowded enough for all the colognes and perfumes to mix in an unpleasant way, too sweet and potent, and the music was too loud for easy conversation. Sara bantered for a few minutes with their beverage benefactors, then shut them out by turning her attention to Jolene.

"Remember when George fell asleep on the couch watching Cinemax and woke up thinking the dog licking his chin was me?" Sara giggled with a hand clamped over her mouth.

Jolene inwardly smirked at Sara using the English form of Jorge as the name of her fictional ex-husband. Sara was brilliant at improvisation.

"How about when he clogged the toilet in your parents' bathroom that one Thanksgiving?" Jolene found herself inspired to attempt a game of one-upmanship. Sara, of course, recognized the challenge immediately.

She tossed back her head and gave a throaty laugh just a bit bigger and brighter than the real one in Jolene's apartment a few hours before. This laugh radiated from her, a siren song to every heterosexual male in the entire establishment. If they were in a musical, men would have swooned and dropped around her in a pattern like flower petals.

The image made Jolene snort-laugh, and that set off Sara, who bent over laughing, grabbing Jolene's forearm to steady herself.

Sara's memories blossomed in Jolene's head, sort of. A large gold sphere took up the entire landscape of Sara's mind. It shimmered as if iridescent. She had never seen a metallic bubble before, and she guessed this was Sara's persona's story—fake and real mixed together. Sara had told her more than once that believing your own cover was the surest way to pull it off.

Despite Jolene's no-reading-friends policy, she almost touched the bubble. Could a memory surgeon be fooled if a person believed hard enough? Would it still be wrong to peek if the memory wasn't real?

Sara moved her hand before Jolene sacrificed her morals on the altar of curiosity, and a thought intruded, as if it'd been waiting for the opportunity to pounce: What if she couldn't get even one code?

Jolene laughed a moment too late, but only Sara noticed. She picked up her Jack and Diet Coke and clinked it to Jolene's glass of mostly ice. "You worry too much."

Jolene nodded. This was the best plan with the talents and experience she possessed. Inside, the bitch part of her screamed it wasn't enough and Stadler was right about her lack of attention. She gave that negativity the middle finger. She would don a horsehair bra later. Now, she needed to focus.

The doors to the private room had opened, and party attendees were putting on coats or meandering to the bar. More than a few noticed the crowd and the significant number of women present.

Sara straightened on her stool and pulled back her shoulders, effectively thrusting her breasts forward. "You know what I'm going to do?"

"I'm afraid to ask." Jolene couldn't hold back a grin. Anything might pop out of Sara's mouth.

"Get laid. I am going to get some tonight, and it's going to be amaaaaazing." She brushed her Nordic white-blond hair away from her neck, letting it cascade to her shoulder blades. "What do you think the chances are we'll run into twins? I want to go home with twin gymnasts."

Jolene squinted at Sara. "Gymnasts are usually pretty short."

"That's okay. They're strong and bendy, so they can stack themselves on top of each other, then on top of me."

Jolene stared at her for a few seconds, then shrugged. "All right. I'll be on the lookout."

Sara clapped her hands together and cast her gaze about the bar. She didn't need to look far. Most men in their immediate circumference tried to catch her eye, but Sara rebuffed them all with sweet charm. Jolene wondered which of them would appeal to Sara if she weren't on a job. Did she like average, thin, smart men, like Jorge, or had she chosen Jorge because she could be herself with him?

The sudden tick of interest in Sara's eyes told Jolene that someone from the party was approaching the bar. Sara giggled and spilled her drink, likely on purpose. The distinct smell of Jack Daniel's made Jolene's stomach quiver, as if she feared the alcohol might jump into her mouth of its own volition.

The first three men from the Stefano organization to talk to them weren't on their hit list. Sara charmed everyone, but held herself a little aloof, waiting. Finally, Jolene spotted a viable target. Gustov Flemming, the head of Stefano's security, stood across the room.

Her vision went a little wonky as her heart scrambled, and her thoughts wouldn't hold firm. She wasn't ready. She wouldn't know what to say. He didn't work out at Gold Coast Health Club, so initiating contact with him wouldn't fit with the plan. But if she didn't try, she'd be kicked off the team for certain.

Flemming walked up to a beefy guy she did recognize from the club, though he also wasn't on their list. She knocked back the watery dregs of her carbonated nastiness.

"Hey, I see someone from GCHC," Jolene said to Sara in what she hoped was a casual tone. "I think I'd better do some networking. You okay on your own for a few minutes?"

Sara grinned. "I'm sure someone will keep me company until you get back."

"No doubt," Jolene muttered as she slid off her barstool. She strode through the crowd with purpose, imagining herself as an ass-kicking heroine in a martial arts movie . . . until she stepped on a particularly sticky patch on the parquet floor and almost tripped. She kept her composure and soldiered on.

"Excuse me," she said, interrupting the two men, her focus on the stranger. "Hi, I recognize you from GCHC." Jolene stuck out her hand and grinned. "June North. I'm a personal trainer there."

The guy looked her up and down in a way so obvious it bordered on satire. "Larry." He slid his eyes over her one more time. "Yeah, I seen you around there." His memory bubbles as he gripped her hand were thick and murky.

"You guys look like you're having fun," she said, eyeing Flemming. "This your brother?"

Jolene inwardly winced. Flemming was old enough to be Larry's dad, and she'd sounded like a creeper.

Larry's memories shifted, and a bubble so dark red it was almost black flashed. Jolene skimmed her awareness over it and saw Gustov Flemming inside, the recollection a combination of fear and fury. She pushed through her wariness and entered the memory.

* * *

"Are *you a fucking moron?" That vein in Gustov's temple pulsed, though his face hadn't darkened from red to purple yet.*

"No, sir." Larry couldn't not respond, but it was best to keep answers as short as possible.

"Then why was your phone sitting unlocked at the table?"

"I was checking—"

"No, you weren't, because you'd stepped away."

"I just left for—"

"The screen was open. O-pen. Anybody could have picked up your cell and had full access."

Panic tripped his stutter. "S-s-s-sorry, s-sir. It won't—"

"If it ever does, you won't just be fired. Do you get what I'm saying?"

* * *

JOLENE RELEASED LARRY'S HAND AS HE SAID, "THIS IS MY BOSS, MR. Flemming."

"Hey," she said, barely acknowledging Gustov to avoid raising his suspicion. It was easy, since Larry's fear still pinged around her chest. She gave Larry her game-show smile. "Can I take a picture of us together for Instagram? You're not one of my clients, but you're exactly the look I'm going for, you know?"

Larry looked her up and down *again*. She held her cell out to Flemming. "Would you mind taking our photo?"

"No need," Larry said, snatching the phone out of her hand. "I got long arms."

"It won't look as professional." She wanted to look at Gustov again, but she thought she might have already blown her chance to catch his attention. "But it's fine."

"Can you enter your passcode?" Larry asked.

"Oh, I don't have one."

Out of the corner of her eye, she saw Gustov flinch. Damn it. If she'd managed to get a hand on him, she was certain she would have gotten exactly what they needed, but he stood too far away. How did she naturally touch him?

"You need to have a lock on your phone," Larry said in a condescending tone. "Without it, you could be easily hacked."

She shrugged. "Who'd want to hack me?"

"Everyone," Gustov said, a more authoritarian version of Larry, and finally stepped in her touch range. "A decent criminal can steal your contact list, credit card numbers, and identity through your phone. But by all means, hand your unprotected cell over to strangers."

"Oh." It wasn't hard to look cowed. "How do I add a passcode?" She directed the question to Gustov and held her phone out to him so their fingers could brush.

But she hadn't snagged him. He made a scoffing noise and walked away. Larry took her phone and showed her how to enter a lock code. She placed her hand over his and bent to look at her screen. Once again, she dipped into his memories and found another to skim. He was in his car and lost, cursing at the GPS.

Damn it. She needed a *passcode.*

The word *passcode* echoed, and then several small bubbles pulsed.

No. Fucking. Way.

Jolene reached out to the first one.

* * *

Larry paced through his bedroom, the carpet warm under his bare feet. "six-three-five-two-zero-six, six-three-five-two-zero-six, six-three-five-two-zero-six." Fucking stupid to change passwords every fucking two weeks like fucking lunatics. This code was a combination of his dad's and mom's birth months and years. He didn't have many dates memorized. How the hell was he going to come up with a new code every other week? Fucking Gustov had a ball-busting bitchfit, too, if anyone forgot. Fuuuuuuck.

* * *

Larry took the photo and then added his contact information to her phone with a smirk. At least he didn't wink. "See you soon."

"I hope so," she lied and backed away.

The press of the bar crowd and the smell of booze and overly sweet perfume road-rashed her nerves. She'd discovered she could sort of search memories inside minds with a keyword, but she hadn't gotten Flemming's code. She'd never get close to him again tonight.

This wasn't going to work. None of it was going to work.

Cass and his calm blossomed in her mind as Jolene took a few moments in the bathroom to breathe and shake out her hands, but her thoughts wouldn't settle.

Sara arched both eyebrows at Jolene when she squeezed back onto the barstool next to her.

Jolene said, "Not everyone wants a personal trainer, if you can believe it."

"You didn't really expect everything was going to simply fall into your lap without any problems, right?" Sara asked, patting Jolene on the shoulder, briefly losing her balance before righting herself. She played a drunk brilliantly, and it reminded Jolene how much more talented everyone else on the team was.

Jolene bit her lip. "Shouldn't someone be interested?"

Sara laughed. "It's early." She resettled herself on her stool. "Guess what? I had some nice eye contact with a hot guy." She crossed her eyes for a moment, then she pasted on a sloppy smile. "So cute. Twenties, I think. Tatted up just the right amount, you get me?"

Mario Bulaggio, one of their targets, a grunt.

"Oh yeah? Moving away from older men, then?"

Sara blew a raspberry. "Every newly divorced woman should have a boy toy for at least an evening and a half, don't you think?"

"At a bare minimum." Jolene clapped her hands in mock delight, trying too hard. She pulled back the enthusiasm. "You should introduce me to your friend. Get a second opinion."

Sara used one of her patented head tilts, and Mario practically pushed people out of his way to get to her.

Jolene hadn't seen prime targets like Benjamin Gold, Stefano's secretary, or Diego Kenneth, Stefano's top advisor, yet. She hoped they'd ditched the party altogether, then it wouldn't be her fault when the entire operation failed. She should care more about the success of the mission than how others would perceive her competence, but she didn't.

Finally, inspiration hit. "Photo!" she sang out to Sara.

Pulling her phone from her back pocket, she purposely flubbed entering the new code. "Aw, shit," she hissed. Then she gave Sara puppy eyes. "Some stern dude made me put in a passcode, and now I can't remember it."

Sara laughed, bending at the waist, showing off more cleavage. "That's okay." She tilted her chin to Mario. "Hey, doll, will you take a photo of us and then text it to me?"

"Sure, babe." Mario's voice was as deep as his chest was wide. His fat fingers fished his cell out of his pocket. Jolene squashed the impulse to clamp a hand on his wrist and pluck the code from his mind as he entered a six-digit number with his thumb. "Smile, girls."

Jolene slung her arm over Sara's shoulder as Sara did the same to her. Sara's mind was opaque, even the gold sphere gone. Interesting.

"Let me see," Jolene said the moment Mario lowered his hand, her fingers touching the spot of skin below the cuff of his merlot-colored dress shirt.

Mario's memories were neon bright, a shocking contrast to Sara's wasteland. Jolene took the half-formed bubble of the current moment and tried to shape the connection into a line she might follow backward to the passcode.

Passcode, she sent into his consciousness. And she found it, shimmering like a cherry Jolly Rancher and thick with lust for Sara. Jolene dipped into the memory.

* * *

Mario pictured the blue-eyed goddess impaled on his shaft, rising and lowering over him, the fit blond naked and sucking on her friend's tits.

0-1-3-6-5-2

This was just the beginning of what he intended to film.

* * *

JOLENE STRUGGLED TO KEEP HER FACE IN THE SAME EXPRESSION AS adrenaline dumped into her bloodstream and his arousal tripped her own. No matter. She got the first code!

But seriously, did every male have the same Neanderthal brain? The guy was in for a very disappointing evening. "We look so cute!" Jolene said to Sara, tilting the screen.

"Hey, pretty lady, can I take one with you?" Mario asked Sara, then handed his unlocked phone to Jolene. Gustov would have had a fit.

"Oh yeah. I hope George is stalking my Instagram." Sara pressed herself against Mario, hand on his chest, molding her body to his like her catsuit molded to her.

Jolene took three photos and smirked. "Got it." She looked at Mario, but the words were for Sara. Her thoughts slid toward Cass, Mario's desire still affecting her own, but she course corrected fast back to the job.

Sara sneaked a peak at the last photo and beamed. "Hell yeah, you did."

It took Sara twenty minutes to ditch Mario by convincing him she was into cock-and-ball torture, all with a straight face. About then, Ryan slipped his way up to the bar and gave Jolene a very obvious once-over.

She arched her eyebrows at him, enjoying the fiction of being strangers. They'd ultimately decided three friends at the bar would be too much, and Ryan might scare off some of the men.

"Gold Coast Health Club?" he asked.

"June North," she replied, holding out her hand.

Ryan kissed the back of her hand. "Allow me to introduce myself." His memories were tight and orderly, sitting behind a veil, and his bubbles didn't flash or pulse. "Ryan Caldwell the Third."

Jolene almost spluttered at "the third" but managed to keep her reaction to a smile. "Charmed to make your acquaintance."

He released his hold, and the connection blinked out of existence. "That, my dear, is a lovely watch," he said, eyeing the Cartier Crash Salvador Dali watch he'd picked out for her.

She grinned. "Isn't it? This was a gift from one of my clients in LA."

"That's quite the largesse."

Ryan bought a round of drinks, and Jolene sipped another club soda as Ryan savored some fancy whiskey, and Sara sucked down what Jolene hoped was a watered-down Jack and Diet Coke. Then Ryan slipped into the crowd.

Jolene didn't dare keep track of Ryan, so he surprised her when he sidled up a few minutes later with Benjamin Gold, Stefano Sr.'s secretary, in tow. "I'm telling you, it's a Cartier Crash," he said to Gold, who collected watches, according to his file.

"Hey, June, can you show my friend here your watch?" Ryan played the part perfectly.

Her usual Fitbit had been replaced by an 18K rose gold watch with a Salvador Dali "melted" watch face surrounded by tiny diamonds. "Sure." She held her wrist out at an odd angle, hoping Benjamin would turn it.

Gold peered at the watch and nodded but didn't try to touch it or her. "So it is. Lovely."

Jolene pretended to catch sight of Benjamin's watch. "Is that a Jacob & Co.?" she asked.

Benjamin's eyebrows spiked. "Yes, it is." He pulled up the cuff of his shirt but didn't move any closer to Jolene. "It's an Astronomia Solar."

"Nice." And it was. Large, also circled in 18K rose gold, it contained a crystal miniature solar system that circled the watch every ten minutes beneath the clear, domed face. Jolene brushed past Ryan. "Can I take a closer look?"

Benjamin eyed her for a full three seconds, which seemed like three hours, before giving her one, sharp nod.

Jolene touched the ends of his fingers, guessing he wouldn't want her hands anywhere near his watch, and adjusted the angle of his wrist. He stiffened but didn't pull away. Benjamin's memories were remarkably similar to Ryan's, orderly and behind an even thicker veil. Jolene didn't have time to ponder options. She either busted through the wall now or tried again later when he might be inebriated and, therefore, more open. She couldn't count on another opportunity.

As if reading her distress, Sara stumbled and bumped her into Benjamin. Jolene gripped Benjamin's hand and shoulder and prepared to shove her way into his memories.

Passcode, she called out.

Bright flickers popped up everywhere. How many passcodes did this guy have? She wished she knew what his cell looked like, but she didn't, so she pictured entering the passcode on her own phone, hoping for some resonance.

"Sorry," Jolene said.

Sara grasped Benjamin's other arm and said, "Oh my God, I am so clumsy. Are you okay?"

With Benjamin's focus temporarily on Sara, he didn't notice Jolene still had hold of his hand. The memories shifted, and only a few brass-colored bubbles appeared. Jolene charged into the closest one, the bubble giving way only after a hard push.

* * *

"I'm not taking chances. I want my password changed every week," Benjamin said to Flemming, though he shouldn't have to tell the head of security how to properly do his job.

"Good," Flemming replied in an equally crisp voice. He spoke only to Benjamin like that, and Benjamin understood it was a slight. Flemming might have been in his thirties, but he acted like an adolescent. "I wish everyone was so . . . dedicated."

* * *

Getting out of the memory also took a concerted effort. Benjamin's hand twitched in hers. She'd get one more shot, if that. She leaped for a bubble close to the one forming in the moment. God, that was a handy trick. Her mental scramble created enough momentum she battered into it too hard.

"Ow!" She clutched Benjamin tighter and pretended Sara had stepped on her foot.

"Oops, sorry," Sara said, her response seamless. "I keep doing that."

* * *

Six-eight-nine-three-eight—

* * *

The memory didn't disappear like it should have but cut off like a slammed door. Benjamin jerked away his hand. A sharp pain exploded behind Jolene's right eye from the impact of the closed connection.

"Excuse me," Benjamin said and backed away from them with a curled lip, patting his suit coat over the inner pocket.

Jolene grabbed on to Sara as the room spun, agony shredding her mind, her stomach threatening to heave.

"Hey, are you okay?" Sara said, all the pretense dropping from her face.

Jolene's brain felt as if it were unraveling, thoughts spilling everywhere, nothing contained.

"Do you need some help?" Ryan said to Sara—or maybe to Jolene.

"Yeah. I think we should grab a Lyft. She gets these nasty cluster headaches." Sara giggled, but her grip on Jolene never faltered. "We don't want her spewing all over."

A few men still hanging around backed off at that, giving Jolene more room to breathe. She needed it, her lungs seeming to contract far more than expand. Black dots encroached on the edges of her vision. Colognes mixed with the stench of stale beer reminded her of past mistakes.

"I need air," Jolene said, her voice as rusty as old farm equipment.

Ryan and Sara each took an arm and slipped her out of there as if they were all on rails.

Jolene had never traveled on Amtrak. She imagined riding a train, anticipating the rocking and reverberating hum, the sound and constant motion lulling passengers to sleep.

Sleeping on a public train was dangerous. It was too easy for people to steal your shit or touch you. You might not realize it. You could be violated and never know. You could walk around like a normal person, like a regular woman who hadn't experienced sorrow or fear—

"Jolene?" Sara's voice was higher than usual.

"Climb every mountain," Jolene said, sure that was what Sara needed to hear.

"What, honey?" She gripped Jolene's waist tight enough to pinch. "Did you drink anything funny?"

Jolene shook her head. "Not alcohol. It's—" She couldn't talk about memories, but she couldn't remember why. "It's something . . . that went wrong."

"Damn it," Ryan hissed under his breath. "What do we do?"

Nothing ever flustered Ryan. They must be in big trouble if he was swearing and sounding worried.

"It'll pass. Don't worry," Jolene said. A little nap, and she could handle anything. She always knew she could be that person, and now she would be.

"Forget Lyft. I'll give you ladies a ride," Ryan said as the cold night air brushed through Jolene's clothing. He slipped an arm around her, his hand brushing her sore ribs. She whimpered, and Ryan flinched. "Are you hurt?"

"Stadler." Sara didn't say more.

Jolene tilted her hot face into the breeze. It didn't clear her head, but it did ease some of the stabbing behind her eye. Sara and Ryan weren't careful as they shoved her into the back of Ryan's silver SUV.

"Not nice," Jolene said.

Sara scooted next to her in the back seat and looped her arm across Jolene's shoulders.

"You're so pretty." Jolene tried to scratch her nose but hit her cheek, which was fine, because her cheek kind of itched too. "It's not always fun, though, right? Does it ever make you sad?"

Sara brushed a lock of hair away from Jolene's face. "I'm not a sad kind of person."

Jolene snorted and closed her eyes.

Sara nudged her. "Keep talking to me."

Jolene opened her eyes. "I met an artist. Did I tell you that?" Jolene knew she hadn't but didn't want to seem as if she'd been purposely holding back. "He's beautiful and chill."

"Wow. Beautiful *and* chill."

"He just wants to be friends, but he kissed me. His name is Cass. Ryan, do you ever kiss your friends?"

"Nope," Ryan said.

Jolene sighed. "His last girlfriend was a sex addict and cheated on him." She rested her head on Sara's shoulder. "I think that's so sad. He's got a snaggletooth."

"What?" Sara brushed Jolene's hair back again, and her cool hand felt nice.

"I'm just saying he isn't perfect." Jolene closed the eye that hurt, making her a winker too. Memories inside her—others' memories and some of her own—shifted as if they might blossom open but finally settled. Her mind slowed to a faint whir. "I think I'm going to be okay."

"You fucking better be," Sara replied. "Seriously, Jolene. I don't know what you did, but never do that again."

"Motherfucker hurled the door in my face." She sighed. "Rude."

"While you were . . .?" Ryan asked.

"It took some elbow grease to get in there. When he clammed up, his internal barriers shut down hard, and my mind was sort of stuck inside his.

It hurt. Kind of like losing a few fingers by having a car door slammed on your hand."

"Jesus," Sara said in a sigh. "Can you, uh, grow back those fingers?"

"Yep. I'm a psychic lizard." She hoped. Since this had never happened before, she was talking out her ass, but the words felt true, so she didn't consider it a lie. "I'm going to take a nap. Wake me when we get there."

"Did you reach Stadler?" Sara asked Ryan.

"He'll meet us at Jolene's," Ryan replied.

"Aw, man," Jolene said, her head lolling to rest on the window. "He's going to be so pissed."

"Why do you think that?" Ryan asked.

Jolene closed her eyes. "You know how much he hates surprises."

"You couldn't have known that would happen," Ryan said.

"He expects me to predict everything." Jolene yawned.

"You think he *expected* you to get all four codes on the first try?" Ryan asked in a very accusing tone.

"Of course he didn't. He thought I'd fail," Jolene said. She hadn't pulled her weight, and Stadler was going to tell her all about it. "This was my one shot."

Sara rubbed her arm. "Stadler likes to be a hard-ass to push you to do your best, but getting even one code is amazing."

"Hmph." Jolene's lids were heavy, sleep yanking her down.

"Tell me more about this Cass guy," Sara said with a nudge.

"Very hot." It was unfair to characterize him by only the outside packaging. "Easy to be around. He makes me laugh, so maybe he's funny?" Was he funny, or did they just get each other? "He's a super listener. He hears what isn't being said, and that's rare. He's a qigong master."

"I want to meet him and make sure he's good enough for you," Sara said.

"Sara." Ryan's voice carried a warning, but Jolene was too busy saying "sure" to think too much of it.

Ryan double-parked in front of Jolene's apartment, and Stadler opened the back passenger door, letting in a slap of cold air. Jolene peered up at him as he eased her out of the car.

"What the fuck happened?" Stadler asked, his voice tight.

Jolene didn't respond. She wanted to avoid his attention. Grumpy Stadler tended to leave bruises.

"I don't know," Sara said. "She said Gold sort of slammed the door shut while she was in his mind. She's acting like she's on a bad acid trip. We should take her to the ER, but Ryan decided you should make that call."

When the hell had they discussed hospitalization? "I don't need medical attention, just some sleep," Jolene said.

"You don't know that," Sara snapped.

"What crawled up your butt?"

Sara threw up her hands. "See? Does that seem like Jolene?"

"Let's get inside," Stadler said, still attached to Jolene's elbow. "Did Gold know you were in there?"

Was that possible? Nobody had ever felt anything—that was memory surgeon canon. But then she'd done things she shouldn't have been able to do. "Uh . . ."

"Would Gold have let her leave if he'd suspected anything?" Ryan asked.

"No," Stadler replied.

Jolene suspected something in the conversation should upset her, but she couldn't access her emotions.

Once they were settled in her apartment, Stadler held her chin still as he shone the flashlight on his phone into her eyes, making her headache roar in protest. As soon as he released her, she curled into a ball, moaning.

"Really?" Sara said from several feet away, sounding like dust at the end of a crawl space. "What made you think that was a good idea?"

"Shut up," Stadler said, much closer.

Jolene didn't want Stadler seeing her cowering. He respected stoicism and toughness and the ability to keep one's face blank.

From her spot in the corner of the sofa, Jolene managed, "I got one whole code from the list. Mario."

"Yeah?" Stadler tossed a blanket over her and held the back of his hand to her forehead as if checking for a fever.

"And I got a partial from Benjamin, but he knocked me out of the memory before I caught the last digit."

"That's okay. We'll figure out the sixth." Stadler sounded like himself now.

"This guy is anal and fussy. Probably, it's random or a mathematical puzzle or some shit. And that dude changes his code every week." The spike in her eyeball continued to stab her, but she risked a glance at Stadler.

He frowned.

Her mouth kept moving. "I got Larry's digits, too, but he's not on the list."

"Larry who?"

"How should I know? He isn't on the list." She really wanted them to leave. "All of you go home, and we'll finish this tomorrow. I'm fine, Stadler."

"Sorry, babe, but no can do. I'm staying until I'm sure you're okay."

She might have hated his presence, but it comforted her too. He wouldn't let her choke on her own vomit if she passed out. She wasn't alone.

She fell asleep sitting up on the couch, her head feeling better when she was upright rather than lying flat. Stadler woke her every few hours as if she'd sustained a concussion. The first time, she told him to fuck off. The next, she almost cried because her eyes stung so sharply. Finally, the smell of bacon frying and too much light in the living room awakened her. Her headache wasn't gone, but it had faded enough she could think.

"I like this alarm much better than the arm shove," Jolene said to Stadler as she leaned against the kitchen entryway.

Stadler grunted and flipped bacon in the spitting pan. He wore a white dress shirt tight in the biceps and rolled to his elbows, three buttons undone.

Jolene studied her socks. When had she taken off her shoes? Stadler was in his socks too.

He eyed her as if visually diagnosing her. "After you eat this, sleep in your bed. You need to rest."

"I'm scheduled to work this afternoon."

"Ryan called you in sick at the gym."

"But if anyone from the party—"

"Jolene."

"I'm fine."

"I need to be sure." He pulled the bacon out one piece at a time, shaking the grease off of each one, then blotting the strips on a paper towel. His feet were shoulder-width apart, like a fighting stance. "Nobody knew what the fuck happened to you or what to do to help, and it's not like we have anyone to ask. Could Benjamin Gold be a memory surgeon too?"

"I'm positive he isn't. The . . . assault came from, like, a different part of his mind. Nothing about the attack was sentient." She pressed her fingers into her eyes. "I can't explain any better than that."

He nodded. "Okay. Fine." He looked as if he hadn't slept in a week. "Eat and rest. Ryan's calling you in sick tomorrow too. Please don't argue."

He wasn't one to throw out a *please* willy-nilly, and she didn't want to put any more darkness under his eyes. "All right. Bacon and sleep would be awesome."

Jolene might have felt on the shitty side, but she didn't mind, because she and Stadler had made eighty-five percent peace with each other. She wanted it to last.

CHAPTER EIGHTEEN

Jolene

JOLENE WOKE ALONE LATE SUNDAY MORNING TO the lowing-cow sound of her cell on vibrate and a head more bass than treble, but better than the day before. Cass had sent her another of his epic text threads, the phone nonstop buzzing.

Hey sweet cheeks

I call you that because you have a nice ass

which is something a friend would absolutely tell another friend

when am I going to see said ass again?

why aren't you texting back?

Jolene laughed out loud, as he'd given her no time at all to respond.

I'm talking too much right?

It's not that I'm avoiding painting

I could paint anytime I want

Any

Time

Happy Halloween. Oooohhhh.

Whatcha doin?

Are you hungry?

I could bring you candy.

Or a hearty stew

It's hearty stew weather

where can I find some ready-made stew?

Do you miss me?

Jolene waited a full minute before deciding he was done blowing up her phone. She smiled, despite her shitstorm of a life, and kicked off her covers. Gingerly, she maneuvered herself into a sitting position. Her head throbbed extra hard for a few beats before sinking into low-level aching.

When she felt stabilized, she responded, *Who dis?*

Dots started, then stopped, then began anew.

You have no idea how close you just came to getting a dick pic.

She laughed and sent a crying face, though she wasn't sure if she was crying because she hadn't gotten a dick pic or because he'd almost sent one.

Seriously, though. Are you working? Want to meet for lunch or dinner? It's been a while.

Exactly two weeks. She chewed on her lip and thought about her vow to Stadler to focus exclusively on work and the delicacy of their work relationship right then.

Sorry. I'm not feeling well enough to work or go out.

Her phone rang. Cass.

"Hey," she said, regretting she'd said anything, because he would be far harder to resist on a phone call than in a few texts.

"Are you okay?"

Jolene wanted to curl up and sleep around the care in his voice. "I think so. Massive migraine." Migraine was close enough to the truth.

"Can I bring you anything? Medicine? Food? I wasn't kidding about the stew—well, kind of, because I don't know where to find any, but it's Chicago in fall, someone's selling stew. Should I fetch you some?"

Cass always asked what she needed, never assuming he knew best. Surely, it was okay to see him when she couldn't work anyway, what with her brain the building equivalent of a box of tissues. Besides, Halloween was a holiday. She needed supplies, medicinal and social, and relying on Cass was textbook time management.

"Campbell's Chicken Noodle Soup and some crackers?" It was what she'd eaten as a child when she'd felt poorly. "Do you think I'll get trick-or-treaters here? Maybe you should bring candy just in case."

* * *

Cass showed up in less than an hour, bringing his scent of citrus and leather and spice and comfort. His Blackhawks T-shirt fit perfectly, formfitting without being too tight, like his faded jeans.

He hung his leather jacket next to hers on a peg by the door and then delivered his Jewel bag of groceries straight to her kitchen. He unloaded two bags of candy, seven cans of soup, and a package of low-sodium oyster crackers onto the counter.

"Seven cans?" she asked with a laugh.

He rubbed the back of his neck, drawing attention to his thick, beautiful hair. "Better to have too many than not enough."

Jolene kissed his cheek. "Thanks."

He'd brought her a bag of suckers and a variety of miniature candy bars. She didn't care for hard candy, so the suckers would be safe, but he'd have to take any leftover chocolate home with him.

"How're your ribs?" He sounded casual, but his mouth was tight and his eyes too sharp.

"Much better." She leaned against the counter. "So, painting not going well?"

He blew air through his lips like a horse. "Nothing feels right or looks right. I'm trying to push through, but I can't stop thinking I'm wasting canvas." He grinned at her. "I brought you a present."

Her chest flushed cold, then hot, and she broke out in a sweat. "You did?" Nobody ever gave her presents.

"Ta-da!" He extracted a cat-ears headband from the bag.

They were cute and fun and completely pointless. "Thank you."

He gestured toward the living room. "Why don't you sit down, and I'll heat up some soup for us?"

She slid the headband on as she retreated to the couch.

Cass followed like a devoted servant, fluffing a blanket over her once she'd situated herself. "Want something to drink? Water?"

"Sure, thanks."

Cass was a world-class pamperer, tucking and fussing. He brought her a glass of water with three ice cubes. "Can I grab you a book to read?"

She chuckled. "Dude, it takes two minutes to heat up soup."

"I don't expect you to entertain me." He squeezed her foot through the blanket. "I'm here to make sure you're okay and to keep you company."

"You're here because you can't paint and want a distraction," she countered.

"Believe me, Jolene, I have a list as long as my legs of things I can do to procrastinate when I'm creatively blocked. I'm here because you're not feeling well, and I missed you."

"You did?" She sounded altogether too needy, but his attention made her crave more.

His gaze grew soft, his lips hinting at a smile, and something flipped in her chest. He reached out and tucked a stray lock of hair behind her ear, his fingers caressing the curve of her jaw. The intensity of feeling welling in her gut made her look down to keep from blurting out God knew what. Everything.

Cass kissed the top of her head, and she reminded herself he was affectionate that way. It didn't mean he wanted more. She imagined how marvelous it would feel, if only for a little while, to have Cass love her.

"Here you go," Cass said two minutes later, setting a bowl of soup on the coffee table, a small ramekin of oyster crackers next to it.

"Where's yours?"

He grinned. "It's heating up now."

She waited for him, and they slurped their soup side by side, bent over the coffee table. It was as delicious as she remembered.

Cass spent the entire day with her. Every moment felt both right and wrong. Stadler texted twice to check on her, and each time, her stomach dipped and twisted. But she'd missed Cass so much, she didn't contemplate sending him away.

Sara texted a GIF of a cat with an ice pack balanced on its head and asked how she was doing. Jolene told Sara she'd just eaten soup, and Sara wanted to know how she'd gotten it—because she was a snoopy bitch who'd apparently cataloged the contents of Jolene's kitchen.

Jolene told Sara that Cass was there and hoped she wouldn't tell Stadler. Sara did seem like a sisters-before-misters kind of woman, but she also liked to stir up trouble.

As soon as Jolene sent the text, she realized she should have said she'd had soup delivered via DoorDash.

Sara sent a *squee!* GIF and a request for photographic proof.

"My friend wants me to send a picture of you." Jolene winced at the grade-school vibe, though she wouldn't mind having a photo of Cass for herself.

"Face pic or dick pic?"

Jolene laughed. "What's with you and dick pics today? She'd definitely prefer a dick pic, but I'm not going to encourage her." She held up her phone, suddenly feeling awkward. "I don't have to; she's not the boss of me."

He grinned and shrugged. "Go ahead."

It took four tries to get a decent photo. Of course, in that take, he looked amazing. Then he wrapped his arm around her and pulled her into his chest.

"Take one of us together," he said, resting his cheek on top of her head. Cass wanted her to send a copy to him, so she did. It took most of her willpower not to assume anything because he wanted a photo of them.

They looked like a couple, a happy couple. She sent the good one of Cass alone to Sara, not comfortable with how she might respond to the photo of her and Cass together.

Sara responded with several emojis, including bug-eyes and quite a few eggplants. *Must meat. On my way.*

Ha, meat. Then Jolene considered what would happen next. Shit.

Jolene squinted at Cass. "She's coming over, and I can't stop her. That woman is a force of chaos. Do you want to go?"

"No way. I want to meet her." He pulled Jolene's feet onto his lap, dug into her instep, and spoke no more words.

She focused on the firm hold he had on her foot and the delicious pressure of his thumbs. Her headache turned a corner, one step toward the background of her mind. Part of her wanted him to meet Sara, to take the step of introducing him to her friends.

She imagined living with Cass and having some version of this every night. Some nights, though, she would rub his hands, which would be cramped from all the painting. Or his neck and shoulders. They might run together in the mornings or evenings. She might learn to cook, to assist him in the kitchen or do the meal prep and cleaning. They'd need a king-sized bed, because Jolene occasionally thrashed in her sleep, but they would fall asleep curled into each other, his breath on the back of her neck, his arm around her waist, the breadth of his chest pressed into her back.

* * *

Sara arrived dressed like a sexy vampire, complete with a cape, carrying one of those old-fashioned ice packs like the one her GIF cat had worn and a get-well card featuring an old guy in a surgical gown that gaped in the back, his saggy ass cheeks on display.

Jolene laughed and hissed, "Don't fuck this up for me," as she hugged Sara before gesturing to Cass. "Sara, this is Cass. Cass, this is Sara."

Cass extended his hand. "Nice to meet you."

"You too." Sara shook his hand. "I've heard so much about you." Her voice was a teasing purr, and Jolene almost smacked herself for introducing Cass to the most beautiful woman she had ever met.

"Mostly positive things, I hope?" Cass smiled at Sara, but he wasn't cartoon-bug-eyed staring.

"Oh yeah. She's quite the fan." Sara laughed and grinned at Jolene, then tweaked her cat ears.

Shut. Up.

Jolene glared hard at Sara—so hard her headache returned like a curtain call. "Let's sit down."

"It's mutual fandom," Cass replied, sitting next to Jolene on the couch. "How do you guys know each other?"

"We work together," Sara said, ignoring the armchair and pulling the coffee table back a foot to sit there instead, probably to mess with Jolene with her proximity. Sara loved to do the unexpected. "Best buddies. I've known Jolene for years, so if you want to hear any embarrassing stories, I am here for you."

What was Sara up to? She didn't have any misadventures at work to share. Except for the incident with Colton, of course, and nothing about that was *embarrassing* or remotely sharable. Had Stadler warned Sara about Cass with orders to scare him off to force Jolene to focus on the mission?

Cass skated a hand up and down Jolene's back, the contact light and comforting. "I think she's been traumatized enough for one day," Cass said. "So, you work for the medical-billing company? Or are you a personal trainer too?"

Sara laughed her throaty laugh. "I'm not really an exerciser. I just have good genes." She winked at Cass and, perhaps sensing her impending murder, shifted her focus to Jolene. "How're you feeling?"

"Better."

"Did you just move to Chicago too?" Cass asked.

Sara didn't hesitate. "Oh, no, I've lived here for years. Jolene and I were virtual friends from the moment she started with the company. And now we're in the same city, so we can be real, live pals."

Cass smiled. Jolene worked hard not to show her anxiety. Sara was spinning a tale without any idea what Jolene might have already said.

She should be letting Jolene take the lead, but Sara couldn't help her recklessness. She had a Loki nature, and if she were caught in a lie, there would be no consequences for her.

Jolene stood. "Sara, can I talk to you a second in the kitchen?"

"No need," Sara said with a contradictory smirk. "I'll be good."

Cass watched them like a ping-pong match.

"Kitchen." Jolene shoved the heel of her hand into her eye socket to counter the sharp pain that speared her.

"You said you were better." All the mischief died in Sara's eyes. "I thought you—you're not fully recovered?"

"I'm fine, just tired."

"Should we go?" Sara asked.

We? Jolene wanted to tell Sara that *she* should go. She was already pushing her luck by allowing Sara to witness her breaking the rules—not that Sara knew about the deal or would narc if she did. But if Sara let slip to Stadler that Cass had been in her apartment, he might cut out all access.

"Probably a good idea. I have to get ready for trick-or-treaters, anyway." She walked her guests to the door.

"I'm going to do some trick-or-treating before I go home," Sara said. "Do you think it's too early?"

Jolene laughed, unsurprised Sara had no qualms about going from house to house by herself, as an adult, looking for candy.

Cass shrugged. "It's after five and close enough to dark. I think you can go for it."

They walked out together, talking about favorite Halloween costumes, leaving Jolene alone with sweets she couldn't eat and a chest that wouldn't stop aching.

CHAPTER NINETEEN

Jolene

JOLENE CONTINUED HER COVER AT THE HEALTH club as they waited for Jorge to do whatever he did with the information she had collected after the birthday party. Meanwhile, she worked to cozy up to anyone at the gym with a connection to the Stefano organization, needing a work victory to counter her thoughts of Cass.

Unfortunately, the Stefano crew kept to themselves, and every inquiry or friendliness she threw out was smacked back hard. Stefano Jr. came in every Friday, but he brought two giant bodyguards with him who screamed *fuck off* without saying a word. She couldn't get close enough to determine even the color of his eyes before being curtly rebuffed.

There were huge chunks of time with no clients. When she wasn't lifting or running, she occupied herself with some form of moving meditation. The movements settled her mind but also reminded her of Cass.

She forwarded him articles about painter's block, and he sent her strange photos, like the corner of a painted canvas and his tattooed arm from the elbow down holding a paintbrush or stirring something in the kitchen. The lighting varied, giving some photos a haunted quality and others an effervescent glow. He created moods and interesting compositions. She prodded him to let her see his artwork.

In the meantime, she looked him up online, finding several images of him and his work. Despite knowing he would hate it, she studied his paintings. Most were monochromatic but with multiple shades and hues. Zooming in, she spotted textures both rough and smooth, along with shapes—no, *shapes* wasn't the right word. There weren't identifiable circles or squares, but swirls and swoops and angles.

Jolene hadn't the discernment to tell if he was talented, but she couldn't stop looking at his work. She wanted to see a painting in person, run her fingertips over the surface and touch what he'd created. She wanted him to trust her enough to share his art. Then again, why should he trust her when she hadn't trusted him with her secret?

She'd never wanted to tell anyone she was a memory surgeon—until now. If she told Cass about her gift, maybe he would show her his work.

Would it be worth the risk?

By the end of the week, she began to think it might be.

* * *

CASS STOPPED OVER ONE NIGHT AFTER NINE, CLAIMING HE NEEDED TO ascertain how she was progressing with her qigong practice. She didn't turn him away, though she knew it violated her agreement with Stadler, and she didn't have any sort of illness excuse this time. But his presence awakened something inside her, something she wanted to cultivate.

He guided her through a series of movements for half an hour, their bodies syncing. Jolene's frenzied mind flattened like a lake without wind, an unbroken reflection of the sky.

Afterward, they sat cross-legged on the floor and worked through a few breathing exercises. Jolene propped her back against the couch. Cass faced her two feet away.

"Tell me one thing nobody knows about you," Cass said after they'd finished. He sounded halfway to sleep.

This was her chance. But when she opened her mouth, the words stuck inside like a dry-swallowed horse pill.

She could work up to the memory-surgeon reveal. Until then, she would tell him something she hadn't told anyone, a recollection painful enough to make her squirm to avoid sharing.

"When I was eleven, I was walking home from school and there was this bigger kid on the sidewalk with a box of kittens his family was giving away for free. There were only two left, and I asked if I could have both so they wouldn't be lonely."

Cass shifted to watch her, chest forward, elbows on his knees, as she told the story, and she found his attention comforting.

"I named them Bernadette and Hank, after my parents who died when I was five."

"I'm sorry," Cass said, resting his hand on her knee.

Jolene waved her hand. "It was a long time ago." She swallowed, though the ghost of the pill remained. "Anyway, I brought the kittens home, and my grandmother sort of looked at me and these two kittens in a box, and then she went out and bought all the cat stuff you need—dishes, litterbox, toys."

"Uh-huh."

"She was pretty cool that way. But when I told her what I'd named them, she got this look on her face and told me it was spiteful to name animals after them. I hadn't done it because of that, but I got so angry at her—for making assumptions, for lecturing me, for being so protective of—" She blew out a breath and unfolded her legs to hug her knees to her chest. "I don't know. I was eleven and resentful and embarrassed, so I said that if they didn't want to be pets, then they shouldn't have died." She smiled at Cass and grimaced. "Didn't go over so well."

"Did she make you give up your cats?"

Jolene shook her head. "That's not the point of the story." Resting her chin on her knees, she closed her eyes and tried to remember and not remember. "I named them after my parents because I couldn't recall much of them. All I know is my mom used to sing me bedtime stories, just make them up and a tune to match. She had long, brown hair and the kind of smile that showed her gums. That's it. My dad—he had a scratchy voice, like a cowboy who smoked, and a laugh that was more of a wheeze. He was tall. They loved me, I think, but I don't remember."

Cass scooted closer and wrapped his hands around her ankles, his face near hers. "That must have been hard."

She nodded. "Here's the . . . the point to the story, the secret, if you will. I didn't think the kittens were my parents reincarnated. But . . . I also didn't *not* think that. Part of my kid brain thought their spirits or whatever might be attracted to them because the animals had their names, and although it wasn't likely, it was *possible* that through the kittens they might, you know, share something with me. Like, cats feel things and want things, like food and sleep and attention, and people feel and want some of the same things, and there had to be these moments when they felt like my parents had felt. And even if I didn't know at that moment I was connected to my parents, at least consciously, it would still be . . . something."

Jolene tapped her forehead and chuckled. "It made sense to my kid self."

"And did you? Feel those things?" He stroked a hand up and down her calf, the contact soothing and only tangentially sexual.

She sighed. "Turned out I was allergic to cats. I wanted to keep them anyway, not caring about the red eyes and congestion or headaches. I told my grandmother I was fine, but in retrospect, I clearly wasn't. It was a pretty bad reaction. One day, I came home from school, and they were gone." Tears pricked her eyes, so unexpected and insistent that she couldn't shut them down. She blinked and swallowed until a measure of control returned. "So, I kind of lost my parents a second time." She sniffed and canted her head to the side. "And I never got to say goodbye. Again."

Cass rose onto his knees and slipped a hand behind her neck, holding her in place as he kissed her tear-streaked face, cheeks to eyelids, his chest pressed to her still-folded legs. He didn't say anything, though, which she appreciated. For some situations, there were no words.

"What about you?" she asked. She hadn't shared her gift, but she'd revealed deep muscle tissue, and she wanted him to stop looking at it.

Cass stroked her hair and gave her a soft kiss. The sensations coursing through her ran fathomless and thick, something desperate and comforting, like love. Her lungs were shaky, her fingertips numb from gripping one another. The kiss was more than casual but less than sexual, and it blanketed her in warmth and want.

He scooted next to her, his back also against the couch now, though he stretched his legs in front of him, his white socks a decent focal point for Jolene.

"During one of my tours in Afghanistan, I was deployed with my spotter, Tom Daniels, who everybody called Brick—it's a long story. But anyway, Brick and I had been out there for over a month, not seeing enough action, and we were itching for it. You do all that training, and you naturally want to use it. Excitement and dread build up rather than cancel each other out. It's weird. We didn't want to die or kill people, but we wanted to be part of something. Right before the first big mission we had—three platoons in a synchronized attack—I caught some nasty-ass bug. High fever and it was coming out every which way."

Jolene winced in sympathy.

"I couldn't go. It killed me to see all those guys kitted up and balls-to-the-wall ready, and I was struggling to keep down water." He shook his head. "Man, I tried to go, but Sergeant Varga took one look at me and ordered me to lie down before he sent me to the MTF—that's like an army hospital. Everything in me hurt to watch them go without me, and all I could do was sprawl on my ass and wait. Couldn't even go down to the ready room and listen." Cass threaded his fingers with hers. "And, as I'm sure you've already guessed, the mission didn't go down as planned. It went FUBAR fast."

"FUBAR?"

He smirked. "Fucked up beyond all repair."

"Can only military people use that? Because that fits my life perfectly." She only partially kidded.

"I don't think they've trademarked it, so go ahead."

She squeezed his hand. "Sorry, I interrupted. Go on."

"It was an ambush, and here's the thing . . ." He swallowed with a clicking noise. "Snipers are sent in for two reasons: to take out HVTs—that's high-value targets—and to cover our guys. We're there mostly for protection, but we usually take out more enemy combatants than anyone else, so we're often among the first targeted by the other side."

She didn't like where this story was headed, meandering into loss and heartbreak.

"Brick was mad-skilled, but if you don't have the right position, you're just fucked." Cass slanted a glance at Jolene. "He didn't die—you look worried, so—so—" He took a moment, stillness wrapped around him like armor. "We lost one of ours and sustained a few injuries, including Brick. He got shot in the thigh, but our medics are badass motherfuckers, and they saved him. But eventually, his leg—infection and—"

Jolene waited, unsure if he needed something from her or just a few seconds to compose himself.

"I couldn't stop thinking that I should have been there and wondering what would have turned out differently. Brick . . . He wasn't mad or anything. I physically could not have gone on that mission, but that fact doesn't prevent my mind from perpetually running over the situation, picturing how I could have saved the other guy and prevented Brick's injury."

"Or been killed yourself," Jolene said.

"True." He leaned his arm against hers. "I'd rather have been there, no matter how it would have turned out. And I hate how I'll never know if I could have made a difference. Sometimes I think if I run it through my mind often enough, I can figure it out, even if it doesn't make rational sense." Cass tilted his head to rest on her shoulder. "Adults also have that inner child in us who have these mystical ideas of what might be achieved or accomplished, even when we should know better."

"How's Brick now? Do you keep in touch?"

Cass nestled his nose against her throat, and Jolene closed her eyes to capture the moment. "He's adjusted to it, but I still struggle. We've seen each other a bunch of times. He's one of those positive people who keeps a sense of humor and perspective through everything."

Like Sara.

"He told me there's nothing he could do before that he can't do with his prosthesis, and he's glad to be alive. I believe it, too, that he's grateful he lived, but something so life-changing . . . I don't think it's something you just accept and then you're done. I think you have to accept it over and over again."

Jolene basked in the tickle of his breath on her neck. "All trauma is like that, I think. You have to keep acknowledging it too. Nobody can save everyone, and some people are lucky if they can save themselves."

"True."

They sat that way for almost an hour, and Jolene might have remained there longer if her right ass cheek hadn't gone numb. She'd never done that before, communed with someone in silence, letting their companionship ease something delicate inside her. Regrets dominated her life, but sitting with Cass made each sting a little less potent, his presence a balm and a gift.

And having him in her life was worth the risk—from Stadler and from her heart.

CHAPTER TWENTY

Jolene

On Friday, Jolene sat at her favorite spot in the AA circle, thinking about Cass and picking at a hangnail, vowing to moisturize better. She looked up when Stefano Jr. entered the room.

He had a lean lankiness that lent him elegance and the impression he was smooth enough to slip under doors or through keyholes. He had the aura of a master thief. His sandy-blond hair was cut short, probably because of the fineness, which would lie too limp or fluffy if he grew it out.

When Jolene noticed him, she gaped for a second, two tops. Unlike at the gym, he had no bodyguards, and the AA meeting worked its magic on him like it did on everyone else. Out in the world, they all had the pressure of appearances and expectations. At a meeting, the only expectation was harsh honesty. It stripped a person, which alcoholics needed. Lies to yourself easily festered and led to drinking.

Stefano wore an expensive suit with oxfords that shone, and his demons lurked on his face in the lines around his mouth.

"I'm Stef," he said.

"Hi, Stef," the group replied.

"I've been sober eight months, one week, and two days," he said.

Jolene smiled despite her heart darting around like a cat with its tail on fire. She remembered counting each minute and hour of her sobriety, building a tower of days tall enough that she no longer felt mired down. Not that that feeling ever went away.

"It's been stressful," Stefano said.

The cat inside her stilled, then ran faster. Was it possible she'd garner some juicy intelligence without using her gift at all? Probably not. An AA meeting might be a judgment-free zone, but she doubted he would talk about his involvement in a criminal empire.

"My father is pushing me. I've made a decision to make a change, but . . . I'm still not sure I'm doing the right thing."

What? Stefano Jr. planned to break away from his father? Her team had heard nothing about that, as far as she knew. What kind of change? Her palms grew slick. How could she use this to push his thoughts?

"Loyalty is everything to my family," Stefano went on, "but I . . ." He shook his head. "Isn't it crucial to do what's right?"

Digging into people's stories was verboten in AA, so she swallowed questions down, where they heated her stomach. She'd burst soon.

"I want a drink so badly," Stefano said. "Just one, you know? To ease my nerves."

The room was filled with heads shaking—*don't do it*—and heads nodding—*yeah, I get that*. Jolene found herself in the nodding group. Alcohol actually fixed a lot in the moment. It just didn't keep things fixed, and then it made everything worse.

After the meeting, people would likely give Stefano encouragement and warnings, support and little barbs to remind him of the perils and stakes. Jolene wouldn't ordinarily do that, but this was an opportunity for her to crack underneath Stef's pain for the greater good.

Jolene didn't always share at these meetings. Most of the time, she soaked in the camaraderie, the collective trauma of having failed everyone, the lack of judgment. But if she shared, maybe he'd be open to her approach after the meeting, and when she touched him, she might find something useful.

Except . . . damn it all. Could she violate someone in recovery like her?

Nietzsche said, *Fear is the mother of morality.* Jolene always thought that meant the fear of being ostracized if you didn't conform shaped many of society's morals. But right then, she experienced a more sinister interpretation. Her fear of failure was tilting her moral compass into the red, tempting her deeper into karmic debt. She could end-justify-the-means herself into becoming someone she couldn't respect . . . again. There had to be an uncrossable line.

Finally, she had the opportunity to speak. "Hello, everyone, I'm June." She still hated using her cover name at these meetings, though now that Stefano Jr. had shown up, it was good she did.

As usual, she stuck to the truth as much as possible. "I've been struggling at work." Would Stefano recognize her from GCHC? Guys like him rarely noticed others unless they wanted something from them. "Fitness is my new addiction, and I have to admit I'm pretty smug about it, like physical activity taken to an extreme is somehow still healthy." She swallowed. "Every time I try to take a day off, I get this itching under my skin. Like, if I stop moving, I'll fall right back into drinking. It's been five years, and I'm so grateful for that, but . . . I'm so tired of the terror of failing, of being afraid I'll misplace focus for one moment and lose everything."

Everyone nodded, even Stefano, though Jolene made an effort to look at nobody for very long except the facilitator. "But I feel better when I'm here. I mean, if a drink were to magically appear to tempt me, I'm sure someone here would smack it out of my hand."

A few people smiled. One middle-aged guy in a suit that rivaled Stefano's laughed, a short bark she liked for how unsophisticated it sounded. A laugh like that had to be genuine.

She shrugged. "Anyway, nothing pressing or anything. I'm just glad to have this break."

Stefano had said something similar, and she hoped that might initiate a potential bond.

After the meeting, she maneuvered herself close to the refreshment table near the door, the burned-coffee smell bolstering her. If Stefano wanted a quick exit, she could snag him, and if he lingered, she could drift his way in a seemingly natural manner. He didn't bolt for the door, but he kept his eyes down, as if shy, ashamed, or struggling internally. Or all three.

Jolene shook hands with a few others, priming the psychic pump. Each time, memories flared and pulsed. Eventually, she and Stefano faced each other.

"I appreciate what you shared," she said, holding out her hand. "June."

He looked at her hand but didn't shake it.

She kept talking. "I have issues with both my parents, so I get it." The mention of her parents stabbed through her rib cage, as it always did, but her words broke the spell, and Stefano put his hand in hers.

"Yeah? Sorry to hear that."

In his mind, she found the biggest memory bubble she'd ever seen. Taller than her, scarlet red, and fluttering, it zoomed toward her, as if Stefano could barely contain it. The edges of his consciousness groaned as if wanting to close. It reminded her of Gold's consciousness before it had slammed down on her. But this was her white whale, and she had to try.

* * *

"What if someone wants to pat me down?" Stefano asked as Agent Wild taped the wire to his bare skin. His armpits were slick, and his deodorant was failing, the stink of fear pouring out of his pores, and this was only a test run. What would he do when he was at the Merchandise Mart with his father, most of his crew, and those out-of-town allies?

"You and your father are showing up at the last minute. They aren't going to stop to frisk the two of you," Wild said with a confidence he could afford because he didn't actually know Stefano's father.

"What if my dad finds it?" Stefano wanted out of this world but not at the cost of his life. He couldn't pull it off. His father had an uncanny nose for deceit. When in his entire life had he ever gotten anything over on his old man? He couldn't act natural with panic hijacking his veins.

"We'll protect you," Wild said, though the words failed to reassure Stefano. Anytime anyone assumed something with his father would be easy, it blew up in their face. "At the first sign of trouble, we'll come."

"But I don't have the details—the time, the floor and room, the route. They'll probably block off part of the building and have guys everywhere." Stefano attempted to curb his panic. He'd already asked more than once, but he tried again. "Can't you just take the computer stuff and make a case from that?" It would be over once they analyzed the bookkeeping.

"We will, but we have an opportunity here to do more." Wild displayed no signs of irritation, only sympathy. "With evidence of what you say is going to happen, we can damage at least four different crime organizations. It's only an extra week, but it's your call."

Bile splashed up his throat. They were going to get him killed. The Feds. The goddamned Feds.

* * *

STEFANO'S ANXIETY SWALLOWED HER. STEFANO JR. WAS WORKING WITH—

"The Feds," Jolene muttered, confusion tackling her anxiety, mixing it with a giddy sort of disbelief. Stefano—

"What did you just say?" Stefano Jr.'s face turned the color of bone, his lips a too-vivid red. He jerked his hand away.

Oh shit. Shit, shit, shit.

She had to fix this. Jolene squeezed her hand against her thigh, as if to prevent it from going rogue. "I said . . . the . . . fest thing you can do is be true to yourself."

He needed to believe she'd said *best* and not *Fed,* so she'd split the difference. It could work to cover her mistake. The words were close. Close-ish.

Stefano frowned at her as if she were toxic and not at all as if he'd bought her revised word.

"What are you talking about?" His complexion had gone beyond white to a pale shade of green.

Fuck.

They were on the same side, but Jolene lacked the qualifications to swim in the political river of governmental agencies. She couldn't share her role in the Agency, but Stefano Jr. appeared seconds away from a panic attack.

She tried a sympathetic hand on his shoulder, but he jerked away.

Jolene smiled, acting as if she didn't notice his discomfort. "I was just commiserating with your position." From his wide eyes, she'd said the wrong thing again. "With your family's expectations. I can relate. Do the next right thing, yeah?"

Those words didn't comfort him. His forehead glistened with sweat.

Jolene had no clue how to ease his worry and hold her cover. Stefano Jr.'s terror still rang through her mind, his adrenaline tripping her own body to pump out stress hormones. If he comprehended that another agency had their eyes on him, it would spiral his paranoia. He wouldn't be wrong either, because the more people who knew, the more opportunities for the secret to slip into the wrong ears.

What made everything worse was that the next right thing for her was clear. Come clean to him and Stadler and let the various bosses work it out.

She intended to do neither.

A fuckup on this level would bench her, and not in Chicago. Stadler would send her back to Virginia, and there'd be no more Cass, and no more atoning for her past on the scale she needed. And for what? So Stefano Jr.'s anxiety could escalate until his panic triggered a misstep. No, keeping quiet may not be the "right" thing, but it was the safest—for everyone.

Jolene needed to believe that.

"Do you know who I am?" Stefano Jr. asked.

She doubled down on her ignorance. "Stef, right?" Thank God she remembered his introduction. "But, really, who we are doesn't matter, right?"

She had to stop saying *right*.

"But you-you said—"

"You're not alone." He didn't look any happier to hear those words as he did the others. "All I was trying to say is that I'm a friend, and I take the anonymous part of AA seriously. Your secrets are safe."

"You guys okay?" the meeting facilitator asked. Tom? Tim? Yes, Tim.

"Yeah," Jolene and Stefano Jr. said simultaneously.

Tim looked between them and nodded. "Didn't mean to interrupt. I'm just going to start putting up the chairs."

"I gotta go," Stefano Jr. said, his voice a little louder than necessary. Then he scrambled out the door like a rat with a ferret chasing him.

Jolene picked up a chair and began a stack to add to Tim's. He smiled at her efforts.

What she'd learned from Stefano was progress. But the quandry of how to tell Stadler what she'd learned, while avoiding sharing that she'd let *The Feds* slip out of her mouth, made her stomach yowl like a newborn. He'd only given her one more chance.

CHAPTER TWENTY ONE

Walther

WALTHER STARED OUT THE WINDOW JUST beyond Darby's shoulder, not caring if his boss thought he was paying attention or not. The view from Walther's shit position with his back to the conference room door was an iron sky and the roof of the building next door.

The neighborhood was working class, but Darby had sunk serious dough into rehabbing the interior of this building, giving his office a high-end, glass-and-steel look. It didn't match Darby's personality, but it wasn't meant to.

Ultimately, the space was designed to give Darby a sophistication he didn't possess on his own. He was old-school, crass, and craggy, a blunt, bloody instrument that couldn't appear otherwise, no matter how fancy the drawer that held him.

Walther had been trying his boss's patience, and he didn't care. His mother had died two years ago, and his brother had been dead not even two months. Walther had no family left, and what was more important than family?

"We boring you?" Darby asked. He was all nose and hunched shoulders. In his sixties, Darby hadn't aged well.

Walther should have been embarrassed at being called out in front of another lieutenant, of fucking up his responsibilities within the Red Flames. Darby wasn't the forgiving sort, and he'd already cut Walther a good deal of slack. Walther yanked his thoughts back to the room and attempted to concentrate.

"I got a lot on my mind is all," he said.

Pat Lawsom, the only other person in the room, snorted. "I know what's got his panties all bunched."

Walther turned his wintry stare to the other man, an atomic rage splintering the ice around his control. The man was only five years older than Walther, but he'd already sprouted a middle-aged paunch, and his face had turned fleshy, especially around the eyes, giving him a piglike appearance.

Mention his name, you fat fuck. Say it.

Lawsom had somehow lost his talent for detecting and evading trouble. Walther needed to kill someone, and Lawsom would do.

"I seen the photo, and I was like, 'Ain't that Saff?' And sure enough, there she is with her tits all smashed into some goon's chest. I mean, it's one thing to move on, and something else to lift your skirts to muscle." Lawsom chuckled, his face pinking with pleasure.

Walther registered his words. "You saw a picture of Saffron?"

"Yeah, out in Chicago with one of Stefano's goons. Posted it on the Instagram for everyone to see. You don't forget a body like that. Sweet Jesus, it had to hurt to lose that piece of ass." Lawsom snorted again, his amusement hiding a thin blade inside it.

Stupid fuck. He'd just given Walther exactly what he'd been searching for. He stood up, and both men jerked in reaction. Walther strode over, grabbed Lawsom's face, and planted a kiss on his forehead.

Walther barely managed a goodbye. He had a flight to Chicago to book.

CHAPTER TWENTY TWO

Jolene

By the time Jolene unlocked her door, she hadn't come up with a good enough story yet, but she'd sent a text to Stadler. Telling him she had a headache but would check in with him tomorrow bought her some time to formulate the perfect story and to decide exactly how much of Stefano Jr.'s memory to share.

She decided to soak in an epsom salt bath for her achy muscles from too much exercise and let relaxation stoke her creative side. Aside from the asinine blurt, she'd done good, carried her own weight. Her gift had exposed information sure to aid them in their mission. If she could sidestep the mistake, she'd be looking uber competent.

Before filling the tub, she sent a semi-flirty text to Cass, telling him she missed him. They might wrap up this case soon, and she intended to take a few weeks off. She was going to ask if he'd be willing to try dating properly.

Jolene used Spotify to play some pump-up-the-volume music that conflicted greatly with the idea of relaxing but lit a peony-scented candle to compensate. She closed her eyes and let the excitement of everything coming together vibrate through her like Frankenstein's monster struck by lightning.

"It's alive," she whisper-yelled to herself.

Her cell rang, cutting off the music.

Cass.

"Hey," she said, letting her smile infuse her voice. She tried not to slosh or splash to give away her location.

"Hey yourself, beautiful," he replied. His voice on speakerphone echoed in the bathroom. "Listen, I finished a painting for a showing."

"That's great!"

"I think I'm ready. I know you asked for space, but is there any chance you can come over and see it?"

She giggled. "Yes."

This was exactly what she needed to push the dread away and embrace how awesome a discovery she'd unearthed. Just the timbre of his voice infused her with hope and excitement. She couldn't stop grinning or wiggling her feet in the hot water.

"I'll make us dinner, anything you want," Cass said. "I get you're busy—"

"I already said yes." She'd earned herself as much time with him as she wanted. "Are you plying me with food because the painting is that awful or that awesome?"

"You'll have to tell me."

She should have asked for a chicken breast and fresh salad, but this was a double celebration, even if he didn't know it. "Steak and potatoes?"

"You got it. When can you come over?"

His calling was a sign everything would work out. It was as if the universe had whispered to him about her change in fate, and he was as eager as she to move forward. Every shitty thing that had ever happened to her would now be cast in a rosy glow because of where she'd landed.

Tonight, she'd tell him she was a memory surgeon. No more excuses. She trusted him—they trusted each other—and this would only bring them closer.

"I can be there in an hour."

* * *

LOUD MUSIC CAME FROM THE MASTER BEDROOM, AND JOLENE WONDERED if he'd been adding finishing touches to the painting. Cass still wore his working clothes—worn, paint-spattered jeans and a likewise streaked white T-shirt. The fit of both was relaxed, but neither hid his athletic body.

His eyes were bloodshot, hair loose, a bit unkempt, and tumbling over one eye. She launched a hug his way, assuming his enthusiasm would match her own, but he'd clearly lost his ebullient mood. She wondered how many hours in a row he'd labored over his work. The force of the embrace couldn't be curbed in time, but she eased her arms around his neck instead of wrapping herself around him like a spider monkey.

The scent of roasting meat made her salivate and her stomach gurgle. "Hi, stranger." She held herself back from nibbling on the plump earlobe so close to her mouth.

"Hey," he said, his smile wide but lacking something.

"What's wrong?" she asked.

His face fell, and he bit his lip, his eyes cutting to the studio room. "I—I don't want to show you my work just yet."

"Okay." She grabbed his shoulders and gave him a playful shake. "You worry too much." The idea that she was berating someone else for worrying made her smile.

He nodded. "I know."

She followed him into his galley kitchen and perched on the counter, swinging her feet. Cass completed each task of preparing dinner as if he were being graded.

"Hey, if I don't like the painting, I can offer you a blow job."

Cass stopped in mid-search of a drawer for utensils to mix the salad she hadn't requested.

She shrugged. "That way, you can relax. The worst thing to come out of this evening would be a blow job. Pretty sweet, right?" Now that she was free—mostly—she saw they'd always been more than friends. Oral sex wasn't the best place to start when trying to begin a real relationship, but at least it snagged his attention.

He snorted, then shook his head. "You're nuts."

"Hey, this is a low-bar testimonial, but I've never gotten any complaints on my oral skills." She was going to push until he laughed or passed out from embarrassment.

"Good to know," he said, back to searching the drawer, his movements jerky and self-conscious.

"One guy even said it made my personality tolerable." A man really had said that to her once, and it had stung at the time, but it didn't now. Now, it was funny.

But not funny enough.

"You need to find a better class of lover, Jolene."

She was trying to, but he was *not* helping. "I said it was a low bar." She chuffed a laugh. "It wasn't even during my alcoholic days. I was—"

Holy shit, she'd almost told him she was a memory surgeon. She'd almost blabbed that she'd gone through a brief period when she'd screwed on the regular as a way to keep the torture memories at bay. That wasn't how she wanted to tell him.

She had to recover. *Ha, recover.* "You may find this hard to believe, but this is the most together I've ever been."

He still didn't smile. "Why wouldn't I believe that?"

"Cass." For once in her life, she thought she might have enough happiness for two. Jolene wanted to be open with him. "Your friendship means more to me than you'll ever know. I feel like you see me without judging. I can be myself—no, not just myself, but my best self. It's—"

His shoulders stiffened.

"I'm being too mushy, I know. I just want you to understand you're not the unfocused mess you tell yourself—"

A crimson haze blurred her vision. At first, all she saw was an image—a black gun with a silencer tucked behind a canvas. Then details pinged her. Glock 17 with a threaded barrel and suppressor. Anxiety. A heart that wouldn't slow. Orders. Duty. Death.

Cass's memory hit her like a backfist to the jaw.

* * *

"Stefano called Agent Wild and reported she said 'Feds' and told him he wasn't alone, right after they shook hands," Shaun said, his voice just as unyielding as when they'd been kids, even over the phone. "She must have found out about the impending bust. It's the only explanation for her cryptic words. With a handshake, Cass. Only a brief touch of their hands. Did you know they could do that?"

"They can't access other people's memories without consent." At least, that's what Cass had learned in his training. "You're being paranoid."

* * *

How was this happening? She wasn't touching him. The next memory jumped into her, linked to the previous one like children running together down a hill, holding hands.

She couldn't stop the onslaught of more memories . . .

* * *

"What are you saying?" Though Cass knew exactly what his boss meant. Behmann thought it would be easy for Cass to eliminate Jolene. Just another day in the life of a killer.

"Your brother's been overseeing this case for over two years. The lives we can save with this bust are worth more than one memory surgeon. This is why we exist, to make these hard calls."

"There's no proof she's a danger."

Cass's boss wanted all memory surgeons incarcerated and eliminated. Behmann's reasoning, per usual, was unsound. This wasn't the answer. This wasn't why Cass had signed on to the mission.

"Does Shaun know you want a hit?" Cass asked.

"You guys were specifically trained for this eventuality. This is an official order,

Stuart. Although you may not like it, you understand duty. So does your brother."

The FBI would never sanction a termination, particularly that of a US citizen. Never. But Cass imagined his brother would be relieved that his case was salvaged if Cass's agency made that call.

Behmann continued, "Tonight. There'll be a crew on standby for cleanup. Dr. Muller wants you to avoid a headshot, if possible. He can't extract much data from a dead brain, but there are tests he can do if it's intact."

Cass's gut soured and tumbled as he pictured it—a double tap to the chest. He could use his art room, the tarp already laid out on the floor. Jolene would walk in there, her back to him, her eyes on his painting.

She wouldn't feel a thing.

* * *

Jolene's body flash-froze, the image of herself sprawled on the ground, eyes vacant, blood pooling around her, two small holes in her chest stuck in her mind. She was going to die.

Cass.

He'd quieted her demons because he was the biggest demon of them all.

Her eyes rose to his, and as always, he pierced through her, all the way to the cellular level. He smiled, and at best, she grimaced.

His gun was in the studio, but she'd have to get past him to reach the door. Her face wouldn't move, wouldn't fix itself the way she needed so she could live. Her hand shook as she reached behind her to pull out her cell to fake getting a call.

If she couldn't calm herself down, she was dead.

She bobbled the phone, and it fell to the kitchen floor, face up, so she couldn't fake that call now. *Get out. Get out. Get out.*

"I was told you had to touch people to read their minds," Cass said, all pretense gone.

She couldn't swallow or blink. All that time. All those debates. He'd known all along she was a memory surgeon. "I don't read minds." Not exactly.

He arched his eyebrows. "Your face says otherwise." Cass scratched his jaw, eyes darting away. "What did you see?"

"You were imagining my death," she said. "Double tap to the chest. Seemed like you were pretty upset to be killing again, didn't appreciate the idea that some people think that's all you're good for."

Cass stared at her, his eyes filling with something volatile but not violent. "I wouldn't have done it."

Wouldn't have. What about now?

He'd never believe this was the only time she'd ever gotten anything from anyone without touch. She'd never have the chance to figure out why. "Who do you work for?" she asked.

"How do you not know?"

"Memory doesn't tell me everything. Your brother is your boss or boss's boss, or you're some kind of contractor. It's confusing. He's somehow involved with Stefano Jr. and his flipping, but if you worked for the government, your superiors wouldn't want me dead." Could she talk her way out of this? He didn't seem inclined to want to hurt her.

Cass snorted. "The FBI *doesn't* do that sort of shit, it's true. That's why he needed to use someone from PIA."

"What the hell is pia?"

"P-I-A. Paranormal Intelligence Agency. We operate as part of Homeland Security under the Office of Intelligence and Analysis. Unofficially."

She frowned. "I'm employed by the government too. Unofficially."

He squinted at her. "You work for the Agency."

Jolene almost rolled her eyes, but she wanted to live. "The Agency is"—she wasn't willing to die over that secret, or any secret—"an off-the-books department, but we're under the DEA and legit."

He looked at her for so long without speaking sweat slid all the way down her back.

"Jolene, the Agency is one of the biggest criminal organizations in the country."

She barked a laugh. "What are you talking about? We're making serious headway on cutting down the drug trade."

He stared. Her stomach rolled and dropped, and she swallowed down something thick and bitter. The tremor in her hands grew until her entire body shook. It was like the one time she'd smoked pot, finding herself floating and disengaged, almost like watching herself from the outside. No matter how much she wanted it to end, she couldn't pull free.

"Come with me," he said, his voice soft.

Her face prickled as if it had been pelted with buckshot made of ice. "No." She'd beg. Already, the pleas and tears built up in her chest and throat. Even knowing it wouldn't change anything, she'd plead for her pathetic life.

"I'm not going to hurt you."

Part of her believed him, twenty percent, but then, she'd also thought they might have a life together. Oh God, she was to him what Colton had been to her—just a job—and she was mooning over him even though they'd never fucked. Cass probably hadn't even had the painful breakup he'd told her about.

He stepped to her, and she flinched. He closed his eyes for a second, then took her hand. His warmth did nothing to relieve her chill. She followed him to her death like the pathetic, devoted dog she was.

Cass pulled her into his bedroom instead of his studio, where his gun was. Her heart careened around in her chest, desperate to escape. Images of being tied to the bed, raped, and cut popped into her mind from a past memory surgery. More recollections blazed through her head, of broken fingers, waterboarding, sounds and lights that never stopped, dark places, tight spaces. Apparently, before a memory surgeon died, other people's lives flashed before their eyes.

He released her hand and took a key from inside a spider plant on top of the bureau and unlocked the bottom drawer of his nightstand. Did he have another gun there? She couldn't breathe, her lungs paralyzed.

He withdrew a thick manila folder and held it out to her. She didn't want it, didn't want to know what was inside. All she wanted was to forget everything.

"Open it," he said.

She did. At first, she didn't understand what she was seeing in the photo. The dead body lay sprawled in an alley. Wadded paper and cigarette butts haloed his head, which bore two bullet holes.

Colton. Colton was dead.

He'd been *double tapped.*

"You killed Colton?" she asked. Jolene didn't want him to be dead, even if he hadn't been a good person. The knowledge made her queasy in a way she hadn't experienced since she'd gotten clean.

"No, Jolene. *The Agency* did that less than a week after you left Boston."

"What?" *No. No. No.* "No."

"This is their MO."

"He was fine the last time I saw him. There was no reason—" She dug her nails into her thighs. "Why would they do that?"

"You tell me."

She shook her head. Nothing made sense.

He sighed and guided her by the elbow to sit on the edge of his bed. He had a black and white comforter that reminded her of prison bars, though she supposed the bars were actually trees. A forest in winter?

Cass took the file from her numb fingers and flipped through pages. She didn't want to see any more, her mind at capacity for fucked-up-ness, unable to handle one thing more. He laid down four photos, two police reports, and a copy of her Chicago lease.

"The Agency is slowly taking over the drug trade in Austin, Pittsburgh, Boston, and Annapolis," Cass said.

She'd been to all those places on jobs. It didn't make any sense. "We're dismantling—"

"And then moving in. You're not working for the government but crooks."

Jolene leaped up, stumbled, and slammed her shoulder into the doorframe in her mad scramble for the bathroom. She dove to her knees, sliding and lifting the lid as her stomach erupted.

Since she hadn't eaten anything in several hours, she was surprised by the volume of vomit. She hadn't missed this part of drinking.

Cass knelt next to her and gently pulled her hair back. When she finished, he leaned away then close enough to brush her arm with something soft. "Here."

She took the hand towel, a sunny, yellow-and-white-striped fluffy thing too cheery for the occasion. Or perhaps it was perfect, she thought as she wiped her tragedy of a face, ruining the happy color. She blew her nose a few times on generous squares of toilet paper, then tossed them into the toilet.

The whole time, Cass rubbed barely there circles on her back. She wanted to wash her face and brush her teeth but settled for pushing to her feet and flushing. The room had a sickly sweet, just-puked smell. Cass stepped away to give her some breathing room.

She didn't look at him as she eased out of the bathroom, her legs taking turns trying to buckle, turning her walk into a lurch. "Let's see this finished painting," she said, her voice ground to stardust.

Jolene walked into the middle of his studio, her chest quivering in the aftermath of vomiting, or maybe from the cold inside her. The music pounded loud enough to concuss her ribs.

Cass didn't look at her as he stepped to the Bluetooth speaker playing the song "Bodies" by Drowning Pool. Apropos.

When he turned it off, silence echoed more loudly than the music.

She tucked her hands under her armpits, goose bumps itchy under her cotton shirt. "Wait!" she said, though Cass only stood there. "You wait!"

He watched her, his face not blank, but she couldn't decipher his expression. Her brain stopped working, her thoughts a whirlpool of snippets of pictures and the conviction that everything she'd done in the last five years to atone for all her mistakes hadn't been moving her soul into the black, but so deep into the red she'd never break even, let alone make a positive impact in the world.

"Wait," she said again, her throat contracting in painful pulses, tears clogging her nose and washing out her vision. She had to untuck her icy hands to swipe at her inferno of a face. "Don't—don't you dare do it when I'm like this." Her voice came out so choked she wasn't sure he would understand her.

"Jolene." His own eyes swam—or her wonky eyesight made it seem that way.

"Please," she said, swallowing down tightness, trying to catch her breath. This was important, the last thing that would matter. "Wait until I calm . . . the fuck down . . . Don't . . ." Jolene had no question about who she wanted to be at the end. "Don't kill me until I wrangle my shit together." She swallowed, gathering all the scattered parts of herself.

"Jolene." His face was pale, with sharp swatches of red across his beautiful cheekbones. He shook his head, but she didn't think it was in response to her request. "I'm not going—I was *never* going to—" Cass squatted almost to the floor, his elbows on his thighs, his weight on the balls of his feet. He dug the heels of his hands into his eyes. "I couldn't kill you if I wanted to, and I don't."

Lies. Everyone lied to her.

"I won't get on my knees, and I'm not going to look away. You are goddamned going to have to look at my fucking face when you—when you—" She couldn't say it.

He looked up at her, his eyes red, his face stripped of all confidence. With a small, tight nod, he straightened to his feet. He walked to the canvas on the side of the room, the one that hid his Glock 17 with the threaded barrel and suppressor. She watched, shoring up her strength, desperately trying to rein in her tears and sobs. If he didn't want to wait, she couldn't stop him.

Cass pulled out the gun by the long barrel and held it out to her, grip first. "I'm not going to hurt you."

"Too late," she said, snatching the firearm before he snapped it away and shot her in one motion.

His weapon and gravity tugged her arm, impossibly heavy. She wanted to drop it but couldn't in case Cass changed his mind. "Who the fuck are you, really?"

"I *am* an artist. I make my living by painting and teaching a few private students. I didn't lie about that." He pulled his hair into a ponytail and secured it with the ever-present elastic around his wrist. "And I was a sniper in the army. My brother works for the FBI, and he's in charge of the Stefano case. When he found out the Agency had a memory surgeon asking about the Red Flames, and Colton told a *lot* of people, he asked my branch of Homeland Security to look into it." He held up his hands as if to say, *What can you do?* "Stalking is a specialty of mine, and we're trained in memory surgeons. I watched you for a few days, and you always went to Starbucks around the same time every day. So, I did too."

Her skin retroactively crawled at the idea of eyes unknowingly scraping over her day after day. "Just you?"

"From PIA, yeah, but there were others surveilling from the FBI. A few neighbors."

All those eyes digging into her flesh. She thought she might vomit again, but her stomach was empty.

"And Skip?" Had the coffee-slinging douche at Starbucks been a plant?

"Serendipity." His chest visibly rose and fell, belying his calm. "I—we—just met. And once we did, it's not as if I could blend into the background after that."

"You're too hot to blend. You could never blend." Her voice was too loud, her pulse too fast. Her life had hit a patch of black ice and careened over an embankment.

"We need a plan," he said.

She looked down at the firearm in her hand. Someone in her headspace shouldn't be holding a loaded gun. Wasn't that the perfect metaphor for her life right now? She didn't want to hold the loaded weapon, but if she let go, even for a moment, she might die.

The photo he'd shown her of Colton popped into her mind, along with the report of three dead in the apartment at the address in Austin she'd procured from a passed-out middleman. How many others had she gotten iced? *Iced.* As if she were some sort of gangster after the fact. None of them had been innocent men, but that didn't exonerate her role in their deaths.

On some level, she should have known. She'd comprehended that Stadler was a killer the moment they'd met, but she'd also thought he was a government operative, so she'd accepted it. Cass was a killer, too—possibly her killer. Also supposedly working for the government.

What had he just said? "Huh?"

He took careful steps toward her. She could shoot him with his own gun. It would be self-defense, wouldn't it?

His eyes were wide. "I said we need a plan."

"A plan for what?"

"To keep you alive and safe."

She stared at him, trying to see truth but seeing only lies. "And what would you get out of that?"

He tapped the outside of his thigh with his fingers. "I get to keep you living." His tapping stilled. "I know where we can go. Do you trust me?"

"No."

He nodded as if he should have expected that response. "But I trust you, and not just because"—he gestured between them—"I have a knowing about you."

"What the hell is 'a knowing'?"

Cass sighed. "Sometimes I just know things. My gut twists, and I become sure—and I mean absolutely sure—about something. And whenever I thought—when I went through the mechanics of what they asked of me, preparing mentally, I couldn't. No doubt hurting you would have been a mistake. There was zero chance I would have killed you, with or without you reading my mind."

"I don't read minds. Just memories. It only seems like—" She shook her head, but her brain wouldn't wrap around anything. God, she'd spent so much time wanting to share with him that she had a gift, but not only had he already known, he had some sort of psychic ability too. Unless he was fucking with her. "I don't read minds." If she could, she'd read his right then.

"I want to take you to my grandparents' place in Northbrook. They've moved to their winter place in Sedona early. We can spend the weekend coming up with a solution to all this. Let's go."

"You think I'm just going to get in a car with you?" She snorted. Forty percent chance he was in earnest. "Are there any deserted woods en route to your grandmother's house? Hungry wolves? You must think I'm an idiot."

Cass stared over her shoulder for several seconds. "You can sit in the back seat with my gun. If I take you anywhere that screams 'dump site', shoot me in the back."

"I'm not as callous as you about shooting people."

"Okay, stay in Chicago, then. PIA is going to send someone else after you, and you won't know who or when. Or your own people will take you out and leave your body in a vacant alley. Either of those very probable scenarios is obviously a better choice than getting in the car with me while you are armed and prepared."

He was right, and she could use a hidden location to think without spotting assassins on every corner. "Okay. I need to go home to grab—"

"No. We leave now and take nothing. Not worth the risk." Cass jogged out of the room and came back, carrying the folder, the contents poking out as if he'd stuffed everything inside in a hurry. He grabbed his laptop and coat. "Let's go."

CHAPTER TWENTY THREE

Cass

My God, how had he fucked everything up so badly?

Cass wasn't surprised Jolene accepted his offer to sit behind him in the car. He hoped she had enough sense not to keep her finger on the trigger. He didn't need a pothole on I-94 to spook her into sending a bullet into his back.

She'd read his mind—or memory—without so much as a brush against his skin. Nobody in PIA knew memory surgeons could do that. It was one of the tenets of PIA's training: Agents were safe as long as they kept their thoughts locked down and their contact minimal. Her simple handshake with Stefano Jr. had blown everyone into a tizzy, as the current belief was that memory surgeons couldn't do their thing without either a willingness on the target's part or a compromised state of mind. Stefano had been sober, the contact lasting only seconds.

Cass suspected the kill order had come so fast, and without proper discussions, because she'd read Stefano so easily. To his boss and his own brother, Jolene was a liability and a criminal. He couldn't imagine what the response would be if he told anyone that Jolene had read him without touching him at all. She had long-range abilities.

His insides blazed as if he'd swallowed a halogen spotlight, which was now attempting to shine a hole through his body. He'd had knowings before, but nothing like this. Usually, the knowing came in a flash, accompanied by a cramping pain and a simple thought. *Don't get in that car. Check the third door. Something is wrong.*

This knowing wouldn't shut down, and it tied itself to his feelings for Jolene, as if his subconscious feared his sense of duty would override his—

He couldn't love her. Neither of them had been honest with the other, so the connection—

Real.

Jolene hadn't known the Agency was a criminal organization. She'd thought she was one of the good guys and finding out she wasn't was shredding her world. Cass couldn't help her with that, but he would protect her.

Of course he would. So why was his gut churning and glowing inside like a nuclear power plant?

Because she's not safe. Not yet.

They didn't talk as they rode in silence up I-94, the traffic bearable, streetlights and headlights illuminating them both at regular intervals. He considered turning on the radio, but he wanted to give her space to think, and if thinking made her antsy, he wanted her to speak to him. She didn't crack.

This was an opportunity. If he leveraged her employer's deception to turn her, he could save her life and bring her into PIA as a new source. If he persuaded his brother and boss she wasn't a threat, but a valuable tool . . . Too many ifs. This would require patience.

His grandparents lived on a quiet block in a modest house in the affluent suburb of Northbrook. Cass didn't have a key, but he knew a spare key hid in the hat of the most disturbing garden gnome. There were several posed in the front yard, none in good condition, their red hats chipped, noses cut short, and a cracked leg or two.

If you clicked a button on the side of the gnome and pushed backward, the hat opened to reveal the key. Cass didn't think anyone had ever used it until tonight. The gnomes were surrounded by solar ground lighting, casting their faces into grotesque shadows. The air crackled with a cold that stung his nose but cleared his head.

Jolene leaned against his car and watched him. She still held his gun, though she didn't point it at him.

Had he broken her?

She didn't strike him as someone easy to break—or maybe that was his desperate desire not to drown in guilt. Why had she seen him contemplating the hit, but not how much he couldn't do it? Then again, he didn't understand himself what he was feeling, so it wouldn't have mattered, other than she would have comprehended how he could never hurt her.

The Agency wouldn't release her. She was an asset or a liability, nothing in between. Right now, his own bosses weren't any better, terrified of her ability to uncover spies, reveal truths, and look into their black hearts. His black heart.

He extracted the key and carefully wove his way through the mums and flowering kale the gardening service planted every fall, though his grandparents were around only a month or so a year to enjoy it.

Cass held up the key to Jolene as if she hadn't witnessed the retrieval process. "Come on."

Jolene kept the gun in her hand, and he wondered if she would sleep with it under her pillow, if she slept at all. She followed him, a hollowed-out version of herself. Cass left his laptop and the file in the car for now, wanting to settle her first.

The lights ran on a timer, so the house wasn't dark when they entered. It had that stale, abandoned smell, though his grandparents had been gone for only a few weeks. The entire first floor was themed "heather gray" by his grandma, who redecorated every three years on a schedule. It was an open-concept space with a generous kitchen and a welcoming living room with seating for several people. No television there because his grandma hated the distraction from talking to others.

"If this is your grandparents' house," Jolene said, gaping at the modern aesthetic, "where are the plastic flowers, hand-crocheted doilies, and huge television from the eighties?"

Cass chuckled. "You're lucky my grandma isn't here. She'd be mortified at the thought."

"My grandmother's house looked like a thrift-store showroom."

"Oh yeah?" He hoped that would get her talking, but it didn't.

Jolene trailed through the sofa, the divan, and two armchairs, sitting on each one as if she were Goldilocks, gun forgotten but not released. She stroked all the fabrics and bounced on every seat. "Needs a fainting couch," she finally said.

Cass smiled. "There's one in the library upstairs."

Her eyebrows perked. "Your grandparents have a library?"

"It's probably not as impressive as you're imagining. There aren't rolling ladders or anything, and I swear it's half full of gardening books."

She looked around, spinning in a slow circle. "It doesn't match the outside. How could someone with this aesthetic keep all those creepy gnomes?"

"My grandma liked them for a brief period, and the family went overboard with the gnome gifts. After so many years of having them, they've become part of the home. I don't think she even sees them anymore."

"My grandmother collected these thick, chunky magnets of flowers on the fridge, and she'd use them to hold my drawings there every once in a while."

"You drew?"

Jolene shook her head. "Not well, and it wasn't like she had favorites." When she looked down at her feet, her hair slid forward, hiding most of her face. "She'd put my artwork on the fridge when she didn't want to take the time to look at it. I think she thought putting them up would fool me into thinking she gave a shit."

His first impulse was to tell her that her grandma did appreciate her art, but he couldn't say for certain. According to Jolene's file, Marigold Newlander had worked at a methadone clinic for over forty years, organized food drives, opened her home to troubled teens. But every time Jolene had referenced her grandma, there'd been a thread of resentment.

"Maybe she wasn't a person who appreciated art," he said, trying to give Jolene a way to couch her grandma's actions in a way that wouldn't hurt as much.

"I think it was having a granddaughter like me she didn't appreciate."

"Because of the memory-surgeon thing?"

She snorted. "God, no. She loved that, thought it was a gift bestowed on me so I could martyr myself to the masses, like every proper person does. When I was doing the refugee stuff, taking away memories of torture, she was proud of me then. The only time in my whole life, I think. Well, allowing the government testing was also a 'good life choice'." She didn't make actual air quotes, but Cass heard them. "She approved of all those blood samples and CT scans and MRIs. Anytime I hurt myself for someone else's benefit, I got her approval and her cursory attention."

Cass didn't say anything. His own family was nothing but supportive no matter what he did—army or artist, checkout clerk or box office ticket seller. Sure, Shaun got most of the glory, but Cass always felt unconditional love from his parents. "You get that's fucked up, right?"

She shrugged. "My grandmother was well loved in the community. Everyone assumed my life was filled with homemade cookies and endless hugs." Jolene looked up at him, her expression rawer than he'd ever seen it, including that moment when she'd read his mind—memories—whatever. "I never wanted to be like her, but I still want to *want* to be like her."

"Some cold bitch who cared more about other people than her own granddaughter?" He instantly regretted calling her grandma a bitch—that wasn't his place—but he didn't stop. "How the hell were you supposed to be this paragon of love when you grew up neglected?"

Jolene squinted at him as if she had to translate his words. "I wasn't neglected. She had a lot on her plate and selfless goals. My mother and father were like that too."

"I thought you said they died when you were five."

"They did."

"And at five, you were able to give them a full personality assessment?"

She huffed a laugh. "Fine, but they were killed by a mudslide while doing humanitarian aid, so the circumstantial evidence is pretty strong."

"All right, but the same could be said about you. Memory surgeries for torture victims, participating in those early governmental studies . . ." He paused, but then pushed through. "Presumably working for a government agency to fight the drug trade."

She collapsed onto the sofa closest to the fireplace, gun in her lap. Cass contemplated starting a fire but decided to push it off for another hour or so, depending on how the conversation went. He sat across from her in his grandpa's favorite bomber-jacket-brown recliner.

Jolene buried her head in her hands. "I'm FUBAR."

"Not you, just your life."

She peered up at him through her fingers, one side of her mouth quirked as if she wanted to smile. "Same thing."

"We can fix this." His gut twinged. Too soon to talk details. "We just need some time to consider all our options."

"*Our* options?"

Blood throbbed behind his eyes, making his head ache. "Yes. There will be repercussions for both of us."

"Isn't your brother your boss?"

The information she'd garnered apparently was spotty, and that surprised him. "No. He's in charge of the Stefano case, but PIA agents are consultants when we assist government agencies." A formal reprimand would be the least of his punishments. He suspected he'd get fired, regardless of all the money PIA had sunk into his training. No soldier worth a cent disobeyed a direct order like he had.

"Any brothers with a combined name like Shaun Cassidy have to be tight. All that shared trauma. I'm sure he'll help you."

Cass ignored the twist in his heart and studied her. Jolene leaned her cheek against the sofa's arm, blond hair cascading over her chin to cover her throat. With her back to the floor lamp, her face was cast in shadow, making her appear tired. The glistening of her rosewood eyes made her seem young and vulnerable. He hadn't seen an alternative path he could have taken to save her this pain.

"I wouldn't have hurt you," he said, for probably the hundredth time. He hoped she wouldn't repeat her words too. *Too late.*

"That doesn't matter as much as you think it should." She put his gun on the coffee table between them, stared at him for a full three seconds, and closed her eyes. Her body shifted, and she curled into herself, a tight ball on the sofa.

Her voice came muffled. "Do you think whoever invented Rohypnol or GHB feels guilty? I mean, they were created to help people with insomnia and anxiety, and then . . . wham. Women being slipped the stuff into their drinks, being raped, all their memories stolen, nobody believing their stories, no way to discover who'd violated them. Sometimes they die. Do you think the inventors feel responsible? Could they have hurt more people than they helped?"

Cass moved to sit on the coffee table in front of her. His gut didn't tell him to stop, so he brushed her silky hair away from her face, then ran a hand down her arm. "You didn't know."

Her eyes opened, wet and so deep he thought he might be trapped forever. "I should have known, or maybe I did know but didn't let myself consciously admit it."

Once she untangled herself from the lies, she would come around. He'd bring her onto their side, preserve her life, and take down the Agency (at least part of it). Cass would demonstrate how he could save the day without violence.

He plopped himself on the floor and stroked her soft hair. For so long, he'd wanted to spend the night with her, but certainly not like this. If she fell asleep, he'd cover her with a blanket and start a fire in the fireplace. No more conversation tonight. He'd given her a lot to ponder, and now he'd give her the space to work through her situation and find her way back to him.

CHAPTER TWENTY FOUR

Jolene

HER SHREDDED SOUL BECKONED HER TO SLEEP, TO give herself a few hours of respite. Everything she'd believed had been obliterated, and once again, she could trust no one, especially herself.

Her eyelids dropped like weighted curtains, but the idea of too-on-topic dreams made her resist the downward pull. Cass joined her on the couch in the space left beyond her feet, his profile to the fireplace, his focus solely on her. His attention had always been tangible, but what she'd taken for attraction turned out to be something entirely different.

Cass tugged a couch cushion onto his lap and pulled gently on her shirt sleeve. She flipped around and crawled until her head reached the pillow. He smoothed her hair and then combed across her scalp in a gentle wave, petting her as if she were the world's most-spoiled housecat. Every so often, he twirled a lock of her hair or slipped his fingers through a section. She wondered why he touched her so sweetly. Was he still manipulating her? God, she wanted this connection between them to be real.

The sensation sent shivers from her head to her shoulders and chest. Jolene ignored the inappropriateness of pleasure amidst the charred remains of her life and let her eyes slide shut, just for a moment, just to rest.

A roughened finger brushed across her cheekbone. Her lids were stronger than her curiosity, and she couldn't open her eyes. The touch traced down to her jaw and under her chin. Cass circled small patterns, light and soft, like a spring breeze.

Nobody had ever touched her like that. It was contact that didn't ask for anything in return. She wondered if this was what being loved felt like. Not that her grandmother or her parents hadn't cared about her. They'd simply been too distracted by everyone else in the world to think about her. Cass saw her, protected her, cared about her—maybe. At the moment, *maybe* was enough.

Her eyes opened, no longer heavy or sealed shut. He'd been watching her. "I tried so hard not to touch you," he whispered.

"You kissed me. After our run. I wanted to, but you were the one—"

"I didn't kiss you to get you to trust me." His green eyes were obsidian in the dim light of the living room. Dark truths or dark lies.

"Because you didn't need to. It seems I've been trusting all the wrong people."

"No. I'll keep you safe." His hands returned to her hair, smoothing it over the cushion.

"There's no safety in this game, Cass. The Agency killed Colton, and PIA ordered you to kill me." Death everywhere, wedged beneath her nails, coating her nose, burrowing into her ears.

"I wouldn't hurt you."

"Thanks to your magic gut." Sometime between her discovery of Cass's true identity and now, she'd come to believe he had a gift—like hers, only different. When memory surgeons first began appearing less than a decade ago, everyone had scoffed. But if she experienced others' memories, why couldn't Cass decipher intentions or personalities?

She should stop busting his balls over his ability but wouldn't.

"Double tap to the chest to nail my heart and instantly kill me. Like a fucking coward."

"I wouldn't—"

"Sawing off my head so the scientists could study it."

He stood, dislodging her, and started to pace in front of the couch. "Stop it. I—"

"—wasn't going to do it? Of course not." She leaped up, not allowing him to tower over her as he continued to gaslight her. "Without your *knowing*, you'd have killed me and made someone else dump my body. The plastic tarp would have been easily rolled away, taking all traces of me with it. Nobody would find my body, and the Agency would be left wondering if maybe I'd simply bolted."

"They would have found out."

"How? Were you going to send them my empty cranium as a kind of warning to back off?" She was only upsetting herself but couldn't stop. "You think being conflicted makes it okay."

"It's not fair of you to use my raw, emotional thoughts in such a high-stress situation against me. Those weren't my only thoughts and feelings." His voice rose enough to be considered shouting. "What the fuck, Jolene? I just rescued you—"

"From *you*."

"No, from the government."

"I didn't realize the threat was over."

"Fuck you."

"Sorry, Cass, but fuck you."

His face tightened, and he gripped her shoulders, fingers digging into her muscles. Jolene didn't mind, wanting him to show himself as the monster he was.

Cass kissed her instead, his lips crushing hers, his growl vibrating into her. He sucked all the oxygen from her, leaving her disoriented.

Jolene could have broken his hold, but she didn't want him to release her. Being held by him felt too right. She returned his kiss, made it more violent, their teeth bumping before she bit into his lip. He moaned into her mouth and yanked her tight to his body.

"Goddamn it," he panted as he drew back. "I'm sorry. You're not thinking straight."

A red haze rolled through her vision. The term *seeing red*, it turned out, was literal. "Tell me again how I'm feeling and what I need."

He blinked and backed up a step.

She followed, tracking him like the wildebeest at the water hole he was. "No, seriously, Cass—if that is your real name. Right now, I'm feeling everything, every emotion that's ever existed since the dawn of time. I didn't realize this whole time that you're here to tell me what I'm *really* feeling and what I *actually* need. I mean, I thought fucking might ease some tension, but luckily, I have you here to safeguard me from myself. Assassin savior to the rescue."

"I'm only trying to do what's right," he said, because he was an idiot who didn't listen.

"For me," she said, all statement. "You're disregarding what I want because you think you know better."

He interlaced his fingers behind his neck, still moving away from her. "I just don't want you to regret anything in the morning."

She laughed, the deranged sound fueling her even as it scared her. "There is absolutely nothing you can do or not do that's going to make me wake up to tomorrow regret free."

Cass threw out his arms. "It's not just your judgment that might be impaired, you know."

"So, you're covering your insecurities with fake concern for mine?"

"My consideration isn't—" He growled and tugged at his hair. "I—cannot—stop—fucking—this—up." His growl turned into a roar as he kicked a chair, then stormed out the front door, not stopping to grab his jacket.

Jolene had never seen Cass lose his temper before. It comforted her, in a way, that his patience had limits. She stared at the slammed door for a full minute before trudging up the stairs, where she commandeered the master bedroom. The room smelled faintly of a too-sweet perfume she couldn't identify, either because Saks hadn't carried it or her brain was on a timeout.

She snooped everywhere because she could and because she'd worked almost five years for a criminal organization and gotten people killed. So who the hell cared if she pawed through a stranger's underwear drawer? If she saw anything she liked, she might shove it into her pocket. Run off with the family silver. She snorted and yanked out a white cotton nightgown with a ruffled collar and long sleeves—very *Wuthering Heights* and at least twenty years too old for her. Perfect.

The voice that had faded with time roared to life louder than it had in the last five years. *Might as well have a drink. Your life has exploded, so why bother torturing yourself? Remember the relief of that first sip? You've already fucked up. You're probably going to die soon. Why hold back?*

Sleep. Unconsciousness might ease some of the pressure or at least give her a break. Fuck any bad dreams.

With a flourish, she yanked back the covers on the king-sized bed. The jacquard pattern of raspberry and gold looked trying-too-hard. An apt fit for her. She kept the comforter pulled away and slipped under the thin sheet that was just as white as her nightgown.

White. The color of purity, good intentions, and ghosts.

CHAPTER TWENTY FIVE

Cass

CASS WALKED ONLY THE BLOCK, BUT BY THE TIME he returned to the house, Jolene had escaped upstairs. His grandparents' bedroom door was shut, probably locked. If he'd been her, he would have shut him out of the entire house.

Jolene had a psychedelic drug effect on him, making him feel all the wrong things, as if she'd turned his insides ninety degrees to the left. He should have felt trapped. Hell, he couldn't remember a time in the years since he'd gotten out of the army when he hadn't gagged from the feelings of suffocation, the world no longer black and white, but every hue and shade, and now he'd run off with her. Jail wasn't an impossibility.

Yet, he wasn't conflicted at all about that decision. He couldn't kill her and wouldn't allow anyone else to hurt her. She possessed a rare talent and—

No, he wouldn't lie to himself and pretend he'd absconded with her for any reason other than he loved her. How it happened didn't matter, but he kept picking at the idea as if it were a fresh scab. Somehow, she'd blown through all his defenses, and now he had to protect her regardless of how much she hated him.

He. Could. Not. Fuck. Her.

Not until they'd resolved this situation. Not until she believed he genuinely cared. Not until he had enough control to do it right.

Cass changed into an old pair of sweatpants and lay down in the guest room he'd used as a boy, but he couldn't relax. If someone came for them, he'd be hard-pressed to hear anything upstairs. Grabbing a blanket and pillow, he settled down on the living room couch.

* * *

CASS WOKE COMPLETELY BUT WITHOUT ALARM, HEARING SOFT FOOTFALLS in the kitchen, the slight sucking sound indicating bare feet. Jolene raiding the fridge?

The clink of condiment bottles confirmed his suspicion, though he knew his grandma wouldn't have left behind anything perishable. He pictured Jolene staring into the mostly empty refrigerator, cold air wafting over her face, the harsh light making her squint.

He padded into the kitchen, intent on brewing her a cup of tea and plating some of the Lorna Doone cookies his grandpa hid in the pantry behind the kale chips. The white nightgown hung loose on her, the hem reaching just below her knees. He recognized it as his grandma's, but that knowledge didn't affect his erection one bit. The fridge light outlined her body, somehow more erotic than if she'd been naked.

Her long blond hair stuck up on top as if she'd been tossing and turning—or having sex. He stared at her bare feet and sculpted calves, exposed and vulnerable, then let his gaze travel up her body, snagging on the ruffles at her neckline. They should have been frumpy and ridiculous, but the rounded neck was loose enough he suspected he could easily pull it off her shoulder and expose a breast.

"You're staring," she said without looking at him. "Are you pissed I'm wearing your grandmother's clothes?"

"No." His voice came out husky, as if he'd spent the last three days on a bender. "She'd want you to help yourself."

"I tried to help myself earlier, and you weren't having it." She closed the fridge and brushed past him, apparently planning to head back to her room.

He grabbed her arm to stop her, immediately realized what he'd done, and released his grip. "Sorry," he muttered.

Jolene whipped around and fisted his hair, pulling his face close to hers. He couldn't move, his head held immobile and the rest of his body freezing.

"Jolene—"

"Shut up." Her voice was soft and hard all at once. "Don't talk, Cass. It only makes me want to slap you."

Silence fell as they waited—him for whatever she would do next, and her for . . . something. Probably waiting for him to ruin the moment. For once, he didn't.

She smirked and tightened her grip on his hair. He easily ignored the pain but not his clamoring heartbeat. His composure fractured at the edges as she brought her lips a millimeter from his. Being held back when she was so close opened a wicked room inside him. He welcomed the scream of his scalp as he strained forward to brush her lips. She allowed it for only a breath before moving an inch away.

"I didn't give you permission to do that," she said, her voice a rumble in the dark.

"Please." He was so hard it hurt. Something desperate clawed up his throat. "Jolene, please."

"Hmm."

Her evil purr skittered down his spine, and his balls tightened. He wondered if he might come just from . . . whatever this was.

"I don't know, Cass." She sounded unlike herself, possessed, her voice slow and slick, like a snake slithering through silk. "I'd hate for you to wake up feeling as if I took advantage of you in this . . . vulnerable state."

Oh, that bitch. She gripped his hair, but really had him by the balls. He would have done anything for the barest touch. "Why don't we both manage our own regrets?"

She raised her eyebrows. "That sounded suspiciously like consent."

He grabbed her hips as he pushed his pelvis forward. They slammed together in a satisfying connection. "Is this what you want?"

She squeaked and lost her hold on his hair as their lips collided. He shifted his hands to her waist and hefted her so the vee of her thighs fit his cock perfectly. She wrapped her arms around his neck and her legs around his body. Cass turned them and pressed her against the refrigerator to pin her in place. Magnets clicked together, and pictures fluttered to the floor.

Jolene grunted from the impact, and he pulled back to assess the damage. Had he hurt her?

"Don't even think about stopping," she said with a glower that spoke of impending annihilation.

He chuckled. "Yeah, but shouldn't we share our feelings first?"

"Irritation. You?"

"Hungry." He kissed her smirk. She hadn't been wrong. He'd made assumptions about her based on his need not to be an asshole. Maybe fucking *would* clear her head. Just because it would surely muddle his thoughts didn't mean she would react the same way. Really, though, his dick was too hard for him to care about anything beyond making her come.

Cass ground into her again, swallowing her moan through their locked lips. He had enough upper-body strength to pin her for a while, but not enough to hold her there and somehow divest them both of enough clothing to fuck. His fear of her changing her mind prevented him from breaking their kiss, and in moments, their nipping teeth and thrusting hips fell into a kind of rhythm.

Jolene's legs tightened around his waist, and her fingers dug into his shoulders. All the places in the house where they could fuck flashed through his mind.

Cass pulled back enough to gulp in a few breaths of air. He wouldn't screw this up.

He set her on the ground and tilted up her chin. "Bedroom?"

"Too far away."

He kissed her again. He'd suspected the forbidden aspect of their physical relationship was what made it so hot. But now no lies separated them, the need had grown instead of eased.

Her hands slipped under his paint-splattered T-shirt to his bare skin, the coolness rapturous against the inferno of his body. He wanted to possess her completely, crack her open, and protect her. She'd probably hate every one of those things.

He bit her lower lip, held it in his teeth, and eased back, testing to see if she'd resist or follow. As usual, she surprised him. Her mouth crashed into his. She broke the kiss and fisted his shirt. With a savage yank, she off-balanced him, sending him to his knees.

Cass wanted to bite into the flat of her stomach and press his fingers into her hip bones. Nothing existed beyond the now. Their eyes fell into each other, and Cass's body became so hypersensitized the seams of his clothing itched against his skin.

"Take off your shirt," Jolene said, as if reading his mind. Maybe she had.

He didn't care. He obeyed and waited for what she wanted next. *Anything*, he said with his eyes. *Anything, sweetheart.*

"You're a bit of a sick fuck. You know that, right?" she asked in the voice of a phone-sex operator. "I mean, getting hard while I'm wearing your grandmother's nightgown? What does that say about you?"

His hands snaked under the nightgown, the bottom as frilly as the top. The wrongness of her words, her clothing, the entire situation only made him harder and more desperate for her. She didn't move or say anything as he raised the nightgown to midthigh, his hands traveling all the way to her waist and her underwear. He dipped his fingers just inside the waistband and traced along the edge over her hips. He bent forward and nipped just above her left knee. "I want to taste you," he said, not recognizing his own thick voice.

"Who's stopping you?" She stared down at him like a goddess, and he looked up at her like a supplicant.

He pulled her underwear down, working it over her amazing ass and tugging it from where the material clung between her legs. He was going to draw out every moment until she turned into a sobbing mess of want.

She drove her fingers into his hair. He expected her to jerk him into the apex of her thighs, but she did nothing more than run her nails over his scalp in a way that excited as it soothed. He kissed her inner thighs, one side, then the other, licking and sucking, scraping his teeth over her skin, determined to mark her everywhere.

Her hips jerked and rolled a few times, and her legs trembled. He wanted to draw the moment out longer but couldn't. Cass dragged his tongue through the center of her, starting low so he could flick the tip of his tongue over her clit at the end.

Jolene gasped and thrust her hips forward. She said nothing, though her fingers occasionally gripped his hair tighter. She held his head still and ground into his mouth. The movement was domineering, particularly with him on his knees, and he couldn't believe how much he liked it or how much harder his dick had become.

Her breathing hitched as she panted and shook. Cass flicked her clit and slid a finger inside her, groaning at how hot and slick she'd grown, so wet that his intrusion made an obscene squelching sound.

"Oh fuck," she hissed as he added another finger and curled it to find her G-spot. When he felt the rough surface, he rubbed back and forth with his middle finger and sucked on her clit.

Jolene's hands slapped backward onto the fridge as she shrieked. "Don't stop."

She clamped her hand on his shoulder, then in his hair again. A high whine came out of her mouth, and her pussy tightened around him.

"I—I—Cass—Cass—"

The sound of his name when she was so close to coming almost made him orgasm himself. This unrestrained version of Jolene, the way she gave over to his lips, his touch, was sexy as hell.

"Please. Oh please. I need—I need to—don't stop. Don't you fucking—"

Her entire body locked up, and her cunt clamped down so hard on his fingers he could barely move them. She screamed his name as her head knocked back into the fridge. Then her body milked his fingers, fluttering and gripping in a steady rhythm. Finally, her legs buckled, and she almost didn't catch herself.

"I . . . have to sit . . . or . . ."

"Take that off and sit on the kitchen table," he said, almost toppling himself when he stood. His knees complained, but they were easily ignored with all the blood flooding his cock. He needed her more than he'd ever needed anything, and he couldn't wait a moment longer.

Now, now, now.

Jolene grabbed near the hem of the nightgown and drew it over her head. Holy hell was she beautiful. Her toned body sloped and flared in all the right places. Her arms and thighs had visible bands of muscle, and her breasts fit the palms of his hands. He wanted to paint her just like that—naked, flushed, and overcome with lust. Paint directly onto her body, swirling purple around her breasts, pink down the arcs of her hips, a smiley face in the crook of her arm. And the other side . . .

"Turn around," he said, needing to see her naked backside.

"Why?" she croaked.

"Because I love nothing more in this world than your ass."

Jolene rolled her eyes but turned. She spread her legs a few inches and arched her back, sticking out her rear. Her limbs continued to tremble. Cass groaned and cupped himself through his sweatpants.

"Is this all right?" she asked in a tone that failed at innocence.

He'd fantasized about her ass from the first moment he'd seen her, before they'd even spoken. That kink had never intrigued him before, and he'd expected it to be a passing thought. However, the compulsion gripped him so intensely he'd done internet research on spanking techniques.

He didn't want to hurt her, and surely a woman fluent in trauma didn't want someone spanking her bare, exposed, luscious posterior. But maybe she'd at least let him grab and knead those gorgeous globes.

"So fucking perfect," he groaned. "Bend over the table. I need my hands on that ass now."

She looked at him over her shoulder, assessing, then did as he'd demanded.

CHAPTER TWENTY SIX

Jolene

THE MAN WHO'D ALMOST KILLED HER HAD JUST given her the best orgasm of her life. And now Jolene was going to fuck him. Part of her reveled in the destructiveness of the choice.

It wasn't a decision someone with a clear head and self-respect would make. This delicious high was better than alcohol or drugs. She was already addicted.

She collapsed her upper body on top of the oak table, in between two spindle chairs. The wood was cool, though not as chilly as glass or marble would have been. She turned her head to the left and rested it on her hands, then closed her eyes.

He stroked his hand from the backs of her knees to the tops of her thighs, his touch so light she barely felt it. She told herself she didn't care what he did to her. Anything. Everything. Pleasure. Pain. Destruction.

Cass leaned over her, naked, flesh to flesh, the warmth of him a shock. His cock rested against her ass, hotter than the rest of him, stiff and heavy. He brushed her hair forward and kissed her from the top of her spine down, his hair dragging over her skin like a feather. She shivered and pressed the pads of her fingers into the wood to ground herself.

He dislodged enough parts of her psyche she could disappear or float away. When he reached her lower back, he rested his hands on the dip of her waist. Goose bumps exploded over her skin, the light touch reawakening her lust, which should have been sated. Her hips rolled and her heels rose with her body's automatic attempt to increase her contact with him.

One hand had moved to her tailbone, his thumb lightly stroking. "Fuck me, you're beautiful," Cass said, his voice quiet, reverent.

She couldn't react at all. Only wait. Her lungs struggled for air, and she lifted her chest off the table for a few seconds to catch her breath. Only her nipples touched the table, stiff and aching. She rocked her body, enjoying the friction.

"So hot," Cass crooned, his other hand stroking over the cheeks of her ass. "Do you have any idea how many times I had to jerk off after spending time with you?"

"No."

"Every time." His fingers dug into the flesh of her butt. "I want to spank you, Jolene. Are you going to let me do that?"

"Yes."

He gripped her with both hands and pulled her cheeks apart. She felt the stretching sensation in her pussy. She gasped.

"Good girl."

She shivered, confused by the thrill running through her body. She wasn't a goddamned dog—and yet, the compulsion to please him, to relinquish her control made her achy and wet. Life was always unpredictable, but purposely giving Cass power over her made her secure in a way that defied logic.

"I have a condom, but it's in my glove compartment—"

"Not necessary. Tubes tied, remember?" She fought to catch her breath. "I'm clean." Too clean. And she didn't care if he was disease-free or not. Her life spun so hard, she clung to danger and giving zero fucks—at least for now.

He chuckled. "You want me to fuck you raw?" His voice lowered an octave, and she shivered again.

"Yes."

"Come inside you?" He slipped a finger into her.

"Yes." Her muscles clenched, and she moaned. She wanted him in her with a desperation that tripped all her warning sensors. "Yes."

He slapped her ass, the nip sharp and unexpected. She squeaked, which she instantly wanted to retract.

His hand massaged the spot he'd struck, spreading the sting toward her pussy, turning it from discomfort to pleasure. Before she processed the changing sensations, he slapped the other side, then the first again. The sounds weren't cracks, but they were still loud and sharp, the heat and prickle following like lightning after thunder. As soon as pain registered, he rubbed it away, and her body consumed every thought. Her mind, always so cramped and whirling, stilled as if she were in the eye of a hurricane.

"You okay?" Cass's voice sounded as if he'd aged fifty years and suffered from emphysema.

"Yes. Better than qigong."

He chuckled and slipped his fingers into her again. "Fuck, you're wet. Is that for me?" He finger-fucked her for several seconds. "All that hot, wet cunt. Did I do that?"

"Yes."

"Are you ready for me to fuck you now?"

"Yes."

"Turn over." He backed away, but he kept a hand on her hip, as if needing to maintain contact.

She straightened and turned. He cupped the back of her head. The raw vulnerability on his face startled her, and she tried not to think about how much her own expression revealed.

He kissed her, gentle and sweet. His erection pulsed on her naked stomach, hot and hard. She shifted her hips enough to have the space to grab his shaft and stroke. Her backside pressed into the table, smarting the skin of her ass. Had his spanking left marks?

Cass groaned, and his grip on her neck tightened. "This isn't how I want to come," he wheezed and took a half step backward, his hands dropping as he watched her fist his cock.

"Too dry," Jolene said and pushed him back another step. Then she bent at the waist, pulling her abs tight to support her back, until she reached the head of his dick and licked.

"Jesus!" His hips bucked, and his hand moved into her hair. He allowed her to swallow him and suck him for two strokes before he pried her mouth off his cock. "Lie back."

She released her hold on him and obeyed. She dug her heels into the edge of the table, keeping her legs spread as wide as possible. The position was obscene and dirty and, somehow, empowering.

Cass grabbed her ankles and pulled them to the tops of his shoulders. He lined his cock up to her entrance and stared down at her. "Still good?"

She flopped her arms up over her head and stretched, arching her back.

"Fuck me," Cass said, staring at her body, reaching down to trace his fingers over her hard nipples.

"I've been ready for a long time," she finally said.

He pushed inside her with a sustained press, her body tight but yielding.

"Yes," she said when he paused, as if waiting for her emotions to catch up to her body. But she had no emotions, only the moment. Her psyche was filled with Cass as much as her body was filled by him.

He pulled back and thrust in again, a firm, gentle glide. Jolene closed her eyes, and Cass's mind blossomed in her head, expanding so wide the technicolor bubbles of his memories were brighter than any she'd ever seen. She couldn't *not* trust him when looking at the vividness of his consciousness. The vibrancy meant he'd completely exposed himself to her, nothing locked down.

Jolene opened her eyes and still saw his memory spheres, but she didn't touch them. She didn't want to leave her own moment in time. There was nowhere better to be.

He fucked her slowly, his gaze roving from her face to their joining. His eyes on her made her hotter and wetter, and she wanted to desecrate his grandparents' house with sex in every room, on every surface, in every position.

"Harder," she croaked.

He thrust twice, brutal and fast, then slowed. "Touch yourself while I fuck you."

She slid her hand between them and circled her clit as Cass pistoned in and out of her. He gripped her hips hard enough they would likely bruise. She liked the idea of evidence of sex with him on her body.

"God, Jolene, I can't hold out much longer. You need—hurry, baby, hurry."

She adored the sound of her name in his mouth and when he called her *baby* or *sweetheart*. He tilted his hips to give her more space, and the change in angle hit her perfectly. She tensed, her orgasm coiling tight and fast.

Her world paused, her body tightening, but she was already so taut the increased clenching felt more like stasis than movement. And yet. Everything around her spun and wavered as her core bore down, down, down, and the rest of her prepared to blast into the cosmos, turning her to particles and radioactive chemicals.

Eventually, her two competing thrills merged in an explosive orgasm. Jolene screamed a chant of Cass's name, her back arching as she rode the rippling pleasure of her body squeezing his cock inside her.

"Holy fuck," Cass gasped, before hunching over her and biting the juncture of her neck and shoulder. She was too flooded with endorphins to feel any pain, only more sensation as the bite prolonged her orgasm so long she wondered if it would ever end.

It did.

The blessed distraction of sex mostly stayed. She remembered her situation but didn't care. He let her legs flop off his shoulders, but he didn't move away.

Cass pulled her up to sit, all while kissing along her throat, over her jaw, ending at her mouth, where he kissed her for several minutes. He slipped out of her, but he didn't stop kissing. Her feet hit the floor, and she was unsure of her balance, as if she'd been on a boat for a month and had just returned to shore.

Her sea legs carried her to the bathroom. When she saw her reflection, she paused. Her hair was nestlike, her eyes round and glossy, almost as if she'd been weeping, but not her typical ugly-crying. Her lips were swollen and darker than usual, and strawberry-colored marks trailed down her throat. A sizable hickey sat between her neck and shoulder. She looked wrecked—in the best possible way.

She wouldn't allow the euphoria and relief to paint over everything he'd done before they'd arrived at this house. The sex hadn't been enough of a balm or enough of a punishment or any sort of answer.

CHAPTER TWENTY SEVEN

Cass

JOLENE RETURNED FROM THE BATHROOM AS disheveled as when she'd left, which he found damn sexy. She eyed him and his reclothed state, then swiped his grandmother's nightgown off the back of the chair where he'd folded it. The garment was loose enough it fell over her body without any fussing on her part. "Where's my underwear?"

Cass pulled her panties out of his pocket.

"I need those. I'll probably be leaking pretty bad for the next few hours."

His semi-thickened dick lengthened more. He wanted her in his bed, on top of him, on her hands and knees. "I'd love to plug your leak."

"Cool your jets," she said with a chuckle. She shivered after drinking the glass of water he had waiting for her. It was freezing in the kitchen, the thermostat programmed for cooler temperatures in light of the house's occupants being away. "The sex was damn fine, but nothing has changed."

Just because she was right didn't make it sting less. "Who'd have thought you were such a romantic?"

She didn't look at him. "I'm trying to be practical." Her right hand curled into a fist, and she tapped it on a chairback. "It doesn't mean anything."

Her words hit him like a bitch slap. Their sex hadn't meant anything to her. And the hint of accusation in her voice grated, as if he'd fucked her as a manipulation.

"I'll see you in the morning," he said, leaving her to sort through her feelings. He resumed his post on the couch to contemplate his own.

* * *

CASS WOKE WITH A CRICK IN HIS NECK AND A JAGGED STONE IN HIS GUT. He had to fix the distance between him and Jolene. She might not want to admit it, but the sex had meant something more than simply scratching an itch or blowing off steam.

Jolene slept (or hid) for another hour before coming downstairs in her jeans from yesterday and a fuzzy raspberry sweater that had to be his grandma's.

"You want to know if you can trust me?" He held out his hand. "Go ahead."

Jolene sucked in a breath and pushed his hand away. "Trust isn't binary, Cass." She curled her fingers under the hem of her sweater. "There's more than trust or mistrust. People are complicated and often contradictory."

Cass pulled the elastic from his hair, letting it fall around his shoulders, and scrubbed his scalp. "How do I make you believe in me? Help me out here, sweetheart."

"'Make' me? Dude, you need to choose your words more carefully."

He closed his eyes, wrangling all the squiggling worries inside him into one corner of his mind. This moment was too important.

She stroked her fingertips down his arm. "I want to trust you."

"What can I do?"

She stepped into him and wrapped her arms around his neck. He dropped his face into her shoulder and hugged her body close.

"I hear sex builds trust," he said, hoping the joke wouldn't detonate in his face.

Jolene laughed, and an alien buzzing filled his chest.

She sank into his embrace. "Do we have to do this now? Can't we—I don't know—pretend everything's fine? Act normal? For a little while?"

So that's what they did. They watched TV and played card games: Texas Hold 'Em, war, and slapjack. Whenever she looked at him for longer than three seconds, he pulled her into him. They didn't talk about the past or the future, only timeless things like her hatred of coconut and his distaste for neon colors.

* * *

"LET'S GET A LITTLE SLEEP, YEAH?" HE ASKED AS THEY LAY TANGLED ON the sofa after their third round of sex, which did seem to help build trust. It was early afternoon, and she looked as if she'd slept as little last night as he had. All he wanted was to lie down next to her and think about nothing.

"Okay." She led the way, walking to his grandparents' room.

"Oh." He stopped. "Let's go to my room."

She snorted. "There's only a full-sized bed there. Do you not want to sleep in the master bedroom because your grandparents have sex there?"

"Oh God!" He backed up. "Why would you put that in my head?" Cass refused to think of his grandparents naked in the bed, which of course meant the image hit him like a flash-bang, robbing him of both sight and sound for a moment. "You are evil."

She laughed, and they fell into bed, kicking down the comforter before burrowing under the sheet. They tumbled into each other, fitting as if they'd been sleeping together for years.

It wasn't everything, but Cass hoped it was enough.

* * *

CASS WOKE WITH HIS HAIR SPILLED OVER HIS FACE AND JOLENE'S HAIR IN his mouth. He'd slept deeply enough his body had become an immovable mass.

They continued to lay mashed up, her legs between his and on top. Jolene groaned and stretched against him, her breasts pressing into his chest. Her arms encircled his waist, and she held him as he embraced her. Cass wanted to stay in the moment, just for a while.

"I think we slept too long," she said, her voice hoarse, her breath tickling his neck. "Or not long enough? What time is it?"

The sparse light of the room gave no hint of the time. "Don't know," he mumbled, though it came out more like *dunno.*

Jolene made a yawning-sighing-snorting sound. "I kind of like sleepy Cass."

"Sleepy Cass likes you too."

"Did you just refer to yourself in the third person?"

"Sorry, sleepy Cass is an arrogant bastard."

She chuckled and tucked her face into his neck. "We need to go back."

"They won't—" They were back to real life, and he had to get these words right. "Stefano Jr. is handing the feds a bust that will not simply make careers, but will rock the drug trade. There's more than one way you could ruin everything. That's why PIA took such drastic action to take you out—or tried to, anyway."

She rested a hand on his cheek. "*Listen.* If I don't go back, then the Agency is going to dig in deep and search. They're keeping track of Stefano Jr. It's likely they already know he and I attended the same AA meeting. I went to your place right before I disappeared. They're going to hyperfocus on you and Stefano Jr."

"You have a point."

"I have several. They know something big is brewing, and when they start turning over stones, they might very well interfere with the FBI's mission—if I haven't already done that. What if they somehow prevent the meeting or interrupt before the feds get there?"

Cass pulled his hair back, jerking his scalp. "Shit."

"I get that your people don't trust me, but the best course of action is everyone doing what they've been doing. We find a holding pattern until Friday—that's less than a week—then the feds can get that megabust they want."

"And what about you?" They were close. The heat and solidity of her body drew him closer. "What do you plan to do?"

The pause that followed filled the air with tension. She sighed. "If I stay with the Agency and play it cool until after the FBI makes the arrests, will I be able to go free?"

He wouldn't lie. "Maybe. The DOJ decides who gets charged and with what, but they'll likely cut you a deal only if you give a statement and agree to testify."

"Which would get me killed."

"You could work for—"

"I want to get far away from this shitstorm." She flopped onto her back, her shoulder brushing his. "I won't work for the government or anyone else ever again."

"You don't need to decide yet. I can get the kill order struck." Cass would ensure it. "But that doesn't mean the feds won't take you off the playing board. Incarceration is definitely a possibility."

After a long pause, she asked, "What do I do?"

That she'd asked him meant she had faith in him—at least a little. He wouldn't squander it.

He checked his Apple Watch. It was Sunday morning. Cass had an idea.

* * *

"Hey, Mom," Cass said and kissed his mother on the cheek. Her black hair was held up with a clip, a few stray hairs breaking free. Her graying roots were barely visible. "This is my girlfriend, Jolene. Jolene, this is my mother, Christine."

Jolene froze for a second before his mother tackled her in a hug.

"Oh, Jolene, it is so great to finally meet you!" His mother stepped back, keeping a hand on Jolene's shoulders. "Let me have a look at you."

"Mom," Cass said, trying to shift her focus back to him.

"She's lovely," his mom said, then called out, "Victor, come over here! Cass has a girlfriend." His mom took their coats and piled them on the filled coat rack. The house smelled like his childhood—tomato sauce and garlic—which relaxed him but not Jolene.

Cass wrapped an arm around her. "Sorry."

His mother waved a hand. "For what? I love her already." She looked over her shoulder. "Vic!"

Jolene pulled off her boots and set them in the row of footwear beside the entryway. Cass followed.

She seemed dazed over his mother's warm reception. "Um, nice to meet you too."

Cass's father slipped in behind his mom, his height and broadness not as intimidating with the elevated ceiling of the foyer. "What's this?"

"This is Jolene, Cass's *girlfriend*," his mother said, beaming.

Was she? He wanted that.

"Really?" his dad said, his thick, dark brows climbing high enough to be lost in the gray hair that flopped over his eyes

"Could you not act as if I've never dated before?" Cass asked. "What's for lunch, anyway? We're starving." They'd burned many calories and hadn't replenished enough.

"Oh." His mother scrambled toward the kitchen, talking over her shoulder. "I should make more garlic bread. We're having lasagna. If I'd known you were coming, Cassidy, I'd be more prepared."

"Surprise." He turned to Jolene, who'd paled slightly. Not bad considering what an overload his family could be. "Hey, Dad, is Shaun showing up today?"

"We're expecting him and Mia any minute."

They crowded into the kitchen around the butcherblock island, all of them standing because there were only two chairs. Cass's mother slathered butter on an extra loaf of French bread.

Cass missed aspects of his childhood home, the routine and the coziness, but he didn't miss Batavia. City life suited him far better than the suburbs.

He couldn't picture Jolene living in anything remotely suburban or rural. If they had to go on the run, though, she might have to adapt.

Jolene told his parents she was a personal trainer and asked about their professions in return. His mom brushed off the question, as she brushed garlic butter on the bread, as if being a retired lawyer turned homemaker were nothing, while his dad said evasive things about his military consulting work.

By the time Shaun and his wife arrived, Jolene was entertaining his parents with tales of male clients making fools of themselves to impress the female trainers. Cass had no sense if the stories were true and decided it didn't matter.

"What's going on?" Mia asked as she entered the kitchen. She looked as she always did, like a primary school teacher in her cream cashmere sweater, long brown skirt, and matching boots. Mia never took her shoes off at the door.

"Cass has a girlfriend!" His mother gestured to Jolene, as if Mia might not figure out who she was talking about. "This is Jolene."

Mia's smile lit her face. "Hi. It's great to meet you."

"Meet who?" Shaun said, walking in with a case of beer and a bottle of wine. He stopped abruptly when he saw Jolene.

"This is Jolene," his mom said with another wide grin. "Cass's girlfriend."

Shaun jerked his head back in shock.

"Don't be a dick about it," Cass said, pinning his brother with a glare. "I'm allowed to have a girlfriend."

"Of course you are," his mother said, not picking up on the heat between the siblings.

Shaun set the drinks on the counter and glared at Cass. "I need to speak with you," he said through gritted teeth.

"Sure, but you need to meet Jolene first," Cass said.

"No, I don't."

"Shaun!" Mia and their mother admonished him at the same time.

"Sorry, I just need to talk to Cass. *Right now.*" Shaun stalked out of the kitchen, heading for the front door so they'd be assured privacy.

Cass had just reached the driveway, his coat unzipped, his shoes untied, when Shaun said, "Are you out of your motherfucking mind? You brought that woman to our parents' house? My wife is with me, asshole."

"What is it you think she's going to do, steal Mia's chicken cacciatore recipe? I hate to break it to you, bro, but it's not all that theft-worthy."

Shaun's eye twitched, and Cass wondered if his brother was going to take a swing at him. They'd both served in the army, but Shaun had gone into military intelligence, while Cass had gone into Special Forces. Both of them stayed in shape, but Cass was sure he could take Shaun.

"Do you have *any* idea how much shit you're in right now?" Shaun's face turned coral. "When operatives found your apartment empty, we thought the Agency might have taken you out. You haven't answered any of my thirty phone calls. No tracking on your cell. I thought I was going to have to sit through Sunday fucking lunch thinking you were dead while Mom and Dad had no clue. Instead, you show up here with your *target*." He pitched his voice particularly low on *target*.

"Yeah, let's talk about the hit order. She's innocent," Cass said. When Shaun gaped at him, he continued, "Look, she thought she was working for the government; they kept her in the dark about their real goals. I couldn't do it, Shaun. I mean that literally." Shaun was the only person he'd ever told about the knowings. His brother believed only when it suited him, despite Cass giving him some heavy circumstantial evidence.

"Come on, man, that's not your gut talking, that's your dick. You think I missed those hickeys all over her neck? What the fuck is wrong with you?" Shaun paced a few feet and back, too restless to stand still in the driveway.

The neighbor's garage hummed open before a white SUV circled the cul-de-sac and pulled inside. The vague scent of car exhaust briefly overpowered the aroma of fresh air and fall. A sudden breeze fluttered through the tall maples, downing several red and gold leaves.

Cass wasn't about to tell his brother he was in love with Jolene, but he had to change his mind. "She doesn't deserve to die. You're about to spend Sunday lunch with her, and I dare you to let the order stand when it's over." He stepped into Shaun's path.

"You know I didn't give that order."

"And yet, you did nothing to stop it, and we both know you could. Look," Cass said slapping a hand onto Shaun's shoulder a smidge harder than necessary. "I get that the kill order was given spur of the moment and without the necessary forethought, but now you've got time to consider all the angles. Is killing her really the best solution? Think of the sort of intel you could get from having someone inside the Agency while everything is going down. She can warn us if their organization intends to interfere. Having her on our side can only make you look good."

"Sure, until she goes triple agent on me and obliterates years' worth of work and makes me look like an incompetent asshole."

Cass stared at him, wishing he could slap Shaun upside the head with his thoughts. That would have been an awesome talent.

"She's untrustworthy, and I can't have such a huge unknown out in the field."

"Make Behmann pull the order. If you don't and PIA sends someone else to do it, I'm going to tell Mom it's your fault she's dead."

Shaun laughed. "You're going to tell Mommy on me?"

"Yep. I'm going to tell Mom you did nothing to prevent the murder because you felt threatened by Jolene because she's different." Cass's gut hummed, telling him this was the right leverage. Shaun cared about nothing more than their parents' approval.

"She's a threat to the biggest criminal-organization bust of the decade! She's freaky powerful and an unknown complication. We at least need to take her in for questioning. My reputation is on the line." Shaun groaned and tilted his face to the sky. "You were just supposed to watch her."

Cass rolled his eyes. "When the opportunity arose for me to get closer to her, you were thrilled." The FBI couldn't have done what Cass had done. If an agent had made contact with Jolene, a target of surveillance, like Cass had at Starbucks, the fed would have had to fill out an FD-302 report and back off.

"That's when I thought you were objective."

"Just because I'm not objective doesn't mean I'm wrong. She can help us, Shaun, if you'd pull your head out of your ass."

"Fucker. I should have you arrested."

"Mm. You should. Maybe in the middle of Sunday lunch." Cass inched closer to Shaun until they were almost nose to nose. Shaun's cologne was leather and musk and too heavy. "I'm sure the family would be totally understanding."

Veins pulsed in Shaun's temples, and he turned from coral to strawberry. "I can't stay here with that *woman*. Who knows what the hell she'll pick up from me?"

"Jesus, you sound like Jerry." His boss, Jerry Behmann, was terrified of memory surgeons, though he couched it as concern about their abuse of power. He had no business supervising PIA agents. "He might have been the one to make the call to take her out instead of looking for alternative solutions, but you said nothing."

Shaun winced. His personal ethics had to be affecting him.

"You're not interested at all in what she might have to share? How she might help us on her end?" Cass asked. If he could persuade the FBI to recognize Jolene's value, she could likely avoid jail.

"Turn her into a snitch? Possibly when this case is over, but right now, we're focusing on shutting down multiple criminal organizations. We don't need her to do that."

"Fine. I'm going to go have lunch with my family. You can fuck off."

"Cass," Shaun growled. "I'll get the order canceled, but you'll have to bring her in. If you don't, they'll have someone else do it, and I doubt they'll be as nice to her as you are."

"And when the Agency starts flipping over stones and sticking their noses everywhere, asking questions and calling attention to themselves, then what?" Cass raised his eyebrows and stared down his brother.

Shaun laced his fingers behind his neck and bent over for several seconds before straightening. "Goddamn it. If this blows up, I'll see that you're held personally responsible."

Cass gave him a two-fingered, mock salute. "Noted."

CHAPTER TWENTY EIGHT

Jolene

While Cass and Shaun talked outside, Jolene and the rest of the Stuart family gathered around the kitchen table, which was tucked in a windowed alcove with a view of the large backyard and its perfect grass and smattering of mature trees. Three piles of colorful leaves gave the place a bucolic feel.

Although Jolene smiled and answered questions, she participated in the conversation on autopilot. She was more interested in what decisions Cass and Shaun were making that would affect her.

When Cass finally returned, his cheeks pink and jaw tense, Christine asked, "You boys okay?"

"No, your eldest is an ass," Cass replied.

"Language," Christine said, though it held no heat. "Problems?"

Cass's eyes met Jolene's for a moment. "More personal than anything else."

Shaun bustled in behind him, his focus solely on his wife. "Work thing, babe. We gotta go."

Mia arched an eyebrow. "We just got here."

"We're happy to drop you at home later, if you want to stay, Mia," Cass said with a warm smile.

Shaun looked as if he'd run into an invisible wall, his entire body tensing. "No, she's coming with me."

Silence rang through the kitchen, Shaun's barking tone reverberating.

"Thanks, Cass, that would be great," Mia said, then physically turned her body to her mother-in-law. "What can I help with, Mom?"

Christine looked from a fuming Shaun to an irate Mia and mumbled, "Nothing left to do, sweetheart."

"Mia, can I talk to you for a second?" Shaun asked through gritted teeth.

"I can talk, but all you can do is issue orders—first with Cass and then with me. Go work, Shaun. I'll see you at the house later, and we can discuss this when I'm less likely to whack my heel up your ass." Mia's voice was calm.

Jolene liked her, and Christine must have, too, because she didn't reprimand Mia for her language.

"Honey, please," Shaun said, trying for a placating tone and not quite hitting it. "Come with me."

Mia stood, and Jolene lost some respect for her, which wasn't fair, since Jolene didn't know the ramifications of Mia defying Shaun. But then Mia rested her fists on the table and stared down her husband. "No."

"But—"

"We made a commitment to be here. If you have to work, fine, whatever, but I'm staying. If you think you can order me around like I'm one of your minions, then let me disabuse you of that notion right here and now."

"You're making a scene," Shaun said.

"No, Shaun, you're the one making a scene." Mia's posture had gone so rigid she probably grew an inch.

"She's a memory surgeon!" Shaun said, pointing an accusing finger at Jolene like a Puritan decrying a witch.

The entire family looked at Jolene. Her face flashed hot enough to make sweat dot her forehead.

"So what?" Cass said, the only one in the room unfazed. He collapsed into the chair next to Jolene.

Shaun sputtered, then found some words. "So, she—she—she can read our thoughts."

"Not from over there, she can't," Cass said, his voice sounding unnaturally calm compared with Shaun's outburst. He placed his elbows on the table and leaned his chin on a cupped fist. "I can shoot a person in the head from four hundred yards, and yet, you eat with me all the time."

Shaun glared at Cass. "She's not trustworthy."

"Shaun Paul Stuart," Christine's mom voice cut through the tension and added its own. "We don't judge people based on preconceived notions."

Jolene waited for Shaun to tell them she'd been a lapdog for a big-time drug operation. He'd already outed her as a memory surgeon, so she had no hope for his discretion.

"But, Mom—"

"No, Shaun. Jolene is your brother's guest, and this is my home. You're being abominably rude on nothing more than hearsay and speculation. Nobody has any evidence that memory surgeons are any less trustworthy than anyone else. If you actually have to work, then go, but if you're going to stay, you're going to be polite."

Jolene wasn't used to people sticking up for her. Cass had great parents, and she didn't want to ruin that for him. "I should go."

"Yes!" Shaun said.

Everyone else said, "No!"

"Son." Victor stood. Though he had to be in his fifties, he looked fit enough to lift a tank with one hand and had a military snap to his voice. "In my study."

Shaun ducked his head, obviously not daring to *but, Dad* his father. He followed the older man out of the kitchen and down the hall.

"People still have studies?" Jolene asked, the need to fill the silence a compulsion.

"Oh, 'study' is just a pretentious word for 'home office'," Christine said with a wave of her hand. "Sorry about that, Jolene. Shaun's just . . ."

"An uptight asshole," Mia finished.

"Those weren't the words I was going to use, but yes." Christine patted Jolene's hand. The trust implied in the gesture made the backs of Jolene's eyes prickle. "I had a great-aunt who predicted fires."

"You did?" Jolene, Cass, and Mia all asked.

Christine nodded. "Aunt Flossie. People accused her of setting the fires to get attention, consorting with the devil, and being a communist." She shrugged. "All she wanted to do was help. People in general like to demonize what they don't understand. It's hard to fight public opinion without proper representation."

Jolene thought about Cass and his own presumed ability. Did he come from a line of psychics of some flavor or other? Did she? Her grandmother had always lamented that nobody else in the family had possessed any sort of psychic gift.

"Anyway, your gift is nothing to be ashamed of," Christine said. "This is a safe space."

Maybe Cass had been right to bring them here, because her entire body relaxed. Cass wouldn't have brought her to his family's home unless he'd been honest about wanting to protect her. He wouldn't have killed her. Not everything between them had been a lie.

"Can I ask you questions, or would that be rude?" Mia asked Jolene.

"It depends on the questions but go ahead."

"Is it true a person has to let you in before you can see a memory?"

"Yes." That was a flat-out lie. Even so, Cass nodded to back up her claim. Lying was necessary to protect herself and other memory surgeons from persecution and prejudice. She hated that she'd made Cass complicit. "The only exception is when someone is mentally vulnerable by drugs or alcohol." Or sleep, meditation, trust.

"Have you seen any of Cass's memories?" Mia asked with a wide smile, as if Jolene might have spied something flattering or romantic.

The image of Cass imagining gunshot wounds in her chest belched into her mind. "I try not to violate people's privacy like that."

"Oh, I'd be reading Shaun's thoughts nonstop," Mia said. "I'd find out for sure if he likes my chicken cacciatore or not."

Everyone laughed, though Jolene faked hers. "You might not like what you learn."

Cass reached over and squeezed her hand.

Shaun and Victor returned. Victor walked over and kissed Christine on the top of her head, the gesture both rote and romantic.

"Jolene, I apologize for my words and behavior earlier," Shaun said like a recalcitrant child. "Mom, sorry I was disrespectful in your home."

"That's okay. We're all continually learning," Christine said.

Jolene didn't bother to acknowledge or accept Shaun's apology, since it was bullshit.

"Where's my apology?" Mia asked, hands on her hips.

Shaun gave her a crooked smile, the left side of his lips pulling higher than the right. "I'll apologize properly when we get home."

Mia sniffed. "You wish."

"TMI," Christine said, and everyone laughed.

* * *

Cass's family wasn't TV-sitcom awesome, but the ease and genuine affection were apparent. They were their own unit or bubble, somehow forming a whole. Jolene wondered what her life would have been like with relatives like that. Her family consisted of her, her grandmother, and the world, something too vast to provide anything so warm and cozy.

Shaun never warmed up to her. Cass kept a hand on her thigh through most of the meal, and it felt like companionship more than comfort. Best of all—or worst of all—it seemed real and not for show.

She didn't deserve to be a part of this family meal. Shaun was right—not about how she was an abomination because of her gift—but she understood why he wanted her far from his loved ones.

If she ended up having to go on the run, Cass might agree to go with her, and that would break up this happy unit. They wouldn't think so highly of her then. But she'd take Cass, wanting to be the woman he seemed to see.

CHAPTER TWENTY NINE

Cass

CASS WAS UNSURE IF IT WAS WHAT HIS FATHER HAD said to Shaun or if sharing a meal had done it, but Shaun pulled him aside as they were preparing to leave and relented on his harsh stance about Jolene. She'd have to give up intel, testify, and work as a source, but Shaun thought he could keep her out of prison and further studies.

It was a fair deal, and she'd see that in time. If she accepted it. For now, he'd keep the details to himself. No sense mentioning it before the bosses approved anyway. Besides, the weight of all she'd have to do might make her crack.

On their way back to the city, Cass asked, "Have you thought about how you're going to handle things with the Agency?"

She sighed. "Not really. Stadler's going to be pissed I went radio silent for the weekend, especially when he hears I met Stefano Jr. on Friday."

"Why would you tell him that?" Cass asked, his chest flinching as if he'd been punched. "They can't know—"

"Stefano's under surveillance," Jolene said. "If the Agency knows he was at the same AA meeting as me, and I don't mention it, we're screwed. They're going to *know* I'm holding things back. It'll work better if I tell them I interacted with him but didn't get anything."

"Good thinking. I've seen what happens when you disappoint your handler."

"Hopefully, Stadler isn't so pissed off he pulls me off the mission." She bit one of her thumbnails.

"Shaun's willing to push for immunity, but you'll have to give the feds information in return." He held his breath, waiting to see how she'd handle that news.

"I get that, I do, but I'm not in charge, and the others might be as in the dark as I am. What if I get them in trouble and they're innocent?"

According to Jolene, Stadler had always treated her differently. The others knew, but she might not have been ready to face that yet. "Just be part of the game. Find an angle, leverage your unique contribution and what you already know. Don't pussy out because it's easier."

Jolene snorted. "Yes, sir." She pushed his shoulder. "And what are you going to be doing on your end?"

He smiled. "I've still got to keep an eye on you, don't I?"

The closer they got to Chicago, the more traffic slowed them down.

"How did you find out about me, anyway?" she asked, focusing on her folded hands in her lap.

Cass had expected the question much sooner, and though it might hurt her, he told her the truth. "Colton talked to several people about memory surgeons and how one had stolen his girlfriend. That flagged our section of Homeland Security. When we looked into it, we found your address at the time in his contact list, but of course, you'd abandoned the apartment by then, but the company that rented the place was a known Agency proxy. The landlord hadn't yet cleaned the place for the next tenants, and we got fingerprints that matched someone in our system." He glanced over at her and smiled. "Doreen St. John, a memory surgeon killed in a fire about five years ago. From Colton's connection to the Red Flames and mentions of the Stefano Organization, it was deemed prudent to keep an eye on you. By monitoring the same proxy company, we found your new lease in Chicago, and since I already live ridiculously close and my brother is in charge of the feds case, I was assigned to the mission."

"Quite the coincidence, don't you think?"

He hated that she would have to face the Agency on her own. He'd play backup, but he'd have no clear sight lines. Cass reached over and took her cold hand in his. "There's something special about us, don't you think?"

Jolene looked at him then, the streetlights striping across her face. He saw more than most, and she saw more than most, and at that moment, they each saw the other. "You're not wrong."

CHAPTER THIRTY

Jolene

JOLENE HADN'T PROCESSED EVERYTHING—OR, really, anything. She'd been too distracted by almost dying followed by life-altering sex. For a while, she'd managed to block out the majority of her turmoil.

Now that they were returning to Chicago, her mind swirled with thoughts of Cass, the Agency, Stadler, Ryan, Jorge, and Sara. If they weren't who she thought they were, was she who she thought she was? She'd worked hard to fashion an identity for herself, and now it was crumpled and aflame.

Cass moved his hand to the back of her neck and squeezed. He didn't pause before making direct skin contact. She didn't see anything, though, because she'd closed herself off. She'd seen enough for a while.

"Uh-oh," Cass said as he pulled up next to her building. "You've got lights on inside."

Stadler was waiting for her. She should have known. "Better not stick around."

He slipped a burner phone he'd purchased in Northbrook into her inner coat pocket. "Call me if you need help."

"Okay."

"I mean it, Jolene."

Did she trust him?

Eighty percent, she decided. A miracle, considering their past.

His eyes dropped to her mouth, and the pull she always felt around him supercharged. She didn't fight it, letting instinct tilt her face to his. He met her in the middle, his lips as warm as his hands, soft and gentle.

"You do whatever you have to do to protect yourself, okay?" he said. "Promise me."

That he valued her vow made her stomach dip. "I promise."

* * *

"Where the ever-loving fuck have you been?" Stadler asked from just inside the door, his icy voice a harbinger of something deadly to come.

"Give her a second," Sara said, starting to pull Stadler back, but then, apparently thinking better of it, she dropped her hand. "You okay, sweetie?"

Jolene's cover story died on her lips. She'd never convince them she'd taken a romantic weekend away—the idea was too frivolous, selfish, and unlike her. She had to adjust. "I was with Cass."

Stadler's eyes were so hot she couldn't hold his gaze. "Try again."

In her training, she'd learned that sticking as close to the truth as possible was easiest in terms of believability. "I met his family."

"Sara, wait downstairs for me."

Jolene's body flipped into fight-or-flight mode, tripping heavily into flight. "No," Jolene blurted. She didn't want to be alone with him. "I freaked out, okay?" The adrenaline coursing through her shoved words out of her mouth like paratroopers. "Stefano showed up at my AA meeting, and I thought, you know, 'Wow, this is my big chance.' Afterward, I introduced myself." Stadler's posture didn't change. "I got nothing. I shook his hand, and nothing. He seemed more horrified than comforted that someone from the health club was there. I don't think—he's not going to let me get within touching distance again."

"We can fix that, no problem," Sara said. "That's why we have the team."

"You didn't see the way he looked at me." All of that was true. "So, when Cass reached out, I thought, 'Fuck it.' And when he saw how upset I was, he suggested we get out of town for the weekend. It's such a normal thing to do, and I never get to do normal anymore. It was just what I needed, if that matters."

"It doesn't," Stadler said. "You missed two days of work."

"Well, I—"

"Shut up." Stadler's voice was cutting, like a switchblade to her Achilles's tendon.

She obeyed like a cowed dog.

"Where's your stuff?"

Shit. Shit. Shit. "I told you, we just ran off. I borrowed Cass's clothes." She looked at Sara for help. "It was more romantic than it sounds."

Sara clasped and unclasped her hands and wouldn't meet Jolene's eyes.

"Give me your phone." Stadler extended his hand.

Jolene moved slowly and carefully, extracting her cell and holding it out to Stadler.

He took it with equal solemnity and switched it on. Silence choked the room while the three of them waited for the cell to boot. Alert chimes cascaded. Stadler scrolled to her recent calls and selected Cass's number.

Jolene's gut sloshed and squeezed, sending stomach acid up her throat. She leaned her back against the door and hoped Cass wouldn't say anything incriminating when he answered.

Stadler put the phone on speaker as it rang.

Cass picked up on the second ring. "Hey."

Stadler glared at Jolene, as if she should know what he wanted her to say.

"I can't see you again." Her voice propelled the words at time-and-a-half speed.

"Why not? I thought we had a great weekend together."

Jolene closed her eyes, relieved he understood the situation. "I'm exhausted," she said at last. "I shouldn't have blown off work, and I don't have the energy or time to devote to you. You're high maintenance, Cass, which is fine, but . . ."

"You don't want to put in the effort."

"It's not that I don't want to; I can't." And that was sort of true too. "I'm in recovery, as I told you before, and that means I have to keep life as simple as possible."

"So, the rest of your life you're going to avoid interpersonal relationships? Or just me? I think your excuses are hollow and lame." His performance was so perfect, it tripped genuine anger in her.

"It's not an excuse, asshole, it's a reason, and I don't owe you even one of those. I don't want to see you again, period. It doesn't matter if you like it or find it acceptable." She dug her nails into the palms of her hands and looked only at the phone Stadler held. "I'm sorry, Cass. Truly. I wish only the best for you, and believe me, this is what's best for both of us."

He *would* be much better off without her and the danger she brought, but she couldn't bear the thought of actually letting him go.

"Jolene, please, don't do this. Meet me one more time?"

Stadler shook his head once.

"Sorry, I can't. Don't call again. I'm blocking your number when we're done here."

"Then stay on the phone with me for just a little while."

Stadler ended the call, then blocked Cass's number. Jolene blinked back wetness in her eyes. She was alone, an island surrounded by shark-infested waters—though, hopefully, not for much longer, but that hardly improved the needlelike pains in her heart and behind her eyes.

"Happy?" she asked Stadler.

Sara sucked in a gasp.

Stadler grabbed her throat, pinning her to the door. His breath smelled of mint and coffee. "I don't know what the ever-loving fuck is going on with you, Nova, but I don't have time to adjust your attitude. Maybe we picked the wrong memory surgeon. I doubt Brayleigh would have given us this much trouble."

Jolene's entire body recoiled at the thought of Stadler approaching Kiera. "No. You promised to leave her out of this."

He released her but didn't back away. "While you were out diddling around, we got important intel from Gold's computer."

Gold? What about Kiera? Then she remembered Stefano Sr.'s secretary, who'd pinched her mind when he'd slammed his memories shut. He liked fancy watches.

"There's going to be some kind of epic meeting," Sara said, bouncing on her toes as if no tension existed. "Five days from now at the Merchandise Mart. We're only missing the time of day and specific instructions. This is an amazing opportunity to cut off the head entirely."

"Okay," Jolene said, her mind shooting off in too many directions. "All we have to do is—?"

"You've got three days to find out the time of the meeting," Stadler said.

"Me?" She sounded like a dumbass, but she couldn't stop. "By myself? Why is that so important? Couldn't we just watch the Merchandise Mart all day"

Stadler looked at her as if she were addled. "I don't ask for shit that doesn't matter. It's your responsibility, but the rest of us work as a team, so if you need assistance, reach out, which is the opposite of disappearing."

"No problem for you, I'm sure," Sara said, moving toward the door to effectively step between Jolene and Stadler.

Jolene swallowed. "All right."

"If I don't have those details by five o'clock on Wednesday, you're worthless to me. You'll ride out your last few months at the lab." Stadler pushed past her and out the door.

Sara followed, giving her an exaggerated grimace and a tiny wave goodbye.

Jolene locked the door and pressed her forehead against the smooth wood. Now she knew the Agency wasn't a government agency, his threat to relegate her to the lab morphed into something more ominous. She could disappear forever.

CHAPTER THIRTY ONE

Cass

CASS CLOSED HIS EYES AND STUFFED DOWN ALL the impulses pushing him to action. Stadler's choice of repercussions—she could no longer see Cass—indicated he'd believed whatever story she'd given him. Though he could have been testing her, or maybe he was biding his time before springing something worse on her.

They should have run.

No.

Running would ensure someone, somewhere, would catch them eventually. Playing the game was the only route to freedom. He swept his condo for bugs and found none.

After changing into his flannel pajama bottoms and a fitted T-shirt, he called his brother on his secure line. "She's back and in place. You got the kill order rescinded, right?"

"This is a mistake," Shaun replied.

"Shaun—"

"Yeah. I talked to Behmann, and he agreed to strike the termination."

"Good." Cass wanted to ask him what their dad had said but decided not to risk the question blowing up in his face. "She's trying to make things right."

"She's trying to save her own ass. She's charmed Mom and seduced you, and that only makes her more suspicious."

He refrained from telling his brother to go fuck himself. "When have I ever been wrong about a person?"

Shaun grumbled, "Does your first time have to be on my case?"

* * *

Cass's insomnia returned with a vengeance, and he distracted himself with painting at three in the morning. Eventually, he stopped working and stared into space, letting the scent of turpentine burn his nostrils.

A text message at five thirty a.m. from the burner phone he'd given Jolene broke him out of his stupor.

Jolene: *Hey. I'm ok. They know about meeting date and location but not time. New assignment to find the time. Have until Wednesday 5 pm or off case. You ok?*

Cass: *I'm okay. Where are you?*

Jolene: *Bathroom stall at GCHC.*

Cass chuckled. *Call me. I want to hear your voice.*

Jolene: *Can't risk. Probably followed/watched.*

She likely wasn't wrong.

Jolene: *You call me.*

She needed him.

Jolene answered on the first ring but said nothing. He couldn't even hear her breathe.

"Hey, sweetheart," he said.

She didn't reply, but he heard her exhale.

Something warm and too tight circled his belly and shot up to his chest. "I'm worried about you." Cass stood and paced around his studio. The room was illuminated by a naked-bulb lamp, which he liked for the starkness of the light. Outside, the sky remained bruise black. His bare feet stuck briefly to the tarp still covering the floor.

In many ways, they were alone in the world, connected by this slim piece of technology.

"I couldn't sleep last night. I don't think I mentioned to you that I have insomnia. No matter how tired I get, it's difficult to fall asleep, and I never get more than a few hours." He thought about how deeply he'd slept with her next to him. "Part of it is the army stuff. Special Forces snipers are always on alert. Even after being out for years, I still tend to sleep light."

She continued to say nothing, couldn't say anything.

"You hang up when you have to go. Don't feel bad about it." He padded into his bedroom and lay down on top of the covers, one paint-speckled hand resting on his abdomen. He crossed one ankle over the other. "I excelled at marksmanship, obviously, and ferreting out the enemy. There's something noticeable about someone looking to do violence." He closed his eyes. "It's often in the eyes, but sometimes it's in the set of the shoulders or an inner focus."

He pictured the sand and heat, the streams of people, the man in white, exactly like so many others. "I shot this man from twenty yards . . . out of nowhere. I hadn't consciously decided. Checkpoints weren't my normal duty, but every so often, I'd be assigned a shift. One day, I was watching all these people walking by, trying to spot enemy combatants, who look exactly like civilians. Suddenly, my gut twisted, and I shot this man. People screamed and scattered, and the guys working the checkpoint with me were like, 'What the fuck, dude?' And I thought my life and career were over, and then . . . we discovered he had a bomb strapped to his chest under his clothes."

Cass didn't want to remember more, but he wanted Jolene to understand. "Seemed like the knowing was some kind of premonition. Or maybe I just got lucky. The guys started calling me Psych, after the TV show. It made me uncomfortable, probably because I liked it. I liked that I'd stopped that guy before he hurt God knows how many people. I liked being a soldier and a sniper. I liked protecting. But the outside world sees things differently. I'm a person who's taken human life, and I don't feel guilty about it. But that's not all I'm good for. It's not my fucking purpose, and I am more than that."

She grunted, a small sound he understood as her way of saying she didn't see him that way, not even when he'd been assigned to kill her—or perhaps because of that. Because he hadn't killed her, and he'd die making sure nobody else did either.

"I'd take out someone to save myself." Something about his words hit him wrong. "Well, I mean, I wouldn't use someone as a human shield or anything. All I'm saying is if someone comes after me, or mine . . ." Because she was his, and he wanted her to comprehend deep in her bones that he had her back. "I'm going to do whatever is necessary, and I'm not going to feel guilty about it. Even if that makes me a bad person."

Her breaths were coming faster and harder, and he thought she might be crying. "I'm right here. Always," he said in a hushed voice. "You're not alone, okay?"

"Okay," she whispered.

He heard a flush. Their conversation had to end. "I miss you, sweetheart." Cass rubbed his chest, as if he could scrub away the ache there. "You can reach out to me anytime. *Any*time."

Her breath hitched, and she was gone.

CHAPTER THIRTY TWO

Jolene

JOLENE WORKED OUT IN THE LARGER FREE-WEIGHT room with a direct line of sight to the smaller area, which had been taken over by Stefano Jr. and his thugs. Did he have the meeting details she needed? She had to try, and once she had the information, she would decide if she would share it with Stadler.

Regardless, Cass would remain by her side. She wasn't alone.

Out of the corner of her eye, she spotted something pale. Sara's hair in a low ponytail. She wore a sports bra with cutouts and crisscrossed straps in the back and tiny spandex shorts. Gazes followed her everywhere.

"Hey, friend," she said when she reached Jolene.

Jolene stopped her bench press and sat up, casual-like. "Hi."

"I think I need a little personal training," she said, leaning on the weight rack. "Help a girl out?" Sara giggled at Jolene's frown. "Come on." She tugged on the end of Jolene's high ponytail. "It'll be fun."

"Why do you have to jinx it like that?" Jolene groaned before stopping the workout timing on her Fitbit and leading Sara to the treadmills, which smelled a little less like sweat than the free-weight areas and a little more like disinfectant.

Sara had probably lied to Jolene like the rest of them. Still, she'd buffered Jolene from Stadler when he'd turned scary, and she was a decent friend.

Jolene trusted Sara fifty-one percent.

Jolene set the treadmill in motion. "Ten minutes. Work up to five miles an hour within the first two minutes."

"Aren't you going to do it too?"

Jolene rolled her eyes. "I already warmed up. I'll be back for you, and if I see you've slacked, you are going to be sore as hell tomorrow."

"That's what he said," Sara called to Jolene's back.

Jolene laughed but didn't turn around. She finished her chest set. If she turned over information to the feds, would they jail Sara? Jorge and Ryan? Were they as duped as she'd been? Not likely. They'd worked closely together for years, and Jorge with his technical skills would certainly have figured out what the Agency really was.

She didn't want to work for a criminal organization, and she didn't want to hurt the members of her team. Even if they were crooks and villains, she couldn't stop thinking of them as family. Needing to focus on the job—jobs?—she pushed away thoughts of choices and their consequences.

When Jolene checked, Sara had worked herself into enough of a sweat to mollify Jolene. Sara grinned at Jolene no different than she always did as they started walking the gym's track together.

"How'd you get brought onto the team?" Jolene asked, hoping for clues to Sara's level of ignorance.

Sara wiped off her generous cleavage with a gym towel. "Stadler recruited me."

"From where?"

"Off the streets, actually. He was the first person to treat me like I was more than my looks. I know he comes off like an asshole—well, he is an asshole—but he looks out for the team. He's got your back, even if he's a dick while he does it." She tossed her sweaty arm over Jolene. "Don't worry. You'll come through, and it'll be like those little blips never happened."

Jolene needed a plan for extracting more information. They walked past where the Stefano people were lifting, and Sara squealed in recognition of the biggest guy, breaking the mood.

"Hey, hot thing," the man called, his biceps looking like boulders in his sleeveless sweatshirt. Steroids were a definite possibility.

Sara ran over and gave 'roid dude a full-body hug, despite his sweaty-sock aroma. He grabbed her waist and gripped her to him for a few seconds. Jolene cleared her throat, and Sara pulled back a scant inch.

"June, this is . . ." Sara bit her lip.

"Tomas," the man said, smirking at Sara.

"Hi." Jolene held out her hand to him, hoping he might know something. She could redeem Stadler's good opinion right then. Or at least earn some breathing space.

"Hey, Tomas!" Stefano Jr. boomed. "This isn't social hour. Get back to work." He glared at Jolene hard enough she worried his goons might ask questions.

Tomas instantly obeyed Stefano Jr., leaving Jolene's hand untouched.

Sara shrugged and waggled her fingers at Tomas. "Later, babe."

"You need some core exercises," Jolene said, desperate to pull Sara away from there before she realized Stefano Jr. had just warned Tomas away from Jolene.

When they reached the mats, Sara collapsed onto the ground with a *thwack* and snorted. "Does he think you're going to run around and tell everyone he's an alcoholic? Jeez."

"People can be sensitive, particularly when they have a reputation to uphold. Alcoholism is often considered a weakness." Jolene didn't necessarily disagree with that, though she didn't think it was a character defect. At least Sara assumed the animosity was due to the alcoholic secret and not the memory-reading secret.

Too many secrets.

CHAPTER THIRTY THREE

Cass

After Cass relayed to his brother that the Agency knew the date and location of the massive meeting, Shaun growled and disconnected.

Cass decided to confront Shaun in person and stopped by the FBI office, where he and a few other PIA agents also had cubicles—though they worked mostly in the field. His neck prickled in apprehension when he spotted his boss, Jerry Behmann, in with Shaun. Both men looked away from him.

They were sidelining him. Or worse.

Cass walked to his desk, logged on to the computer there, and clicked through his emails just to have something to do until he was escorted from the building. His fingers were clumsy, and he kept making typing mistakes. The woman in the cubicle next to his spoke on the phone, arranging a meeting. Cass's stomach rumbled with a combination of hunger and nerves that made him glad he hadn't eaten anything yet today.

He'd never been fired from a job. He excelled, worked extra hours, focused on getting everything right. And now he was going to be canned by his own brother. Sort of. What would his parents think? They might not pick an official side, but they'd both have opinions. Not that he knew for certain he was getting fired—except he did. Not today, but they would start the process.

Phones rang. Papers shuffled. People talked to one another in garbled voices. Someone popped popcorn in the breakroom microwave.

Shaun and Behmann both stepped into his cubicle. Cass looked past the two men to scrutinize the two security guards who accompanied them. They expected trouble.

This was worse than being fired. *They want to detain me.* His body lit up with adrenaline.

The world slowed so every breath took several seconds. Cass stood. Behmann kept his face blank, but malicious glee poured off him in waves. Shaun, by contrast, wilted, torn by contrasting emotions.

Cass's rush of energy circled in a holding pattern. This wasn't his moment. Sweat prickled along the back of his neck, and he ignored the urge to pull back his hair.

"Hey, Shaun, what's up?" Cass asked, his voice revealing none of his apprehension.

"You need to come with us," Shaun replied, his tone devoid of emotion, though it spouted off his body like an ammonia-bleach mix. Family meant more than anything in their home when they'd been kids, and now Shaun was violating that principle. It didn't matter if he considered his actions justified.

Jolene would have to manage the situation on her own. The Agency wouldn't let her fall into the government's hands. They'd kill her. He stared at Shaun. "You'll keep her safe?"

"That's what you give a shit about?" Behmann said with a sneer he usually reserved for private meetings. "Some memory whore?"

"Jerry," Shaun said, his voice finally animated. "If you can't remain professional, I'll ask for you to be pulled too."

"All of this could have been prevented if he'd done his goddamned job," Behmann replied.

"I don't disagree," Shaun, the traitor, said. "But he made a valid point about us jumping to the most severe plan of action without considering less . . . permanent options."

"Why take the risk?" Behmann hissed, angrier than Cass had ever seen him.

He wants all memory surgeons taken out.

Shaun sighed, as if the outburst was a long-standing irritation and not cause for concern. "Because she's still a US citizen. I'm not going over this again. We bring her in and hopefully she'll allow us to debrief her and keep her off the playing board until the bust is finished. She'll either give us valuable intel and we can cut a deal, or she's looking at potential incarceration. She brought this on herself."

Cass's vision went wonky, as if he were seeing the world from underwater. If the FBI turned Jolene over to PIA, there was a chance she might never be free again. As an off-the-books agency, they could send her to some black site, experiment and test her like a lab rat until they pushed too far and broke her. He hadn't forgotten Behmann's comment about extracting information from her brain for that sick fuck Muller to study. And Cass would likely never track her down, now that he was on the outside.

"Come on, Cass," Shaun said, stepping back and gesturing to his office. "You're just taking a break. If you fight me on this, we're prepared to press charges. Please don't test me."

The two security guards pressed a little closer. They seemed to want Cass to try to make a run for it. As if he'd try anything that obvious.

"A break for how long? What charges?" he asked as he threaded his way through the cubicle maze.

Shaun gave him a don't-be-stupid look. "Obstruction. You'll be free to go once we have Ms. Nova in custody."

He couldn't even say *Jolene*. Cass studied his brother, tunneling deep inside himself to try to find his gift, the one that would know what to do.

Play along.

But what if he did and then ran out of options?

If I fight them on this, they'll put me in a cell.

It wouldn't take long for them to scoop up Jolene. Maybe they should have run.

"You promise she won't be hurt?" he asked Shaun, his eyes flicking to his boss as he pretended to reluctantly acquiesce.

Shaun's shoulders relaxed. "I swear we'll keep her safe. Bringing her in might save her life. The Agency isn't going to sit back and let go of such a valuable asset."

Would PIA?

"Okay." As they approached Shaun's office, Cass scrambled to come up with a plan. "I need to hit the head."

Shaun said nothing for several seconds, staring at Cass as if trying to ascertain a threat. Cass rolled his eyes and handed over his cell phone. Shaun snatched it but still said nothing. Cass held out his arms. "You want the gun too?" He bent down to reach his ankle holster.

"No, that's fine."

"Oh no, if it makes you feel better while I take a shit, then it's a small sacrifice. Want to cram into the stall with me?" Cass extended his Glock, the grip facing his brother.

"Fuck you," Shaun said, waving off the offering. He pushed Cass through the men's room door. "We'll meet you in your office, Jerry." He addressed the guards next. "You guys can go back to your regular duties."

The guards left immediately, but Behmann lingered, huffing out a breath. "I'll wait out here."

In the restroom, Cass asked, "Are you sure you don't want to keep your backup?"

"Shut up, asshole, and do your thing," Shaun said.

"Want to watch me through the gap in the door?"

"I'm trying to save your career, you ungrateful shit." Shaun went to the urinals.

Cass pulled out his prepaid phone. He opened his texts to Jolene and wrote one word: *RUN*.

Then he started a new text to the only person who could help him.

CHAPTER THIRTY FOUR

Jolene

IN THE GYM'S LOCKER ROOM, JOLENE CHANGED INTO her street clothing—jeans and a thin, oversized turtleneck. She had an hour to kill before the AA meeting, and she considered if she'd rather spend it at Starbucks or walking the neighborhood. Out of habit, she checked her cell. No messages. She looked at the burner phone.

RUN

Her heart lurched to the side as if avoiding a bullet. Adrenaline pushed her to run, to break into a sprint and not stop until she reached . . . where? Instead, Jolene gripped her locker, the cool metal digging into her fingers.

She had to have a plan. Otherwise, she risked running right into a net set by the FBI or PIA or somebody she hadn't noticed.

After breathing deeply for two minutes, she laid out her next steps. She left her Agency cell with her workout clothing in her locker. On her burner phone, she logged in to her banking app to transfer money from her overseas account to her local one.

Balance: $50.03.

Jolene stared and stared, waiting for several more zeros to show up. Her face snapped numb as sweat pooled between her breasts and a trickle rolled down her stomach.

Her savings were gone.

Her savings were *gone*. Almost half a million dollars reduced to less than a hundred. She'd earned that goddamned money. Who would steal it? The IRS? She'd been told Agency employees were exempt. Obviously, that was a lie, but didn't they freeze accounts instead of taking everything?

Stadler. He hadn't bought her story, at least not all the way. How stupid had she been, using the Agency computer to do her banking? Of course, Jorge had some kind of spyware on there, tracking everything she did. He'd have access to all her passwords.

Not only had the Agency stolen from her, they'd effectively trapped her. She had forty-two dollars and change on her, and a credit card she didn't dare use.

Jolene pressed an icy hand to her forehead. The scented soap at the club, chemical-floral, seemed to clog her nose, and she had to breathe through her mouth.

Kiera. Jolene had lost her number years ago, not that Kiera would believe her if she called claiming to be her dead friend. She'd have to go to Kiera's condo.

What if she'd moved? Kiera had made herself untraceable, so if she no longer lived in the same place, Jolene would never find her.

If Jolene attempted to reach Kiera and failed, she was screwed. She'd never fool Stadler with another story. If she'd even fooled him the last time.

Jolene splashed cold water on her face. Cass had told her to run, which meant he couldn't help her now. With little money, a fake ID, and nowhere to go, her choices were few—go to Kiera for assistance in escaping, tell Stadler everything and hope he let her live, or let the government take her out.

Really, she had only the one choice.

She pulled up the hood on her jacket and slipped through the gym's back exit, walked two blocks, then sprinted to a Brown Line train, forgoing the Red Line she needed just in case someone followed her. She bought a new Ventra transit card, using some of her precious cash. She switched cars. She switched directions. She got off at a stop and ensured the crowd cleared before getting on the next train. Once she reached the Loop, she walked north and east, checking over her shoulder every few minutes. She went inside Water Tower Place and exited through a side door.

Then Jolene returned from the dead to ask her best friend for help.

* * *

KIERA HAD A PENTHOUSE CONDO RIGHT ON LAKE SHORE DRIVE—AT least she had. The lobby hadn't changed, with the half-high white wood paneling trimmed in a pink that managed not to look awful. The odor of the fresh lilies on the front desk made Jolene's head spin. When she recognized the doorman, she almost cried in relief.

"Manny," she said to the man who had gained a few pounds but hadn't aged. "Can you call up to Kiera?"

He frowned at her, trying to place her, big hands rubbing across the wood counter.

"Doreen. Remember? It's been a while, and I think I was a brunette when you last saw me." *Please remember me.*

"Miss Doreen, yes." He didn't smile. "I'm sorry."

Jolene's lip started quivering. She was fucked. She was completely—

"Ms. Brayleigh is out at the moment."

She blinked several times to try to bring herself into the present moment. "She's out?" Kiera never used to go out. Unless she had therapy? "Do you know when she's expected back?"

He looked away. "I can't say. Residents—"

"Of course," Jolene said. "I'll just—I can wait here, right?" She wasn't sure what she'd do if he refused.

Manny looked at his phone in contemplation. Was he considering calling the cops? Jolene readied to run, even as common sense told her she was overreacting. He hadn't even asked her to leave.

"Her fiancé is home. Maybe he wouldn't mind if you waited for her upstairs."

Jolene's mouth fell open, and her brain blanked for a moment. Luckily, the cortisol in her bloodstream prodded her to respond, "Uh, yeah, sure."

Kiera had a fiancé? She was beautiful, smart, funny, and rich. But she was also brittle, paranoid, and not inclined to trust. How had someone gotten through such a strong defensive system? Then again, Cass had broken through Jolene's barriers.

Manny called upstairs. Jolene tried to picture the kind of man Kiera would marry. She wished she had gum to wash out the tang of fear from her mouth and give her something to do.

He kept his voice down, but Jolene caught snatches of what he said. "It's Doreen. I recognize her, Dean."

Dean.

Manny looked at Jolene. "Definitely not dead."

Jolene laughed, though it sounded fake to her own ears. "The stories of my death have been greatly exaggerated."

"Okay," Manny said and disconnected. "He's coming down."

CHAPTER THIRTY FIVE

Cass

THE FURY HAD TO GO SOMEWHERE, SO ALTHOUGH Cass managed not to lose his shit on his brother and former boss, his hands shook. Was Jolene heeding his warning right now? Fleeing with no one to protect her?

Cass interlaced his fingers and tucked them between his thighs. They asked the same goddamned questions in a loop, attempting to bully him into admitting Jolene had duped him and had by now told the Agency that Stefano Jr. was working with the FBI to take down Stefano Sr.'s organization.

Their perspective made no sense. If Jolene had turned over everything she knew about Stefano Jr. and the feds to the Agency, she'd have no reason to be scared of Stadler. She wasn't faking her fear, and she wasn't playing both sides. If he didn't have a knowing about it—a surety so bright it was almost visible—he could have been persuaded to admit it was *possible.*

After two hours, Behmann shook his head. The heat had kicked on, pushing dusty-scented hot air into Shaun's office, turning it stuffy and uncomfortable. "Maybe she's turned him."

Shaun pointed a finger at Behmann. "Cass may have made some rash decisions, but at least he didn't err on the side of ordering the murder of a US citizen."

"Which is his whole *purpose*. If you don't take him into custody, he's going to warn the memory—" Behmann finally caught himself. A bead of sweat trickled down his temple. "*surgeon*. He'll jeopardize everything. You can't let them stay in contact."

"I know," Shaun said.

Cass closed his eyes, hoping the two men would continue to argue and not ask him any more questions. He had to hold out just a little bit longer. But time was turning thin. If Jolene ditched her burner, or his was discovered and confiscated, he might never see her again. He swallowed down the panic and set his mind to living in the now.

Behmann left the office in a huff, claiming to need some fresh air.

"You're making a mistake," Cass said.

"Shut the fuck up," Shaun said, his hands on top of his head, looking as if he were about to be arrested. "Do you realize what a shitty position you've put me in? I've got to officially question my own brother because you're too pussy-whipped to just do your goddamned job."

"Nice, bro," Cass said, the leash on his anger fraying. He didn't stand, but he straightened his spine until he thought it might crack. "You're seeing what you expect to see. You don't know her."

"And you do? You've both been lying to each other the entire time, but you think you've seen through it all to the sweet, wholesome core of her?" Shaun kicked his desk. "She's playing you, and it's appalling to me that you can't see it. Was she back even five minutes before she told them everything? Now, I'll have to consider pulling the plug on the bust that could have dismantled the Stefano organization. Do you comprehend the magnitude of your fuckup?"

"She didn't know the Agency was a criminal organization," Cass said for the eighth time.

"Is she stupid? Because she didn't seem stupid to me." Shaun rubbed his temples.

How different the situation would have been if they'd worked together. The Stuart brothers would have been unstoppable, but now they might never recover from this.

Luckily, help finally arrived.

* * *

"WHAT'S THIS I HEAR ABOUT DETAINING CASS WITHOUT CHARGING him?" their mom, the former criminal lawyer, asked, her glare directed at her eldest. They were sitting in a conference room no bigger than a standard office.

Cass bit back a smile at his brother's discomfort. Shaun took their mother's ire and tried to deflect it to Cass. "Ask him. His actions have jeopardized a federal investigation. I can't tell you more than that, Mom."

Her glower didn't diminish one watt. "If that's the case, then charge him with something." She gestured to the lawyer she'd brought, a short, neat man in his forties with a goatee so perfect it looked painted on. He smelled like saddle leather and freshly mowed grass. "Mr. Wesson will be present for any further interrogations."

Shaun twisted his body toward their mother, but he focused on Cass. "We're just asking questions. Don't make this worse. I can't protect you if—"

"Protect me?" Cass asked.

"You want so much to be the hero that you're ignoring what's right in front of your face."

That one hit him like a punch to the throat. "I know what I know. She's innocent."

"I agree," his mother said. "Are you going to charge him with something, or can we go?"

Shaun looked between his mother and brother, his face a mottled red. "Mom, you're making a mistake. You aren't privy to all the particulars."

Their mother didn't budge. "You're doing what you think is right, but you're wrong about this one, and you have no legal standing."

Shaun threw up his hands. "How can you know that without knowing the details?"

She shook her head. "Sometimes, Shaun, you just *know*."

Cass had never told his parents about his knowings and hadn't entertained the thought his gift might be present in either of his parents.

Aunt Flossie and the fires.

When Cass looked over at his mother, he wondered if she had the answers he lacked. He thought about her track record when she'd been a criminal lawyer. Had she won so many cases because she'd *known* who was guilty or innocent, lying or telling the truth?

"Cass," Shaun said, breaking into the spiral of his thoughts. "If you interfere, if you attempt in any way to aid her, I will have you arrested and prosecuted for obstruction. Do you understand me? If you want to improve your situation, you need to help bring her in."

"See you on Thanksgiving," Cass said to his brother. It was possible he smirked.

* * *

CASS LEFT WITHOUT HIS CREDENTIALS, SOMETHING THAT ADDED WEIGHT instead of removing it. He had no access to the government's plans and no hope of influencing their decisions.

"You need to be careful," his mother said. "He was serious."

"Thanks for coming, Mom." He kissed her cheek. "I'll be as cautious as I can."

She nodded. He thought she was going to leave, but she didn't move. Whatever she was considering saying must have been heavy, because she hesitated. "I like her," she said. "But don't let her get you killed, okay?"

CHAPTER THIRTY SIX

Jolene

KIERA'S FIANCÉ WASN'T WHAT JOLENE EXPECTED, which was funny since she hadn't expected anything. He was on the tall side, blond, almost lanky but with a posture that said he was in charge. His gaze was intense, as if he inspected Jolene for a disguise or an ulterior motive. The paranoia made sense—that was right for Kiera.

If she was what he'd imagined, she couldn't tell. His face gave away little. "You're Doreen?" he asked, his body language similar to a cat about to pounce.

"Yes," she said, the admission almost painful. Was she Doreen? Jolene? Anyone at all? "I go by Jolene now."

"Why? Where have you been? Why does Kiera think you're dead? She said you overdosed or died in a fire." He shook his head. "Something like that."

Jolene looked around the small lobby, which was empty. Manny was too far away to overhear, but Jolene didn't like the exposure. Too many tall, narrow windows. "When will Kiera be back? I'd rather tell her directly."

"No," he said. "You need to convince me you're who you say you are before I let you anywhere near her. I'm not letting you mess with her head without a damn compelling reason."

Jolene death-ray eyed him. "Who the fuck do you think you are?" She stopped. She needed to rein in her words, but something dark inside her burst. "We've been through more together than you can imagine. You can't understand what it's like to be a memory surgeon, to experience the things we lived through." A thought struck her like a spear through the liver. "Did her parents send you? Are you keeping away everyone who cares about her so they can worm their way back into her life? She deserved—*deserves* better than that, you manipulative prick. And I'm going to help her see the truth, and there isn't a goddamned thing you can do about it." She looked him up and down with new eyes.

A small smile ticked up his mouth. He had dimples. "Dean," he said, holding out his hand.

She took his hand and grabbed the first memory she saw.

* * *

Kiera kept her face tucked into his chest, her fists gripping his T-shirt. He kissed the top of her head. "You don't have to tell me, babe."

"It's okay," she said. "It still hurts, but not as much. Maybe I'll never get over it. She—"

Dean tightened his hold, careful not to make her uncomfortable. Being held too tightly made her feel claustrophobic. He rubbed her back with one hand.

"She understood me. You have no idea what that meant to me. Everyone else kept telling me what I should do and how much I owed the world because I had this gift, and I was selfish—"

"Babe, you know that's bullshit. You're one of the least selfish people I know."

She snorted. "Yeah, a regular saint. Let's not get too carried away." When Kiera tilted up her face, her cheeks were wet, but she smiled. She nipped the underside of his chin, and Dean thought his heart would explode with how much he loved her. "I guess the terrible thing is that she saved me, and I couldn't save her back."

"But you saved me." He kissed away her tears and stroked her sharp jaw.

* * *

JOLENE RELEASED DEAN'S HAND AND THREW HER ARMS AROUND HIS neck. "Thank you for taking care of her."

As Dean stiffened, Jolene released him and leaped back. What the hell had she been thinking?

"What the fuck?" Kiera said from Jolene's right.

Jolene and Dean both whipped their heads toward her. Kiera's scowl morphed into shock, her eyebrows popping to the top of her forehead. "D-Doreen?"

Dean rushed to her side, sliding an arm around her waist. "It's really her?"

Jolene was distracted for a moment by how comfortable Kiera was with Dean's touch. Back when Jolene had known her, she had always been weird about human contact. What else had changed in five years?

"Hey, kid," Jolene said.

"Not a kid." Kiera's practiced response came out as if no time had passed between them. "I never thought I'd hear that again." She burst into tears.

* * *

JOLENE FOLLOWED KIERA INTO THE LIBRARY, WHICH LOOKED EXACTLY AS she remembered: dark wood shelves, tissue boxes everywhere, glass coffee table between Kiera's favorite nest chair and . . . Wait, the armchair across from Kiera's favorite spot was different. It used to be a black leather monstrosity that fit one-and-a-half people, but now it was a muddy-brown, narrow chair with a high back and rolled armrests.

It was boring as hell, but she didn't say so, because Kiera would only reply that if Jolene had wanted a say in her furnishings, then she shouldn't have left.

She shouldn't have left? She shouldn't have come back. She was endangering Kiera—though at least now she could warn her friend. Stadler would come here eventually, because he'd just mentioned her, and where else would Jolene go? First, though, she'd take a minute to catch up with her friend.

"So, whatcha been up to?" Jolene asked.

Kiera barked a laugh. "Same old shit, mostly. I'm still doing memory surgeries, though I'm more particular about what clients I take and how often. What's new is I've been working on memory recovery."

Jolene found her interest perked, even with her drama unfolding. "Like repressed memories?"

"Worse." Kiera's jaw bulged before she exhaled in a long rush. "Dean has a lawyer friend who's got a class action suit against some memory-surgeon fuckhead who had a fake couple's therapy practice. Doucheholes would bring their wives and girlfriends in to forget about lies, cheatings, beatings, and inheritance stealing."

Jolene gritted her teeth. "He should be in jail."

"Ha! That's what I said, but they don't have laws against that yet, mostly because they'd have to legitimatize us then. That's what I think."

Jolene grunted in agreement. "And you can get their memories back?"

Kiera sighed. "No, but I can confirm he took memories, find the edges of what he stole and sort of shore them up. Sometimes, that gives them an inkling of what was taken or a place to look for evidence, like a person to talk to or an email to find."

"That sounds almost pointless," Jolene said, then winced at her insensitivity.

Kiera only nodded. "I thought that too when Jack—Dean's friend—suggested it. It's funny, but them finding even tiny snippets or clues made almost all of them feel better. Gave them back some of their power, you know? They're able to do *something*, and I get to help with that."

Jolene smiled. "I'm glad you've got that."

"Yeah, beats the rapes and tortures every time."

The familiarity, the way they fell right back into the rhythm completely their own made Jolene's insides pull dangerously apart. "I'm sorry," she said, as inadequate as it sounded.

Kiera curled into her nest chair, tucking her knees under her cashmere sweater. "For what?"

Jolene pressed her palms into her face. "Everything."

"I'm not accepting some generic-ass apology. I *needed* you, and it's not like you didn't know it." Kiera's voice cracked at the end.

"It seemed like the only way." Jolene forced herself to look at Kiera. She owed her that. "I was only a few months sober and so . . . lost and bitter and directionless. Mistrustful. You can't succeed in recovery without a purpose of some kind, any kind. And this 'agent' came to me—"

"See, I don't believe that." Kiera slipped her sleeves over her hands and tapped them together. "You are the most paranoid person I've ever met. No way would you fall for some fake shadow-government line."

She shrugged. "It was my blind spot. Did I think there were secret agencies with dark agendas? Absolutely. They gave me exactly what I expected . . ." Jolene trailed off, thinking of Sara's advice, that people always believed when given what they anticipated. Fuck.

"So why didn't you tell me? You trusted me so little?"

"It was *me* I didn't trust. If I told you, we'd have kept in touch, and they'd convinced me someone was watching us, and if you weren't believable as a grieving friend, you'd be in danger. I *felt* it, Kier, their eyes on both of us. It burrowed into my brain, and—and I thought I was protecting you."

Kiera snorted.

Jolene flinched. "Sorry. Do you want me to go?"

Kiera scowled at her. "If I wanted you to go, I'd have told you to fuck off downstairs. What I want is for you to have never left."

After clamping down on her emotions hard enough to crack a tooth to reach Kiera without imploding, Jolene couldn't hold back the tsunami backlash. She knew intellectually not *every* decision she'd ever made had been a mistake, but it felt as if she'd done nothing but ruin things her entire life.

"I thought I was doing the right thing," she whimpered, tears streaming everywhere. She collapsed her face into her hands, trying to push feelings back inside her, where they belonged.

"Goddamn it, don't cry," Kiera said, her voice shaky. "You know I'm a professional-level sympathetic crier."

Jolene lifted her head, studying a blurry Kiera. She spluttered a laugh, which sounded entirely too wet with her running nose. Nothing was funny, but the familiar rhythm of their conversation made her feel both old and new. With a dramatic exhale, she pressed a wrist to her forehead and in her best/worst Southern accent said, "I've suffered."

Kiera curled into her chair and watched Jolene with a smile tugging her lips. "I had a client interview the other day, and she didn't come right out and say it, but she intimated I was *a bit* selfish for not doing more memory surgeries."

Jolene wiped at her face and pulled a Puffs Plus Lotion tissue from the box on the coffee table and blew her nose. "It's so refreshing to have that sort of helpful feedback, someone looking out for you instead of themselves."

"It builds a real sense of community."

"Makes the world a bitter place—I mean, a better place."

They cackled together.

"I'm okay," Kiera said suddenly, breaking their repartee. "You should feel shitty, but not wrist-slitty shitty. Things were bad for a while, then really, *really* bad, but I came out on the other side with Dean, so . . . there's that."

"What happened?" Jolene asked, wanting to smack herself for not asking Kiera more questions about her life. She'd come busting in there thinking only of herself and her situation. Talk about selfish.

Kiera snorted and shook her head. "We don't have time for that story." She bit her lip. "You didn't hear about it? Like, at all?"

Jolene's stomach slid into a dangerous turn, like a car about to flip over the guardrail and roll down a steep embankment. "Something newsworthy happened?" She thought back to the times the Agency had made her go full dark on media and internet while she was deep into training or some study, sometimes without warning. What had she missed?

"Yeah. It made all the news." She unleashed a huge sigh. "Which you know I loved. I mean, what's the point of life unless reporters are pawing through your garbage or calling you sixty-seven times a day?"

"How'd they get your number?" Okay. That was *not* what was important, but with her mind spinning, it was hard to pin down individual thoughts. "I mean—" Kiera had already said she didn't have the time, or possibly even the inclination, to talk about it right now. "You're all right, though? Now?"

"Being with Dean helped me see life in a different way, and he's . . . I've moved forward in my life, and as you might recall, that's not something I ever thought I'd be able to do. I thought I'd be my usual, fucked-up self forever. Now I'm a slightly improved fucked-up version of myself. He makes me a better, happier person. So, yeah, I'm all right." Kiera steepled her fingers, elbows resting on her folded knees. "What about you? You don't seem as meth-head twitchy as you were."

Jolene dug her fists into her scalp to keep her head from exploding. With all the recent revelations, she wasn't sure she was a better or happier version of herself. "Sometimes I think I'm destined to fail no matter what I do. There's something inside of me set up to self-destruct anytime I make any progress. I don't know what happiness would look like."

But then her burner phone rang, and Jolene thought she had some idea.

CHAPTER THIRTY SEVEN

Cass

Cass arranged to meet Jolene at Daley Plaza downtown. He arrived in less than an hour, even after ditching his car and hopping on the 'L.' The area around the civic center was busy, which he preferred. He let his senses sharpen and soften at once, feeling for anything off.

He sat on a concrete bench facing the fifty-foot Picasso sculpture, watching people passing, looking for the only one who mattered. Relief that she'd answered the phone, that she hadn't cut him off entirely had yet to fade. The air had cooled enough to prickle his fingers, but he embraced the sensation.

Jolene didn't show up for another half hour. He saw her first, looking disheveled but fine—beautiful as always. She walked past the fountain, heading toward the statue, attention flitting all around. A couple flanked her. He recognized the woman—Kiera Brayleigh, the most famous memory surgeon in the US, maybe the world and a known associate from Jolene's file. He had no intel on who the man might be—friend? boyfriend?—though he had a military look about him, which made Cass relax.

With a last look around, pinging for anything suspicious, he headed on an intercept course. Jolene stopped walking when she saw him, her face relaxing and brightening. Cass's chest squeezed with a pleasure-pain that made him want to sprint the rest of the way to her. He walked faster but careful not to draw attention.

When they met, Jolene's eyes darted around, and she licked her lips. He wanted to pull her into him, hold her, kiss her, move her someplace safe so she could rest.

"Are you all right?" he asked.

Jolene nodded. "Kind of like walking a tightrope without a net and limited training. I can't figure a way this doesn't end badly." She lowered her voice. "You okay?"

Cass shrugged, though he didn't feel at all casual about his failure. "I'm just—I'm telling myself it's better to get fired protecting you than to keep the job and see you detained, or worse."

Jolene shook her head. "Oh shit. Sorry."

Cass stroked a finger under her chin, encouraging her to lift it. "I'm not."

"Day ain't over yet," she drawled, then leaned her body into him, her face rising to his, a small smile ticking up one side of her lips.

"Do you have any kind of plan?" he asked, his mouth an inch from hers.

Jolene maintained the space between them. Before he could kiss her, she stepped back. "First of all, we need to cut loose these losers." She held out an arm like a game-show hostess. "Cass, this is Dean and . . . Kiera." Her voice grew soft on her friend's name.

"Good luck with that," Kiera said with a huff.

Cass shook Dean's hand and nodded at Kiera. He wasn't about to touch another memory surgeon, not with so much on the line, and he hoped she wasn't offended. She seemed relieved, returning his nod like a pro.

The four of them stood in a kind of formation, nobody sure what to do. Jolene looked around. "I don't like talking in the open, but I want to be sure we're not overheard."

They ended up at Elephant & Castle, an English pub and restaurant on Wabash with a British hunting club feel and dim lighting.

Kiera slipped the hostess a hundred-dollar bill. "We need some privacy."

The hostess pocketed the money and escorted them to a booth across from the bar area. Nobody was seated at any of the nearby tables. This would work.

The aroma of fried foods, fish and chips most likely, made Cass's stomach rumble, but they weren't here to eat. He rested his hand on Jolene's thigh, wanting to absorb her body into his. "Have you made any plans?"

Dean huffed out a breath. "She should turn herself in to the FBI."

Jolene and Kiera exchanged a look. Cass agreed with Dean, but his instincts told him not to share his opinion on that just yet.

One of the waitstaff set four tall glasses of water on the table, but they indicated they weren't ready to order. Cass sipped his water and waited.

Kiera narrowed her eyes at Dean. "She's officially dead. Who would miss her? They could make her disappear, and what would we do then? Get a lawyer to demand they let us speak to a deceased woman?"

"There's no reason to believe they'd do that. Arrest her, maybe, but they've offered a deal before so . . . Besides," Dean said, rubbing the back of his neck, "they have files on all of you. If they find out Doreen—sorry, Jolene—is still alive, the feds are going to come looking at us sooner rather than later."

"What do you mean they have files on us?" Kiera slowly lowered her palms flat to the table. "Are you telling me you've known the FBI is . . . what, watching me? And you've never bothered to tell me?"

"The feds already know that Jolene is Doreen," Cass interjected. "That's how I got pulled into the mission. Her prints were discovered in Boston, and the feds tracked her to Chicago. The connection between Jolene and Kiera is not a secret."

Jolene pressed her fingers into her temples. "They could show up at any moment. I mean, you're my only friend. Where else would I go?"

"We can't count on my brother," Cass said, jumping in to keep them on point. "He's a goodish guy, just . . . very by the book, and he'll put the case first." He hated what a terrible impression Shaun continued to make. "But I do have a few army buddies scattered throughout the US and one in London who can help find us a few places to hopscotch before we land somewhere to lie low for a while. It has to be a location with no connection to any of us."

Jolene dug her knuckles into her eyes and sighed. "This table here? These are my only connections . . . You know, other than the Agency."

"That's not a failing on your part," Cass said, reaching for her hand and threading his fingers with hers. "They kept you isolated on purpose."

She lowered her head. "I can't contribute anything. They took all my money, Cass, drained the account."

"Fuckers," he hissed under his breath, though he wasn't surprised. He squeezed her hand. "I've got some cash saved and—"

"Please," Kiera huffed. "I'm funding this escape. I can give you more than enough to get you situated and work out fake identities and whatnot. We don't have to worry about money, so let's move on."

"I'm not going to run," Jolene said.

CHAPTER THIRTY EIGHT

Jolene

"If I run, the Agency or the FBI, or both, will go after Kiera," Jolene said. "They'll use her to get to me. The Agency in particular knows she was my only friend before they faked my death."

Dean laid his arm on the back of the bench, and Kiera tucked herself next to him. They appeared so comfortable together, happy even.

Cass rubbed his chin with his thumb. "Shit. Jolene's not wrong about the Agency using brutal methods to get what they want. They're not above a snatch-and-grab. And if they can't get to Kiera, they'd take you, Dean."

"I'm a Chicago police detective," Dean said. "They wouldn't dare come after me."

"It's not beyond them," Cass said, and his surety made Jolene's throat dry.

If Jolene got Dean killed, Kiera would never forgive her, even if she wasn't directly responsible. "They might set fire to your building," Jolene said, thinking of her own home being burned to the ground when they faked her death.

Kiera grabbed Dean's hand, squeezing hard enough to whiten her knuckles.

"Look, Stadler is a vindictive motherfucker," Jolene said. "We can't leave any trace of a connection between Kiera and me." Protecting Kiera had to be a priority.

"You're not ditching me again." Kiera gave Jolene her death glare, which had only improved with age.

An idea suddenly occurred to Jolene, and Kiera must have seen it on her face, because she said, "You're not thinking about killing him, are you?"

Jolene tried to laugh, but the noise she made sounded like a car refusing to start. "Of course not. If I can get into Stadler's mind, you'll be safe, we'll work out the fed situation, and we won't have to lose touch ever again."

Kiera slapped her hands on the table. "We didn't *lose touch*. You fucking *died*. I mourned you to this day, fuck-knuckle."

"Are you going to bring that up every time we see each other?"

Kiera stabbed a finger in her direction. "You are a Cunt of the First Order, and I am so fucking pissed at you I could punch you in the face, and I'm *definitely* bringing this up every time I see you until the end of time. I might even have an embroidered pillow commissioned."

Jolene loved Kiera with a fierceness bordering on primal. "I mourned you too."

Dean massaged the back of Kiera's neck. "We should focus—"

"Shut your pie hole." Kiera shrugged her shoulders free of his contact. "Just give me a second."

Dean leaned over and kissed her temple, not saying a word. Kiera's eyes flicked to him and held, her face twitching through a series of unidentifiable emotions. The connection between them pulsed strong enough for Jolene to feel the tickle in her belly. Her body thrummed with adrenaline, flushing her face and shooting tremors into her hands.

The server returned. "Are you ready to order?"

The group mumbled another general lack of readiness, and the waitress disappeared.

"All right, say we take this Stadler out of the mix. What about the FBI? They might arrest you," Kiera said.

"Let's worry about that after we deal with the Agency. Stadler is the bigger threat," Jolene replied.

The ambient sounds of dishes clicking and kitchen staff laughing filled the silence as they contemplated their next move.

"What if we shot him with a tranquilizer dart?" Kiera said.

"Where are we going to get a tranquilizer gun and darts?" Dean replied with a grin. "You read too many bullshit books."

"We need something stealthier," Cass said, squeezing Jolene's leg.

Jolene almost jumped out of her seat from both the contact and an idea. "What if I drug his coffee? If he's woozy, I can take him physically and get in his mind." She thought of Colton and how horribly wrong that had gone when Sara had tried it, but she pushed that memory away. This could work.

Cass frowned. "How would you get him to drink drugged coffee?"

"Consolation coffee. It's this unofficial thing we do after we've had a disagreement. Stadler doesn't apologize, like, ever, but when he's been a prick, he brings me tea. If I bring him a coffee, he'll assume I'm apologizing."

"Dude!" Kiera squirmed and bounced. "I have Ambien. We crush a couple pills in there, and he's toast."

Cass gripped the leather seat of the booth, making it creak. "You want to confront him *alone*?"

"He's certainly not going to drink the coffee if you're there." She brushed her shoulder against his, trying to project nonchalance. He smelled delectable enough for her to want to bury her face in his neck and hide forever. "I'll have to be thorough to ensure he has no memory of my connection to Kiera, so I can't rush it with a touch here and there. This will work. The man loves his coffee."

In truth, she envisioned him making her take a few swallows to prove it wasn't poisoned. It was just the sort of test he loved to give, prove that he was more cunning than her. She could handle a few sips of Ambien coffee.

"Once he's totally out, maybe you could come in, Kiera, to make sure I got everything and help me cover my tracks?" Jolene asked.

"No." Dean's voice slashed through the room.

Jolene expected Kiera to detonate at his commanding tone, but she only reached up and stroked his jaw. "It'll be fine. You can come with and be there the whole time," she said.

"But if it doesn't work, it could put you more firmly on his radar," Dean said. "The feds can—"

"We can't trust the government," Jolene said. "And she's already on his radar. He mentioned her by name just this week."

"Okay, but he's not working alone. Kiera will still be known to the Agency," Cass said, his words careful, as if he were delivering a terminal diagnosis. "Is it worth the risk?"

Jolene ran her finger along the edge of the burgundy, fake-leather menu, trying to read the selections but unable. "I've asked Stadler a bunch of times about how we get jobs and who he reports to, and, he's always been vague, only mentioning a director but no name. He once told me the Agency works in cells. We were accountable to 'management' but operate with considerable autonomy. Stadler picks our targets, assembles his team, creates his own plans. He wouldn't go to them for a plan of attack."

"That's if he was telling the truth," Cass said. He held up a finger, and Jolene watched the approaching waitress change direction.

Jolene tapped the menu to her forehead. "The only way to find out for sure is to see for ourselves. Maybe I can't go into his mind once and be done, but I won't know until I take a look." She dropped the menu and wrapped her hand around Cass's wrist. "I can't go on the lam until I suss out any plans Stadler has for Kiera. We can't leave with her in danger, especially when it's all my fault."

Cass shook his head. "What if we all run? Then there's nobody for them to find."

Dean ran his hands through his hair, but it was Kiera who shut down that plan, as Jolene knew she would. "No way. I'm not leaving my safe space. And Dean can't just—"

"I could ask for a leave of absence," Dean said.

Kiera leaned into him. "No. We'll hire security, if it comes to that, but I can't just," her voice cracked as she waved her hand, "run around out there."

"Okay, babe." Dean tucked her into his side. "We'll do it your way. Maybe you can also find something to give the feds," Dean added. "I'd feel a lot better with that bastard in jail."

Kiera grinned up at him. "You're such a cop."

He pinched her chin and kissed her. "Not out of my sight. Not for a second."

Kiera nodded, a ghost of a smile on her lips.

Jolene had to look away.

CHAPTER THIRTY NINE

Cass

KIERA AND DEAN RETURNED HOME FOR THE NIGHT to keep up the appearance of normalcy for them. Cass and Jolene had to find a hotel that didn't require a credit card, which hadn't been easy.

It wasn't the nicest place, but it was tolerable. The bedspread had once been burgundy with a wavy pattern stitched into it, but half the stitching had come out, and the underside was scratchy, the covers thin and ill-used. He'd hate to see how the room would look when sprayed with luminol and hit with a black light.

They set down the Target bags with the clothing and necessities they'd bought, as well as a few snacks, most of the sugary variety.

"It's not too late for you to back out of the whole thing," Jolene said. "You don't have to blow up your future for me."

"And what do I tell myself if your body ends up in an alley?" It wasn't smart to interject doubt just before a mission, but he was willing to risk it if it meant she'd reconsider.

She didn't flinch. "You tell yourself you're not responsible for my choices and actions. Then you cry a little, but in a manly way, like a single tear or something." Jolene flopped onto the bed, which had entirely too much bounce to it. "You do *not* get drunk or pour a beer over my grave. Go for a sweet run on the 606 and remember better times. Then you move on with your life, find a nice girl, knock her up, and name your dog after me." She held out her hands as if she'd handily taken care of all his concerns.

"What about Kiera?" he asked.

Jolene pulled her new clothes out of the bag and tucked them in a rickety dresser farthest from the door. "She buried me once; she can do it again."

"It'll do a helluva lot more damage the second time, and I think you know that."

She slammed the drawer shut. "I'd rather have her suffering and alive than dead because Stadler used her to try to get to me. And he would too. One of my conditions of employment was they never recruit her."

"And you thought they would honor that?" He sat in a desk chair that creaked ominously. "You seriously believed it all?"

Jolene walked over to him and grabbed his hair, wrenching his head back. The move sent a thrill through his body. She loomed over him and tugged with each word. "Stop. Second. Guessing. The. Plan."

It shouldn't have turned him on, not with all they'd been through and all that awaited them tomorrow. Still, he was harder than he'd ever been, his cock so swollen his brain wouldn't function. This was life and death, but his dick didn't care.

She had this way of looking into him as if she saw not his memories but his very soul—or maybe the soul was nothing more than a collection of memories. Regardless, her eyes on him made him feel seen and never judged. Even within her flinty glare.

"Don't you smolder at me," she said, one corner of her mouth ticking up for a second. "You can't change my mind."

He trailed his fingers from her waist to her hip before skirting around to her ass. "Okay, what about a distraction? Can I do that?"

She smirked. "I don't know, can you?"

Cass yanked her to him, his chin hitting her stomach. He bit softly into her belly and shook his head like a dog with a bone. His fingers dug into her ass, kneading and lifting. Her hands rested on his shoulders, gripping tight. He released her just long enough to lift the hem of her turtleneck and slip his head inside.

He rubbed his stubbled cheek against her bare skin. She stroked his hair through the sweater as he drew her flesh into his mouth to lick and suck, marking his territory.

Cass slipped his hands up her back, then around to her breasts. He tugged down the cups of her bra to circle her nipples with his thumbs. They hardened enough he suspected they hurt as much as his cock straining in his pants.

"You're stretching out my clothes," she said around a gasp.

"Hm. Should I stop, then?" He tweaked her nipples one more time.

"No." She wiggled in place, then pulled the sweater off. "Problem solved."

Jolene straddled his lap as he unhooked her bra. They fit together perfectly, her pussy snug against his hard cock. He could fuck her anytime, anyplace, with no fears of getting her pregnant. For a moment, he thought of when she'd been a young woman who'd been so sure she'd never want kids that she'd had surgery. For all her insecurities, she was a woman who knew what she wanted.

A bite on his earlobe brought him back to the moment. Jolene pressed her breasts into his chest and rode her pussy up and down his erection through their clothing, all while licking and nibbling his ear and neck. Her teeth sank into the side of his throat, and she sucked his skin into her mouth.

He wanted to touch every part of her at once, consume her whole. But he had only two hands and one mouth, so he groaned and slid his hands under her ass, pulling her in tighter, lifting and lowering her faster.

She interlaced her fingers behind his neck and tilted back her head, exposing her upper body. He covered first one nipple with his mouth, flicking with his tongue before sucking. Her lower half jerked in his hands. He moved to the other side.

"Oh fuck, that's good." She gripped him tighter, letting him maneuver her body how he wanted.

"Look at me." He needed to see the lust in her face, the flush creeping over her chest.

She did as he asked, lowering her forehead to his, whispering, "Anything you want."

He stood, and she wrapped her legs around his waist. He crawled them onto the bed, covering her body with his. They squirmed into each other, finding dips and filling them, discovering swells and riding them. Together, they sank their bodies closer.

Cass pulled off her pants as she unbuttoned his. He removed his own pants and fell over her again, only his boxer briefs and her panties between them. He could have fucked her now—they were both ready—but he wanted to linger and stroke her skin with just that little bit of fabric preventing penetration.

Her leg slid up his body, changing the angle of her hips to better brush against him. He kissed her collarbones and down her sternum. Jolene sank her fingers into his hair, pulling it back, letting it slip through her fingers. His scalp tingled with delight, and he hummed into her skin. They indulged in each other for several minutes before he needed more.

Cass rolled to the side to give himself better access before sliding a hand into her panties. She was soaked, and his finger slid easily inside her. He circled her clit with his thumb as he finger-fucked her until she writhed under his hand.

"Get naked," she gasped, pulling his hand away.

He grunted but acquiesced. When they were both naked, the air crackled with a primordial energy, something uncontrollable and inevitable. She straddled him, looming above him like an avenging goddess. He submitted to her, his arms outstretched, allowing her to do as she wanted.

She grabbed his cock and pumped him twice before lining him up with her entrance. "Yes?" she asked, as if it were possible to change his mind.

"Yes. Please."

Jolene sank down on him, and he regretted all those weeks of striving for something platonic when they could have been doing this the entire time. He never wanted to be doing anything else as long as he lived.

She rose and fell, using her thigh muscles, her nails scratching up his chest light enough to make goose bumps pop everywhere.

His nipples were sensitive but not a particular favorite erogenous zone—or so he'd thought. She pinched his nipples, pulling them, and moving them in small circles. A bolt of pleasure struck him up through his balls to his shaft. He gasped and rocketed his hips hard into her.

"You like that?" She did it again with a little more pressure.

"Too much," he panted. Then he groaned as she lightened her grip and rotated them in the opposite direction.

She bent down and sucked his left nipple into her mouth, the suction light, then ran her tongue over the peak, alternating sucking and swirling. He'd shifted his hands to her hips and helped lift her body so she could fuck him faster. The building sensations rushed him forward even as he warned himself to enjoy the moment, to slow down.

He couldn't. The excitement growing inside him demanded a release. The intensity of the rising euphoria almost hurt. He should wait for her, make her come first—probably should have done that before they'd started fucking—but it was too late, everything a foregone conclusion. If the hotel caught on fire, he wouldn't pause. If his parents barged into the room, he wouldn't slow.

"I can't stop," he murmured like a confession. "I need—need—you—oh fuck, Jolene. Jolene." His balls squeezed and rose, moments from exploding.

She pinched his nipples so hard everything stopped. "Ow!"

"Sorry!" Jolene snatched her hands away. "I thought—oh God, did I hurt you?"

He rolled them over, chuckling, careful they didn't fall off the bed. "I can't believe you just purple-nurpled me." He withdrew and spread his thighs between her legs, spreading hers even more. "I should thank you, but goddamn, that stings."

She slapped a hand over her mouth and winced.

He kissed a trail down between her breasts, over her stomach, and to the sweet spot he craved. His dick had its own pulse from his near orgasm.

Her wetness coated his tongue with the first lick. She tasted of earth and sky and lust. She melted in his mouth and squirmed with every swipe of his tongue. He suckled her clit, using gentle pressure and occasional flicks of his tongue. Her arms slammed onto the mattress as her hips rose to meet him. She threaded her fingers through his hair and held him, not riding his face or yanking him to her, but holding on, as if she needed the support.

Her breath came out in audible pants. He slipped two fingers into her soaked pussy at once, and her walls clenched them tightly. He found her G-spot and a rhythm for fucking he matched with his lips.

She cried out, a throaty bellow that could probably be heard three doors down. He wanted them to hear her. He wanted the world to hear her. He wanted her feeling so turned on that nothing existed but the two of them.

"Please. Oh. Yes. Yes. YES. Uh, uh, uh. Fuck. Please. Don't. Yes. I need. I need. Cass. Cass, please." Her chanting grew hotter and faster, her body undulating under his mouth, her insides tightening around his fingers so hard it was difficult for him to move them. Her moans turned high-pitched, like a cat in heat, the sound broken, unlovely, and so fucking hot he, again, almost came. The pressure of his weight pressing his cock into the mattress brought him to the edge. If he moved at all, he'd spew for certain.

She came with a shriek, fisting the covers. He didn't wait for her orgasm to finish. Once she'd peaked, he picked her up and flipped her to her hands and knees. He entered her in one energetic thrust, holding her hips for more leverage. Her cunt tightened around him and fluttered.

"Oh fuck!" She was coming again.

Cass slapped her ass, just once, careful to strike the fleshy part and not too high. Jolene shrieked again, her body bucking as she continued to come.

"Yes!" Her voice was thick, as if she were crying.

He cracked her other cheek, loving the way her flesh jiggled, the skin pinking, her pussy clamping on to him. "You like that, don't you? That's it, come for me again. Come harder." He slapped the same side again, using mostly his fingers, but a stinging blow.

She cried out, a deep sound echoing from her throat like a foghorn. It shouldn't have been sexy. If he'd heard a porn actress make that sound, he might have laughed, but it hit him squarely in the dick. No woman had ever made that noise with him before, but his body instinctively understood the primal pleasure.

The tickling began in his lower back and traveled up his balls. He thought he might die, that he might suffocate or implode. The urgent need for release climbed up his cock, time slowing as if every second were a minute.

He made his own nonsensical sounds as her cunt gripped him. The orgasm grew and grew, the need more desperate than pleasurable until a switch flipped, and it was only pleasure. He spurted, the climax better than anything he'd ever felt. It rocketed out like a gunshot, each spurt another bullet killing him. Tonight was a six-shot night.

Jolene shuddered, her pussy finally stilling. Cass continued to move in and out of her, trying to ease himself back to reality. Sweat covered their bodies, aiding in the delicious slide. He wanted to savor all that lovely salt, but his body drooped from exhaustion and drained energy.

CHAPTER FORTY

Jolene

THIS WAS GOING TO WORK. SHE'D KNOWN STADLER for years. They'd spent many days together—she would *not* think of the nights they'd passed together—and she knew him as well as he knew her.

They'd trained, sparred, shared meals, and he'd looked out for her. Yes, he was going to be furious she'd ditched her phone and disappeared—again—but his anger would make him colder, more calculating. As long as she fed him something, he would play along.

All she had to do was wait him out, and the drugs would take care of the rest.

Cass, Dean, and Kiera stood by in Dean's car on Western Avenue, waiting for her all-clear call. They'd promised to give her half an hour, but she suspected Cass wouldn't hold back that long.

Jolene walked down Iowa on her own, the side street quiet and unassuming. The apartment was in a red-brick two-story building, no different than its neighbors. Stadler lived on the second floor, and the first floor housed Sara. Part of her wanted to go to Sara first, fish around, procrastinate. But the countdown had begun. Stadler needed to be thoroughly drugged by the time her backup arrived on the scene.

She wished she'd had her phone so she could have called ahead. What if he wasn't home? What if he wasn't alone? Too many unknowns and too little planning, but she was out of time.

When Jolene hit Stadler's intercom, the door immediately buzzed. Was he expecting her or someone else? Jolene stepped inside. Before the door closed, she slapped a piece of duct tape over the latch to prevent the door from locking, a fancy one-handed maneuver since she carried the Ambien-dosed drink caddy with the other. Now her backup could waltz inside—or fox-trot, if they preferred. It was almost over.

At the turn to the second floor, she saw Stadler. He stood at his door, wearing a plain, white T-shirt stretched at the biceps, as always, and jeans. He stared down at her as she ascended the stairs, his face scary-blank.

She held up the Starbucks offering. "I brought beverages."

He said nothing but stepped aside—or mostly aside—to let her pass—or mostly pass. Her shoulder brushed him, and he wrapped his hand around her upper arm and dragged her to the living room, almost spilling the drinks, and deposited her on a ruby-red sofa, the material ancient and bare in places, the color nonetheless vibrant. It didn't fit Stadler, but then, he'd probably shopped at thrift stores to furnish the place, like she had with hers.

Jolene set the coffee caddy on the scratched-up coffee table.

"Well?" he prompted, standing a foot from her. He smelled of clean sweat and hand sanitizer.

She didn't offer him the coffee, though her insides were chanting like they were at a frat party—*drink, drink, drink, drink.* In her mind, she'd played this scene out sixty-seven hundred times, but she won only when he drank.

"Well, yourself. Don't you have something you want to say about where the fuck you've been?" She held his gaze, though the intensity made her eyes water.

"How about my disappointment in you?" he offered.

"How about *my* disappointment in *you.*"

Silence clonked down at their feet, thick and heavy, sucking in all the air. He waited. She waited. For once, she had more pieces of the puzzle than he did. Gavin Stadler would talk first.

"You're unhappy, and instead of coming directly to me, you—"

"Why did you need to fake my death?" She'd been remade in the Agency's image, but she suspected it was more than that.

"Covert work is—"

"Stop lying to me." She'd meant to shout it, pound on his chest, but it came out more of a plea. She reached over, scooped up the tea, and took a sip, hoping it would cue Stadler to also drink. Her tea was the perfect drinking temperature.

Stadler pulled the tea out of her hand and set it back in the tray, then handed her the coffee. Ha! "Drink it."

"Gross, no." After allowing him to warm her face with his glare for several seconds, she grabbed the drink. "What the fuck, Stadler." Then she took a swallow, making a face as the acrid flavor of the black coffee hit her. At least she couldn't detect the Ambien under all that bitterness "Damn, that's nasty. How do you drink that? Do you hate yourself that much?"

She held the coffee out to him. He took it. And set it next to the tea.

"You want the truth?" he asked.

"Yes."

"We faked your death to isolate you. You have no identity except the one we gave you, no work history, school records, and—you'll find out soon enough—no money. We own you. You have no friends or family or support. What are you going to do, Doreen?"

She flinched. "I'm not that woman anymore."

"And who saw to that? We gave you a fresh start, a chance to make the world a better place."

"You're a drug syndicate!"

He smirked. "So what?"

She gaped.

Stadler crossed his arms over his chest, his biceps bulging. "We're still helping people. You think drugs can be eradicated from our society?"

"No, but—"

"Most deaths are caused by fentanyl. Everyone is cutting their heroin with it. It's cheaper and heightens the effect and addictiveness. It's why ambulances stock up on Narcan, though they're often too late. We provide a clean product." Stadler held up his palms. "We're saving lives."

"What about Colton? The Agency has his death on their hands."

"*Their* hands? *Our* hands. You've been a part of the Agency for almost five years." His eyes twinkled in amusement, and Jolene wondered if she could kick him in the balls before he reacted. Stadler edged closer, as if daring her to try. "Colton shot his mouth off regularly. Any number of parties could have silenced him."

Jolene reached around him, grabbed her tea, and took another sip. *Come on, Stadler. Yummy, yummy coffee.*

"What did you think would happen here?" Stadler asked.

She shrugged. "I thought maybe you'd feel bad for lying to me for so many years."

"I never lied to you. You made assumptions, and I didn't correct them." He picked up the coffee, and Jolene almost smiled, but then he set it back in the cardboard caddy and did the same with her tea, pushing them to the side as he sat on the coffee table. "You made a difference, a positive difference. So, don't go beating yourself up about it."

"It's not me I want to beat up."

He smirked. "You want to go a round?"

No, I want you to drink the fucking coffee.

She covered her face with her hands. If he comforted her, she might find something in that split moment to help her.

He grabbed her wrists and pulled them away from her face. All she saw were muted bubbles that disappeared when he released her. "Look at me," Stadler said.

She did.

"I don't know what you thought you would accomplish, but here's how it's going to be." He was too close to her, their knees less than an inch apart.

"Mansplain away." She scrunched her toes in her sneakers to ground herself.

"You're going to tell me everything, *everything* about Stefano Jr., your little boyfriend, and any government involvement. Depending on what I hear, you're either going to continue to be a useful tool in the Agency arsenal or neutralized." His voice didn't change, and his face showed no signs he gave half a shit about her.

Her chest clenched when he said *government involvement.* Did he already know everything?

"And if I don't tell you anything?" She wasn't built to withstand torture, but she needed to buy time. Her best hope now was escape.

He grabbed her calf and yanked her off the couch to the floor. Before she could react, he flipped her onto her stomach, squishing her face against the leg of the sofa. When she flailed, her ankle hit the edge of the coffee table causing a bright spark of pain. And then he zip-tied her wrists behind her back, pressing down extra hard as if to make a point.

Stadler hauled her to her feet with little effort and placed her on the red-and-white-checked armchair on the other side of the coffee table. With her hands bound behind her, she had to perch on the edge.

"What—what the fuck are you doing?" Jolene tried to sound outraged, but her voice came out diminished, as if she'd run it through a strainer first, and only the thinnest part came through.

"I'm getting the truth."

"And you have to tie me up to do that? I wanted answers from you, but you don't see me tying you up."

He blew out a puff of air, almost a laugh. "Because you can't."

Stadler understood her so well she thought she might die, just split in half and fall over in two big chunks. "So, ask your questions, asshole."

She wouldn't cry.

"I will."

Jolene's knee bounced, and she allowed it, needing some way to expend the energy roaring through her. If she got loose, she'd run so fast only a smoke trail would be visible. But she couldn't run. She was trapped. Memories pressed inside her from torture-session surgeries she'd removed. Blood. Fear. Pain. Rage. Loss.

She had twenty minutes. No, fifteen at the most. Possibly ten. Cass would come early. All she had to do was distract Stadler until then.

She let the silence settle. Waiting was her friend. The more pauses between questions and comments, the better.

Anticipation tickled through her belly like some sort of parasite. Stadler watched her, an empty shell of a person, while her leg jiggled as if she were having a seizure. Her armpits turned swampy.

"What are you waiting for?" she finally asked.

Stadler bent down, careful to stay out of the range of her legs. "Did you think you were the only memory surgeon we had?"

It was like being slapped in the face with a frozen towel. "No." Panic parasites wiggled and chewed her nerves in an attempt to eat through her epidermis. "Stadler, no."

Stadler shook his head. "Pull yourself together, Nova. That's not the worst news you're getting today."

"Fuck you." She jerked her wrists, not caring she had no chance of breaking free. "You can't do this." Words fell out of her mouth like the dialogue from every bad movie she'd ever seen, as if she couldn't escape the script.

Stadler walked past her into the kitchen. Jolene ran to the door, needing to at least try to escape. The deadbolt was engaged. The scent of WD-40 hit her. Had he oiled the lock? She tried to maneuver her shoulder under the deadbolt.

"You're embarrassing yourself. Sit down," Stadler said from right behind her.

"No." Her brain wasn't helping her at all.

Stadler grabbed her by the hair and dragged her back, slamming her into the chair. "You know what you need?"

Jolene stomach threatened to unload everything. She swallowed and swallowed, trying to keep herself from vomiting everywhere.

"A nice . . . stiff . . . drink."

The world stopped. Jolene watched dust motes floating in the room, revealed by the sliver of sun that had suddenly glowed to life through the gloom of the day. Stadler hadn't shaved that morning, and he had a few gray hairs in his wispy mustache and more in his stubble. She'd touched his jaw a few times, enjoying the squareness of it. She remembered thinking he must like having such a masculine jaw. She tried to crawl into the memory—any memory—anything to escape the moment to come.

"I won't do it," she whispered.

Stadler held up the vodka he'd retrieved from the kitchen. The oversized bottle had a blue and white label, but she couldn't read the name as tears poured down her face.

Part of her roared, part of her curled into a ball, and part of her stretched and reached for the alcohol, wanting the balm it promised. She could dive inside the bottle and never return. It was the sobriety that made being drunk so awful.

Stadler grabbed her jaw and sank his fingers into her flesh. She gasped and jerked, but he slammed her head into the back of the chair, pinning her, the bottle held aloft like a sword, ready to behead or knight.

Jolene tried to shake her head, but his grip was too firm. She kicked out, but he side-stepped her and squeezed harder. When she screamed, he poured the alcohol over her mouth, splashing her face, shirt, chair, and floor. She spit out what she could, but some of the alcohol burned down her throat.

Vodka supposedly had no smell, but alcoholics know that wasn't true. It smelled like relief and destiny. Hadn't she always understood this time would come? Certainly not like this, but—

"Spit it out again, and I'll shove the bottle hard enough to break your teeth." His voice was calm, almost friendly. "Understand?"

She whimpered, the last dregs of her willpower and grit washing away.

He grabbed her jaw in the exact same place, the spots already tender. She gasped. He poured.

Jolene swallowed, hating him. Hating life. Hating herself.

CHAPTER FORTY ONE

Cass

"YOU CAN'T GO IN THERE. SHE'D DO ANYTHING to protect you," Kiera said, glaring at him from the other side of the headrest as they waited in Dean's Cadillac sedan.

"No, she'd do anything to protect *you*," Cass countered, tapping his fingers near the door handle. His gut told him they were both correct. He and Kiera were Jolene's greatest weaknesses. "In a fight, what are you going to do?"

"I'm going to rip out his memories. Dor—Jolene and I worked it out."

"And you can do that from across the room?"

Kiera looked at Dean. "No."

"What if he's not unconscious? Jolene might think he'll drink that coffee, but I'm not convinced. He's been at this a long time, and he's not going to drink something someone he's suspicious of brings him." He waited a moment for that to sink in, for Kiera to absorb all the danger.

On the other side of Western, a black SUV with tinted windows slowed and turned right, heading toward Stadler's place. Cass's gut pinched, then lurched. "We've got to go. Now!" He jumped out of the back of the car.

His stomach twinged. *Don't bring the gun.* Cass pulled the holster off his belt and handed it, gun and all to Dean, who'd popped out and rounded the car.

"What? Why?" Dean took the proffered weapon, though he didn't stick it in the car or on his person. "You might need it."

"It would make things worse." He started forward, but Dean put a hand to Cass's chest to stop him.

"We'll endanger her more if we go in at the wrong time."

Cass waited, because if he didn't, Dean might fuck up everything. "That SUV that just turned toward Stadler's is an Agency vehicle." He wasn't sure how he knew, but that was the way of his knowings.

Luckily, Dean assumed Cass had incontrovertible evidence. "Oh shit."

"What?" Kiera stepped out of the car too. "What's going on?"

"Bad-guy backup," Dean replied, opening the passenger door and stuffing Cass's firearm into his glove compartment.

"That's it, I'm calling 911," Kiera said, scrabbling for her phone.

"No." Dean muttered a series of curses. "Let's get eyes first. Officers arriving might make the Agency people act rashly, and that could get Jolene killed. Let's assess. If there are available cars, officers can be there in less than five minutes."

At the next break in traffic, they ran across the four lanes of Western Avenue and onto Iowa Street, a quiet one-way side street.

Dean brushed a hand through his hair as they power-walked down the sidewalk. Kiera had her phone ready in her hand. Cass stayed silent, his gut and head bickering, his heart ready to explode.

And there was the SUV, parked directly across from Stadler's two-flat.

"Fuck," Cass hissed, his lungs revving his body to run, to get to her before it was too late, though he feared it was already too late.

"She's all alone in there." Kiera's voice was high-pitched and taut.

Dean embraced her, kissing the top of her head. "Let's play it cool. We don't want to spook them into killing her in a panic."

Kiera sniffed. "Don't say that."

Cass and Dean exchanged a look, both understanding how impossible it was to predict what would happen. They had too few facts and too little time. Busting in there themselves or the police could save or kill Jolene.

Where the ever-loving fuck had his knowings gone? This was the moment he needed them most.

"I'm going in there." Cass wished this nonplan of his had come from his gut—or even his head—but it was his heart running the show.

"So they can use you as leverage?" Dean asked. "We already talked about this."

"They aren't going to have time to make her do anything. Call 911 ten minutes after I'm inside."

"It takes less than two seconds to shoot you both. All you're doing is providing them with an extra hostage or pawn," Dean said. "What's your plan?"

All fair points. Cass shrugged. "I'll figure it out once I've scouted the situation." Surely, his gift would flare to life once his ass was on the line. It always had.

Dean frowned. "I don't think—"

"Shut up, both of you," Kiera growled. "I'm setting an alarm for five minutes, then I'm going to make the call. Ten minutes total, Cass. That's all you get, so make it count."

* * *

Cass pushed open the door, the duct tape Jolene had used working perfectly. At least that part of the plan had worked. He crept up the stairs to the second floor and knocked twice, trying for casual authority.

"Jolene, did you invite company?" a man, presumably Stadler, asked in an overly friendly voice from the other side of the door.

Cass played the game and used an even friendlier voice. "Thanks for having me, Gavin."

The door opened. Cass stepped inside the apartment and tried to see everything at once. With the open space and little furniture, it wasn't difficult.

Stadler was to the left of the door, and two men stood at the back of the living room in front of a faux fireplace. The white brick of the back wall would show blood spatter well.

He recognized the first man, a tall, dark-skinned Black man in a suit and camel hair coat that together must have cost four to five figures, as Ryan Caldwell, a member of Stadler's team. Caldwell was well groomed, his eyebrows professionally shaped, jaw stubble curated. His eyes were tight, lips pinched.

Cass didn't recognize the second man, white, early to mid-twenties, with a trimmed, russet beard that didn't match his sandy-brown hair. His arms were crossed over his chest, his chin tilted down, but his eyes sparked with vicious defiance.

And then there was Jolene. She sat in an armchair, hands behind her back, tears and snot running down her bruised face, her long-sleeved shirt soaked, her eyes glassy, and a half smile on her face. "You might have been right about my plan sucking," she said, her words slightly slurred.

He'd drugged her. That motherfucker had—

The strike came from the back. Cass shifted to the side, too slow to avoid the blow entirely, so the butt of Stadler's gun hammered into his shoulder. He grunted and twisted, his fist coming in for an uppercut. Stadler's head snapped back, but he didn't drop the weapon. Instead, he stumbled around the red couch, managing to find enough space to raise his firearm as Cass lurched forward to duck behind the couch.

"No!" Jolene attempted to stand but fell back into the chair before she could manage it, capturing Stadler's attention. He stepped behind her, holding the gun a foot from her head. They both knew Stadler had won.

"This isn't what we planned," Ryan said.

Stadler gave him a stare that weighed about a hundred pounds.

Ryan looked away, sucking in his cheeks. He cared about Jolene—or at least cared about what Jolene thought of him. In a fight, he'd hesitate to hurt her, though he wouldn't show Cass the same courtesy.

Jolene whimpered and continually mumbled, "No," but if Stadler had wanted to kill him, he would have shot him already. Cass would be useful as leverage over Jolene.

"Frisk and cuff him," Stadler said to Ryan and tossed him a zip tie.

Ryan caught the plastic. His pat down was thorough, and Cass was glad he hadn't brought his firearm, which would have ended up in Ryan's hands. Ryan had Cass put his wrists behind his back.

Although Cass could have taken Ryan, Stadler's gun kept Cass compliant. For the moment. He held his wrists tightly together. Ryan slipped the stem of the cable tie through the head and ratcheted it, but not very tightly. Cass needed the tie tight to have any chance of escaping later.

Cass snorted. "My grandma pulls tighter than that."

Ryan, as expected, tightened the bonds to the point of pain and stepped back, shoving Cass's shoulder until he dropped to his knees. Cass immediately angled his body as if trying to take in the room while he maneuvered the tie around until the head was between his wrists. He was ninety percent sure he could break the cuffs as they were now, hopefully in one go. Now he needed to wait for his moment.

"Can we get started?" the man Cass didn't know asked. He was shorter than everyone in the room except Jolene. He shuffled closer to her. His posture was stooped and rounded, like a dog expecting a kick, but his voice held a note of arrogance.

Jolene stiffened. Cass watched the man, scrolling through the possibilities of what he was doing there. He didn't ping as a torturer, and nobody acknowledged him.

"Just when you think it can't get any worse," Stadler said, looking down on Jolene. "Am I right?"

"How could you?" she asked, her voice timid like a child's. "Why not give me sleeping pills?"

Cass scooted until his back was to the wall, giving himself some room. The movement caught Jolene's eye. The round bruises on her jaw made him ache to gut Stadler. That prick had dug his fingers into her face. Cass vowed right then to kill him.

His gift roared to life, shoving the thinking and feeling part of his brain to the side, focusing on the moment and everything around him.

Stadler tucked his gun into his back waistband. Big motherfucker. He had another weapon in an ankle holster and a knife in his front jeans pocket. His right quadriceps was tight. An injury of some sort from less than a week ago. *Strongly right-handed*, which didn't fit with someone well trained. He must have seriously injured his left hand at some point, forcing him to rely heavily on his right.

Stadler's posture and interest were all turned toward Jolene, but his right foot angled back toward Cass. The man was aware of everything. Cass could get out of the zip ties, but he'd have to stand up to do it, and that might take three seconds, which wouldn't be fast enough.

He had to wait.

Jolene was barely in the room, staring at the two Starbucks drinks sitting on the glass coffee table. *Full.* Stadler hadn't drunk anything.

"You aren't going to fight him," Stadler said to Jolene in a soothing tone as he moved in front of her. "But as your mentor, I want you to fully grasp the lesson." He curled an index finger and placed it under her chin, lifting her face to his. "Open your mind."

Oh. The hunched, arrogant man was also a memory surgeon.

Jolene shook her head. "Please, don't. You don't need it. Stadler. Gavin. Please."

Cass watched, helpless, as Jolene fell apart. Stadler ignored her pleas, but Ryan turned away, heading to the door.

"Caldwell," Stadler said, his interest never wavering from Jolene. Stadler didn't enjoy her torment, but she wasn't giving him what he wanted.

"Come on, man," Ryan said, his voice harsh and pleading, though he used it to mask something. *Anger. Disgust.*

"We have a job to do," Stadler replied.

"Then stop playing around." He managed to say it without challenging Stadler's authority. They were well acquainted.

This was the "family" she'd embraced, the people she'd been hesitant to rat out to the FBI, even after they'd lied to her so thoroughly. Stadler held a bottle of vodka, about double the size of a regular bottle. It was half empty, but Jolene clearly wore some of it. The floor around her was splashed with liquid, and the chair cushion appeared soaked.

"No more," Jolene gasped. "You don't need more."

Stadler's jaw clenched, just once. He reached behind his back, then raised his gun at Cass, his eyes cold and empty.

"Okay, okay, I'll drink it. Give it to me."

Jolene's rasp snapped something in Stadler. He brought it to her mouth. "Good girls swallow."

Stadler poured mouthful after mouthful down her throat, so much that Cass feared she'd have to have her stomach pumped later. His gut wrenched, an indication he needed to make a move soon.

"Stop!" Cass shouted.

"Should I kill him now or later?" Stadler asked Jolene, his hand digging into her face in the exact places he'd abused earlier.

"Since when does what I want matter?" she replied, her head lolling in a tight circle. She smiled at him, a tiny, genuine gesture. "You can't trust anyone."

"You can't." Stadler put his gun back into his waistband, then addressed the memory surgeon. "You're up, Mickey."

"Mitchell," the kid corrected.

"He does that on purpose," Jolene slurred. "You'll be Mickey from now on, Mickey, so you better get used to it."

"I don't—"

"M-I-C," Jolene sang with a drunk solemnity that would have been funny in a different situation.

"Shut up," Mickey snapped. Then he stomped over and held out a hand, trying to decide where to touch her. Her face was too personal for Mickey's comfort, and her hands were secured behind her back. Seeing how his predecessor was treated seemed to be giving Mickey pause.

Mickey won't fight, if it comes to that.

"Jesus," Stadler muttered under his breath. "Her neck."

Mickey flinched so hard he stumbled back a step.

Stadler crossed his arms over his chest. "I didn't say choke her, moron."

"I usually just touch hands," Mickey mumbled.

"Ain't this your lucky day, then? Hurry, before she passes out."

"If she's passed out, I won't have any trouble—"

"We don't have all day for you to root around." Stadler gestured at Jolene. "I'll ask questions. You pull out answers."

"Oh," Mickey said, placing both hands around Jolene's neck. "Like a smash-and-grab."

Cass put Mickey on his hit list. When Ryan slipped into the kitchen, muttering, clearly unwilling to watch, Cass decided he might let Ryan live. Beyond the kitchen was a door that led to the back stairs. Ryan paused in the kitchen as if contemplating escape.

Stadler bent to look Jolene in the eye. "She's going to give you whatever I ask because if she doesn't, I'm going to shoot her boyfriend in the gut. It's a slow and painful death."

Jolene hiccupped and started mumbling about stars and rivers, her words hard to distinguish with the thick tears inside them.

"Show me everything that happened at the AA meeting with Stefano Jr." Stadler had already guessed where the meat of what she was hiding lay.

Cass saw Stadler so clearly. Ambitious. Driven. Jolene had disappointed him. He probably didn't admit to himself how much he cared about her opinion. She was paying for his discomfort.

"Whoa," Mickey said only a few seconds later. "Whoa." He giggled.

"What?" Stadler snapped.

"That Stefano Jr. dude is working for the FBI. Pretty fucked up, turning against his old man like that." Mickey chuckled.

Every single detail poured out. Cass had already heard some of it, but Mickey also revealed what had been shared by both Stefano Jr. and Jolene at the meeting. Tears dripped off Jolene's jaw to disappear into her already-soaked shirt.

Mickey's face squashed together like he was taking an epic shit. "She's—she's hiding something." His grip tightened on her neck. "Hey, you can't do that."

"Jolene." Stadler's soft voice seemed to strike her like a blow.

"There." Mickey grinned and nodded. "Got it. It's—" He let go of her and whipped his head toward Cass. "Holy shit."

Cass's face heated. Mickey shook his hands out and hit the heels of his hands against his head a few times, not hard, but in some sort of OCD pattern.

"What?" Stadler prompted.

"He was supposed to kill her." Mickey looked between Cass and Jolene and then told the story of Cass's duplicity in broad strokes, her pain echoing through Mickey's words due to the nature of his gift. Lies. Truth. Neither.

Stadler slapped Jolene across the face. "You didn't come to me?"

"Everybody lies," she said, nonplussed. "I thought we were doing big things. I was going to do what my grandmother couldn't. I was going to make her legacy obsolete." She cackled and hummed, so unlike herself the hair on Cass's arms rose. "Burn that clinic she worked for to the ground. Stupid linoleum and particleboard would have caught quick and made a toxic cloud."

Stadler cocked his head. "What else?"

"What the fuck else is there?" Her voice squeaked. "I win, and she loses. I get the last motherfucking laugh. You know what the last thing she ever said to me was? 'I'm so disappointed in you.' Who's the disappointment now, Granny?" She giggled, then started sobbing. "It's still me, isn't it? I'm the disappointment."

Jolene cared about the drug trade and making the world a safer place. Most of all, though, she wanted to do more on the drug front than her grandmother, to make a bigger contribution. To prove her value.

She wants to be worthy of love.

The sounds of sirens split through the room. Cass wasn't sure yet if that was a good or bad choice by CPD.

Everyone looked to Stadler, and Stadler stared at Cass.

HOLD.

Cass didn't move, his mind cleared of everything but this moment. His gut spun as if trying to figure out a direction.

"Wipe her memory of this meeting and let's go," Stadler said, turning his attention to the window.

A police cruiser arrived outside, its siren cutting off.

Despite only a profile view, Cass saw the shift in Stadler's shoulder as he pulled the knife from his front pocket. Mickey saw it too and jumped back with a yelp.

MOVE.

Cass shifted his weight and jumped to his feet, keeping bent at the waist as he jerked his arms up as high as he could with his hands behind his back. He slammed them against his backside as hard as possible. The zip ties broke apart on the first try, which was fortunate, because Stadler had his firearm pulled. The knife Stadler had been holding clattered to the floor, allowing him a more stable two-handed hold on his weapon.

Cass dove to the right, expecting to take a hit. But Jolene let out a scream and shouldered into Stadler. They crashed together, and the gun fell from Stadler's hand. Jolene nailed Stadler right in the nose with a head butt. Mickey scrambled into the corner of the room, hands covering his face.

Stadler grabbed Jolene by the throat and pulled her in front of him. Cass scrabbled to find the gun. Jolene wrenched her body to the side, dropping all her weight onto one knee. Stadler didn't release her, but he was pulled off-balance. Cass spotted the gun sticking out from under the couch.

"Don't move," Ryan barked from the kitchen.

"Shoot him!" Stadler commanded.

"Not with the cops here. Run," Ryan countered and raced to the back door.

Stadler still held Jolene as a human shield, maneuvering toward the kitchen, as Mickey scurried ahead. *He intends to take her with him.*

Cass managed a roundhouse kick around Jolene into Stadler's right quad, the tight one, and his entire leg buckled. Stadler shoved Jolene as he crumpled, and Cass chose to catch her rather than kill Stadler. By the time he steadied her, Stadler had disappeared through the kitchen.

Later, Cass might regret not shooting the prick, but for the moment, his heart held only gratitude that they'd survived.

CHAPTER FORTY TWO

Jolene

JOLENE WOKE TO LIGHT STABBING HER EYES AND aches everywhere. Her head throbbed, her face stung, and her throat burned as if she'd swallowed paint thinner.

Or alcohol.

Everything slammed into her, like a traumatic memory consumed whole, all the pain hitting at once, though the details evaded her. Tears gushed out of her eyes, and her throat pain intensified as she tried to swallow. She touched her face—tender, swollen.

She'd failed before in life—many times—but if half of what she remembered was true, this was a new low.

"Jolene." His voice was deep, thick with an emotion she was incapable of deciphering. Not that it mattered.

"What happened? Where am I?"

Cass knelt on the mattress where she lay, no frame or box spring, just a mattress sitting on a concrete floor—the smooth, poured kind, not the unfinished-basement kind. The room was tiny, like an upscale prison cell with nothing but the bed with maroon-striped sheets and a natty mud-colored blanket of some man-made material.

"Stadler made you drink an obscene amount of vodka and had a memory surgeon pull out your memories of Stefano Jr. . . . and me. Kiera and Dean called in the cops, who spooked them, and they ran off. You saved me, and I saved you. We also took off to avoid having to face the police ourselves."

He gently brushed the hair away from her face, but she refused to look at him. Her tongue felt swollen and tasted sour. She needed water but couldn't bear to ask for anything.

Cass rested a warm hand on her arm. "I . . . encouraged you to throw up when we reached the back alley. Dean brought the car around, and Kiera and I kept you sitting up and talking, got you some water and Pedialyte. We debated the hospital to have your stomach pumped, but you were adamant we not do that. You said it wasn't safe, and Kiera agreed."

From his tone, Jolene thought perhaps Cass had had a different opinion. "Where are we?" Jolene asked, eyes squeezed shut to avoid seeing him looking at her. She buried her face in the blanket, which smelled of must and something slightly chemical.

He carefully brushed a hand down her flank. "We're at a gallery space near the Goose Island Brewery. It's where I was supposed to have my art show, but with the mission, it got pushed back. We should have it to ourselves for at least a week. You're safe here, sweetheart."

No, no, no. "Cass." Just saying his name made her body shriek in grief. Her chest spasmed, and she could barely breathe. "I need a few minutes to myself."

"I don't want to leave you alone." His voice shook, and she hated she'd done that to him, exposed him to the rot of her life. "Please, let me stay. I won't talk."

"I need the bathroom," she said, her voice rising. She couldn't fall apart in front of him, and she couldn't hold it together for much longer.

"Jolene, can you at least look at me?"

He was killing her, a rusty knife through her stomach and intestines, twisting and twisting. "Please. I can't. Just . . ." Her croak finally must have worked, because he rose.

"There's a bathroom right through there." Cass left with the click of a closed door.

At last, she turned toward where he'd gone, staring at the particleboard surface of the door, unpainted and unadorned. The ceiling, by contrast, was covered in decorative tin, smaller squares in an art deco pattern reminiscent of seashells. She crashed her face into the flat pillow and screamed. The action ripped up her throat, but she didn't care. The pain meant something, though she couldn't say what. She shrieked again and choked on her own phlegm.

She should have died. Part of her had always assumed that's how she would end—in a bottle. It hadn't been her choice, unless she considered all of her choices had led her to that moment, so, in a way, it was her fault. Stadler had beaten her at everything—always had—so why had she believed she could trick him? He knew her every bit as well as she knew him—more, actually, since he'd held the truth, and she'd held his lies.

Stadler.

Her mentor, the one she'd turned to over and over again for the past five years. Destroyed her but left her alive. Not because he cared, but because he wanted her to suffer. Her five years of sobriety, gone. Stadler obliterating her will like a spoiled brat swatting away all the game pieces. He hadn't even been losing.

Zero days sober.

She stumbled on shaky legs to a tiny white bathroom with only a toilet and sink, the lighting nothing but a bare bulb. The warped mirror she avoided, unprepared to witness her physical devastation. The edge of the sink held a toothbrush and a travel-sized tube of tooth-whitening Colgate.

This moment. This awful, soul-stripping moment was nothing more than her bill coming due. Karma was a bitch, but she was, by nature, fair.

After using the toilet, she leaned with her hands propped on the concrete block wall, still avoiding her reflection. Jolene brushed her teeth with the new-looking toothbrush, red and soft-bristled, that was left back against the lip of the sink.

Jolene had dedicated almost five years of her life blindly supporting the drug trade, working for the cruelest people. Sure, the universe was totally going to give her a devoted lover and partner, some kind of happy ending.

When she couldn't brush any longer, she spit and rinsed and drank a few handfuls of water.

A knock came on the bedroom door. "Can I come in?"

"Go away!" she shrieked, her voice cutting out halfway through, the pain sharp and brutal. She tasted copper through the mint of the toothpaste.

"Baby, please," he replied, his own voice soft and tender. A dull thump meant he'd either slapped a palm or his head against the door.

She wasn't ready to face him yet and collapsed back on the bed. "I'll come out when I'm ready." Which might be never.

"Okay." Nothing but a wisp of sound. "There's Motrin and some Pedialyte next to the bed. Promise me you'll drink the entire bottle, and I'll give you a little more time. I'll make you some toast, but, Jolene . . . I'm worried. I'm—I'm scared. Please don't shut me out."

She peered over the side of the mattress to see the bottle of cherry pomegranate Pedialyte next to a Costco-sized bottle of Motrin. Even better was the box of Puffs Plus Lotion tissues, the perforated cardboard cover already pulled free. "I'll drink this and be out soon," she said, though *soon* was likely a lie.

Jolene yanked out three tissues at once and blew out a gallon of mucous. She tossed the slimy ball of misery to the floor and grabbed two more tissues. Her nose was plugged, her face hot and sore, her head pounding, her stomach feathery and delicate. The Pedialyte cap had already been unscrewed and then closed again. Cass. Making everything as easy as possible for her. Taking care of her. She took several deep gulps. The beverage was cool but not cold, the liquid welcome, so far, in her belly and down her throat, though the taste in her freshly washed mouth was too sickly sweet.

She had to let him go. Her choices had whittled down to one: running. Cass would probably offer to give up his work, friends, and his wonderful, supportive family to save Jolene from a situation she'd put herself into by her own stupidity. What could she give him in return? Intense neediness and insecurity? Her sparkling personality?

At some point, he'd realize how much better he could do than her.

CHAPTER FORTY THREE

Cass

WITH SHAKING FINGERS, HE PULLED OUT HIS prepaid phone and texted Kiera. *She's awake. It's not good.*

Her reply came immediately. *Does she need a doctor? I'm already on my way.*

Cass wanted time alone with Jolene, but what Jolene needed was Kiera. *I don't think so. She kicked me out of the room and won't talk to me.* Typing the words made the backs of his eyes burn. Jolene wasn't the only one in need of comforting.

Meditation was a great tool, but nothing cleared thoughts and brought perspective like a battle. Yesterday, everything had become clear: nothing mattered more than Jolene. Her unique mixture of strength and vulnerability fit him so perfectly. He could lean on her—lean hard—and she could handle it. He had the fortitude to hold her up in return. If only she would let him.

Shit. I'll be there in 10-15 minutes.

Cass closed his eyes, his back against the thin door between him and the woman he loved. They'd never been further apart.

Time was slipping, the clock ticking, their options dwindling. Cass killing Stadler or running. Or both—he could take out Stadler, and then they could run.

Though he wasn't sure Jolene would want Stadler dead, even after he'd spectacularly mind-fucked her. But Cass still imagined setting up a situation in which he lured Stadler close enough Cass could convince the state's attorney and Jolene that he'd had no other option but to kill that motherfucker.

So satisfying to imagine. And possible.

The sounds of choked sobs gripped his intestines until he almost doubled over. He had to *do* something. Toast. Lamest support move ever, but still . . .

Cass moved to the kitchenette across the hall and popped two pieces of white bread into the toaster as he poked around his "feels."

Guilt, of course, but along with that, a familiar exhilaration. He deeply regretted Jolene's abuse, but he'd felt wholly alive when they'd been trapped in that apartment. He'd liked the danger, the strategy, the fight, and he'd adored the sensation of being Jolene's protector, of saving her. It reminded him of what he'd loved best about serving, the sheer magnitude of the difference he'd made. He'd saved his army brothers' lives, no doubt. Saving Jolene's meant even more, though. The danger surrounding her wasn't a turnoff at all, but the after-dinner mint following a ten-course meal.

The toast popped. He pulled the slices out two-fingered, ignoring the biting burn, and plopped them onto a thin paper plate. No butter, so dry it would remain.

Obviously, Jolene didn't want to be in a position where she needed saving. Perhaps that was why she'd shut him out so thoroughly. She'd seen the killer in him, the alpha male he mostly kept caged, and after everything she'd been through, maybe she didn't want that—want him—in her life.

But the more he contemplated it, the more confident he became he was exactly what she needed. They'd both lived at the edges of life's experiences and fell victim to society's expectations. If he was more than a killer, then she was more than a broken tool. He only had to find a way to prove it to her.

I'm here. Kiera's text propelled him into motion, clamping hard to the distraction. He was only a few steps from the back door, which they'd agreed was the safest ingress for spotting any tails.

Cass set the paper plate on the small Formica counter and opened the door for Kiera. Wearing oversized sunglasses, an oversized sweater, and pale blue jeans worn through in places, she carried four stuffed canvas bags and a smaller plastic sack, the handles all looped over her forearms.

"Hey," she said, holding out one arm to him.

He began unloading. The first canvas bag contained a mini pharmacy: hydrogen peroxide, Band-Aids, bandages, Alka-Seltzer, cold compresses, ginger tea, ginger ale, ginger snaps, a tiny bottle labeled Rescue Remedy, vitamins C and D, echinacea, zinc, Saint John's wort, a broad-spectrum probiotic, and an oversized plastic case of Ferrero Rocher chocolates.

Another sack contained twelve paperback novels, most with supernatural creatures like dragons and vampires on the covers and a few with naked male chests. Cass chuffed a laugh. "Just how long do you think we'll be here?" Forget a week. They wouldn't stay more than three days.

"We don't know what the hell she'll be in the mood to read."

Kiera unpacked the remaining two canvas bags, which were filled with clothing for both him and Jolene. Everything she'd brought looked soft, even the jeans, which were artistically well-worn. Nothing looked cheap. She held out a smaller, plastic bag with a finger, letting it swing. "Unmentionables."

Cass snatched it and peered inside at the boxer briefs. Saxx. Tom Ford. And a no-name brand covered in toadstools. He snort-laughed. "Thanks." Her presence breathed hope into the dark space they'd fallen into.

"Jolene's down-under bits are in that pile," she said, pointing to a stack of black clothing. "Don't peek."

He gripped the back of his neck, trying to massage out the kinks. "She's in there crying. She won't let me in."

Kiera hugged herself and looked away. "She just lived through her worst nightmare, losing her sobriety—and trust me, that's how she'll see this—and abused by someone she trusted. You witnessed the whole thing. It's no wonder she doesn't want you watching her fall apart. That's not how she wants to be seen."

Cass shook his head. "You weren't there. He—cruel doesn't begin to describe what he did to her, and she was devastated, but still . . . still, she had the presence of mind to knock him off-balance when she had the chance. She saved my life. Now she's in there, suffering alone when she doesn't need to be. I can't force my company on her, but I also can't do nothing."

Kiera stared at him for a few seconds, then nodded. "Agreed. I'll go into the cave of the beast and clear the way for you."

"Here." Cass snagged the now-cold toast and handed it to her. He bit his lip. He wanted to be the one to hold Jolene while she pulled herself together, convince her she needed him as much as he needed her. But this wasn't about him. "Tell her I love her."

"Why? Do you have a terminal illness?" She rolled her eyes. "Nut up and tell her yourself." Kiera grabbed the stack of clothes for Jolene with her free hand and knocked on the door twice, almost spilling the pile. "It's me. Make yourself decent."

Jolene didn't respond, and Kiera didn't wait. She disappeared into the little bedroom, leaving Cass on the outside, heart breaking. He was used to action, making decisions, solving problems. But Jolene wasn't a problem. Cass interlaced his fingers and squeezed until the pain cleared some of his helplessness. He closed his eyes and breathed deeply, calming himself for Jolene. When she was ready, he would be too.

CHAPTER FORTY FOUR

Jolene

"WELL, FUCK ME, I DO NOT LIKE THE LOOK ON your face." Kiera strode the few steps to the bed and dumped a stack of clothing onto Jolene's lap as she sat next to her, setting a paper plate of golden, dry toast on the edge of the mattress.

"What look is that?" Jolene turned her attention to the shirts, yoga pants, and jeans, all black and in fabrics so soft touching them was like stroking a bunny. Kiera's clothing style had always been comfort first. The jeans Kiera wore were probably as cozy as cashmere.

"It's an expression that says you're ready to fuck up everything."

Jolene checked the label on a boat-neck sweater. Bamboo. "Been there, done that. And now I've got a shirt."

Kiera laughed. "Girlfriend, yesterday was someone else fucking up your life. Now it's your turn to fuck or unfuck it, and I'm here to badger you into the latter course of action."

Jolene shook her head but glanced at Kiera out of the corner of her eye. Her friend stared at her with a frank, open expression, her jaw set but her eyes soft.

"I don't think it matters what I do. Every choice I make turns out to be a mistake," Jolene said.

"What about Cass? Is he a mistake?"

Jolene shut her eyes. "The biggest one of all." She'd gotten herself attached and him ensnared in her problems, and she couldn't allow her selfishness to ruin his life.

"Oh yeah, I can see that." Kiera rolled her eyes. "A hot badass who risked his life to save you. Those guys are the *worst*."

"I don't want someone to do that!"

Kiera looked at her then, her eyes cutting through Jolene's defenses, albeit battered, and striking her directly in the heart. "That's all you've ever wanted."

Tears overflowed Jolene's eyes, the pressure in her head building to stroke-level bursting. Her shaking fingers whisked away the moisture, but not fast enough. She blew her nose again and again, but the tears wouldn't stop and everything hurt so damn much and her face felt bloated like a balloon.

Her friend watched her with a wary patience, handing her the half-empty bottle of Pedialyte but saying nothing.

Jolene pressed her fingers into her eyes. "I fucked up everything." She bit her lip and tried to summon numbness to surround her. "I almost got him killed, Kier. I don't remember everything, and I don't know if that memory fucker took something or if—if it was the alcohol. Stadler. He—he—he—"

Kiera leaned over and hugged her. The floral-vanilla scent of Kiera's body lotion popped open the memories of their friendship. "He forced you to drink."

"Why would he do that to me?"

"Because he's a cunt-quistador trying to put you in your place." Kiera pulled back, her chin rising an inch. "The fuck-weasel thinks if he does the worst thing to you, you'll just fall apart like a shattered doll."

"I did."

"Of course you did!" Kiera rolled her eyes again. "The point isn't being broken; the point is not *staying* broken. He doesn't get to be the one who defines your life."

Jolene gave her a watery smile. How the hell had she lived without her friend for so many years? She—

The world clarified.

"Oh shit," Jolene said, easing away from Kiera to cup her own face. "I let my grandmother do that."

Kiera raised her brows, waiting for Jolene to finish the epiphany bursting through her brain.

"Everything I've ever done was either to make her proud or piss her off, even after she died. I've used her life as some sort of ethical yardstick. She defined me. Why would I do that when I never approved of her values, not really? What the fuck is wrong with me?"

"Bitch, please, there are not enough hours in the day to answer that." Kiera smirked as Jolene barked a laugh. Kiera exhaled. "Good parents shape their kids in fucked-up ways, too, apparently, with their blind faith and high expectations."

"Sounds like a first-world problem to me." Jolene had craved that sort of conviction from her grandmother.

Kiera looked away. "I used to think that, too, but . . . Dean twisted himself around for years trying to live up to his parents' admiration. Who the fuck are we to judge?"

Jolene tilted her head in acknowledgement because Kiera was right. "What do we do?"

"Turn your anger away from yourself and put it where it belongs." She shrugged and smirked. "Therapy helps."

"Not this again." They hadn't argued about it in over five years. "You'd been in therapy for years, and you were still fucked up."

"And I'm *still* fucked up, just less so. Part of the problem is when you're a headcase, you just assume if something isn't working, it's on you. Turns out—get this—therapists are people too. Some of them suck, both personally and professionally. You need the right one."

Jolene chuckled. Parts of herself drifted together, reforming into something resembling a human being. "I have AA meetings." Saying that brought the recollection of Mitchell, aka Mickey, prying into her brain, trying to glean more than the Stefano Jr. memory. He—

"Oh shit."

"What?" Kiera sat up straighter, looking ready to grab a pitchfork and storm Stadler's castle.

"I took something." Jolene shoved the heels of her hands into her temples. The hangover made even the simplest tasks impossible. "Fuck. Where would I have put it?"

"Your pocket?"

"No, dumbass. I took a memory."

Kiera grinned and clapped her hands. "Oh, girlfriend, you have come to the right place."

"What do you mean?"

"Remember I told you I've been helping those victims of that couples-therapy scam artist?"

"Yeah."

"Most of what I do is shore up what memories they do have and find little wisps of remembrances that dickface missed. If anyone can find that shit inside your brain, it's me." Kiera held out her hands.

Jolene placed her hands in Kiera's, closing her eyes and trying to find the memory. Actively thinking about it should help Kiera find it. Jolene wondered how long it—

"Got it," Kiera said. "I'm going to sort of reboot it for you."

* * *

Mitchell regretted taking the tall chair because he had to either scoot to the end of the seat like a girl or let his feet swing like a kid. The old man glaring at him didn't help with his comfort at all. Stefano looked like a white-haired bulldog with his sagging jowls and beady eyes. A well-dressed bulldog. Mitchell planned to buy some flashy suits when he cashed out. He'd never been a suit kind of guy before, but he was about to become rich.

Underneath his bravado, however, ran a ribbon of pinched nerves, causing his palms to sweat and his bowels to rumble in an alarming way. "Dude, they've broken into your files once already, with the help of another memory surgeon," Mitchell said. Stefano didn't acknowledge this key piece of intel. This wasn't at all how Mitchell had expected the meeting to go. "They hacked in through a Benjamin Gold guy's computer."

That got a reaction. He narrowed his eyes. "I find that hard to believe."

"He likes watches, right?"

Stefano's face opened like a crack of thunder. "He does. Did they bribe him with a watch?"

"No." Mitchell hadn't considered Stefano might be a skeptic. "She was, like, pretending to admire his watch and shit and touched his wrist. Then she pulled five digits of his passcode, and with random luck, their tech dude got the sixth on his second try. Their other people took a glass he'd drunk out of and got his prints. That's all they needed."

"Why are you here?"

Mitchell swallowed. In his mind, Stefano had begged him to join their crew, had gotten on the phone to brag to the other drug lords about his valuable find. He'd set Mitchell up in a downtown skyscraper with a built-in bar and a line of credit for high-end prostitutes and an assortment of recreational drugs. He hadn't had to propose anything.

"I—I thought you might want a memory surgeon of your own." It sounded pathetic. He should have practiced looking tough in the mirror.

"What for? I already know what everybody around me is thinking." He had a clichéd bad-guy voice, deep and rough as if he'd injured his vocal cords in his twenties during some sort of turf war.

It occurred to Mitchell he might have put himself in a worse position. "Okay . . . but what about your enemies?"

Stefano laughed, one of those condescending laughs meant to knock a person down. "I know what they're thinking too. Power. Money. Pussy. There ain't nothing else in life. Everyone wants more, and they all want what's mine."

Mitchell wanted to dive into Stefano's mind. Was he truly this TV-show gangster, or was it all an act? Did he think Mitchell's information was free? "What about loyalty?"

Stefano's face dropped any sign of humor. "What do you know?"

Shit. He didn't know anything. "I . . ." It came to him, the perfect edge. "If you had a memory surgeon, you could ensure the loyalty of every single one of your people. And if any were disloyal, you'd know who and how much." He should have opened with that angle.

"Prove it."

* * *

MITCHELL HAD DOUBLE-CROSSED STADLER. JOLENE DIDN'T ENVY WHAT would happen to him once Stadler found out. She almost laughed when her conscience caught up with her random thoughts. "Oh shit. Stefano Jr."

Jolene leaped to her feet to fetch Cass, but Kiera called out, "Wait!"

"What?"

"One more thing." She shook out her hands and blinked too many times. "Someone's been in your head, Dor—Jolene. It's subtle, but I've been working on this for so long, I noticed the signs. Some of your memories have some kind of . . . residue, for lack of a better word. I'm not sure it was that Mitchell guy—he feels like a hack. But some asshole at some point has been looking at your memories and taking a few pieces."

"Oh my God, how far down does this well go?" Every time she thought she'd hit the bottom, it turned out, no, there were actually more shitty things. She wondered how many memory surgeons worked for the Agency. Had they mined her memories regularly, then erased their footprints? Or had something horrible happened to her? The idea someone had taken her memories without her permission and without her noticing made her already-fragile stomach threaten to unload all the Pedialyte.

She'd never stolen personal memories, only removing moments of herself after questioning, but she'd been tempted, and she'd crossed lines. But she'd also held some lines, and she wouldn't let herself forget that.

Though it could go either way, she bit into the toast, hoping it would settle her gut. She'd linger on the violation later. Right now, she had an FBI asset to protect.

CHAPTER FORTY FIVE

Cass

"CASS!" JOLENE CALLED.

He opened the door immediately and darted into the room, searching for the cause of her panic. "What's wrong?"

Jolene rubbed her temples. "You need to call your brother and have him get Stefano Jr. into protective custody. Mitchell went to Stefano Sr. when he found out the Agency was trying to move in on Stefano's territory. He'll definitely tell him his son is working with the FBI. Stefano Jr.'s life is in danger."

"I called Shaun yesterday, the minute we were safe in Dean's car. It's okay, baby, Junior's already been taken in." Cass edged close and pushed her hair away from her face, stroking his fingers down the strands. They were thick and a bit tangled, but he didn't mind. Jolene was finally allowing him to touch her.

She wouldn't meet his gaze. "All right."

Kiera waved her hand in a *continue* motion from her spot on the edge of the bed.

"I want to hold you," he said. "I won't believe you're okay until I do." His hand slid beneath her hair to the back of her neck, his fingers making small circles, but he held the distance between them. She had to come to him first. "Please, Jolene."

Jolene leaned forward, and he practically tackled her with the speed he brought her to his chest. Holding her was exquisite in its torture and comfort. He stroked her hair and murmured into her ear every soothing word available, including *you're safe* and *it's over*, even if they weren't true yet.

She wasn't safe, and it certainly wasn't over, but he hoped the timbre of his voice might lull her into a temporary feeling of safety. Jolene dug her fingers into his back to pin him close. He couldn't crush her to him with her injuries, but he banded his arms around her, enclosing her against him, reminding her—he hoped—he would always put his body between hers and danger.

Kiera tapped her foot against the concrete floor. "Sorry to intrude, but we have a little more to discuss."

Cass loosened his grip enough to allow Jolene to pull away, but she didn't go far. She threaded her fingers through his and scooted closer to him until her head rested on his shoulder as they faced Kiera.

Kiera rubbed her hands together as if they were cold. "Dean and I have been figuring out the best way to funnel you guys money. Do you think you could protect a backpack of money? It's the least traceable but most easily stolen option. We figure half in cash and half electronically transferred to some offshore account."

"You don't have to do that," Cass said, the response a reflex.

"Oh," Kiera said, straightening. "I didn't realize you had a sufficient cache of cash ready to keep you safely on the run for the next several years."

He looked away.

"Yeah, that's what I thought," Kiera mumbled. "Don't pretzel-twist your nuts. The greenbacks are for Jolene, not you."

Jolene huffed a laugh. "I don't know—"

"Obviously, but we aren't arguing about it." Kiera stood.

Cass didn't want to take Kiera's money, even if she could afford it, but they desperately needed it. Somehow, they'd repay her.

"I'm not *allowed* to stay here for more than an hour," Kiera said, her lips pursed into a pout. "Which reminds me." She pulled out a phone and sent a text, presumably to Dean. She grinned, her mood shifting. "Now I'm on the clock."

A text dinged, and Kiera frowned at her cell, then snorted. "Asshole." She showed the screen to Jolene, and Cass crowded closer to her to read it too. *You've already been there 15 minutes, so you only have 45 left.*

"He's tracking you?" Jolene asked.

Kiera shrugged. "I don't care. It's not like I go anywhere." She wrapped her arms around herself. "And if anybody ever takes me, he can find me."

"We should do that," Jolene said, looking up at Cass.

"Not necessary, since I'm not letting you out of my sight again," Cass replied.

Jolene flinched, and Cass's gut twisted with the certainty that she planned to flee alone, with nobody at her six, and he wasn't certain he could talk her out of it.

"I can protect cash," he said, picking up Kiera's earlier question. Cass didn't have time for pride or anything that wasn't about Jolene's safety. "And we've got our prepaids. You can buy one, too, and text Jolene the banking information when you have it. We'll set up another account and transfer funds immediately."

"About that," Jolene said. "I think it's better if I head out on my own. They won't expect me to be traveling alone." It was a weak argument, and she had to squish up her face to get the words out.

"No way you're that stupid," Kiera said before Cass could respond.

"It's not stupid," Jolene replied.

Cass lifted his hands, wanting to keep touching her but sensing the timing wasn't good. "I would never force anything on you—"

"I would," Kiera said. She turned to her friend. "You want to save him, right? Protect him? Make sure that prick Stadler doesn't hurt him?"

Jolene closed her eyes for a full second. "Yes. Absolutely, yes."

Kiera smiled, but it wasn't kind. "That's all he wants too. Isn't that sweet, the two of you wanting the same thing?"

Jolene jerked back and swayed on her feet for a moment. Cass steadied her. She scowled and pressed her fingers into her temples. "It's different." She walked over to the almost-empty bottle of Pedialyte and finished it in a few gulps. "Because this is my mess. My decisions put me in danger, so I should be the one to bear that."

Cass and Kiera exchanged a glance, which Jolene caught but didn't comment on.

Kiera reached out and hugged Jolene. Softly, but loud enough for Cass to hear, she said, "Leave him behind, and you make him an open target. And if you won't keep him with you for yourself, do it for me." Then she turned to Cass. "I'll get cash tomorrow first thing. Until then, I'll just let you guys do what you do." She arched her eyebrows on the way out.

Jolene crossed her arms over her chest. "She didn't have to go for another half hour."

He edged closer. "She's giving us space to work out our shit." Cass knelt in front of her. "Tell me straight up what scares you, and I'll give you an absolutely honest response in return. Nothing but truth between us."

CHAPTER FORTY SIX

Jolene

THE WORDS WOULDN'T COME OUT. THEY WERE TOO pathetic, and every time she imagined him hearing what was inside her, she cringed. "If you come with me, it can't be out of obligation or guilt. I—I can't do that again."

Cass frowned.

Total honesty. "Everyone leaves me," she said. "My parents. They cared more about taking care of strangers in a third world country than they cared about me. Who abandons their five-year-old for eight months that turn into forever?" She swallowed. "My grandmother. She didn't really want me. She poured all her love and hope into drug addicts, and there wasn't much left for me. Stadler. He . . ." Joleen shook her head. "You might think you want to run with me right now, but—"

Cass slipped his arm around her shoulders and pulled her gently into him. Jolene curled close, resting her forehead on his chest. He kissed the top of her head. "I don't feel an obligation to you, Jolene, but attachment. My heart only wants you. I fucking *love* you, and I want to go where you go. I want to lie down next to you every night and wake up next to you every morning. We haven't known each other long, but I don't care. I've never, in my entire life, been so happy as when we spend time together. Even right now. In this shitty, awful moment when I couldn't protect you, and you were assaulted, and we have to live our lives always looking behind us—okay, I can't say I'm happy about that, but I'm at peace. There's nothing inside me telling me to stay away or let you go. We belong together, and it's all right if you don't believe me now. One day, you will."

Her eyes glistened, and her resolve sank into oblivion. "You'd have to give up your family, your job." She looked around the tiny bedroom, remembering where they were. "Your art."

He shrugged. "I can paint anywhere and do any number of jobs to make money. My family will understand."

"I've met your family, and they won't understand."

"They won't have a choice."

"Because you choose me?"

Cass cupped her face with both hands, his green eyes bright. "Yes. I will always choose you."

Her heart pounded hard enough she thought it might be fatal. He wanted her. Above anything else. And fuck it, she was going to embrace all the happiness. "Okay."

His smile spread over his handsome face, and she almost couldn't breathe. "Yeah?"

Her smile made her face ache, but she didn't care. "Yes." She coughed a laugh. "How many times do I have to say it?"

Cass cupped her uninjured cheek and stepped into her. She had to tilt up her chin to see him, but she no longer struggled to meet his eyes. He knew what he was getting into by staying with her—hell, he probably knew better than she did about that sort of danger and running—and he still wanted to be with her. His thumb feathered over her bottom lip.

"Tell me one more time," he whispered.

"Together. We'll run together." She wanted to tell him she loved him, too, but she didn't want him to think she said it only because he had. Tomorrow, when they woke in each other's arms, she would tell him.

Cass dipped his face to hers slowly, giving her time to stop him, but she never would. Sure, she was nauseated, aching, devastated, and hunted. But it mattered less because, at last, she wasn't alone.

His kiss was soft but not tentative. He used only his lips for two short kisses before the slide of his tongue entered her mouth. The tempo remained slow as the tension between them grew, as if a spider wove a web back and forth between them, connecting them at so many points, Jolene wasn't sure they could be parted.

She rose on her toes, needing to press closer. Her hands stroked down his chest, feeling the muscles beneath his Henley, his heartbeat.

Mine. This is mine.

Stadler would never beat the two of them together. Even with the alcohol and cold cruelty, all he'd proved was he wasn't the man she'd thought he was. He wasn't a mentor or a friend. He understood her weaknesses very well, but he had no clue about her strengths. If he had, he'd have killed Cass for certain. She wouldn't give him another opportunity.

"We leave tomorrow, as soon as Kiera comes with the money," she said.

Cass grunted and kissed her again. He had a point. As long as they were together, nothing else mattered.

* * *

THUMPING WOKE JOLENE. SHE LOOKED AROUND THE BLACK BEDROOM. Cass was nothing more than a shadow as he strode away, his footsteps sure in the odd hour and the darkness.

"Have they found us?" Jolene asked, her voice creaky from sleep and the earlier damage.

"I doubt they'd be knocking," he said.

Jolene pulled on yoga pants and a long-sleeved tee and padded after Cass, unwilling to let him face whatever had come for them alone. After the narrow hallway, she entered the main gallery space and had a clear view of the glass doors.

Sara stood outside, looking more discombobulated than Jolene had ever seen her as she pounded on the door. She stopped when she saw Cass. Or maybe the gun he held at the side of his leg. When the hell had he gotten that?

Sara didn't run, though, only stepped back so Cass could let her in.

"What—?" Jolene said the moment Sara crossed the threshold.

"You have to go now," Sara said, looking everywhere at once. "They'll be here any moment." She rubbed her hands up and down her arms, looking like a drug addict itching for a fix. "I don't know what the hell Stadler's doing, but I won't be a part of this next-level bullshit. We're a team. You just—"

Cass bolted for the bedroom, presumably to pack up their meager supplies.

"How did you find us?" Jolene asked.

Sara winced. "Tracker on your Fitbit."

How long had they been tracking her? Did they slip it on her when she'd been drunk or had they been following her for years? Then she recalled when Stadler had zip-tied her wrists, that extra push.

Jolene dug her nail into her thigh and stared at Sara. "Did you know?"

"About the tracker or what he was going to do? No to both." Sara stepped to Jolene, her keen eyes landing on her swollen cheek. "Hell no, I didn't. I would have—" She ran a hand over her own face. "I can't say what I would have done, but I'd like to think I would have tried to stop him. This is *fucked* up."

Jolene swallowed hard, and it hurt. "About the Agency? Do you know who they really are?"

Sara bit her lip. "Yeah."

"And you're okay with that? Working for a criminal organization?"

"Yes." Sara wore jeans and a gray sweatshirt, her hair in a sloppy half ponytail. She looked more girl-next-door than femme fatale, except for her eyes. Jolene had seen that hard, flat look many times before. Sara had experienced some shit in her life. "We aren't screwing over good people. That doesn't make it okay, but I was already doing some dodgy stuff just to survive when Stadler found me. He gave me a place, a family of sorts. He might be a prick, but I always thought he had our backs." Her eyes filled with tears. "Now I don't know what to think."

Cass returned with four bloated Target bags stretched to their limit in one hand and Jolene's sneakers and coat in the other. "High speed, low drag. Let's go."

Jolene stuck her arms through the sleeves of her jacket and sat on the floor to put on her shoes, not confident enough in her balance to risk putting them on while standing. She had one shoe on when headlights splashed through the space. All three of them froze. Jolene tried telling herself it was simply a passing car.

"Cass," she said, her voice nothing more than a wisp.

Shadows converged at the door, and a cinder block crashed through, spraying glass everywhere. Stadler kicked the opening with thick boots until it was large enough for him to step through, then he pulled the pin of a grenade. Jolene remained sitting on the floor, one shoe on and one off, her mouth open and her stomach detonating.

Cass moved in front of her, gun pointed at Stadler, who held the grenade's safety lever down. If he'd intended to kill them that way, Stadler would surely have thrown the live grenade into the space and run.

Behind Stadler, Jorge and Mitchell stood just inside the door. Mitchell had his arms crossed over his chest like a smug weasel. Jorge kept his eyes on the floor and looked as if he wanted to be anywhere else.

Stadler's gaze shifted between Jolene and Sara. Jolene's left eye twitched. Sara's attempt to help Jolene might have condemned her as well.

"Hoes before bros?" Stadler asked.

"More like sisters before abusive assholes," Sara retorted. "Haven't you done enough? Good God, Gavin."

Jolene looked up at Cass. He had his gun trained on Stadler but couldn't shoot him without endangering everyone.

CHAPTER FORTY SEVEN

Cass

CASS WANTED TO STEP BACK SEVERAL FEET TO GIVE himself a bigger field of vision, but he couldn't leave Jolene out in the open. Jorge and Mitchell stayed by the door instead of fanning out, indicating they weren't trained for this sort of confrontation, and Stadler likely hadn't had time to plan the details of this attack.

Stadler shifted his icy glare to Sara, his lips pursed. "Is this the side you've chosen?"

Sara's face paled, and her fingernails dug into her thighs. "She's part of the team, so why would there be two sides?"

Stadler shook his head. "There shouldn't be." His left hand gripped the grenade tight. "Here's the deal, Jolene."

Jolene was already on her feet, stuffing her foot into her shoe, using Cass for balance. He angled to the side to keep his body between her and Stadler. Jolene allowed it, which surprised him. She spoke over Cass's shoulder. "Don't hurt her!"

"I don't want to punish either of you. Come with me, and everyone lives. Even you. When your contract expires, you'll be free to do what you like." Stadler's voice was calm and steady, and Cass believed him. Well, he believed Stadler believed his own words.

"After what you did to me and all the lies, you think I'd still work for you? Are you high?" Jolene's voice was rough and broke at the end.

"Continuing the same tasks you've been doing isn't worth Sara's life?" Stadler's cool, rational tone didn't hide the sick fury inside him.

Cass should have shot him, but his gut said to wait. His gut didn't, however, give him any idea if Stadler would shoot Sara or not. Cass should have cared more about that, but he focused only on saving Jolene.

"Just let me go," Jolene said. "We'll leave the city, drop off the radar."

"We?" Stadler asked, one eyebrow rising. "You think you can count on him? He'll bail the moment you no longer need rescuing. One day soon, you'll find yourself completely alone."

Jolene's breath hitched, giving Stadler the satisfaction of knowing he'd hit a sore spot.

"Look at him," Stadler said. "A guy like that isn't going to stay with someone as fucked up as you."

"He might. The pretty ones are sometimes kind of dumb," Jolene replied.

Sara snorted.

Jolene pressed a palm between Cass's shoulder blades in solidarity.

Cass ignored the conversation, keeping his attention on Stadler with an awareness of Mitchell and Jorge. He kept his breathing even, his finger on the trigger. At this close range, he decided on a headshot. Smaller target, but more incapacitating. Of course, there was also the matter of the grenade. It could detonate as fast as two seconds or as long as six, but most likely three to four. Cass was too far away to shoot Stadler and then toss his dead body on top of the grenade before it detonated.

"I'll trade you information for our freedom," Jolene said, her words tumbling out. "I know something very valuable, and I guarantee it's worth it."

"You underestimate your value," Stadler said. "We're more than a team. We—"

"There's a traitor, and I can tell you who if you promise to let us run and not follow," Jolene said.

Cass hid his surprise, but only because he'd practiced. It was both a smart and foolish gambit. Smart because that sort of information might have been worth their freedom, but foolish because the traitor could be only one person, and if Cass knew who it was within seconds, then Stadler probably comprehended his identity instantly.

"Is that true, Mickey?" Stadler asked, confirming Cass's suspicion.

"Dude, of course she's going to accuse me," Mitchell said, his voice a plaintive whine that wasn't going to convince anyone.

"You pulled a memory yesterday?" Stadler asked Jolene, his voice soft, one corner of his mouth ticking up. He was proud of her.

"No fucking way. She was sloppy drunk," Mitchell said.

"Even shitfaced, I'm a better memory surgeon than you." Her voice remained steady. She blew out a breath. "I'll tell you what I found, but you need to let us go."

Mitchell's face turned crimson. "She's a goddamned liar. She—"

Stadler barely glanced at Mitchell before he pulled a Glock out of a side holster and fired one-handed. Two to the chest, one to the head. As Mitchell crumpled to the ground, Cass kept his gun trained on Stadler. He couldn't shoot him when Stadler still held the grenade in his left hand.

The burned-firework smell of a discharged weapon filled the room. Cass's ears rang. Sara edged closer to Cass and Jolene. Jorge took a step toward the door.

"Jolene, come here." Stadler didn't sound as if he'd just killed a man.

"The fuck I will," she said, scrambling backward.

"If you stand between us, we'll both play nice," Stadler said.

"You just shot Mitchell!" Jolene's voice shook. "This was not in the brochure."

Sara giggled, a nervous explosion of tension.

Cass wished he could take his focus off Stadler to comfort Jolene. He understood her gallows humor and her mind's desperation to comprehend the death of a human being. Stadler, like Cass, didn't need a killing refractory period, so Cass kept his mind on the moment at hand.

"What's your plan?" Cass asked Stadler.

"Mutually assured destruction to keep things . . . friendly," Stadler replied. "I'll allow Jolene to hold the grenade."

Cass wanted to refuse and keep his body as her shield, but his gut twisted and burned with the knowing. Stadler wasn't there to kill Jolene. Playing along was the best course of action.

"Go ahead," Cass said.

She moved before Cass assured her.

"Just to be clear, it's Cass I'm trusting, not you." Jolene closed the distance to Stadler.

CHAPTER FORTY EIGHT

Jolene

JOLENE'S HANDS SHOOK, WHICH OF COURSE THEY did. Stadler stepped closer to her, closer than he needed. He'd trained her for tricks and traps and ruthlessness, and the smell of gunpowder reminded her of his capability. She thought she might also smell blood underneath that, metallic and earthy, though she might be imagining she could detect it.

Past memory surgeries with torture victims and assaults with blood sprang up with memories of the stench of death, the thick taste, the splash, and spray. Crunching bone, high-pitched screams, blinding pain.

These violent delights have violent ends. Shakespeare knew.

The grenade was cold metal and heavier than she'd expected. Her fingers overlapped Stadler's to hold the grenade's lever against its body, preventing its lethal countdown. "Where's the pin?" Her voice was at half-mast.

"I'll keep that," Stadler said, his lips quirking up.

He didn't release the grenade, so she was forced to hold it with him. His eyes twinkled. He enjoyed this standoff, the killing, and the negotiating. His ruthlessness battered the air around him, carving out more space than most people ever occupied. Stadler was a killer. She'd always known but somehow had managed never to confront that part of him.

Mitchell had been a sorry excuse for a memory surgeon and a shitty human being, but Jolene didn't think he'd deserved death.

Stadler behaved as if they were at her kitchen table and not in an empty gallery with a dead body a few feet away. "You performed well. You kept me from shooting lover boy and stripped Mitchell while he was inside your mind. Clever. You'll see your one-time day-drinking experience isn't going to turn you back into a raging alcoholic."

Jolene's mouth dropped open. Was he *proud* of her? "I *am* an alcoholic, Stadler. And it's only been a day, so let's not throw a sobriety party quite yet."

"You've been with me for five years. I've seen your best and worst. You've made such progress with your gift. Time to return to the fold."

Stadler didn't do praise, and now she understood why, because it was heady to hear it, to impress someone so exacting.

She shook her head to bring back sense. "How would I ever get past what you did to me? You seem to think it was some sort of tough love and not the actions of an abusive prick. Do you honestly think I'm so fucked in the head I can't tell the difference?"

Her slick hands threatened to slip off Stadler's, and she wanted to be the one directly holding down the lever. His steady gaze made her woozy with how overmatched she was.

"Read my memories, and you'll understand. Experience them and make an informed decision."

"Dude, no matter what I find, in what universe do I work for a drug syndicate? It goes against *everything* I—"

"We'll shift paths," Stadler said.

"What?"

"This is my team, and I can take us in a new direction. We can work within the Agency's legitimate businesses, we—"

"If we could have done that all along, then what the fuck were we doing—"

"For you."

Jolene wondered if his goal was to talk her into insanity. "Why the hell—"

"Why take my word for any of this when you can take a look yourself?"

As he said the words, bubbles blossomed in the back of her mind, muted, a thin barrier between them and her. She didn't want to experience Stadler. Not one minute. But he wouldn't give her a choice.

"What if I want out after I read your memories?"

He stared into her eyes, more open than she'd ever seen him. Oh God, she'd slept with him, and the entire time, he'd been lying to her. How had she forgotten that? Her head pounded, and her hot face prickled.

Nothing she experienced through his point of view would change her mind, but his confidence made her want to run away screaming. Something was wrong. She was missing something that would alter everything, but she was so tired and scared, she couldn't wrangle her focus enough to figure it out.

"When you're finished, I'll respect your decision, as long as lover boy agrees too."

Jolene frowned. "What is it you think he's going to do? Kidnap me and pour a liter of vodka down my throat?" She twisted her lips. "No. That's already been done."

"I don't like this," Cass said behind her, his voice tentative.

"What's plan B?" Jolene asked Stadler.

He smiled a shark grin. "We wrestle for the grenade and see what happens."

"His word is good," Sara said, having edged herself closer to the door and Jorge. Her hands clenched and unclenched, and she seemed unable to determine where she wanted to put them. "I've known him for seven years, and he's never broken an official promise. But you might want to lock down the details."

Stadler's lips quirked up. "Excellent point."

Jolene's chest fluttered. He had always been very my-word-is-my-bond. Maybe she and Cass wouldn't have to run after all. "I take a peek at your memories and then decide if I want to continue to work for you, doing legitimate, legal jobs only. If I choose not to, you and the rest of the Agency and anyone they're associated with will leave me and Cass alone. No harm will come to us, or anyone associated with us, and we'll be left in peace, never to be contacted again."

"I give you my word." Stadler didn't break eye contact as he repeated his vow. "If you stay, then you and Romeo call it quits, permanently. No texts, phone calls, Skype, emails . . . no contact of any kind."

"Agreed," Jolene said.

"Agreed," Cass added without prompting. She wondered if he'd had a knowing.

Stadler arched his eyebrows. "Go ahead."

Jolene looked back at Cass, ensuring he was still with her. He winked. Jolene rolled her eyes but couldn't stop a small smile. She wasn't alone.

Stadler's mind snapped into sharp resolution, almost as if his brain was HD. The thin film popped in and out of view, which she interpreted as Stadler trying to pull down his defenses to give her access.

Jolene studied the various bubbles and noted the ones he pushed forward. As if she'd only look at a curated sample.

She snatched a small, random memory.

* * *

Gavin kept motionless, willing the others not to notice him as he studied Jolene interacting with the rest of the team. Sara wore her genuine smile, though she tended to like everyone. Jorge, as always, split his attention between his computer and the live people in the room, but his lips were relaxed in a quiet grin. It was Ryan who confirmed for Gavin that he was right to add Jolene to the group. Ryan gave Jolene the real story of his upbringing, not his preferred fiction. At last, the team was complete and whole.

* * *

JOLENE REMEMBERED THAT MEETING, HER FIRST WITH EVERYONE, AND she'd felt that same rightness. But even if everything hadn't been a lie, she still—

One bubble caught her interest and held it. It was a strange shape and seemed to move, as if it struggled to hold itself together. It could have been some sort of booby trap, and part of her felt herded toward it, which had warning sirens screaming in her head. The color was a soft rose, so innocuous. When she looked closer, the instability was more apparent. If she peeked, it might pop.

She'd been tricked so many times by this man, enough that walking into that memory blind would be epically stupid, and yet, her instincts pulled her to it. Either looking or not looking could be the mistake. Jolene decided she'd rather be wrong while trusting herself than wrong by not listening to her gut.

When she grabbed on to the memory, it played in a compressed chunk.

* * *

Jolene leaned on the balcony railing, admiring the view of the Pacific Ocean. She wondered what it would be like to live in San Diego permanently, a life full of warm weather and marina views. Could she pull off being a California girl? Probably not. She was awfully dark for so much sunshine.

"What are you doing?" Stadler asked, mimicking her posture, his forearms resting on the railing, his shoulder close to hers, the setting sun softening his hard face.

"It's beautiful, isn't it?" she asked.

"Every place has its beauty," he replied.

"What about Nebraska?"

He smirked in that way he had, amused but not wanting to show it. "Sunrise over green fields. Clean air. Wooden bridges and family-owned diners."

Well, fuck her, that did sound nice. "What's your favorite location?"

"Everywhere." Stadler turned so his back was pressed against the railing. "You should go to as many places as you can. Find what you like instead of what other people like."

"I'm not sure I know how to do that." She tilted her chin to catch the breeze more fully on her face. It smelled more of car exhaust than salt. "I grew up in a very black-and-white world, where there were things acceptable to want and others . . ." Jolene sneaked a look at Stadler, but he continued to face forward, despite there being nothing to study in that direction except the interior of the apartment, a basic studio with minimal furniture. As she was wondering about it, she realized he did that so she would talk freely without feeling scrutinized. For a demanding prick, he had not a soft side, but a sensitivity.

"You think you're ethically defective," Stadler said. He really did understand her.

She closed her eyes and nodded. Even looking away, she knew he'd see it or sense it. "Just selfish."

"I've known a lot of selfish and evil, Jolene, and you couldn't join the league, let alone lead the team." He tilted his face to her. He had a strong jaw she hadn't noted before, distracted by his ridiculous mustache. She swore he kept it just to annoy her—or entertain her. There wasn't much teasable about Stadler. He gave her a rare smile. "You're a valuable person."

It almost hurt to hear those words, words she desperately wanted applied to her. "You didn't know me when I was drinking."

He smiled again. "You are a pain in the ass who doesn't like to take orders and spends altogether too much time trying to decide if you're good enough." Stadler shook his head. "You're ridiculous. Of course you're good enough."

Tears pricked her eyes, but she held them inside with an epic will. When her throat loosened, she said, "Thanks, Gavin. For everything." He'd spent a lot of time training her both physically and mentally, always pushing her as if she was worth the effort.

He nodded. "You call me Gavin in front of anyone else, I'm going to dislocate your kneecaps."

She snorted.

"You can use your gift from a wheelchair. Remember that."

Jolene laughed, watching the sun slide into the ocean.

* * *

THE MEMORY SLOTTED INTO PLACE IN HER MIND. HER MEMORY.

Stadler had one of her memories.

Her belly took a swan dive to her toes as his memories jostled one another, the majority pinks and purples with a large lemon-colored bubble in the front. Stadler was either a memory surgeon himself, or he'd had someone else remove her experience and give it to him.

She knew. In some ways, she'd always known, or at least she should have known. Nobody had understood her as well as Stadler—what scared her, what pissed her off, what motivated her. Every time they'd touched, had he rooted around inside her mind?

Realization struck her like a lightning flash, the electricity hitting the only spot available—her heart. This was his plan. Let her take a leisurely stroll around his brain while he stripped her of every memory that would compel her to reject his offer. He'd never had any intention of giving her free will.

She found a blood-red circle forming in his mind, a sign of a current, short-term memory. Stadler didn't know she could read forming memories, her mind-reading skill. This was her chance to figure out his plan. Jolene stepped into it only to find it filled with Cass, stretching in Churchill Park.

Stadler's present consisted of stealing Cass, and he'd likely already stolen other memories of him, like stripping cars for parts. Jolene snatched back the memory and then tightened their shared grip on the grenade as she slammed down her consciousness, envisioning a two-foot-thick metal door ramming down onto stone.

Stadler made a noise somewhere between a squeak and a groan. Jolene wished Kiera was there to help her try to take back her memories. Cass. She didn't care about the other memories Stadler had taken, anything she'd done in childhood, while drunk, or while working.

Cass was all she cared about. She needed every second she'd spent with him. Being with him had enabled her to discover truths about herself and the Agency. She wouldn't let go. If he left in a month, a year, five, never—it didn't matter. Jolene wanted every moment with him, both past and future.

Her mind blasted into Stadler's, her gift engulfing his memories. This time, she didn't have to say a word, not even his name, before tiny bubbles flowed into her.

The dip of her belly when Cass's hand bumped into hers as they walked.

Thick eyelashes on his cheekbones as he slept on his stomach, one arm under a pillow, the other stretched in front of him. So beautiful.

A playful bite to her big toe as his fingers dug into the arch of her foot.

Eye contact over lunch as neither said a word. Heat popping over her cheeks.

Energy pinging between them as his body crowded her against the door.

Want. Want. Want.

His lips so soft, his kiss so hard.

Teeth. Tongue.

Falling. Falling. Falling.

All those tender moments, all that happiness—Stadler had tried to steal it all from her. He would have gutted her and then stuffed her with lies and false promises—or even real promises. Then he would have murdered Cass. Killed him and taken that from her too. The team would vanish from Chicago, never to return, and Jolene would carry around the devastating loss and never understand why or what was missing.

The Cass-shaped hole in her world would grow only bigger, and then what might she do to try to lessen the emptiness inside? Alcohol? MDMA? Heroin? She might stay clean, embrace the void, but she'd never again be the person she was with Cass.

Jolene reclaimed every moment with Cass and then smacked down Stadler's mind one more time, just for spite. Stadler jerked, and she snatched the grenade from his grasp. The pin had fallen to the floor at some point, and she scrambled her shaking hands around for a few seconds before she grabbed it. She cradled both to her chest as if they were squalling babies.

The dexterity to reunite grenade and pin eluded her.

Cass still pointed his gun at Stadler, but his eyes flicked to Jorge and Sara, who both remained standing by the door, eyes wide, before he looked back at Jolene. "Take your time and put the pin back in. You can do it."

His words seemed to make it so. It took six eternities, but she managed. She handed the grenade to Cass, glad to be rid of the responsibility. He took it in his left hand, his gun finally lowered to beside his leg.

Jolene turned back to Stadler. "Why didn't you tell me?" She hated the hurt evident in her voice, but how could he not tell her he was a memory surgeon?

Stadler blinked at her. "It was the team."

She remembered the disorientation of having her mind crushed. No answers were coming anytime soon—not that she would believe anything he said, anyway.

"I choose to go," Jolene said as Stadler pressed the heel of one hand into his eyes. Maybe she should have felt guilty, or relieved, but she didn't. In fact, rage tunneled up her body until it stuck in her throat. She slapped his face.

Disoriented by her psychic assault, he didn't try to evade the blow at all. A satisfying crack sounded, her hand stung like a bitch, and Stadler's entire head whipped to the right.

Jolene believed he'd keep his word. He would trick, manipulate, and misdirect, but his vows meant something to him. She had meant something, and the team meant everything. What wisps of memories she'd caught had confirmed he'd thought of the group as a family too. But he'd doomed them from the start.

Part of her wanted to step aside and let Cass shoot him. It would ensure he didn't come after them, if his integrity further devolved or if he conjured a loophole in their deal. But Jolene had fucked up enough she didn't like to mete out moral judgments, and she didn't want to decide Stadler's fate.

She turned to Cass, drinking in the whole of him, desperate to fill her memories with more and more of him. "Let's go."

CHAPTER FORTY NINE

Cass

Cass studied Stadler, who rubbed his cheek where Jolene's handprint bloomed red, his eyes bleary and his balance unsteady. Jolene had obviously done something to his mind, and if Stadler considered that cheating, he would also consider their deal void. Stadler would come after them, and Cass couldn't allow that.

Jolene put a hand on his extended arm. "No, it's okay."

"So proud," Stadler mumbled, his bleary eyes on Jolene.

Everyone believed Stadler would keep his word, but looking at Stadler looking at Jolene, Cass wasn't convinced. Yet, if he killed him now with him disoriented and Jolene believing Stadler would let them go, she would think the decision was impulsive or a jealous reaction to the obvious obsession in Stadler's eyes. Jolene was more than a coworker or mentee to Stadler, and one day, he would likely pursue Jolene again. He couldn't count on the feds having enough evidence to arrest, let alone convict Stadler. No knowing occurred to help him make a decision.

Cass couldn't kill him and couldn't *not* kill him.

The hair on Cass's neck rose as his stomach twisted. Something was wrong. Danger. He turned, but it was too late. Two bullets hit Stadler in the head, then two to the chest.

"Walther," Sara gasped.

Cass didn't have time to process his relief someone had taken care of Stadler for him. Three men had somehow entered through the back of the gallery. The tall, thin one in the middle held a Beretta M9 and was obviously in charge. He wore an expensive suit and had wild eyes. Two generic goons flanked him, both huge, all in black, and carrying AR-15s. One had a neck as fat as a tree trunk. The other had no neck at all.

"Hey, kitten. Did you miss me?" asked the man Sara had called Walther, his voice a soft rasp.

Sara took a step back, and Cass took a step to the side to block Jolene.

The movement snagged Walther's attention, and he sneered at Cass. "I don't give a shit about you. All I want are the bitches and their prick boss." He smirked down at Stadler's corpse. "One down. Two to go."

Jolene's hand pressed into Cass's back, warm and gentle, and he suspected she was going to ask him to step away, to leave her to her fate. Her voice was low, only for him. "I'll follow your lead, but if your gut says there's no way out of this, I want you to live."

He almost closed his eyes. She hadn't given up, wasn't trying to blindly sacrifice herself. She trusted him. When he'd worn a uniform, when he'd been surrounded by army buddies, when he'd been on the job, people relied on him. That had been a long time ago. Too many people shied away when they discovered he'd been a sniper. As if he were a murderer and not a protector, as if that was all he was.

Jolene had always accepted the breadth and depth of him. He would save her, if possible, and regardless of her request, he would die trying—last resort only.

Cass studied Walther. Even with several feet between them, Walther's bloodshot eyes were apparent. He had a large shaving nick amongst his stubble, and his gun hand trembled. Not with nerves, because his eyes were hard and pitiless, but with something worse, a crazy sort of fury, which meant he would stop at nothing to get revenge for the death of his brother, Colton. There hadn't been any photos of Colton's family in the PIA's files on Jolene, but Colton's brother had been listed by name, and there weren't a lot of Walthers running around in the world.

"Afraid I can't leave," Cass said to Walther, his voice calm and easy.

Shooting wasn't the answer. Three guns against one, and no cover anywhere. He wasn't sure what to do, and his gut stayed quiet.

Jolene snaked an icy hand underneath his T-shirt and pressed into his lower back. Comfort? A goodbye? He opened his heart and mind to her, giving ten percent of his focus to her touch while the rest remained on the three thugs.

The goons were obviously waiting for Walther to give the order, but Cass had no clue what Walther needed before he decided to kill them.

Walther cast only a cursory glance at Mitchell and smirked. Michell had betrayed their location to Stefano Sr. and Walther. Walther had intended on repaying that tip with death, because Michell was a memory surgeon, and Walther blamed them for his brother's murder. The knowing didn't tell Cass more than that, like how he could escape this clusterfuck.

The Goose Island neighborhood was mostly industrial, but Stadler and Walther had both fired their guns without suppressors. Surely, someone somewhere had heard the gunfire, or maybe they were close enough to a ShotSpotter, which would automatically alert police and give them a general location.

It had been five minutes, and no cops had arrived. That likely meant nobody had reported Stadler's shots. In another five minutes, Cass would know whether Walther's gunshots would bring the police to them. If they had that much time.

"Put your gun down, or my friends here kill everyone," Walther said, his focus finally sticking to Cass. His obsession with Jolene and Sara might be used to distract him, except—

* * *

They don't deserve my time. Shoot them. Drag their bodies to the alley. Leave them in the garbage.

Not enough. They need to suffer for what they did to Colton. Cunts. Stupid, fucking cunts.

* * *

TWENTY-FIVE PERCENT OF CASS'S ATTENTION SHIFTED TO WHAT WERE clearly Walther's thoughts. What the hell? Jolene's hand warmed with his body heat. Jolene. Memory surgeon.

Cass had opened to Jolene. Jolene had opened to Walther. Walther was too overwhelmed by vengeance and grief to contain it all. He was projecting every emotion, and that must have been enough for Jolene to slip inside. And then she'd passed Walther's emotions to Cass. Her gift continued to grow, which didn't surprise him as much as it should.

There had to be a way for him to use this loop.

Too many moving parts, the field of fire offering no cover or concealment. They were ninety-nine percent fucked. But working together, he and Jolene would keep trying to shift the situation to their own advantage. Cass had his weapon, the grenade, Jolene's gift, and his own.

Now would be an excellent time to help, he told his gut.

Nothing.

"On your knees," Walther said, jaw shifting to the right, his gun pointed at Sara. "Come on, bitch. We both know you were born to be there, all the way to the end."

"Baby," Sara said, sounding wounded. "You're scaring me."

Walther laughed without humor. "Are you trying to play me right now?"

"I'm sorry I left the way I did," she said. She seemed genuinely contrite.

Walther's eyelashes fluttered. "We all know you work for the Agency, and you fucked me as part of your job, *Saffron*. Or do you want me to call you Sara now?"

Through Jolene, Cass felt Walther's hesitation even through his harsh words. Somehow, Sara had planted a seed of doubt, buying them a little more time.

"You found me," Sara said, acting as if Walther coming after her to kill her was some sort of compliment.

Walther frowned. His rage blasted through his brain in a smoke so thick Cass almost coughed.

Finally, his gut engaged. Cass released his trigger so he could pull the grenade pin.

"You fucking cunt!" Walther screamed at Sara, his face crimson, spittle flying from his mouth.

The shot echoed through the space, reviving the ringing in Cass's ears. Through their connection, Jolene knew Cass's plan with the grenade. She sprinted toward the door, shouting at a crumpling Sara and Jorge, "Run!"

As they ran, Cass pitched the grenade at Walther. "Catch, motherfucker!" He raced after Jolene, hoping to clear the door and use the building's concrete exterior for cover. He assumed Walther would duck the projectile that otherwise would have smashed him in the face and hoped the goons would be too freaked out by an incoming grenade to shoot at anyone.

He'd been mostly correct, as he reached the door before gunfire sounded. Walther's Beretta. Cass didn't think he'd been hit since he didn't feel anything. Adrenaline could definitely mask a gunshot wound, but he would have expected a burn or push if he'd actually been shot.

"To the right!" he shouted as he caught up to the trio as they burst out of the building. Sara was dragged by Jolene and Jorge, blood spilling from her stomach and over her lower body. Cass crowded them around the corner, glad the building was concrete.

He yanked Jolene to the ground, and she pulled Jorge and Sara with her. Cass covered her body with his own as the grenade exploded behind them. What remained of the glass door shattered with the explosion, the sound so loud Jolene screamed beneath him. Luckily, the building held up, and though a concussive wind blew over Cass's body, no shrapnel caught him.

Cass rolled off Jolene and checked her for injuries. She wouldn't or couldn't blink, and he thought she might be going into shock, but she finally turned to check on Sara.

"Oh fuck! Oh fuck!" Jorge sat next to Sara, curled into a ball.

"Where's Walther?" Sara asked, flat on her back, lungs heaving. "Is he dead?"

Cass pulled off his T-shirt, folding the fabric quickly and pressing it against her wound. Sara hissed in pain, but if he didn't staunch the bleeding, she would die right there on the street.

"Jolene, pull my cell phone out of my back pocket and call 911. Hurry."

Sirens sounded in the distance, and Jolene hesitated.

"Call anyway. We don't know if there's an ambulance coming or just police."

She called emergency services.

"Sara," Cass said, looking down at the woman, the whites of her eyes huge, like those of a freaked-out horse, her pupils consuming her irises. Her face was deathly pale, her lips starting to turn blue. Shock. "Look at me. It hurts and you're scared, but stay with me, okay? Help is on the way. Just a few more minutes."

Cass wanted to clear the building, ensure Walther and the goons were truly dead, but he couldn't leave Sara.

"Here," Jolene said, setting down the cell, nudging him out of the way, and replacing his hands with hers. "I can do that. You go check." In a louder voice, she said into the phone, "I'm applying pressure to the wound."

They made an indomitable team. "Firm pressure, even though it hurts," he said and left Sara in the hands of the woman he loved while he verified their safety.

He was peeking around the destroyed doorway when the first police car arrived, thankfully followed by an ambulance. Inside the gallery, Cass counted five clearly dead bodies—two goons, Walther, Stadler, and Mitchell.

CHAPTER FIFTY

Jolene

THE HANGOVER FROM HELL GOT AN UPGRADE after Jolene witnessed several people dying and almost got killed herself. Once Sara was taken away by the paramedics, the relief and giddiness of being alive made her want to giggle. She had great hope for Sara's recovery. They were taking her to Stroger, the world's best hospital for gunshot victims.

The police separated her from Cass, presumably so they couldn't "get their stories straight," and shortly thereafter, Shaun showed up. The flashing lights, the questions, the smoke, the yellow crime tape, the bitter wind whipping and stilling at odd moments all lulled her into some kind of trance as she sat in the back of a cop car, uncuffed and alone with her thoughts.

Stadler was dead. Gone. She'd never have the chance to ask him what the fuck, find out about his experiences as a memory surgeon and why the Agency had recruited her if they had him.

Well, she knew the answer to the last question. He'd had kept his talent a secret from everyone. Of course he had, not wanting exploitation, and likely using his gift as some sort of armor or weapon. He'd stolen memories from her. Lied. Assaulted. Tortured. Still, a gap remained in her heart where the man she'd imagined him to be used to live.

She'd always be conflicted where Stadler was concerned, torn between her rage at how he'd ultimately treated her and her memories of all the years before that, when she'd believed all the lies, when he'd been her mentor and friend. Or maybe her inclination to forgive stemmed from her desire for forgiveness for herself. And that was okay. Because she understood the difference between Stadler's brand of "care" and real love. Cass had taught her what friendship truly looked like—steadfast and supportive, what love felt like—tender and unselfish, and the difference respect made in both—real versus fake.

She didn't hate him but also didn't mourn him. The world was a better place without him in it, and he'd never hurt anyone else ever again. Freedom always came at a cost, and it was appropriate Stadler had paid for hers, and she didn't feel guilty about it.

* * *

After Shaun talked to the powers that be on the scene, Jolene and Cass gave their statements and were allowed to leave the scene. Cass retrieved his car and took Jolene to his grandparents' house in Northbrook, deciding neither of their places would be safe if the Agency and the Stefano organization weren't through with them.

In the guest bathroom, they showered together, the water hot enough to sting. At first, they stared at each other, Jolene with her back to the spray and Cass in front of her, his hands on her waist, thumbs swirling on her hipbones. They hadn't talked about what had happened, only that, so far, it didn't look as if either of them would be arrested for anything.

Memory surgeons weren't permitted to testify in court about memories they'd experienced or taken, and, therefore, no laws existed for them to be charged for spying or taking memories. Once the investigators finished, they'd confirm she'd been the victim in the shooting and bombing—grenading?—and Shaun had sheepishly admitted that they had nothing tying her to anything criminal in her work for the Agency, probably due to the isolation she used to bitch about.

Stefano's people knew of her through Mitchell, but only what Mitchell had known about her, which couldn't have been much. Stadler didn't share personal information and stories about his team. Regardless, it seemed unlikely they'd waste their resources coming after someone who couldn't hurt them.

"You're thinking too much," Cass said, chest rumbling. "Stop."

"How do you know?" She was the one who read minds.

He snorted. "Because you've been under the spray for a few minutes and haven't washed a damn thing."

"Maybe I was partaking in a qigong breathing exercise."

"If so, you're not doing it right." He grinned and lifted one hand to cup her less-injured cheek. His hand was warm and wet. "Breathe with me?"

"Okay." She'd do anything he asked, and she needed to breathe anyway, so this was a no-brainer.

He put a hand on her chest, almost between her breasts. "Breathe into your chest, then your abdomen to a count of four. Hold for four. Exhale for eight, from the abdomen to the chest. Hold for four, then we'll start again. Got it?"

She nodded. Ordinarily, she'd close her eyes to concentrate, but she didn't want to take her gaze off Cass. They breathed together, Cass talking them through the steps for a few cycles. Her thoughts settled like dust, still there but no longer swirling, and Cass lowered his head to kiss her.

The thought she'd almost never had that closeness again threatened to gut her, but she decided to embrace the idea that finally something had happened in her life where she could revel in how events had turned out rather than how they hadn't. His lips were so soft, like selfless love, his tongue gentle but insistent, their bodies close but not mashed together.

He caressed her hair as water flowed through it like seaweed. She brushed her warm hands over his cooler chest. They'd been in the shower at least ten minutes, and she hadn't shared the spray. Oops. She maneuvered them around until the water beat down on Cass, allowing him the same warmth. Their kiss intensified, fingers digging into flesh, teeth nipping, lips frantic. Until Cass moved his head, and water hit Jolene's face. She jerked back.

Cass stared at her as she wiped the water from her face, then he laughed. "I forgot you don't like water on your face. Not even shower water?"

"Unless it's spraying in my mouth, I don't like it."

"Hm. I've got something to spray into your mouth."

Jolene chuckled. Something loosed inside her chest and gut. The weightless feeling in her body made her light-headed, and she grabbed Cass before she floated away.

They would be okay. *She* would be okay.

* * *

AFTER THEIR SHOWER, CASS WRAPPED HER IN A THICK, TERRYCLOTH robe and put on sweatpants and a Chicago Blackhawks T-shirt. He had Jolene sit on the bed as he combed gently through her wet hair, using the action as a soothing mechanism, kissing the back of her neck a few times.

Afterward, he pulled off his T-shirt and gave it to her to sleep in. It was warm from his body and smelled like his grandmother's vanilla body wash. They snuggled under the covers, facing each other, her leg between his, her nose pressed to his throat. He stroked up and down her spine.

"Do you still want to come with me if it's too dangerous to stay in Chicago?" she asked. After they'd almost died, it seemed stupid to skirt the issue or internalize her fears. "It might be good to spend a couple of weeks somewhere else to test if anyone is looking for us."

"Where you go, I go." One strand of Cass's wet hair lay along the side of his face, flowing over his chin to the bed.

"The French Riviera? Might be a fine place to spend Thanksgiving." It would be warmer than Paris and maybe more romantic. Her first trip out of the country. An adventure.

"Okay, but the French don't celebrate Thanksgiving."

Jolene tucked his hair behind his ear. "If we're together, I can be thankful anywhere."

"Then let's go to France tomorrow."

Even with the lights off, she studied the shape and form of him, made out some of the swirls on his tattooed shoulder. She traced the curved lines, wishing, of all things, she was his tattoo, injected deep under his skin, with him always.

"Do you want to talk about tonight?" he finally asked.

Jolene had been thinking of nothing, which should have scared her, but it was better than a reel of flashbacks or numbness. "What's there to say? We're alive."

"Does it bother you that I killed those guys?" His voice was conversational, but his shoulder muscle tensed under her fingers.

"Are you asking me if I'd rather be dead?" She snorted. "Uh, no."

"You're not . . . afraid of me or anything?"

Jolene almost laughed, but she sensed a real concern behind his easy words. She stroked his cheekbones as she kissed his forehead. "No, love. You make me feel safe in a way I've never known." She continued to trace her fingertips over his face as she kissed his eyebrows, cheeks, jaw, chin. He relaxed into her touch. If she hadn't sensed a barrier in his memories, she might have believed she'd allayed his fears.

She propped herself up on an elbow and peered down at him. Her hair swished down, so she pushed it back. They studied each other in the dark, and Jolene drilled her eyes into his soul, not touching his memories. This moment needed to be old-school soul to soul, heart to heart.

"I'm not going to use tonight to populate my spank bank, but truthfully, the way you were always in control no matter how fucked up things became was a profound kind of hot." She grabbed his chin and lowered her face to his, hovering just far enough away that she didn't have to cross her eyes to look into his. "You weren't killing bad guys. You were protecting the good guys. You can't necessarily control how you feel, but I don't think you should feel guilty."

"I don't. Not even a little. I just—some people don't understand. It's not that I don't value human life, or I won't be haunted by it every now and then. But this isn't something I'm going to have a hard time carrying."

"Their deaths are on them. It's not like they gave us much of a choice." She almost kissed him, letting her lips barely touch his. Slowly, she rubbed her mouth back and forth along his. Their breaths mingled. "I won't have trouble carrying it either."

Cass slipped a warm hand into the dip of her waist but didn't rise up to properly kiss her. When they were both near to panting, she licked her lips and his lips and deepened the contact into a kiss. He pulled her on top of him, the vee of her legs landing perfectly onto his erection.

She rolled her hips, their kisses deep and slow like the swells of the ocean. His fingers threaded into her hair with one hand as the other grabbed her ass and encouraged her to rub against him. Jolene's entire body whizzed and whished, all her aches and pains fading into the background. She wouldn't label herself happy, exactly, but the sense that the universe had somehow ordered itself blanketed her. Jolene had finally found peace.

Nipping his bottom lip, she ground down harder, needing more stimulation, more of Cass. She sat up, still straddling him, and pulled off the T-shirt. His hands covered her breasts, thumbs encouraging her nipples to harden further.

"I love you so much," he said. "You're the most complex, interesting, sexy, gorgeous woman I've ever met."

Her face and body heated at his words. "Yeah, yeah, yeah. Get naked."

He sat up like a released spring, flipping her over. As he pulled down his sweats and underwear, he said, "You too."

She shoved down her panties and rolled back on top of him, nothing between them. He cupped her face, letting her maneuver herself into position.

"Are you wet enough?" he panted, staring at her face.

She chuckled and lowered herself onto him, her slickness obvious in the ease with which he entered her.

"Oh fuck," he groaned. He pulled her face down and kissed her senseless for several seconds. "We should have done this the day we met and every day after that."

"Yes." She kissed him. "Yes." Moving over him, she found the tempo and angle she preferred, throwing her head back, enjoying the stretch of him, the intimate connection.

Cass squeezed her ass and pumped into her. He rose high enough to lick a nipple, alternating licking and sucking until the pleasure made her keen.

He stuck a thumb in her mouth, and she sucked it hard, swirling her tongue, rasping his skin with her teeth. "I just want to be inside you right now," he said, his voice rough and deep. "But later, you're going to suck me off just like that. Aren't you?"

"Yes." She didn't have any other words for Cass. For him, it would always be yes.

He removed his thumb with a pop and lowered it to her clit, massaging in tight, wet circles. Her insides clenched. Cass hissed and muttered a string of profanity that would have made her laugh if she weren't about to come.

"I love you," she gasped, the physical thrill mixing with the clawing need for him, the addictive balm of him, the shuddering stripping of her, of everything between them.

His pleasure bled into her own, and like at the gallery, she opened the channel so he might feel her feeling him. Their pleasure twined as their bodies adjusted in a feedback loop that made her head swim. Cass gripped her hips and contracted his abs, the angle shifting enough that he hit her G-spot.

Jolene had never come from straight penetration, but there was nothing straight about the moment. He was inside her, filling every part of her, and she was inside him, the connection fizzing and popping, rolling and dunking, and taking over every thought and movement. Everything tingled and tightened, their orgasms growing together, his pleasure pushing her higher, her pleasure pushing him higher. Swirling, soaring in her mind but sinking and undulating in her pussy.

She panted and screamed as her orgasm overtook her, running her down before flinging her into an alternate dimension where time slowed enough for her to feel everything at once—the dig of Cass's fingers into her hips, the cooler air on her nipples, her wet hair clinging to her back, the fullness of Cass, the head of his cock as it rocked over the most sensitive spot inside her. Her muscles clamped down on his dick. Clamp. Flutter. Clamp. Clamp. And then she experienced the jet of his release through him, the hot wetness and tight grip of her body, the buzz in his balls, the whiteout of his brain as he came and came and came.

Their minds didn't break apart, but the connection faded as they each floated back to earth, and Jolene found herself in her mind alone.

She understood now how she'd been able to connect without physical contact back when she'd discovered Cass's secret identity, how she'd projected Walther's thoughts to Cass, and how she'd just shared that exquisite moment with him. None of it would have been possible without their mutual openness, their souls' desires to never close to the other.

"You're the strongest person I've met, both inside and out. I'd do anything for you, Cassidy. You deserve every wonderful thing in the world, and I'm going to try to give you as many as I can," she said.

"Yes." His smile lit him, which illuminated her.

"You're mine," she said, lowering her sweaty forehead to his. "Mine."

He tilted his face to kiss her. Their kisses were short and nippy as they both fought to catch their breath. "Yes," he said again.

Maybe that was the only word he had for her too.

ACKNOWLEDGEMENTS

First of all, thanks to my critique group (and beta readers): Carolyn, Dani, Meg, Rae, and Susan. You guys are always so supportive, honest, and amazing writers, and you make all my writing better. In that same vein, much appreciation to my brainstorming/accountability people: Tracy, Lyssa, Sheri, Susan (again), and Tracy.

Shout out to my developmental editor Amanda Bidnall, who helped shape the novel. I also need to express my profound gratitude to my line editor, Joyce Lamb, who turned my sentences from a rusted-out Ford F-Series truck to a brand-new Ford Mustang Mach-E. I had no idea my prose was so clumsy. Also, if not for you, I definitely would have left in that three-paragraph vomiting moment.

Big thanks to my copyeditor Julie Schrader, who graciously let me push back our prearranged date and who made my day by telling me she liked this book better than the first.

I also want to shower gratitude over Olivier Darbonville for the interior design and formatting and Sarah Hansen for the cover design. You guys made my book so beautiful!

I had a lot of people who helped me with some of the research aspects: Melinda Gulledge for the army details, the beta read for the army details, and also giving me the phrase "high speed, low drag;" Dana McNeal for giving me feedback on my FBI stuff and answering all my ridiculous (and non-ridiculous) questions; Dani Hayden for all your insights into AA and recovery; Clark Rowenson for not only your brilliance when it comes to magic systems, but your support and enthusiasm and hardcore brainstorming skills. Muchas gracias, all.

Any mistakes in the book are completely my own.

Very special thank you to the Northbrook Public Library and their Northbrook Writes program, particularly Kate Hall, Michael Hominick, and Jane Huh for informing me about the Soon to Be Famous Illinois Manuscript contest and submitting my first book and all your cheerleading afterward. Your enthusiasm and support gave me so much joy. As promised, I put a little Northbrook into this book just for you guys!

I need to recognize OCWW (Off-Campus Writers' Workshop) for the great speakers, awesome program, and fantastic community. You are like home to me. Likewise, much obliged to all the Just Write Chicago people for showing up on Fridays to talk about writing and support one another.

Mike Austin, much appreciation for coming up with PIA! Much better than the IPP I'd come up with.

Thanks to my friends and family who have been so encouraging with my writing and trying to find extra readers for me. Mike Bush, for always being the first to say he wants to read what I write. I remember that from my first, tentative Facebook post, and it stuck with me.

A most special thanks to Randy and Quinlan—my boys and my heart.

And the biggest thank you to my readers. Without you, I'd probably still write, but it wouldn't be nearly as satisfying.

If you're interested in an epilogue bonus scene or want my earliest updates, please sign up for my newsletter at my website: holliesmurthwaite.com.

www.ingramcontent.com/pod-product-compliance
Lightning Source LLC
Chambersburg PA
CBHW030625310726
48979CB00003B/879

* 9 7 8 1 7 3 7 1 1 8 9 5 4 *